D0952707

THE TEMERAIRE SERIES BY NAOMI NOVIK

His Majesty's Dragon

Throne of Jade

Black Powder War

Empire of Ivory

Victory of Eagles

Tongues of Serpents

Crucible of Gold

Blood of Tyrants

Blood of Tyrants

Blood of Tyrants

Naomi Novik

DEL REY • NEW YORK

Blood of Tyrants is a work of fiction. All incidents and dialogue, and all characters with the exception of some well-known historical and public figures, are products of the author's imagination and are not to be construed as real. Where real-life historical or public figures appear, the situations, incidents, and dialogues concerning those persons are entirely fictional and are not intended to depict actual events or to change the entirely fictional nature of the work. In all other respects, any resemblance to persons living or dead is entirely coincidental.

Published in the United States by Del Rey,
an imprint of The Random House Publishing Group,
a division of Random House, Inc., New York.

Del Rey and the House colophon are registered trademarks
of Random House, Inc.

ISBN 978-0-345-52289-4
eBook ISBN 978-0-345-52291-7

Printed in the United States of America on acid-free paper

www.delreybooks.com

2 4 6 8 9 7 5 3 1

First Edition

To Cynthia Manson, my amazing agent and friend,
with much love and gratitude

ACKNOWLEDGMENTS

With many, many thanks to beta-readers Georgina Paterson, Vanessa Len, Sally McGrath, and Francesca Coppa, all of whom gave me incredibly helpful feedback and inspiration, and helped me improve this book in so many ways.

Thanks again to my wonderful agent, Cynthia Manson, and to my new editor, Anne Groll, who pounded this book into shape.

And now and always, all my love and thanks to my amazing husband, Charles, and also to Evidence, who doesn't quite get what mommy does yet, but is already fond of dragons.

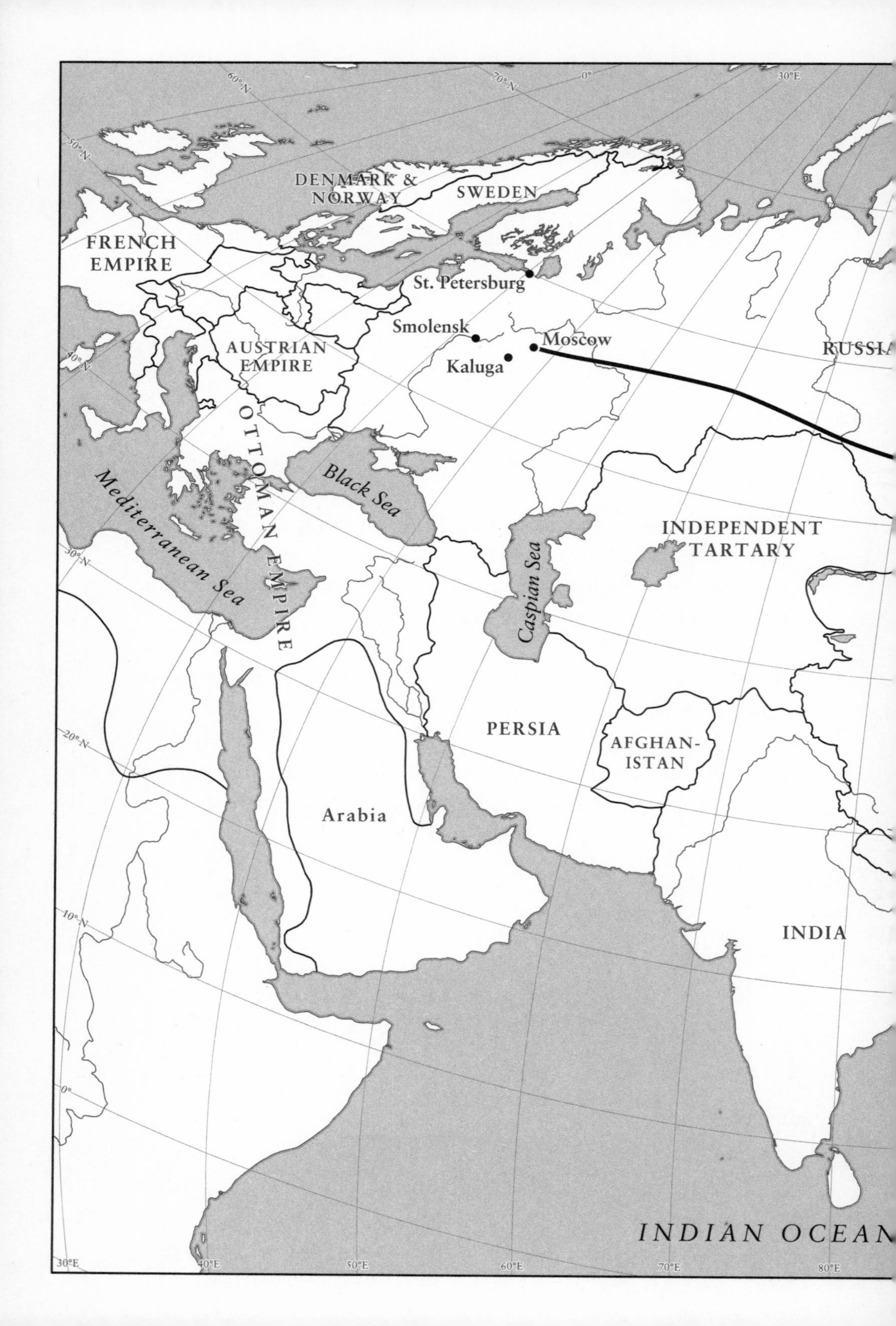

DENMARK & NORWAY
SWEDEN
FRENCH EMPIRE
St. Petersburg
Smolensk
Moscow
Kaluga
AUSTRIAN EMPIRE
RUSSIA
OTTOMAN EMPIRE
Black Sea
Mediterranean Sea
Caspian Sea
INDEPENDENT TARTARY
PERSIA
AFGHAN-ISTAN
Arabia
INDIA
INDIAN OCEAN
60°N
70°N
50°N
40°N
30°N
20°N
10°N
0°
30°E
40°E
50°E
60°E
70°E
80°E

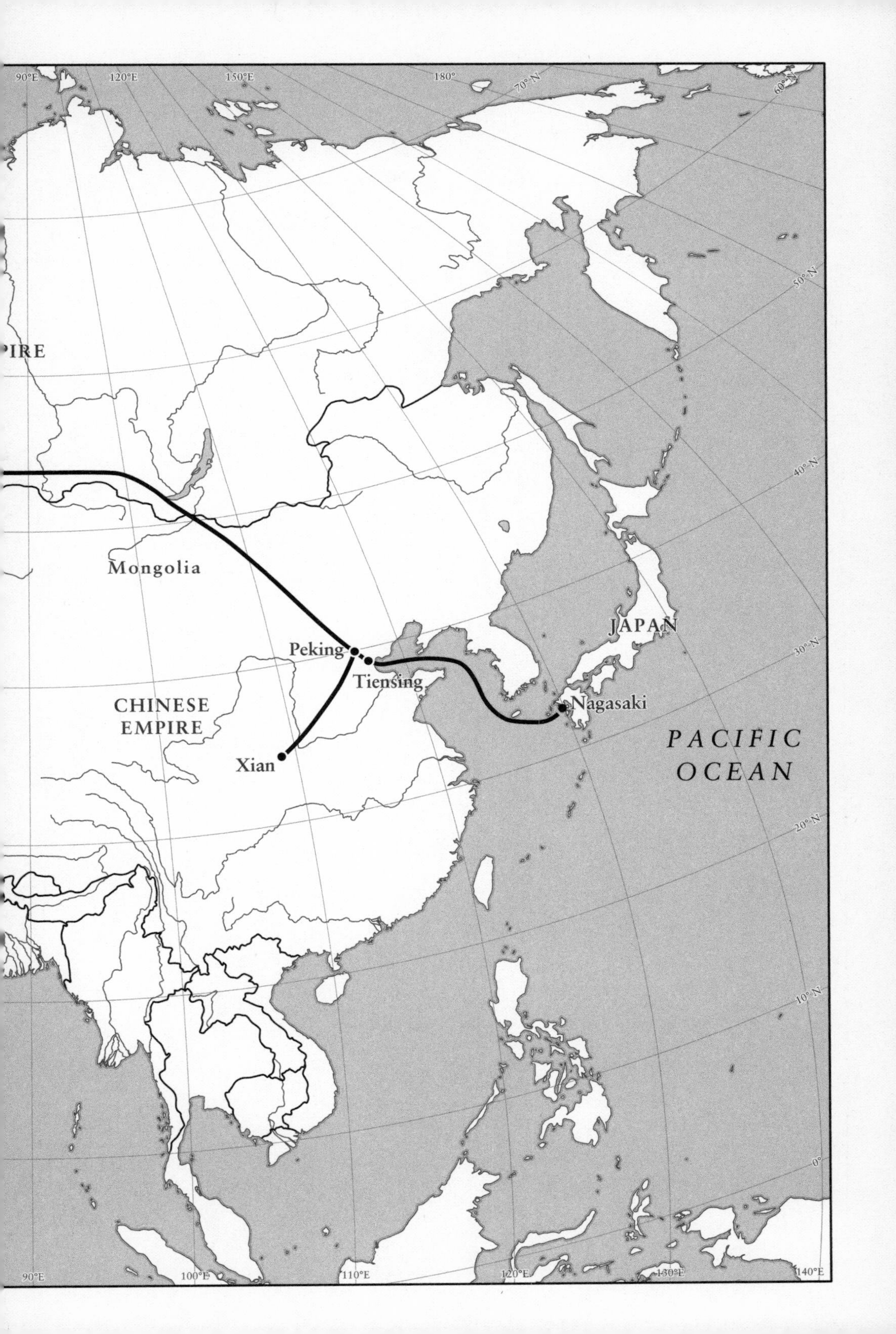
90°E
120°E
150°E
180°
70°N
60°N
50°N
40°N
30°N
20°N
10°N
0°
IRE
Mongolia
Peking
Tiensing
CHINESE
EMPIRE
Xian
JAPAN
Nagasaki
PACIFIC
OCEAN
90°E
100°E
110°E
120°E
130°E
140°E

Part I

Chapter 1

WATER LAPPING SALT AT his cheek roused him, a fresh cold trickle finding its way into the hollow of sand where his face rested. It spurred him: with an effort he pushed to hands and knees and then up, to stagger indecorously along the shore and fall again at the foot of several gnarled old pines clinging to the edge of the beach.

His mouth was dry and cracked, his tongue swollen. His hands were clotted with sand. The wind bit sharply through the sodden wool of his coat, stained black with water, and he was barefoot. Slowly, he unfastened the remnants of a leather harness from around his waist: buckles and clasps of good steel, still bright, but heavily waterlogged; he let it fall to the sand. The sword-belt he kept. The blade when he drew it was bright Damascus steel, the hilt wrapped in black ray-skin, the collar the golden head of a dragon. He stared down at it, without recognition.

He rested it across his knees and leaned back against the tree, half-drifting. The empty ocean stood before him: water cold dark blue, the sky a thin grey; dark clouds receded into the east. He might have emerged onto the sand new-born. He felt as empty as the shore: of strength, of history, of name.

Thirst at last drove him onwards, when little else would have served to rouse him. The stand of trees gave onto a road, well-maintained and showing the signs of heavy use, recent tracks and disturbed dust. He walked slowly and mechanically until he found a narrow stream that crossed the road, traveling towards the sea, and he stopped and cupped water into his mouth urgently until the taste of salt had gone.

He held himself braced on hands and knees, water dripping from his face into the stream. The bank had a little new grass, though the ground was still cold. There was a smell in the air of pine-needles, and the stream ran over the rocks in a steady gurgle, mingling with the more distant sound of the ocean, the scent of salt on the wind. He felt inwardly the sense of something urgent and forgotten like a weight on his back. But his trembling arms slowly gave way. He lay down on the grass of the riverbank where he had knelt to drink and fell again into a heavy torpor; his head ached dully.

The sun climbed, warmed his coat. Travelers went past on the nearby road. He was distantly aware of the jingle of harness and slap of walking feet, the occasional creak of cart wheels, but none of them stopped to bother him or even halted by the stream. A small party of men went by singing off-key, loudly and cheerfully, not in any tongue he knew. At last a larger company came, accompanied by the familiar creaking of an old-fashioned sedan-chair. Some confused corner of his mind offered the image of an older woman, borne by porters through London streets, but even as it came he knew it wrong.

The creaking stopped abruptly; a voice spoke from the chair: a clear tenor with the directness of authority. Prudence would have driven him to his feet, but he had no reserves of strength. In a moment, someone came to inspect him—a servant of some kind? He had some vague impression of a youth bending down over him, but not so low that the face came clear.

The servant paused, and then withdrew quickly to his master and spoke urgently in a clear young voice. There was another pause, and then the master spoke again in yet another tongue, one which he could not put a name to and nevertheless somehow understood: a rising and falling speech, musical. "I will not evade the will of Heaven. Tell me."

"He is Dutch," the servant answered in that same language, reluctance clear in every word.

He might have raised his head to speak—he was not Dutch, and knew that, if very little else; but he was cold, and his limbs heavier with every moment.

"Master, let us go on—"

"Enough," the tenor voice said, quiet but final.

He heard orders given in the unfamiliar language while darkness stole over his vision; there were hands on him, their warmth welcome. He was lifted from the ground and slung into a sheet or a net for carrying; he could not even open his eyes to see. The company moved on; suspended in mid-air, swinging steadily back and forth as they went on, he felt almost as though he were in a hammock, aboard ship, swaying with the water. The movement lulled him; his pain dulled; he knew nothing more.

"William Laurence," he said, and woke with his own name, at least, restored to him: out of a tangled dream full of burning sails and a strange weight of despair, a sinking ship. It faded as he struggled up to sit. He had been lying on a thin pad laid upon a floor of woven straw matting, in a room like none he had ever seen before: one solid wooden wall, the rest of translucent white paper set in frames of wood, and no sign of doors or windows. He had been bathed and dressed in a robe of light cotton; his own clothes were gone, and his sword. He missed the latter more.

He felt adrift, robbed of place and time. The chamber might have been a solitary hut or a room in the center of a great house; it might be set upon a mountaintop or the seashore; he might have slept an hour, a day, a week. A shadow abruptly loomed on the other side of the wall furthest from his bed, and the wall slid open along a track to furnish Laurence a glimpse of a corridor and another room across standing half-open, indistinguishable from his own, save for a window which looked out on a slim cherry-tree with bare dark branches.

A young man, not very tall but gangly with recent growth, perhaps sixteen, came through the opening and folded himself into the low-roofed chamber while Laurence stared at him blankly: he was Oriental. A long face with a sharp chin, clean-shaven and softened with the last remnants of puppy-fat; his dark hair was drawn back into a tail, and he wore an intricately arranged set of robes, creases as sharp as knife-edges.

He sat down on his heels and contemplated Laurence in turn, with an expression bleak enough to be aimed at a plague-carrier. After a moment he spoke, and Laurence thought he recognized the voice—the youth who had wished him left by the road.

"I have not the least notion what you are saying," Laurence said, his voice sounding hoarse in his own ears. He cleared his throat: even that much struck his head with fresh pain. "Can you speak English? Or French? Where am I?" He tried those tongues both, and then hesitating repeated the last over in the other language which the men had spoken on the road.

"You are in Chikuzen Province," the young man said, answering him in kind, "and far from Nagasaki, as you must well know."

There was a sharp bitterness to his voice, but Laurence seized on the one familiar name. "Nagasaki?" he said, half in relief, but the momentary gratification faded: he was no less bewildered to know himself in Japan, the other side of the world from where he ought have been.

The young man—too old for a page, and he wore a sword; an equerry of some sort, or a squire, Laurence could only guess—made no answer, only with a curt gesture motioned him off the mat.

Laurence shifted himself onto the floor, with some awkwardness and pain: the ceiling was too low to have permitted him to stand unless he had hunched over like a toad, and he ached in every part. Two servants came in at the young man's call; they tidied the mat away into a cabinet and offered Laurence fresh garments, baffling in their layers. He felt a clumsy child under their valeting, thrust one way and then another as he put his limbs continuously in the wrong places; then they brought him a tray of food: rice and dried fish and pungent broth, with an array of startling pickles. It was by no means the breakfast he would have chosen, his stomach unsettled, but they had no sooner put it before him than animal hunger became his master. He paused only after having devoured nearly half the meal, and stared at the eating-sticks, which he had picked up and used without thinking of it.

He forced himself to go on more slowly than he wished, still queasy and conscious of being under observation, the young man regarding him coldly and steadily the whole of his meal. "Thank you," Laurence said at last, when he had finished, and the dishes were silently and deftly removed. "I would be grateful if you should give your master my thanks for his hospitality, and tell him I would be glad of an opportunity to repay it."

The youth only compressed his lips together. "This way," he said shortly. Laurence supposed he could have not looked anything but a vagabond, when they had found him.

The corridors of the house were not so stooped as the chambers. Laurence followed him to a back-chamber with a low writing-desk of some sort set upon the floor: another man sat behind it, working smoothly with brush and ink. His forehead and pate were clean-shaven, with a queue of his back hair clubbed tight and bound down doubled, over the bare skin; his garments were more ornate than the young man's, although of the same style. The young man bowed to him from the waist, and spoke briefly in the Japanese tongue, gesturing towards him.

"Junichiro tells me you are recovered, Dutchman," the man said, laying aside his brush. He looked across the desk at Laurence, wearing an expression of formal reserve, but with none of the dismay the young man—Junichiro?—had aimed at him.

"Sir," Laurence said, "I must correct you: I am an Englishman, Captain William Laurence of—" He halted. Hanging from the wall behind the man's head was a large and polished bronze mirror. The face which looked back at him from it was not merely haggard from his recent ordeal but unfamiliar: his hair grown long; a thin white scar running down his cheek, long-healed, which he did not remember; and lines and wear accumulated. He might have aged years since he had seen himself last.

"Perhaps you would be so kind as to explain to me the circumstances of your arrival in this part of the country," the man said, prompting gently.

Laurence managed to say, reeling, "I am Captain William Laurence, of His Majesty's Ship *Reliant,* of the Royal Navy. And I have not the least notion how I have come to be here, except if my ship has suffered some accident, which God forbid."

Laurence did not much know what else he said afterwards. He supposed they saw his confusion and distress, for the questions stopped, and a servant was called to bring in a tray: a flask and small porcelain cups. His host filled one and gave it to him; Laurence took it and drank blindly, glad for the intensity: strong as brandy though light on the tongue. His cup was refilled promptly, and he drank again; the cup was small enough to be a single swallow. But he put it down afterwards. "I beg your pardon," he said, feeling acutely that he had lost control of himself, and all the more awkward in the face of their carefully polite failure to notice it. "I beg your pardon," he said, more strongly. "Sir, to answer your question, I cannot tell you how I came to be here: I must have been swept overboard, is the only possible answer. As for purpose, I have none; I have neither business nor friends in this part of the world."

He hesitated, yet there was no help for it; he could not help but recognize himself utterly a beggar. Pride should have to be sacrificed. "I am sorry to be so bold as to make any further claims on your generosity," he said, "when you have already been more than kind, but I would be glad—I would be very glad indeed for your assistance in making my way to Nagasaki, where I may be reunited with my ship, or find another to return me to England."

But his host was silent. Finally he said, "You are yet too ill for the rigors of a long journey, I think. For now, permit me to invite you to enjoy the hospitality of my house. If there is anything you require for your comfort, Junichiro will see it is done."

All that was courteous, all that was kind, and yet it was a dismissal. Junichiro silently moved to hover behind Laurence at his elbow, plainly waiting for him to leave. Laurence hesitated, but he could not much argue: there was a low hollow thumping in his head, like the sound of bare heels coming down on a deck overhead, and the liquor already had thrown a further haze over his sight.

He followed Junichiro out and down the hall, back to the small chamber where he had awoken. Junichiro drew open the door and stood waiting; his face remained hard and unfriendly, and he fixed his eyes past Laurence like a grande dame giving the cut direct, though he said with cold hauteur, once Laurence had ducked inside, "Send for me if you should require anything."

Laurence looked about the chamber: the empty floor covered with straw mats, the bare and featureless walls, the silence of it; both the siren's promise of immediate rest, and confinement. "My liberty," he said, grimly, half under his breath.

"Be grateful for your life," Junichiro said with sudden venom, "which you have only by my master's benevolence. Perhaps he will think better of it."

He all but hurled the door shut, the frame rattling on its track, and Laurence could only stare after his shadow disappearing on the other side of the translucent wall.

The green, glassy wave broke against the shoals but flung itself rushing on even as it crumpled. The cold foam washed ferociously up Temeraire's hindquarters and left a fresh line of seaweed and splinters clinging to his hide as it finally fell back, exhausted. A low groaning came from the *Potentate*'s hull where she strained against the rocks, pinned and struggling; all around them the ocean stood wide and empty and grey, and the distant curve of land was only a smudge in the distance.

"You may say anything you like," Temeraire said, flatly, "but I do not care in the least. I will go alone, if I must, whether or not anyone will come and help me."

"Oh, Lord," Granby muttered, half under his breath; Captain Berkley, who was clinging to a stanchion to keep his balance on the badly slanted deck, did not bother to keep his own voice low, but bellowed up, "Listen, you mad beast, you don't suppose any of us like it better than you do?"

"I am quite sure I should like it less than anyone, if Laurence were dead," Temeraire said, "but he is not: he is certainly not dead. Of course I am going to go and look for him: I think it outside of everything for you to try and persuade me to any other course."

He did not bother to keep the reproach from his voice, and the anger. "And I do not see why you will all waste time arguing with me, when you had much better be helping me to organize a search: he cannot come to us, as long as we are still fixed out here in this useless position."

He was himself in an equally unpleasant position: perched awkwardly upon the long line of jagged black rocks, with his hindquarters half in the ocean, and peering over onto the dragondeck at the aviators. The *Potentate* had grounded during the storm: a terrific crash which had nearly sent all the dragons sliding off the deck into the ocean and tipped the ship up and over her ends.

There had been no time to think of anything but the mad scrambling effort to untangle themselves from the storm-chains in time, Laurence throwing himself up to where little Nitidus was pinned beneath three knots, frantically sawing them open and letting him at last wriggle free, so the rest of them had room enough to burst loose while the chains and tarpaulins slid down over the prow, into the churning ocean.

"When you are loose, take hold the anchor-chains at stern and bow!" Laurence had roared to him, before climbing up. "You must hold her back and off her beam-ends, else this cross-ocean will pound her apart on the shoals," and as soon as Temeraire had managed to break free he had done it: he and Maximus and Kulingile all working mightily together, straining against the anchor-chains and every rope that Nitidus and Dulcia could bring up to them, to keep the ship upright while the wind shrieked and tried to batter her and them against the rocks. And Temeraire had borne the brunt of it, for he could better maneuver than either of them: though it was quite impossible to hover properly in the storm, at least he could keep to his position more or less, without being flung down into the waves.

No-one had said a word to him, all that time—no-one had mentioned that Laurence was nowhere to be seen, and likely carried overboard with the chains—until he had finally been able to land exhausted on the deck, and look about, and Roland had slowly come and told him softly that Laurence was lost.

Temeraire did not mind admitting that it had been a very dreadful moment, and he had indulged himself in imagining consequences as dire as any of them. He had gone and swept frantically over all the neighboring ocean, every moment a torment as he found not the least sign of the tarpaulins or Laurence anywhere. But he had forced himself to stop searching empty waves—it had already been several hours, and Laurence would certainly not have stayed in the water, but would have struck right out for land, sensibly—and had gone back to the ship to consult maps to determine where best to find Laurence, and organize a better rescue.

It had not occurred to him that anyone would be so ridiculous as to throw some business of politics in his way: this nonsense of Japan being closed to foreign shipping, and unreasonably intolerant of visitors. Of course Hammond might be counted on to try offering him objections on such flimsy grounds, but Temeraire would have thought better of Granby and Captain Harcourt to lend themselves to it, or any of the other dragons' captains.

Temeraire was trying to be just: he did not hold it against anyone, much, that they had not noticed Laurence missing in the great confusion—although he had been trying to save the entire ship, and others had not been in quite so crucial a position; someone else might have looked sooner—"But I do not think it unreasonably selfish of me," he said, "that now the others should keep on without me, until I have found Laurence. And I will certainly go at once."

The storm was gone and the winds had died down, and Maximus and Kulingile could take it in turn to keep the ship from being smashed upon the shoals: Kulingile was aloft even now, doing his turn alone, and the ship was perfectly well. It did not signify if a few waves came over the side; sailors had to be prepared to get a little wet, now and again.

"I do not even mean to be gone very long," Temeraire said. "I am only asking to take perhaps twenty men, or thirty, and fly to the nearest shore and begin a search: certainly we will find him very soon. Particularly if we should make inquiries amongst the populace."

"We must do nothing of the sort," Hammond said, leaning over the rail and mopping his brow with his handkerchief: the weather was pleasantly hot now under the direct sun, which they had not seen for several days. "Nagasaki is the only harbor of Japan even open to any Western trade: the law utterly forbids the entry of any foreigners into the country, and if they should find Captain Laurence thrown up on their shore—" He stopped talking with a choking cough, as Granby stumbled with the swell on the shuddering deck, and knocked him in the side.

"If they do not want any foreigners about, they should be all the happier for us to find Laurence, and depart," Temeraire said, feeling himself on eminently solid ground. "And after all, we can tell them we do not want to be here, either: we are only on our way to China, and if we had not run into that dreadful squall we should not have troubled them in the least."

"Perhaps instead you might proceed at once to Nagasaki," Gong Su said; he did not quail when Temeraire turned a cold glittering eye upon him, although he did add, "I beg your forgiveness for speaking of a course of action which is distasteful to you, but no good can come from failing to follow the proper forms of intercourse. I am sure that an inquiry laid with the harbormaster, with the proper respect, is most likely to yield the fruit which we all desire: the prince's safe return."

"Not much chance of that, certain sure," O'Dea muttered, from where he was sitting not far away, wrapped in an oilskin and huddled up to Iskierka's side for the warmth, pretending to be worming a rope usefully when really he was only listening. "Cruel, I call it, to keep up his hopes: the ocean keeps what she takes."

"Thank you, O'Dea, that is enough," Granby said sharply.

"It *is* enough," Temeraire said. "You need not silence him, when he is only saying what you all think. Well, I do not care. I am not going to Nagasaki; I am not going to China; I am not going anywhere without Laurence, and I am certainly not going to only sit here and wait."

"No, of course you aren't," Granby said under his breath.

"Oh, yes, you are!" said Iskierka cracking open an eye, now of all times. She had slept nearly the entire storm away fastened down in the most comfortable place, between Maximus and Kulingile, with Temeraire curled round and Lily, Messoria, and Immortalis all heaped on top; during the crisis, she had done absolutely nothing but huddle on an exposed rock and watch, grumblingly, while the rest of them had worked. And now the ship was more secure, she had slung herself, very inconveniently for everyone else, around the base of the mizzenmast to keep sleeping all the day.

"I am not, in the least!" Temeraire said to her, with strong indignation: if she were to tell him Laurence was dead, he would clout her across the nose. "Laurence is not dead."

"I don't see why he should be dead," Iskierka said, "what has that to do with anything? But you are not going haring off into the countryside when we are stuck here on these rocks, and anything at all might happen to the ship."

Temeraire thought this ridiculous. The storm was over, and the

Potentate had not sunk yet; she would not sink now. "Whyever ought I stay here, when Laurence is lost somewhere in Japan?"

"Because I am going to have the egg tomorrow," Iskierka said, then paused and tilted her head thoughtfully, "or perhaps to-day: I want something to eat, and then we shall see."

"The *egg*?" Granby said, staring at her. "What egg? What—do you mean to tell me the two of you blighted fiends have been—"

"Well, of course," Iskierka said. "How else could we have made an egg? Although," she added to Temeraire, "it has been a great deal more trouble for me, so once it is out, I think it is only fair you should look after it: anyway you are not going anywhere, until it is quite safe."

Chapter 2

ANOTHER FULL DAY PASSED in sleep and eating restored Laurence to nearly all the outward semblances of comfort, and robbed him more with every passing minute of the inward: he could not conceive of any course which should have deposited him so unceremoniously on the highways of Japan. He could not even be grateful to find himself equipped, apparently by the hand of deity, with the Chinese language to hand: he would have preferred to have been made mute, and known in the confines of his own mind whence he came, even if he could not have communicated that knowledge to his captors.

And captors they certainly were: his request for transport to Nagasaki remained notably unanswered. He had learnt a little more of his situation from Junichiro, who had despite his earlier flash of resentment continued to wait upon him punctiliously. His host's name was Kaneko Hiromasa; his exact rank Laurence could not entirely work out, but he was at the least a reasonably wealthy man of some position, if judged by the size of his house and the number of servants, and engaged on important affairs by the quantity of papers in his study. A country-gentleman, managing his own estates, or perhaps even an official of some sort. Regardless of his rank, however, it was increasingly plain he did not view Laurence as a mere subject of charity, to be fed and washed and sent on his way.

Laurence had not been able to marshal his resources to pursue the matter on the previous day. Confusion and illness had overcome him, and he had spent nearly all the day asleep, stretched his full length upon the bare mats of the floor, rousing only for dinner. But in the morning he awakened feeling himself again, in body at least; and when the servants came with breakfast, he made plain he wished to speak with Kaneko once again. The ordinary maids did not speak Chinese, but when he had repeated their master's name, they went away, and brought Junichiro back with them.

That young man came to the chamber door and stood outside, his face hard and remote. "My master is presently occupied," he said. "Permit me to address your needs." His voice was flat, and he did not look Laurence in the face. There was a strange mingling of formality and palpable resentment in his manner: all the outward shows of courtesy, and no evidence of any real feeling which might have motivated it.

Laurence could not make sense of it. If his presence had meant some great burden for the household, he might better have understood, but Kaneko need not have picked him up from the ground if so, and in any case the largesse which had been shown him, so far, scarcely seemed of a kind which would have troubled the finances of such a house.

But a full understanding was not his present concern: the meat of the matter was that they did not mean to aid him to get back to his ship. "I remain grateful for your master's hospitality," he said, "but my health is recovered, and I will trespass on it no further: I would ask you for the return of my clothing, and my sword, and to show me the way to the road."

Junichiro looked at him with an expression briefly startled, as though Laurence had asked him for a pair of wings. "What would you do?" he said, with sincere confusion. "You cannot speak the language; you are a foreigner and a barbarian—"

"And," Laurence said, cutting him off short; he could not have said how he knew the word had the flavor of an insult, but he did, "if I mean to go to the devil, that is my business, and surely no concern of yours."

He would indeed have been glad of help, but not of the sort which would keep him penned in a room and plied with food and drink. So far, he seemed to figure at once as an unexpected but welcome guest, and a piece of highly inconvenient baggage: Junichiro plainly wished him gone—or never come at all—but even the servants eyed him with sidelong worried looks that required no translation.

At the very least, Laurence hoped his demand to leave might draw out some response which should illuminate matters, and let him know how better to proceed: and indeed Junichiro hesitated; he left and in a little while returned and said, "My master will see you."

Laurence hoped to make a better show of himself, at this second meeting; he had asked for a razor, and conquered the disquiet of looking at his strangely unfamiliar face in the glass long enough to clear away the several days' growth of beard. The servants had brought him to a bathing room, peculiarly divided with a wooden-slatted floor on which they insisted on scrubbing him in the open air, surely unhealthy in the extreme and inviting a chill, before permitting him to step into the large bath, itself excessively hot; at least, he had thought it so, but on emerging he could not deny it had done splendidly to ease his aches.

When ushered into the office this time, he was able to fold himself down in a better imitation of what was evidently the polite kneeling posture; his legs still complained of the position, but he was not so weak he was at every moment in danger of tipping over and having to reach out a hand to steady himself awkwardly against the floor with his fingertips.

Kaneko was frowning, however: Laurence's sword lay on the desk before him, unsheathed, and in the sunlight coming through the open window looked even more splendid than Laurence had recalled: jewels gleamed from the dragon's-head of the hilt, and the blade shone. His fingers itched to hold it again. "Where did you have this from?" Kaneko asked, touching the hilt.

Laurence could not bring himself to make the fantastic if honest answer that he did not recall: in any event, he did not feel himself compelled to answer such a question, personal and unjustified. "Are you proposing, sir," he said, "that I have stolen it? The sword is mine, as are the coat, the shirt, and the trousers you found upon me; I am sorry to be equally unable to provide you with the bills of sale for any of them, if you should require the same to restore them to me."

Kaneko hesitated. "This is a very fine blade," he said, finally.

He seemed to want something more, but Laurence could not provide it. "Yes," he said, unyielding, as he could not be otherwise. "I am a serving-officer of His Majesty's Navy, sir; I rely upon my sword."

He waited; he did not entirely understand what concerned Kaneko so about the blade. Finally, Kaneko said bluntly, "It is of Chinese make," and Laurence inwardly flinched not with surprise, but with the absence of surprise: he realized he knew as much, and had not even thought it strange, before.

"I have another of Spanish," Laurence said, swallowing his confusion, "and one of Prussian. Do you mean to keep it?"

Junichiro twitched as if with indignation, but Kaneko did not answer, only looking down still at the sword: Laurence had an impression he was dissatisfied with the answer, but why he should have cared where the sword had come from, Laurence could not say. "If not," he added, "I would be glad for its return."

"Ah," Kaneko said, and tapped his fingers once upon the desk, before stilling his hand. "The bakufu has directed that only a samurai may bear a long sword."

"If that is, as I suppose, a knight," Laurence said, "I am the third son of the Earl of Allendale and, as I have already said, a ship's captain: I must consider both my birth and my rank adequate to my arms by any reasonable standard. I will speak plainly, sir: if you mean to pillage me, I should be hard-put to prevent you under the circumstances, but I will thank you not to dress it up with justifications as ungentlemanly as they are unwarranted."

"How dare you speak so to my master?" Junichiro flared up, half-rising on his knees. "You should have died, but for his intervention—"

"I did not request your aid," Laurence said flatly, to Kaneko rather than to his squire, "and should rather have had none of it than a pretense at the same: I consider it no favor to be fed and clothed, and held against my will. If you are making yourself my jailor, sir, I should care to know on what grounds I am to meet with such treatment. So far as I know there is peace between our nations, and a shipwreck has in every civilized society all the claims to human sympathy which any man should care to receive, himself being the victim of such a disaster."

"One who breaks the law may desire sympathy and yet not deserve it!" Junichiro said, and then subsided: Kaneko had raised his hand a very little.

"If a man may break the laws of your nation merely by being hurled unwillingly upon your shore," Laurence said dryly, "then they seek to constrain not the will of man, but of God."

"Enough, Junichiro," Kaneko said quietly, when the young man would have answered hotly again. "The objection is just: I have not been of true service to you, as I vowed to be."

He sat in silence a moment, looking down at his desk, while Laurence wondered at *vowed:* he had done nothing to earn any promise of service himself; was Kaneko under some sort of religious obligation?

"The obligations of honor are many," Kaneko said at last, "and often contradictory."

Junichiro made a violent motion of protest, a hand chopped across the air, outstretched as if he meant to catch the words even being spoken. Kaneko glanced at him, and with affection but sternly said, "Enough, Junichiro."

"Master," Junichiro said, "not for *this*. Not—"

Laurence watched them, disturbed: the young man's voice was breaking, though Kaneko seemed as placid as a lake; he felt abruptly as awkward as though he had wandered into a stranger's house, and found it full of family quarrels addressed only obliquely, through hints.

"I must write to Lady Arikawa," Kaneko said, "and offer her my apologies. I see now that I have acted wrongly: I did not have the right to undertake an oath which might expose her to charges of disobedience to the bakufu. I regret that you must endure a delay in my answer," he added to Laurence. "It must be her will, and not mine, whether I am permitted to fulfill my vow with honor by offering you assistance, and then make her my amends."

"Pray Heaven she commands otherwise," Junichiro said.

"You will desire no such thing," Kaneko said, sharply, and after a moment, the young man looked away and muttered, "No."

Kaneko nodded once, and then dismissed them both silently but pointedly by returning his attention to his writing-work as thoroughly as if he had been alone in the chamber.

Laurence hesitated, but the decision seemed made: he followed Junichiro's shoulders, hunched forward a little as though he still felt his master's reproof, back through the corridors to his own chamber. "I should like my own clothing again, at least," he said abruptly, when they had reached the small room, and he had stepped inside, "if there is no objection to that."

"If you wish to look like a ragged beggar, I suppose it can be accomplished," Junichiro said, savagely, and closed the wall-panel behind him. But Laurence for the moment was as glad to be shut in with his own thoughts.

It seemed plain that the law here was inhospitable in the extreme to foreigners, and only some kind of vow—now-regretted—had impelled Kaneko to undertake the forms of charity towards him, evidently at real risk of his own disgrace. This Lady Arikawa, whoever she might be—perhaps his liege, certainly a person of authority—would be under no similar constraint. Kaneko might wish to leave his fate to the will of this lady, and so propitiate her, but Laurence felt not the slightest inclination to accommodate his plans. If return he owed, for hospitality so unwillingly given, then removing himself from the situation was all the return he was prepared to make.

The house was large, but hardly fortified, and he had seen only a few manservants. If the law generally barred the possession of blades, his own lack might not be an insurmountable obstacle if he could not get at the sword; although that, too, might be accomplished. The chief difficulty was not an escape, he thought, but its sequel. He could with an effort summon up the shape of the nation, on a chart, but he had never sailed this way in his life. If he had been asked to find Nagasaki by latitude and longitude, from memory, he might as well have made for Perdition straightaway.

But with any luck he could find his way back to the coast, whence perhaps some fisherman might be prevailed upon to carry him in secret to the port: and if he had not dreamt it in his delirium, the buttons of his coat had been gold. If not, in any case there might be a few coins in a pocket, or slipped through into the lining, if his things had not been pillaged.

They had not. Junichiro returned only a little while later with a servant trailing him, who set down on the floor just inside the room the bundle of clothing. And when the door had closed, and Laurence held the salt-stained and ruined clothes, he found the buttons, still firmly sewn on, were gold; and so, too, were the long narrow bars athwart each shoulder where the epaulettes had ought to be—

—and the coat itself was an aviator's green.

The first order of business was plainly to get the ship afloat again: a ship sitting on rocks was of no use to anyone. "But shan't the ocean get in, once those are underwater?" Lily said, her head tilted to examine the gaping holes where the rocks had pierced the hull and yet stood within, keeping the *Potentate* fixed upon the shoals.

"Oh! by no means," Temeraire said. "They will patch it, with some timber and oakum, I believe; or perhaps with something else, it makes not a particle of difference. That is not *our* affair: that is for the sailors to worry about."

He spoke with impatience, which he was aware Lily did not deserve, but he could not quite help himself. It was so very hard to stay here, especially when he was forced to overhear the officers, who insisted on speaking to one another in the certainty of Laurence's death; even Granby, of whom Temeraire would have expected better, had only said to Hammond, "For Heaven's sake, Hammond, let him think as he likes. It will take him dreadfully, when he *does* believe it."

"Well, I am *not* going to believe it, so there," Temeraire said, to himself; but it certainly did not improve his already-great anxiety to be away, searching for Laurence; and neither did Churki sitting there like a great unhelpful lump and wagging her head seriously and saying, "This is what comes of putting all your heart in just one person! Hammond, I should have mentioned before, I hope *you* are thinking of marriage, and do not fear that I am inclined to be unreasonable. As long as she is young enough to have a great many children, I will be very pleased, whatever your choice."

Temeraire snorted: Churki might be considerably older, and very experienced from her service with the Incan army, but what did she know of it, anyway. He was quite done considering her opinion as particularly worthwhile; at least, on *this* subject.

But he very badly wished to go look for Laurence, anyway: and after all, there was no egg *yet;* there might not be an egg for days, and until there was an egg, it was none of his business but Iskierka's, whatever she might say. And he would have gone, indeed—if only he could have persuaded himself that this explanation would hold the least weight with Laurence.

But Temeraire could just see himself trying to tell Laurence that he had left an egg on a ship swinging about on some rocks, with no-one to look after it but Iskierka. And not just any egg, but his very own egg and Iskierka's: a Celestial and Kazilik cross, which

Granby had said that very afternoon, to Captain Blaise, was likely worth more than the crown jewels of Britain—Temeraire had never seen these, but he was sure they must be impressive—and they must have a great deal of straw and a warm room set aside for it, if he pleased.

"But the ship is not in any *real* danger, at present," Temeraire argued, to an imagined Laurence, "and after all if it did sink, we are close enough to fly to shore. And it is not *only* Iskierka to watch over it: there are Maximus and Lily, too, who would not let anything happen to the egg; and the rest of our formation, and Kulingile and Churki, besides. Really it would be extraordinary if anything should go wrong—"

But the vision of Laurence was unpersuaded, and only looked at him with gentle reproof: it was not *their* responsibility; it was his, and not to be pushed off onto someone else. Temeraire's ruff drooped as he lost the argument with himself once again.

"Anyway," he said to Lily now, out loud, with apology in his tone, "I am sure they will manage that part of the business perfectly well: so pray let us think how we are to get her off the rocks, instead."

He had hoped, at first, that they might simply be able to lift the ship with all of them working together, but the ship's master Mr. Ness had categorically made this impossible as a matter of weight. When he had worked the figures large enough to see clearly, Temeraire had been forced to admit as much: why on earth anyone had put five hundred tons of pig iron and another four hundred of shingle at the very bottom of the *Potentate*'s hold was quite a mystery to him, and he could not in the least work out how she stayed afloat ordinarily, but lifting her straight up by even an inch would certainly be beyond their power.

"If only we might rig a pulley!" he added again, but his best ingenuity had failed at contriving any way to establish a pulley in mid-air, above the ship, out in the middle of the ocean. "Or a lever—"

"Well, what about a lever?" Maximus said, gingerly sitting back on his haunches on the shoals, giving over his own attempts to inspect the holes: the ocean was too rough to see them from any distance. "That is only a stick, put underneath and pushed, ain't it?" and Temeraire paused. He had been stopped, by the size of the ship, but perhaps—

"Where the devil are we to get a lever big enough to move her?" Mr. Ness called down at them, in exasperation. "Why, it should have to be taller than Babel."

"We do not want *one* lever," Temeraire said, with a sudden burst of inspiration. "We want three: one for me, and Maximus, and Kulingile, all to push on at once; and we will get trees from the shore to make them."

Laurence would have given a great deal for a pair of boots. He contented himself, in the meantime, by working out a way of lacing the sandals more closely to his feet with the unraveled remnants of his woolen stockings, braided to make thin ropes. The coat he made into a bundle with his trousers: at least in the native clothing, he hoped he would not be utterly conspicuous at a glance, when he had tied a rag over his hair.

The bundle he left in the corner of the room when the servants came with the evening meal, and despite the reawakening of his sense of taste, he forced himself to eat even the fermented fish with its sour, vinegared rice; he could not anticipate another meal, any time soon. When it was cleared away, and the noises of the house began to die away along with the light filtering in through the rice-paper walls, Laurence debated with himself the merits of going after the sword. All practicality argued against it. He could not be sure the sword would yet be in Kaneko's office, nor that the chamber would be unguarded; if he did retrieve it, the blade should then have to be concealed somehow, or draw unwanted attention. A sword wrapped in a bundle of clothing would be of little use if he were confronted unexpectedly by a few pursuers; and only if he were taken so might he hope to escape.

"Well," Laurence said, standing, "I may as well have a look: if it does not come easy to hand, I may always withdraw." He felt awkward, uneasy in the decision: irrational, when so many sensible arguments stood against it. He could not have said why; some inarticulate feeling only revolted. He did not want to leave the sword.

He mentally told himself to wake at four bells of the middle watch, and slept until the deep of the night, rousing from another strange and unpleasant dream: great chains tangled around his wrists, dragging him through deep water. He took his bundle, slung over a shoulder by his belt, and stepped cautiously out into the hallway: the soft matting did not betray him as he walked, barefoot to keep the slap of the sandals from making any noise.

The walls were a faint luminescent grey, paler than their frames. He kept the very tips of his fingers lightly against the surface of the paper, guiding his steps through the dark. There was a yellow glow of lantern-light somewhere on his right—outside the house, he thought; within, all the rooms were dark. He came to Kaneko's office, and the door slid soundlessly open on its track. He thought at first he had mistaken the room: the desk was gone, and the room entirely bare at first glance. Then Laurence saw the furniture had all been tidied away against the walls, and the writing-desk stood atop a low chest.

He carefully lifted down the desk, and opening the lid found the blade wrapped in a soft silk cloth, which he left behind. He put the sword inside his bundle of clothing, pulling out folds to conceal it from hilt to tip, and restored the chest and desk to their places. He was comforted to have the sword again, and yet distressed for being so: too much as though he could not trust himself, his own feelings, to be as they ought.

Slipping back into the hallway, he looked for a way out, and followed a breath of air to the entryway: a very indifferent sentry drowsed in a corner, and Laurence was past him and had a foot in the gardens when a great roaring came from above, a sound at once familiar and bone-rattling, though he had not heard it since the battle of the Nile: a dragon, overhead, and the lights of all the house flared at his back.

"Buggering mad, the lot of you," Mr. Ness had said, rudely, but Temeraire had with some exasperation demanded a better suggestion of him and, failing to receive any, had nodded firmly.

"Then we shall at least try," he said, "and if it does not work, then I suppose you must begin to take out all that ballast and throw it into the ocean, along with the cannon, until we *can* lift the ship; and while you do that, Iskierka will go to the shore to be safe, and the other dragons will stay with her and the egg, and I will go and find Laurence. You *will* stay with the egg?" he appealed, turning his head.

"Of course we will," Maximus said stoutly, and Lily added, "All of us: except Nitidus will go with you, to carry messages back and forth," an excellent notion. Temeraire was quite sure no-one would give any trouble to Iskierka *and* Lily *and* Maximus.

"Anyway," Lily said, "perhaps it needn't come to that, and I am quite ready to be off these rocks: let us go by all means and fetch some trees."

But they were unable to leave immediately: "I want to come, too!" Kulingile called down, in protest. Certainly Temeraire could not stay, but Maximus stood on seniority and refused to stay behind, either, which bode fair to make a quarrel; and meanwhile Hammond began bleating of the necessity to avoid being seen. Well, Temeraire did not mean to go in blowing on trumpets, but after all, they did need to take away several large trees, and he supposed someone might notice: that would not be his fault.

"We had better come along, then, Hammond; and all your crews, also," Churki said.

Hammond, taken aback, said, "Certainly not—a martial presence, nothing more undesirable—"

But Churki shook her head censoriously at him. "If there are dragons here, they will certainly assume we are here to take their people away if they do not see we have any of our own. And if there are men, they will want men to talk to: that is only the natural order of things, and all the more so if they are like these peculiar sailors you have here on this vessel, who are afraid of dragons."

Hammond paused, doubtful; Temeraire could see the sense in what Churki said, but he did not mean to countenance the delay involved in getting all the crews aboard. He only had a scant few officers himself, but Lily and her formation-dragons had their full crews, and even the aviators could not easily go clambering aboard from the precarious surface which the ship presently offered.

"The captains shall come with us," Temeraire said, "and Ferris shall come with me, which will make a sensible number of men, and not any sort of threatening number; and," to Kulingile, "this time Maximus shall go, and if we cannot get the boat off, then *next* time, you shall: that is surely only fair. And," he added, very handsomely in his opinion, "I will take the lines when we come back to give you a rest before we lever her off, even though it will not be my turn yet."

"I do not need a rest," Kulingile said disconsolately. "This is not very difficult: it is only tiresome, and I want something better to eat, which you are sure to get when you are on land."

"Oh!" Iskierka said, raising up her head from the dragondeck, where she had lain down again, ignoring Granby and Maximus's surgeon Gaiters clambering about her hindquarters, consulting in low voices, "a cow! You shall bring me back a cow, Temeraire; do not forget it."

"Wherever am I to find a cow, which is not someone's property?" Temeraire said in exasperation, and Hammond at once began to speak again—likely the discussion should have been another hour, but Temeraire realized his mistake and said quickly, "but we will bring you both back something good to eat, if we should find anything without anyone seeing us, or objecting: we will save you the very best of what we find, you have my promise."

"Well, that is fair," Kulingile said, mollified, and Temeraire put out a foreleg on the dragondeck for Ferris, who hesitated only a moment before climbing into his grasp, and then launched them before anyone else could object further, or make any more unreasonable demands.

Ferris was very quiet, when he had got astride Temeraire's neck and buckled himself on, while they hovered waiting for the other dragons to take up their captains and come aloft—Temeraire was careful to keep out of ear-shot of the deck. "Are you quite well, Ferris?" Temeraire said, craning about his head.

Ferris hesitated; he looked a great deal better lately, Temeraire had even before now noticed and approved: he could not help but congratulate himself for it, and see in it evidence that he was not a careless guardian of his crew, despite all their trials amongst the Inca and since.

Certainly Ferris was happier than when he had first come back to them in New South Wales; he was not so weary-looking, and the ruddy blotches which had marred his face then had cleared. He looked nearer his four-and-twenty than he had, and if he did not wear a green coat—Temeraire did not understand why Hammond had not straightened out that matter yet—at least the coat which he did wear, brown, was neat and trim and with silver buttons; and he took excellent care of his linen, which was properly white.

"You ought have taken Forthing," Ferris said abruptly.

"Oh, Forthing," Temeraire said, with a flick of his ruff. "Why-ever for? I do not see why I ought to be giving Forthing any special notice: he is very well, I suppose, for ordinary work."

"He is an officer of the Corps," Ferris said, "and I—I am not; he is your first lieutenant."

"You were, before him," Temeraire said, "except for Granby; whom I cannot ask to come away from Iskierka under the circumstances. I do not take any notice of what some silly court-martial may have said, Ferris: I hope you do not think I do, and you ought not, either. Why, they declared Laurence should be put to death; you cannot imagine their judgment holds any water with me, or anyone of sense."

Ferris was silent, and then he said, "You wouldn't be taking Forthing up, no matter what, I suppose."

"Taking him up?" Temeraire said. "I am perfectly happy for him to ride, when the rest of the crew do," although this was not *entirely* true: with as much opportunity as Ferris had been given, during their brief stay in Brazil, Forthing had not bothered to repair any of his wardrobe but what had outright holes in it; his green coat was faded almost to grey, his neckcloth a disgrace, and his trousers frayed at hem and seams. It was an embarrassment, and all Temeraire's hinting had gone unheeded entirely.

"No, I mean," Ferris said, hesitated, and said, "if Captain Laurence—if we should not—"

Temeraire was still quite puzzled a moment; then he understood, and indignation swelled his breast. "I should not take that slovenly third-rate—*piker* for my captain if he were the last person to be had on the earth," he said, heatedly. "Oh! *Him,* to succeed Laurence: I should like to see it! If the Admiralty should dare to propose it, I should go to Whitehall and bring the Navy Offices down about their ears.

"Anyway," he added, in the teeth of his own anxiety, "I am sure Laurence will look after himself very well, until we can come get him: oh! Why are they taking so very long about getting aloft?"

The flight was not a long one, the coast rising ahead of them as they flew, the waters still depthless blue-black beneath. Dulcia and Nitidus sped on ahead in spite of Hammond's cries of protest, but they circled back to meet the rest of them shortly before they all came over the coast: they had seen a few small fishing-boats, they reported, and a great many large half-drowned rice fields, with the beginnings of green shoots.

"But nothing very nice to eat," Nitidus said sadly. "Why, I did not even see a sheep, or a goat."

"Thank Heaven," Temeraire could overhear Hammond say, foolishly: it would have been nice to know sheep might be had, even if they could not easily be got.

Captain Warren fetched Nitidus a buffet to the shoulder, and raised his speaking-trumpet to call over from his back, as they fell back into formation, "More to the point, there's a bay straight-away three points to the north, with pine-trees as handsome as you could like."

The bay was isolate, the glossy black water's surface broken with a great many lumpy protruding rocks which likely made it inconvenient for fishing-boats, and showed no signs of use except a low stone wall which did not seem to have any purpose at all; it only ran along the shore in either direction. Hammond let himself down from Churki's back clumsily but with haste the instant they had landed, and hurried to inspect: it was overgrown with a carpet of pale short green grass. "I see no sign of any other sort of traffic," he said, with great relief, when he had straightened up, "so now pray let us get the trees and be away: at once, at once. I shall account all arrears of Fortune paid off, if only we should escape without notice."

Lily cocked her head, considering, and said, "I suppose we should like them to fall inwards: stand back, all of you, if you please."

"And to the north," Captain Harcourt added, from her back, looking at the narrow wind-socks which stood up from Lily's harness at various points. "Sing out when you are all safe away."

Temeraire waited until Hammond with the rest of the company was moving, hastily, out of any chance of Lily's acid spattering, and then announced, "I will go aloft, and see if I can make out anything more of the countryside: I should not like to disappoint Iskierka."

In point of fact, he was quite willing to disappoint Iskierka if there were no cows to be had; but so long as they were here on land, Temeraire did not see any reason not to have a look around for Laurence. "Of course we are not *likely* to see him," he added to Ferris, over his shoulder, as he flew quickly away before he might have to hear Hammond shouting protests after him, "but if only we should happen to, how convenient that would be: even Hammond could not complain, then. And even if we do not, we will have saved some time, later; we will not have to search here again. We will not go far, we will only go along the coast—"

Indeed, he did not go so far that he did not hear the thundering crash of the first pine, coming down; he did not wish to risk overlooking any sign. The coast was mostly rocky, save for a few other inlets and narrow streams coming down, but not very high. "I do not think it would be *excessively* difficult to get safely ashore, for a man swimming," Temeraire said to Ferris.

Ferris said, "There aren't cliffs, at least," in a consoling way. "Shan't we turn back, now? Those fishermen there are sure to see us if only they look up, and I think that must be a harbor over there—"

"But there are a few more beaches in this direction," Temeraire said. "We shall go and have a look at those, from the air: I am sure they are too busy fishing to pay any attention to—"

He was interrupted in this optimistic speech by a sudden bellowing roar, loud and strangely gargled: he turned back hurriedly. "I do not see anyone in the air," Temeraire said, uncertainly, peering in every direction: the day was clear, and he could not imagine where the roar had come from. "Perhaps it was only another pine coming down—"

"That noise was no tree-fall," Ferris said, urgently, and Temeraire could not disagree however much he wished to do; he turned back towards the bay and crested the trees just in time to find, to his appalled surprise, Maximus and Lily and the others all mantling towards a monstrous sea-serpent rearing itself up out of the bay. The rocks were not rocks at all; they were a part of its body, and it was twice as big as Maximus even only in the parts which Temeraire could see.

And then Temeraire realized he was wrong: it was *not* a serpent; it was a dragon, with forelegs out upon the sand: only it was very long, and with stubby wings. It opened its mouth and made another roaring noise, a deep angry growling demand at the formation, which carried over the water clear enough, but in some language which Temeraire did not recognize.

They stood all amazed a moment, regarding one another, very much like figures upon a war-table from Temeraire's distant view. When none of them answered, the serpent-dragon reached for the second tree, which had struck partway into the water. Lily sprang forward and put her talons upon it; the great dragon made a dismissive snort in her direction, which needed no translation.

Temeraire beat urgently towards them as Lily raised her wings and flared them out a little: the brilliant orange and purple would have warned any European beast, and their immense wingspan, but it was no surprise if the Japanese dragon did not recognize her as a Longwing, or did not know what that meant; and she was not a third his size. Temeraire saw Captain Harcourt, a tiny figure, lean forward on Lily's neck and point to the sand; Lily turned her head and spat a thin demonstrative stream of acid, to make her point.

The serpentine dragon drew back from the hissing black stench and the thin trails of smoke, its own small wings flattening against its back, and then it plunged its head into the water and opened its jaw wide. The dragon, already so massive but slender, began now to rapidly swell up and out to the sides: Temeraire could not understand in the least how he was managing it, and then the dragon reared itself back out and up, and up, and up, and it blasted Lily and all the others with a torrent of water.

"Oh!" Temeraire cried, "Oh, it is a Sui-Riu!" that variety of dragon being known to him from Sir Edward Howe's work on the Oriental breeds, but as he flew towards them as quickly as ever he could, he thought with some strong indignation that Sir Edward might have mentioned the immense—the truly immense—scale; and the book had not in the least conveyed the true impact of the water-spouting.

Even Maximus had been swept off his feet, and was now tangled and struggling up against the tree-line; Lily was coughing and sputtering, having taken the brunt of the torrent, jerking her head, and Nitidus and Dulcia had been carried into the bay itself and were floundering in the waves. Immortalis and Churki were a tumbled sand-clogged mess flung into the woods, trying to get their footing again; Sutton and Messoria, having stationed themselves back and apart, were a little better off and getting into the air.

But the Sui-Riu evidently had no intention of letting them get their bearings back: he had plunged his head back into the water and was inhaling again. He might blast them on the far side, and so sweep more of them into the water, where he would certainly have an advantage, since he could breathe through it: unsporting, except that to be fair he was one against eight.

However, Temeraire could not give him much credit for that: no-one had asked the Sui-Riu to be so unfriendly. Lily had given the most polite warning one could ask for—if *she* had liked to be similarly nasty, she might have taken the Sui-Riu directly in the eye with her shot. Temeraire worked his lungs as he flew, gathering breath, and even as the Sui-Riu drew himself up out of the water again, Temeraire dived towards him, roaring in full and terrible voice.

The waters of the bay shuddered from the divine wind, the surface going for a moment bowl-like and concave; the Sui-Riu was bowled over onto his side with an immense splash, and his torrent erupted involuntarily and spilled harmless over the water, merely adding more turbulence. But the distance was too great, or else perhaps the water somehow absorbed some of the impact; the Sui-Riu managed to right himself in the water, and did not look so dreadfully injured as did most dragons who had borne the direct brunt of the divine wind. Only a little blood trickled black from his right ear, over scales that were a deep greenish black the color of dry seaweed, and his eye on that side was bloodshot: otherwise he seemed quite all right, and great sharp fins were rising up angrily all over his back, like blades.

But Temeraire was hovering off the shore, now, closer; and Maximus and Lily were righting themselves. The others fell into line behind Lily, taking up their formation-positions. Temeraire did not much like formation-fighting, but one could not deny its tactical usefulness, and the Sui-Riu evidently did not have any difficulty recognizing his increasing disadvantage. Shaking away the last of the effects, he looked up at Temeraire, and his eyes—a great slitted pale grey that looked nearly white—drew thin and narrow.

The Sui-Riu rumbled some remarks in a most angry tone, sounding more like a distant thundercloud than anything else. "I do not have any notion what you are saying," Temeraire informed him loudly, in Chinese, "but you needn't complain of us, when you attack people out of nowhere—if you should—"

But as abruptly as he had emerged before, the Sui-Riu was gone: in one smooth motion he plunged beneath the dark murky waters of the bay, clouded even further now by silt and sand raised in their exchange. One long barnacled curve of tail breached the water, and was gone: though Temeraire held position a long time, he did not break the surface again.

Chapter 3

THE LANTERNS WERE COMING alight, one after another, all through the house. Laurence could trace the servants moving in waves as the glow spread behind the walls. The sentry at the door was waking with a snorting start and jerking to his feet, blinking around. Laurence for a moment considered: the man was paunchy and sleep-dazed, armed only with a short blade—a quick struggle might see him through—

But the dragon was descending from aloft—the dragons, rather, for there were two immense black shadows against the milky wash of the moonless night, coming into the lamp-light. One, the larger, had wide green eyes that glowed like a cat's: it was not looking at him presently, but if it could see in the dark, like the Fleur-de-Nuit, nothing could be easier than for the beast to hunt him down while he fumbled over unfamiliar ground in the dark.

Quickly, Laurence turned instead and thrust his small bundle into the ornamental bushes planted against the side of the house, and then went and stood by the door of the house to wait, as though he had been brought there. The sentry looked at him in confusion, but Laurence looked back at him with unmoving face, brazening it out, and the man was in a moment overwhelmed by a sudden flow of servants hurrying out into the garden. Junichiro appeared by Laurence's elbow.

"What are you doing out here?" the young man demanded, but

preoccupied himself did not wait for an answer; instead he seized Laurence by the arm and drew him along with the flow of people. "They have certainly come on your account," he said, "so you may as well stay here."

Kaneko was coming out of the house himself, dressed in formal robes; he wore two blades at his belt and came past his servants, who had arrayed themselves in a square as neat as any infantry troop. Two last men were hurrying around the perimeter of a great flagstoned courtyard, lighting lamps all around it, and then they all knelt together as the dragons came descending into the square, Kaneko out ahead of the rest of the party.

The dragons settled themselves neatly upon the ground; the larger, grey in body and something the size of a middle-weight, wore curious pale green silken dressings the color of its eyes wound about its neck and wing-tips and forelegs, which coming loose made graceful arcs about its body like sails spilling their wind. It had not a single man aboard. The smaller dragon, a brilliant yellow beast larger than a Winchester though not up to combat-weight, carried four: of these, the lead gentleman was dressed in elaborate and formal robes bearing signs of some sort of office, and the others were evidently servants who carried boxes and one an armful of scrolls, and preceding him down unfolded a set of steps to enable him to make a more ponderous and imposing descent.

The grey dragon bent its head towards Kaneko while the men dismounted. It spoke to him in the Japanese tongue, and he bowed more deeply and said something back. Laurence caught the name Arikawa out of it, but he saw no women; perhaps these were Lady Arikawa's emissaries, and he could see nothing to bode well for his future in their cold faces.

There was a little more formal exchange between them, which Laurence could not follow: he was all the more conscious of his utter isolation, of himself as a prisoner among strangers, unable even to pick out a word or to conceive their intentions. The servants were dismissed; the guests and Kaneko went inside the house;

Junichiro took him by the arm and drew him along after them. They turned immediately from the entryway into a chamber on the side, whose entire outer wall was slid back and left wide open to face upon the courtyard where the dragons had settled themselves.

The servants brought great kettles of steaming sharp-nosed tea out to bowls laid before the beasts. The official and Kaneko were served afterwards; they drank, making what Laurence assumed from their tone was mere small conversation, until abruptly he was drawn in front of them, and without hesitation or change of demeanor the official addressed him in Chinese and said, "What is your purpose in coming to our nation?"

"Sir," Laurence said, "I have no purpose but to be restored to my country-men, and my ship if at all possible."

It was the opening salvo of an interrogation which proceeded despite the hour of the night, and was as frustrating to Laurence as it was to his interlocutor. He could not but be conscious of the impossibility of avowing himself unable to *remember* his purpose. Better to be thought a liar than a lunatic, he was sure, but unable to confess this truth, he felt every other word hung upon a knife-edge of honor. He did not know why he was here, and therefore could not say with honest confidence that he meant them no injury. What if the Japanese sheltered some French ship, which he pursued?

"I am a shipwreck: I did not choose to be thrown on your shore, and my presence here is the merest accident," he said again, the best he could do. "And as you have received no declaration of war, from Britain, nor any envoy," he added, hoping as much was true, "then, sir, I hope you will believe I am not here as your enemy. You surely cannot imagine me intended in any way to be a spy, and His Majesty's Government does not behave in so underhanded a manner as to attack another nation with no warning or quarrel."

The official, who had been addressed by the others as Matsudaira, was an older man, with a narrow beard that framed his face in dark lines salted a little with grey; his mouth was thin and hard.

"Indeed," he said, and put down his teacup. "With your gracious permission, Lady Arikawa, we will take the Englishman to Hakata Bay, and consult him upon the evidence there."

Laurence looked in confusion for any new arrival; then the grey dragon answered, in Chinese, "Let it be done," with some reluctance in her tone. Kaneko, frowning slightly, looked at her: the dragon shook her head at him, setting the arcs of green fabric trembling.

The sun was rising, little by little, as they went. Kaneko alone went with the grey dragon—who, Laurence somewhat doubtfully supposed, *was* Lady Arikawa. She bent her foreleg and invited Kaneko upon her back: evidently some sign of great condescension on her part, and one of which Matsudaira did not approve, judged from the tightening of his lips. Laurence himself and the rest of the company went aboard the second, smaller beast.

Junichiro, left behind to watch the house, had watched them go aboard with his eyes darting anxiously from his master to Matsudaira: he, too, saw the magistrate's frowns. Yet he maintained his composure, or nearly so: when the dragons leapt aloft, his face turned up to follow them, betraying for a moment a boyish note of longing. Laurence recognized it as kin to the feeling which he had worn himself as a boy hanging on the prow of his uncle's ship, although he had never thought of attaching such a feeling to dragons.

Laurence was grateful to find both his stomach and his courage easily equal to the journey; he had been able to make his way up the harness without hesitation or awkwardness, and the wind cool and fragrant and crisp in his face was a pleasure despite the great rushing speed. They were near the ocean: dawn broke over the water brilliantly, sunlight a streaming silver path towards them so that Laurence's eyes teared with the glare. The green fabric on Lady Arikawa's back, which she had drawn taut about herself for the flight, was bordered with innumerable small gems which blazed in the new light. She averted her eyes from the sun, however, and dropped back so the smaller dragon's shadow could land upon her head and give her some relief from the light. Laurence noted it with some small gratitude: she would be no very effective searcher during the daylight, perhaps—if he could somehow still manage his escape.

The tenor of Matsudaira's interrogation had left Laurence in no doubt of the increasing urgency of flight. He could curse the ill-fortune that had brought the dragons down at so unexpected an hour, but not berate himself for failure. He had planned his attempt at escape as well as he could, and at least he had avoided giving rise to suspicion—he was neither bound nor chained at present, and Kaneko had not even missed the sword yet.

As soon as another opportunity afforded, even perhaps during this excursion, Laurence meant to try again. He had kept the gold bars tucked into the sash of his garment, so he was not wholly without resources even without his lost bundle. The flight indeed might aid him, for they were aloft more than an hour: Laurence had not realized he had been brought so far from the shore, but Kaneko's house evidently stood perhaps fifteen or even as much as twenty miles inland.

"Hakata Bay" was a promising sound, however: at least he should be on the coast again, and if there were any chance of slipping away, he could more easily hunt out some fishing-boat. So, at least, he told himself; he refused to listen to the grim internal voice which would fain have whispered in his ear at length of the impracticalities of any such plan, and the absurdity of escaping alone from a large and well-armed party accompanied by dragons, no less. Hopelessness was a worse defeat than any other; he did not mean to yield to it.

The countryside below was not unpromising for his purposes. At first the land below was settled; but towards the end of their flight, the dragons turned away from a bustling harbor full of shipping, following the line of an old low stone wall—some sort of coastal defense, perhaps? It resembled nothing so much as some of the defenses thrown up against Napoleon, on Britain's own shores.

It carried them along to a more isolate shore, hidden by the curving of the coastline, where there was only a mere fringe of sand leading up to a thick forest of tree-trunks, which Laurence thought might serve to hide him even from dragons.

But as they landed, the waters of the bay shuddered and broke open, and a monstrous creature came rising from the waves. It was something like the sea-serpents of half-legendary repute, but magnified to a size that put to shame the most outrageous and absurd sea-tales Laurence had ever heard passed off for truth by sailors; he had never even conceived its like.

The smaller dragons landed before it and bowed their heads low to the ground; the men slid to the sand and all knelt deeply before the creature. It climbed a little way out on the shore to meet them, its enormous talons digging great gouges in the sand, so deep that water pooled up in them as it lifted them to claw its way further up the shore. It made a rumbling speech to the party, permitting them to rise, and even inclined its head a very little to Lady Arikawa; but when at last it swung its heavy finned head towards Laurence, a glitter of angry malice shone in its pallid white eyes, one of them shot through with broken black vessels of blood.

"Pray be reasonable," Hammond said, leaning greenish over the rail; he was chewing a great lump of coca leaves in his distended cheek, an effort to make up for the wad he had lost when the Sui-Riu had swamped them: he was still in his sodden clothing. "We *must* go on to Nagasaki, as soon as we may, and there make amends. Only consider: if the beast was not some mere feral creature, and it should report our quarrel, any efforts to find Captain Laurence will certainly be grievously hampered by the opposition of the authorities—"

"What you mean is," Temeraire said, "you want us to run away from that big sea-dragon like cowards, only because you are afraid he will come after the ship."

He did not bother to be polite about it. Captain Blaise had not been the least reluctant to express his own sentiments, when Temeraire and the others had returned, on the subject of the Sui-Riu as it was described to him—sentiments which did not in Temeraire's opinion do him the least credit. "We must get out of these waters at once," Blaise had said, and he had made all the men beat to quarters instantly, though there had not been any sign of the other beast all the long flight back.

"And," Temeraire added, "this after we blacked his eye for him quite thoroughly, to boot; it seems to me you might have a little confidence in us."

They were waiting now only for high tide to finish coming in: the great tree-trunks had been with enormous effort wedged slowly and painfully between the ship and the reef; the anchor-cables were woven in and around Messoria's harness and Immortalis's. Maximus would take one lever, Kulingile the other, and Temeraire the middle. Iskierka would lie about on the rocks doing nothing but criticizing—Temeraire snorted—and Lily would look on, and perhaps strike the shoals with acid, as they tried to get the ship off them, if that should seem useful.

"And if he does show himself, while you are working," Iskierka put in, yawning, "I am perfectly able to breathe flame, even if I do not mean to be exerting myself a great deal presently. He will certainly think better of attacking us, then."

"Dear God," Captain Blaise said, and seized Granby by the arm to object violently to any such proceeding: the sailors were really unreasonable on the subject of fire, Temeraire felt; it was not as though Iskierka had proposed setting the sails alight.

He withdrew along the line of the shoals to wait alone until the tide should rise, and simmered quietly beneath the steady cold wash of the waves. He would *not* go on to Nagasaki. He did not know where precisely Nagasaki was, but it was not near-by; he did not mean to abandon the search for Laurence an instant longer than the ship's rescue required. The egg would be quite safe, once they were afloat again.

The emptiness of the coast he had flown over with Ferris lingered in the back of his mind like an unpleasant aftertaste. It had been three days and nights since Laurence had been swept away—already any visible signs upon the shore might have been lost. Laurence would have gone inland for water, perhaps; or perhaps he had even been lying under some tree for shelter, or calling up to Temeraire from a distance, unheard. Temeraire still had not the least doubt of Laurence's survival, but that alone would be of little use if he could not *find* Laurence.

"Temeraire!" Dulcia landed on his back and knocked him on the shoulder with her head. "We have been calling and calling: it is time to get the ship off the rocks."

"Oh!" Temeraire said, rousing, and found himself very cold and stiff indeed coming out of the great dark circling of his thoughts; the water was almost halfway up his hindquarters, and the short harness about his shoulders was sodden and heavy and dragging as he went into the air, a reminder of his empty back.

Messoria and Immortalis launched themselves with the cables; Dulcia and Nitidus each took another cable, for what help they could give, and Captain Blaise gave the word to throw the sea-anchor over the side beyond them, to help if it might. The tree-tops had been wedged in carefully under the hull, and their long trunks were jutting up from the ocean, froth churning up around them.

"Are you quite ready?" Temeraire asked Maximus and Kulingile.

"I still say there is something strange about this," Demane said, from the dragondeck, gripping the railing hard; he had been reluctant to see Kulingile lent to the attempt at all. "Kulingile, you are sure you will do this? I don't see how it can work—"

"I've told you!" his brother Sipho hissed at him.

Temeraire flattened his ruff: he understood a little Demane's anxiety—there was every reason to believe the Admiralty would be delighted to push him and his brother off if Kulingile were lost: he had still not been confirmed in his rank, and Laurence had been his only patron. But it seemed to Temeraire that this was all the more reason to help him find Laurence and bring him back.

"Oh, I don't mind trying," Kulingile said easily, however. "If it don't work, we will only sit on those logs for a while, and nothing much will happen."

Temeraire drew breath to explain, yet again, why it *would* work, after all; then he forced himself not to argue. "If you are quite ready," he said, and together they flung themselves down upon the levers, and as one exhaled as deeply as they could, from all their air-sacs.

Temeraire had worked it all out on paper, or rather, Sipho had worked it out to his direction, with help from a still-doubtful Ness; but paper made nothing to the experience of plunging deep into the icy cold water, feeling his body pulling at him as though an anchor. He had to scrabble desperately to keep himself upon the lever; his own weight would have dragged him instantly deep beneath the surface of the water.

"Hold on, there, you damned lummox!" Berkley was bellowing, over the railing. "Breathe in again!" Maximus was struggling beside him, and Kulingile was sinking so deep the water was nearly to his fore shoulders.

"Oh, but it is working!" Lily cried, on the far side of the ship, and then with alarm, "Look out—" as the ship came up and off the rocks with almost startling ease, and began to slide down the levers towards them.

Laurence had made one of the party which had taken the *Tonnant*, at the Nile, after the Longwing formation above had made its pass. He remembered the great pitted smoking holes, which had gone through the decks, and the screams of the wretched seaman who had incautiously put his bare foot upon one small spatter, not the size of a shilling. One of his mess-mates had chopped his foot off at once, there upon the deck, and so saved the fellow's life; although the wound had mortified and killed him three days later.

He recognized, therefore, the characteristic spattering of the Longwing acid upon the tree-stumps which they showed him, and the earth surrounding them, and although the stolen trees had provoked such hostility in his captors, Laurence could not help but rejoice that at last he could begin to understand; he could make sense of the intelligence these signs offered him. There was a Longwing near-by, and it had come and taken away three prime pieces of timber.

"Taken for masts, most likely," Laurence said, drawing a picture of a sailing ship in the wet sand to translate the word for them. Three masts on such a scale: a dragon transport for sure, which in any event should have been required to carry a Longwing and its usual formation; and *that,* surely, explained Laurence's own presence. The *Reliant* must have been traveling in company with the larger ship, to serve her as a more agile defender: no-one could call transports easy to handle, for all the massive weight of iron they could bring to bear.

The coat—the green coat—must have come off some aviator's back. Perhaps it had been thrown up on the shore beside him by the same storm that had wrecked the ship's masts, and in the first early moments of cold and delirium Laurence had put it on. He wondered now if the sword, too, had come from another man's hand; but he put that doubt aside. If it had, he could more easily restore it himself than could the Japanese—if he were permitted to go home.

And home was now a real possibility. There was a British ship here, in these very waters. She was not sunk; she was injured, but afloat, and her crew hoped to repair her. The *Allegiance*? Laurence wondered. Or perhaps the *Dominion;* although that ship was ordinarily on the run to Halifax. He still did not know what they had been doing with a transport so near Japan, but those questions were as nothing to the sheer inexpressible relief of knowing himself not, as he had begun to feel, wholly adrift, unmoored from any connection to his own life.

Laurence looked up from the sand, and addressed Matsudaira again. "Sir, I will say on behalf of my country-men that I am sure they intended no offense. They came ashore meaning only to take some necessary material for their ship's repair, from what they must have supposed to be a stand of unused timber."

"And where is this ship, now?" Matsudaira said.

His expression betrayed nothing but the same mild interest he had displayed throughout all the conversation, but the question came very quick. Laurence paused. He had just been thinking he might ask for a map of the coastline, or for a local fisherman to question. A transport had a draught near fifty feet: she could not anchor in shallow waters, and would not risk coming very near the coast. Some haphazard anchorage sheltered from the worst of the ocean by shoals was the most likely; near in straight line flight from this bay. He thought he might be able to guess a likely place, and even direct a boat thence, given some sense of the nearby waters.

He looked at the great serpentine creature looming overhead: the gleam of intelligence in its eye was plain, despite its monstrous size, and it was following their conversation with a keen, cold interest. It had come up from the bay with no warning—evidently it could breathe underwater. Laurence could easily imagine what such a sea-dragon could do to a ship, even one the size of a transport. Come up from below, throw her on her beam-ends, heave a loop of its body over the stern and drag her down—he could envision no easy defense. Perhaps the Longwing might be able to strike the beast, but in time to save the ship?

Its eye was fixed upon him, badly bloodshot. Was that merely some accident, or something else? Laurence glanced around the clearing. The ground was trampled into mud, as though after heavy rains; and when he looked he saw more damage to the trees around, smaller saplings crushed, branches fallen. There had been more than a mere dispute here—there had been fighting.

Laurence rose slowly to his feet. "I cannot hazard a guess," he said grimly, and watched Matsudaira's expression harden.

. . .

Temeraire was very cold. He did not know anything else, at first, and then his head was out in the air, and Iskierka was hissing at him ferociously, her talons sharp and clawing into his shoulders, saying, "Quick, quick, breathe in!"

The water held him like a vise, dragging. Temeraire tried to breathe and could not: his chest clenched and he vomited instead, gouts of water erupting painfully, dribbling away down his neck in long streams. Then at last Temeraire could draw in a thin, struggling stream of air. Lily was swimming beside him, trying to get her head under his foreleg. He clung to her, and scrabbled with his other foreleg at the great side of the ship, rising up before him; he managed to catch at a porthole, but the ship listed towards him alarmingly, and cries of warning came down.

"Oh! Why will you not listen to me?" Iskierka was saying impatiently. "You must get more air in, I cannot lift you if you will be so heavy!" She lowered her head and butted him.

"But I am trying," Temeraire said, only he could not speak for coughing; every breath was a battle. His sides were filling a little more, but the blood was running down his shoulders and he felt so very heavy. His head was ringing in a very peculiar way, and everything seemed colored with a faint greenish light.

Kulingile came up in the water beside him, bulling in under Temeraire's foreleg, so Temeraire could lean upon him and get out of the water a little more, though Kulingile grunted with the effort. "Get under his hindquarters, if you can," Berkley was calling down.

"Come on, Temeraire, scramble up, there's a good chap," Maximus said. Temeraire did not quite see his way clear to doing as much. He coughed again, and let his head sink against Kulingile's back; he was sliding back into the water, but he could not mind that so much. It did not feel so cold anymore, after all—

"Temeraire!" Roland said, leaning over the side, "if you drown, we shall all sail away and leave Laurence behind! You know no-one else thinks he is alive. You must get up, or else Hammond will make us all go."

Temeraire struggled his head up to protest: he was *not* going to drown, at all; he could swim excellently well. And as for leaving Laurence behind—

"You will, too, drown, and then we *shall* leave him, see if we don't!" Iskierka said, and bit him sharply. "Get out of the water. What else do you suppose you are doing?"

He tried to hiss at her, but he had to get another breath in to do it, and when he had that one, he got another. By slow measures, she and the others managed to help him heave up onto the line of the shoals, though the rocks crumbled as he clawed at them, and the waves tried to drag him back down. He crouched huddled on the rocks at last and breathed again in slow delicious sips of sea-air, splendid even though his throat ached badly, getting them in. His wings rattled against his back with cold.

"Well done, my dear one; let him have a rest," he heard Granby saying, faintly, to Iskierka. "We'll get him aboard as soon as he has filled his air out again." The *Potentate* was moving: Temeraire could see it out of one eye, a few sails rigged out on the mizzen, maneuvering away from the rocks. She was listing a little to one side, but not badly. He closed his eyes.

"Idiocy," he heard Gaiters saying, some indeterminate time after. The sun was beating on his back, now, but it did not seem to warm him. "Emptying your air—what made the lot of you take such a notion into your heads? I should have liked to come back to England with three heavy-weights having drowned themselves not fifty miles from shore; I suppose they would have hanged me and every other surgeon of the party for incompetence. Well, make yourselves of use, now: get him onto the deck at once. We must pack his sides with hot rocks, and fire up the galleys below. D'you think because he's a dragon he can't die of pleurisy?"

"I don't see why you fellows must always be complaining about something new," Maximus said. "We did get the ship back into the water, didn't we? And of course Temeraire will not die of a trifling little cold. But you ain't comfortable where you are," he added in

Temeraire's ear, "so do let us get you aboard." His big blunt head came nosing at Temeraire's shoulder.

Temeraire would have preferred not to move very much, at present; his whole body seemed to ache from tail-tip to nose, and his side and his right foreleg felt especially tender and bruised. He did not quite recall what had happened: the ship had come sliding, and he had not been able to get out of the way—diving was quite impossible, and the rocks were too far away to grab a hold of, for he had been on the lever amidships. But nothing after that, except the water, and the cold, and the green glaze that still seemed to hang faintly over all the world.

"Come on, then," Iskierka said crossly, above. "I do not see why you must be making such a fuss at a time like this." She nipped at his hindquarters.

"I am *not* making a fuss," Temeraire wanted to say, but his throat ached so. He let them prod him up onto his haunches, and then Maximus and Kulingile put their shoulders beneath his forelegs.

"Just hop aloft, when you are ready," Maximus said, "and we will go with you, to take some of the weight off: we will see you over to the deck in a trice, see if we do not."

Temeraire did not feel ready, but Iskierka would keep complaining at him, and nipping, and making cutting remarks; and finally he gathered himself and jumped as best he could. "Oh!" he cried, "Oh," for he had *not* been ready, in the least; the pain flaring along his side was like being burnt with a hot poker, to sear a wound after cleaning, but it ran the whole length of his body. His wings snapped tight, and if Kulingile and Maximus had not been beneath him, he should have fallen into the ocean again.

"Ouhff," Kulingile said with a grunt, and wobbled beneath him as they flew. "No, I am all right," he said; Temeraire heard it only distantly: everything had gone greenish and hazy again, and he felt very queer and ill indeed. He clung on blindly only, until they sank all three of them to the deck together and Maximus and Kulingile eased him gently down.

The planks were warm beneath him; the ship rocked with the familiar ocean swell. Temeraire put his head slowly beneath his wing, and shut his eyes, and knew no more.

"Enough!" Matsudaira struck the table before him with the flat of his hand.

They had taken Laurence back to Kaneko's house, and resumed his questioning in the open room off the courtyard, with Lady Arikawa listening in as she devoured the contents of an entire cauldron which had been brought to her smoking-hot and filled with rice, great bowls of beaten egg and fresh fish flung in to cook against the heated sides. The smell was fantastically appealing, enough to make Laurence a little light-headed; the servants had provided a similar meal, on a smaller scale, to Kaneko and Matsudaira, but he had been given nothing.

There had been no chance yet of escape or evasion, but Laurence told himself that at least now he had his bearings, a little. They were on the western coast of Japan—a pity, that; with Nagasaki on the west—and some seven miles as the crow flew from the nearest shore. Laurence worked the map in his mind while they questioned him; it was a refuge from the awareness that they were not likely to give him much future opportunity to put it to use, with a dragon at the door and increased suspicion.

"You persist in telling evident falsehoods," Matsudaira said. "I will be plain with you: Lord Jinai has told us of the true size of your force. He was attacked by eight dragons of war-like style and of great size. These did not come from England on a boat, and neither did a Celestial. Such a dragon has not been seen across the sea for five centuries, since the servants of the Yuan emperor stole the last egg of the Divine Wind line from Hakozaki Shrine as he withdrew in ignominy from his attempt at conquest, his murderous beasts having slain the rest of that noble line."

The foreign names slid over Laurence's mind without purchase, unfamiliar. "A dragon transport is certainly equal to the task of bearing eight beasts; they are designed for twelve," he said. "As for the particular breed, I am no authority on dragons, and can offer you no explanation but to think your identification mistaken. Dragon-husbandry was not undertaken in my nation before the Norman Conquest, scarce eight hundred years ago; we certainly were not responsible for *that* theft."

He spoke dryly; he was beginning to think it not much beyond them to accuse him of such. The magistrate abruptly snapped shut his fan and pointed it at him. "Speak the truth! You are in league with the Chinese!"

Laurence opened his mouth to answer with heated denial, and then halted. The very tongue in his mouth seemed to give him the lie. He could speak Chinese—why? And Japan was not so far off the course for Guangzhou. Perhaps he *had* come here in league with the Chinese. It was not inconceivable that Britain should have sought an alliance with the mandarins—they were a byword for dragon-breeders, of course; Laurence was sure the Admiralty should have been delighted to purchase some of their beasts as breeding stock.

"Ha," Matsudaira said, in answer to Laurence's silence. "Now, Kaneko-san, let us see this Chinese sword, which you have described to me."

Laurence ruefully watched Junichiro leave the room at Kaneko's nod, knowing he would soon return with fresh provocation for his interrogators. "Sir," he said, "perhaps my information is out of date, but so far as I know, you are not at war with China?" Matsudaira looked at him coldly and said nothing, which Laurence took, perhaps with excessive optimism, for confirmation. "Then any friendship between my nation and China can be no concern of yours, if no offense is given you by either."

"No offense!" Matsudaira said. "Indeed, your brazenness knows no bounds. Permit me to inform you, if you imagine us to be so easily deceived, that I have the honor to be related to the governor at Nagasaki, where three years ago your vessel *Phaeton* by deceit took hostages and issued threats against the ships of the harbor, and fired upon the city."

That, Laurence could not conceal, was a blow; he had heard of no such action. The *Phaeton*—he could only vaguely recall the ship to mind. A frigate? Yes, *Minerva*-class, and he thought Captain Wood had her, but—

Matsudaira added coldly, watching his face, "That vessel's dishonorable captain and all his crew repaid their crimes with their lives." Laurence could not but envision with horror a ruin that might well have been achieved by that monstrous sea-dragon, or another such beast: like a kraken rising from beneath the waves, all unsuspected, to drag the ship down and down, shattered, and spilling the men into the waves to be devoured at its leisure, or by the ocean itself.

He shuddered for it, and for their fate; and more that he knew nothing of it. Three years ago? Could he have lost such a span of memory, and not be wholly mad? Certainly no such event could have escaped his notice—even if the events had gone unreported, he must have heard of the loss of the *Phaeton*.

"I cannot account for such an assault, sir, save by some grave misunderstanding, or if intended as an action against Dutch shipping in your harbor," he said, troubled. "They are French allies—"

"More excuses," Matsudaira said, cutting him off with a slash of the hand, and then Junichiro returned in haste, nearly running, to report the sword missing and launch a new uproar, which Laurence almost welcomed as distraction from the questions he was unable to answer even to himself.

"If I have taken it," Laurence said, when they demanded its hiding place, "in doing so I have only been taking my own again, and I do not consider I owe you either apology or explanation in such circumstances. Nor could you rationally expect me to hand it back; yet if I should deny having it, you would call it a lie. I must beg to be excused: I have nothing to say upon the subject."

He had already decided to say as much, if he were questioned.

He thought only a thorough and systematic search of the grounds would uncover his bundle: the ground outside had been trampled by too many feet, since his abortive escape the previous night, to show any trace of his actions.

Matsudaira was by no means conciliated by this reply. "We will see what you have to say when you have been more rigorously questioned," he said angrily. "I will send for a torturer at once—"

Laurence did not flinch, but regarded him with the flat disdain that any such threat merited. "You may question me as you wish," he said. "I have not lied; and I hope I can answer you and die like an Englishman."

To his surprise, however, Lady Arikawa raised her head and rumbled, low, making an objection. "I do not think that necessary yet," she said, a thin translucent ruff around her neck frilling out.

Matsudaira sat up a little further, with rigid shoulders, and said grimly, "I must with the utmost respect disagree, Lady Arikawa."

Laurence could not argue with the man's courage, at least, to so incite a dragon to anger; Lady Arikawa might easily have seized and broken him like a toy without even rising to her feet, and by the swift slitting of her eyes seemed tempted to do so.

"You are charged to carry out a full investigation," Lady Arikawa said. "We have yet no word from Nagasaki regarding any English vessel in the harbor, nor have the Kirin returned from their survey of the coastal waters, near-by. Surely we can wait for this intelligence to reach us before proceeding."

"The foreigner is certainly condemned by the law, regardless," Matsudaira said, after a moment. The grey dragon's wings flared from her back, unsettled, and folded again; the clawed tips shifted back and forth, restlessly.

Sitting beside Matsudaira and sipping tea, Kaneko had shown no expression but level calm all the while; now he said quietly, "My lady, I most deeply regret my error, and—"

"That is enough," she said, interrupting crisply. "What error can there be in the will of the heavens? Certainly it is only a great service to the bakufu that this barbarian is available to be questioned about these matters; it may be that much benefit to the nation may derive from his rescue. It would be a great impiety upon our part to disregard the means by which the gods have delivered him into our hands, through this vow which caused your eyes to light upon him where he lay in the road. If they did not intend him to be well-treated, they would not have arranged matters so. I cannot agree to a course which despises so clear a sign from the spirit world."

She delivered these arguments with an air almost of triumph. Laurence thought he detected in them rather more sophistry than true religious fervor. He remained unable to follow all the undercurrents, but he gathered at the least that she wished to spare her vassal Kaneko whatever embarrassment he might suffer at being forced to renege on his vow of assistance. Laurence could only suppose that embarrassment to have consequences more extreme than he imagined.

Matsudaira did not seem persuaded, but at least her vehemence gave him pause; he said more cautiously, trying to answer her in the same lines, "And yet as a magistrate, I must pursue my duty to the law by every means: the gods would not have delivered him in ignorance of so commonplace a fact."

"The gods would certainly not have expected you to disregard their wishes," Lady Arikawa returned, with scorn. "Which indeed, they may have meant as a warning. Consider: it is well-known that men of other races are weak. The torture which brings truth from a Japanese may perhaps even slay a Western barbarian, and deprive us of further information."

Laurence derived some black humor from the burst of indignation he instinctively felt at the nonsense of being any less fitted to endure pain: a fine and absurd thing it would be, to make a case for his own torture. However, the argument was ill-chosen on Lady Arikawa's part; Matsudaira and Kaneko could not forbear a doubtful glance in his direction. Laurence was a head taller than any other man in the room, and he could have given any of them thirty pounds or more.

Of course, from Lady Arikawa's perspective—near enough to twelve tons, Laurence would have guessed—the distinction was all muchwhatlike. In any event, Laurence closed his mouth on any retort he might have made, and stood wooden beneath their gaze; the weaker and more helpless they chose to think him the better, if they should set a commensurate guard upon him.

"It perhaps would be wise to employ a truly skilled practitioner," Matsudaira said, after a moment, in a conciliatory manner. "I will send to Edo for a specialist in questioning the sick and the elderly. That will necessitate a certain delay, of course. Perhaps in the intervening time, further intelligence will render the questioning unnecessary, or the foreigner may think better of his lies and confess freely."

Lady Arikawa inclined her head. "It will be convenient for you to keep charge of him here at Kaneko's house, in the meantime," she said—a rather strong hinting, there, and Matsudaira did not attempt to argue with her, but bowed his head in agreement.

Two guards were called in: Matsudaira's men, Laurence thought; they wore signs of authority matching his own. They escorted him, but only back to his original chamber; and there was a tray of food set on a low table in the middle of the floor. Laurence did not hesitate to devour it, and then lay himself down on the straw mat to consider and to rest.

He roused from a half-sleep a little while later; there were voices, coming faint but audible through the walls, and speaking Chinese: Lady Arikawa, and Kaneko with her. "There can be no more honorable fate than to die in the service of Japan, even for a barbarian," she was saying, in an anxious tone, low: Laurence could only surmise she preferred not to be overheard by the servants of the house. "Surely in delivering him to such an end, you will have assisted him?"

Kaneko did not immediately answer her, but then said, gently, "Most honorable lady, I regret to disappoint you. I vowed that whomever I found upon the road requiring assistance, whether a beggar or a digger of graves, I would serve him as I would my own grandfather, with honor. To see him dispatched as a low criminal—" He trailed off, and said no more.

"Oh!" Lady Arikawa said eagerly, "but that need not be so! I will speak with the magistrate. Why should he not be permitted *seppuku* instead? And then indeed you will have served him."

Laurence heard no more of the conversation: the heavy crunching tread of the dragon faded, as though they had wandered away through the gardens. The guards were sitting together at the far end of the chamber speaking in low voices over cards: some sort of game of chance. They were armed with short but serviceable blades, and wore a kind of light, handsome armor, crafted of small plates of wood which overlapped one another neatly.

They rose to attention when Kaneko ducked into the chamber, a short while later, and bowing deeply left the room when he dismissed them. Laurence had been engaged in exercising his right arm, which was yet bruised all along its length with markings as of chain links pressed hard against the flesh. He had the movement of it back, however, and he thought he had worked it limber. Laurence did not rise; he had already managed to crack his head on the ceiling several times, and if the King did not require his officers to rise for the loyal salute on board ship, in similar conditions, Laurence was damned if he would do it for his jailor, here.

Kaneko settled himself on the ground with easy grace and regarded Laurence somberly. "I have come to speak plainly with you, Englishman," he said.

"That, sir, cannot be anything but welcome," Laurence said, without much enthusiasm; he had heard enough of the conversation in the garden to guess at Kaneko's intentions: the man was looking for some means of eeling out of his vow, Laurence supposed, and meant to offer him some mean and cowardly alternative to death—imprisonment for life, perhaps, or a kind of indentured servitude.

Kaneko said, "Even if the bakufu had not decreed the death of all foreigners entering the nation without permission, the circumstances of your arrival would be dark. The shameful offense of your country-men in Nagasaki suggests a false character, and a league between your nation and China has been suspected for several years, now. Your ships have been reported in the northern waters near Peking, where no Westerners formerly were welcome—"

The existence of this traffic came as news to Laurence; so far as he knew, only the port of Guangzhou was open at all. "—and now, this appearance of a Celestial, in conjunction with yourself, and this British dragon you have mentioned," Kaneko continued, "more than confirms our most extreme suspicions: the Celestials travel only with the Imperial family."

Laurence could not disagree that such commerce indicated a more intimate connection formed between Britain and China than he recalled; this, however, pressed the bounds of credence. "I should be astonished beyond belief to learn that a member of the Imperial family of China were traveling with my ship. I must continue to believe it more likely that your witness, faced with unfamiliar beasts, mistook some rare British breed for the one you name."

"There is no mistake," Kaneko said. "Lord Jinai is the guardian of the West: he is four hundred years old, and he has seen Celestials before. He was not mistaken."

He spoke flatly, and Laurence did not propose that advanced years might render Lord Jinai's judgment questionable: he remembered too vividly the sharp, deadly look of the sea-dragon's eyes; no signs of creeping age there.

Kaneko added, "And your party have not only stolen timber from our shores, but attacked him: so pronounced an insult cannot be anything but deliberate." He paused, and after a moment said, "You seem a rational man, and though your conduct is not correct, I imagine you are an honorable man, in your own country. Will you offer no explanation?"

Laurence would have liked to pace. He would have given a great deal to be on his quarterdeck, with the sails belled out overhead and wind in his hair, even just long enough to think his way through all the tangled evidence. Failing that, he would have been glad of a pot of strong coffee and a day of quiet—a chance perhaps to write out a letter to Edith Galman; he had often found the exercise to resolve his own thinking, when he had no trusted confidant to hand, as a sea-captain rarely might. Edith—he had a start for a moment; he had not thought of her. He looked at his hand, as yet without a ring.

He pushed that from his mind. He could not allow himself to dwell on such matters now. "I may as well be hanged for a sheep as for a lamb," he said aloud, in English, to himself, and steeling himself for incredulity, gave Kaneko to understand his loss of memory, in as succinct and unadorned a manner as he could.

Kaneko listened to his brief narrative with mingled bewilderment and suspicion; he asked a few questions only, in tones of extreme politeness, which Laurence ruefully feared covered equally extreme skepticism. "You do not recall why you are here," Kaneko said at last, "nor anything of an alliance between your nation and China."

"Whatever injury I have taken has robbed me of more than that," Laurence said. "I have lost years—how many, I cannot be sure, but certainly two or three. I do not suppose, sir, you can tell me what year it is, in the European reckoning?"

"By the latest report of the Dutch, they make the year 1812, if my recollection is not imperfect," Kaneko said, and Laurence stared at him, taken aback in real horror: eight years gone?

He looked away at once, but his distress, which he could not easily master, had at least some small beneficial effect: Kaneko was frowning at him, puzzled but a little more convinced, when Laurence managed to overcome his immediate feelings.

"If I may further trespass," Laurence said, "can you tell me anything of the war? Has Napoleon been defeated?"

Laurence tried as best he could to keep his spirits from sinking entirely, as Kaneko sketched for him the Japanese understanding of circumstances in Europe. Their news was certainly old, and as it came entirely from the Dutch also certainly colored by that nation's self-interest; it had been translated at least twice, and surely much was lost, in the way of nuance.

So he told himself, and Britain at least was free. Laurence clung to that, for what consolation it might be while hearing of Austria fallen, Prussia—Prussia!—fallen, Spain fallen, Russia half-allied with France—the shadow of the tricolor over all of them. Kaneko did not seem to know what had happened in the Netherlands, but Laurence could hardly imagine they had escaped, no matter what the Dutch representatives here might have said. Napoleon was the master of all Europe.

"I can well believe, sir, that you find my explanation difficult to swallow," Laurence said, when he could speak again, "for I can scarcely believe it myself; I have withheld it so far for that very reason, having no desire to figure either as an honest lunatic or a witless liar. But I have told you the truth, and you have served me a very heavy blow; I beg your pardon, but you could scarcely have given me worse news."

His voice failed him, broke, and he did not speak again. Kaneko also said nothing, so they sat together in silence, caught in their own private and separate distress, though by chance entwined. The sun was lowering. A branch outside cast a dappled silhouette upon the rice-paper wall, which lengthened little by little as it traveled over the wall. Soft footsteps moved through the hall outside now and again, the *shush-shush* of sandaled feet; the guards in their creaking armor shifted their weight on the other side of the panel.

At last Kaneko said, "Perhaps I am being foolish, and yet I do believe you. However, I cannot expect the magistrate to do so: indeed, it could scarcely be in keeping with his duty to do so. Nor would this explanation excuse you. A man who, out of his senses, commits a crime, is still guilty: and lacking memory of your own intentions, you cannot even defend them."

"Sir, you have taken it by the horns," Laurence said grimly.

"And no, I do not expect him to believe my explanation in the least."

Kaneko nodded, and then said, quietly, "It may be I can do nothing. The magistrate may insist upon putting you to questioning. But—Lady Arikawa is generous, and her voice is not the least in the councils of the bakufu. She has offered to speak on your behalf, and to request for you the right to commit *seppuku,* if you should desire it—honorable suicide," he added, seeing Laurence's incomprehension. "I would stand for you as your second, if—"

"Good God, no," Laurence said, recoiling, and cut him off. "I will not pretend I have the least desire to be a martyr, sir, but I am a Christian: I will do my best to endure whatever torment God sees fit to try me by, and not turn to self-slaughter like—"

He paused; he had meant to say, like a heathen, but the remark seemed impolite, in addressing one who by his own expression found Laurence's own avowed preference as nearly unthinkable. Laurence abruptly wondered, then, if this same fate lay before Kaneko himself—

"If I cannot fulfill my vow," Kaneko answered, regarding him with somber surprise, "I hope that Lady Arikawa will be generous enough to grant me permission: I am her servant, and she may deny me the right."

"And if she refuses?"

Kaneko looked bleak. "I will be dishonored, and my family as well."

Laurence wished to press him further, to understand more, but refrained; a man's honor could only be in his own keeping, and Laurence could understand, a little. He himself would gladly have accepted death as the price of escaping some dishonorable act, certainly before treason; and he would have preferred death to shameful torment, which would seek to break him. But to endure death was not the same as to seek it by his own hand.

"Sir," he said, "I know of no reason why you should consider yourself so. You *have* been of material assistance to me: without your aid, I should likely have died upon the road, sick and alone, without even what understanding has returned to me. I beg you not to commit such an act on my account. Indeed, if you wished to serve me, you would do better to grant me the satisfaction of knowing you stayed your hand, from what my own faith considers mortal sin."

"My vow was not to you," Kaneko said, cool and a little censorious, rising to his feet. He inclined his head a little and took his leave without another word; the guards came back in.

An evening meal was brought them all—Laurence noticed belatedly that his own meal, as sparse as he would have ordinarily thought it, was considerably more substantial than the simple bowl of soup and noodles offered the guards; he now understood a little better why he was confined in a hospitable and large chamber, waited upon with consideration. Nevertheless he was still a prisoner, and a condemned man. He looked at the guards: both wore short blades on their belts, and though he had reach and weight on them, they were by no means insubstantial fellows. But Laurence was determined, regardless, to hazard again an escape. His circumstances could hardly be the worse for it.

One of the guards lay himself down to rest; the other sat in the corner and yawned. Laurence lay down and closed his eyes to sleep a little while, until it was thoroughly dark.

He roused a few hours later and turned his head to look. The first guard yet snored; the other was idly humming to himself, tuneless, and rolling the dice.

Laurence turned back his head towards the ceiling, gathering himself. He closed his eyes and let his lips form soundlessly a prayer to the Almighty. Almost certainly he would be slain. He meant to try and overcome the first guard before the second awoke, get away the man's blade if he could, and then to somehow get out of the house—perhaps the window of the chamber across the hallway.

Then he would fly for the woods. It was a reckless plan at best, given two men at his back and dragons in the courtyard, but better a clean death than to sit quietly in a room and await torture.

Laurence sat up from his bedding. The guard looked up, narrowly, but then turned away from him; Laurence halted as the door slid open. Junichiro stood outside, swords at his belt, and spoke coldly, gesturing at the sleeping guard. The second guard roused up, abashed; the two men muttered excuses, which Junichiro evidently cut short; he motioned them out of the room, and climbing in made to stand sentry in their place, his face hard and watchful. The men hang-dog went; the door slid shut. Their small light went bobbing away down the corridor, and vanished deeper into the house.

Laurence ought to have been glad of it: shorter odds by far, against one youth not yet at his full growth. But it left an evil taste in his mouth. He had not given his parole to his captors; he felt himself not in the wrong to make the attempt, and if necessary, he could have stomached killing a guard set upon him, in such circumstances. But not an over-eager young man, scarcely more than a boy, one who had done him not the least evil except to love his own master. Half-gathered to spring, Laurence hesitated. Perhaps if he waited, Junichiro might fall asleep himself, later in the night—

Junichiro said quietly, barely more than a whisper, "Get up. Once we are outside, we must go down the slope to the west, quickly, keeping near the stables—the dragons will not be there. Do you understand?"

"What?" Laurence said, taken aback.

Junichiro did not answer; he had taken a bound scroll out of his robes, and set it down precisely in the center of the floor. He went to the outer wall and began to work latches there: abruptly a large section of the lower half of the wall came loose, and the night air breathed in.

Laurence still did not understand in the least; but understanding might wait. He sprang to Junichiro's side and caught the heavy panel, lifting it aside; together they slid through the opening and into the gardens, small pebbles rolling underfoot and a fragrant smell of crushed leaves as they forced their way past a few small pines. Junichiro caught him by the arm. "Quickly, now!" he breathed.

Laurence had no idea what had possessed Junichiro to undertake his rescue, but he could still less easily imagine it some sort of deep-laid strategem. He turned aside for a moment, however, to hunt through the bushes, ignoring Junichiro's attempts to draw him onwards. Then he had the bundle out of the undergrowth where he had left it, and turning said, "Go!"

He followed Junichiro through the gardens, and past a low building smelling of cattle and horse piss; a gentle slope eased away into the woods. Junichiro unerring led them along paths he knew into the trees, jumping fallen logs and streams almost unconscious of their presence. Laurence fixed the bundle over his shoulder, and kept his attention for the forest floor: he had put himself into Junichiro's hands, and he would have certainly done no better evading pursuit alone.

They had been running for nearly half-an-hour when first a dragon roared, behind them and aloft somewhere. Laurence did not turn to look. If Lady Arikawa marked them out for pursuit, they were surely lost, even if she could not come down upon them herself while they remained within the trees. The snap of wings above, so like a sail belling in the wind, seemed strangely loud in his ears. They ran onwards.

Chapter 4

A SHARP POKE IN HIS side roused Temeraire from his torpor; he lifted his head only slowly. The steady rocking of the ship had cradled him in comfortable withdrawal. They had put food in his mouth, from time to time; he had felt the sun creeping over his body, and the heat of the galleys below. "It is time you were awake," a voice said, in Chinese.

"Yes, I am awake," Temeraire said, and put his head back down and closed his eyes once more: the glare of the sun upon the waves ached.

"No, you are not," the stranger said, and prodded him unpleasantly with something sharp and cold in the pit of his shoulder; Temeraire flinched and looked around, frowning. The man, in long grey clothing, looked back at him with a severe expression; a long drooping beard with trailing mustaches hung down from his frowning mouth.

"Stop that," Temeraire said, irritably. "I do not wish to be prodded; take that away."

"Oho, next you will tell me how to mix your medicine," the man said, and poked him once more: he was using for the purpose a very long and narrow silver stick, with a sharpened end. "Up! Up! How do you expect to get well, lying around on hot rocks day after day?" He jabbed Temeraire sharply with the stick, in his hindquarters, and Temeraire indignantly pushed up.

"I am feeling *much* better for having lain here, and it is not hot rocks but the galley, anyway," Temeraire said. "And for that matter—" He stopped short, appalled: behind the stranger, three points to port, a merchantman flying the Dutch flag rode at anchor; and beyond this, only a little way off, the tight-crammed roofs of a city rose away from a curving and beautiful harbor. A ring of Chinese junks surrounded the *Potentate,* bobbing gently with the waves, like a garland made of ships.

"Where am I?" Temeraire cried. "Where have you brought me?" He turned to look furious reproach at Maximus, who was drowsing beside him and did not immediately open his eyes to be confronted: the other dragons were all further out to sea on the other side of the ship, all of them diving at the waves and plucking themselves up some fish.

"You are in Nagasaki Harbor," the stranger said, "and you have been here three days and nights."

Laurence was falling, wet leather slipping between his fingers and a smooth-scaled hide refusing to provide purchase, and he jerked up gasping from beneath the carpeting of leaves. Beside him, Junichiro slept on as soundly as if he had been upon a featherbed in a palace, his cheek pillowed on his arms and his face serene. Laurence ran a hand over his face, wearily, and pushed aside the remants of his covering. The sun was near making noon, he thought, though he could not see it very clearly for the leaves overhead.

They had continued on all the night, stumbling beneath the trees and over rocks. The dragon's roars had pursued them, but her flight had fallen behind; she had turned one direction and another away from their trail, it seemed to Laurence, perhaps led astray by some wild animals leaping in fear from her approach. Fortune had saved them, he could only imagine.

Junichiro had turned aside abruptly, near the dawn, and led Laurence down a narrow barely marked trail to their present resting place: overshadowed by a great standing gate, two enormous pillars joined by bars painted in an orange now faded and peeling. A little beyond it they had found a stand of trees grown wild and engulfed in vines, sheltered from the wind by a great smooth boulder. Laurence rose, brushing himself free of dead vines, and looked up at the gate again. The scale was immense, and yet it seemed to lead nowhere; as far as he could see through the frame in either direction was only wilderness.

In the dim light they had buried themselves beneath dry leaves and slept as the dead. Laurence was yet tired and footsore, but he did not think they dared linger for long. There was a little trickle of a stream running through the woods, ending with a little burbling over rocks in a great clear pool beside the gate. Laurence limped to it and drank deeply, washed hands and face, and took off his sandals and soaked his feet in the cold water as long as he could bear: it was a long time since he had scrambled barefoot over the ropes and planks of a ship as a boy, and the sandals had left him bruised and sore.

He rose at last and tied them back on, then turned to go back to Junichiro and halted, gone very still. The boulder he had noted last night had raised its head and was regarding him with enormous unblinking interest: it was a dragon, hide dark greenish black and with large eyes of pallid grey, which evidently had curled up to sleep against the comfort of the trees.

It yawned, widely, and said something to him in Japanese; Junichiro, still soundly asleep and huddled up against its side, woke with a start and scrambled up and away. The dragon turned and inquired of him, instead; Junichiro answered with a slightly evasive air, backing away towards Laurence. "What is it asking?" Laurence asked him, low, but the dragon overheard.

"Ah! So you can speak!" the dragon said triumphantly, in Chinese. "Are you," it leaned towards him with almost a longing air, "a *Dutchman*?"

"No, sir," Laurence said. "I am an Englishman."

"An Englishman?" The dragon rolled the sound around slowly, tongue flicking out to touch the air. It was only the size of a Yellow Reaper, perhaps, with a wide ruff and long dangling tendrils that hung down about its mouth: something of its appearance seemed strangely familiar, though Laurence had certainly never seen a beast anything like. "I have never heard any English poetry," the dragon announced, after some consideration. "You must tell me some! Come, let us go up to the temple and have something to eat and drink."

He uncurled himself and rose onto four feet, shaking himself out almost as might have a wet dog. He was long and as narrow in the chest as at the base of his tail, with feet widely spaced; his wings were short and peculiarly stubby, folded against his back. He ambled with a swaying stride through the gate itself, stopping briefly to knock his head against one of the posts three times, and went onwards up the rising slope beyond, where now Laurence saw the underbrush was lower, and trampled in places.

He glanced at Junichiro—he was not sure if they ought to take the chance and try to flee. But Junichiro was trailing wide-eyed after the dragon, and the promise of food was a powerful one. The beast at least did not seem to be immediately hostile.

The trail led a winding way through increasingly difficult undergrowth, where at last the dragon paused and looked back and said, "Why, you are falling quite behind. Up you get," and reached out a taloned hand to deposit them each in turn upon his back. Junichiro made a small sound almost of protest, and Laurence would have liked to question him—what was the beast, and why did it seem to have no fear of the same law which bound all others against a foreigner—but he could not find it politic to do so when aboard the very beast's back.

They continued on to a final steeper slope, where at the summit at last a small temple made of wood was found—a tall structure, enough that the dragon could comfortably walk inside, though not very large in plan; and in two great silver bowls at the center stood a pool of clear liquid, smelling very strongly of plums and spirits; and in the other a great heap of rice and meat, still steaming.

"Take cups! Help yourselves!" the dragon said, sprawling himself across the floor—or *herself,* Laurence belatedly corrected, when some portions of anatomy were thereby more exposed to view; he had been mistaken by a series of low finned spines which curved out from the dragon's body along its length. "We will drink to the good fortune of this meeting, and then you will recite some poetry for me. You do *know* some poetry?" the dragon asked, anxiously.

"Ma'am," Laurence said doubtfully, wondering where the attendants were, who had prepared this repast, and how he might hope to make a further escape, "I can give you a little Shakespeare, if that will suit you, but I do not know how it will do in Chinese."

"No, no," the dragon said, coiling back with an air of relief. "I do not want it in Chinese. I already know Li Bai and Wang Wei, and many more besides. I want English poetry."

"But—you cannot speak the tongue?" Laurence asked.

"You will translate it for me afterwards," she said, and nudged across to him with one talon a small empty cup, perhaps a little larger than a thimble, and another for Junichiro.

The excuses a rather shamefaced Granby provided Temeraire for their decampment were threadbare indeed. His health, the lurking unknown danger of the sea-dragon, the uncertainty of their position, the ship's need of further repair, the safety of the egg—

At the thought of the egg, he could not forbear putting his head over the side carefully and peering in, with a single eye, at the porthole which looked into the egg's chamber. This was below the galleys, carefully kept warm, and the egg itself was not visible for being swaddled in a great many velvet and silken dressings, and then hay, and then packed into a crate. But they had shown it to him, when he had first awoken: a splendid smooth pale-cream shell speckled with a very attractive pattern of red and violet spots, and one notable larger marking shaped roughly like a number eight.

"You must see it, surely." Temeraire had pointed it out to Lily, though she had looked at it doubtfully.

"It looks more like a cloud to me," she said, which was absurd; any shape might be a cloud. Temeraire pressed his other friends for their opinion, and finally Kulingile and Dulcia were brought to agree, when he had drawn them the shape of an eight, that it was not unlike; with this he was satisfied to consider his opinion confirmed, and nothing more propitious could be imagined.

Sipho had knocked him up quite a respectable watercolor on a large piece of discarded sailcloth, which was now draped over the crate and might be looked at in lieu of unpacking the egg again—a risk Temeraire quite agreed could not be taken under ordinary circumstances, although he was of course determined Laurence should see the egg as soon as he was found.

"And that," he said stormily, "will be as soon as I can fly back and manage it: I am very sorry indeed, Granby, to have found you so false as to allow the ship to leave Laurence behind; what he must be thinking of me, at present! You may be sure I will not be silent on the subject, when I have seen him again; he will know of this *treachery*."

"Oh! That is quite enough," Iskierka said, cracking an eye. "For Granby did *not* wish to go, at all. He said you would be very upset, and it could do you no good, but Captain Blaise would not stay and the ship is his; and Hammond egged him on, naturally."

"Pray be quiet, wretched creature, you are not making matters any better," Granby said, reproving, and called up, "Temeraire, old fellow, listen to me: you mustn't be so angry. You were very ill, and still are; you couldn't have gone searching for Laurence any road. And Hammond is at this very moment speaking to the local authorities of the port to have them bring us any news of Laurence, I promise you. He must have made a figure of himself, you know—he is a tall fellow, and they haven't yellow hair here; he will stand out a mile. Someone is sure to have taken him up, if—if he has come to shore."

"If Hammond should come back with any news of Laurence at all, it will be a good deal more than I look for," Temeraire said, his resentment unabated, and all the greater for his indeed feeling very ill—very wretched. He did not like the thought of a long flight at present, and disliked still more feeling himself in so weak a condition. "And I *will* go back, if I must fly overland to get there," he added, in defiance of that consciousness.

Wen Shen, the physician, who had been hired to assist in his care, shrugged equably from the deck. "You will drop dead somewhere over the middle of the country, then," he said, and ate an enormous heaping spoon of the rice porridge, flavored with tunny from Kulingile's spare catch, which he had commanded to be worked up supposedly for Temeraire's benefit.

Temeraire did not think much of him, despite his physician's knot. He had insisted on Temeraire's drinking a great vat of some bitter and foul-tasting infusion, and on his flying a full circuit around the ship, though he did not feel at all like flying and his wing-joints ached fiercely afterwards. Wen Shen had also made a great many disparaging remarks on Temeraire's diet and general habits, some of them quite untrue: he did *not* eat an entire roast cow every day. Even if he had liked to, which he did not, they did not have enough cattle aboard for that.

Gong Su had dug up this physician, having rowed over to each one of the Chinese ships in the harbor on their arrival, where he had met with the greatest deference. Since he had openly avowed himself a servant of the Imperial court, he had exchanged his clothing for the formal robes of a scholar; he had shaved his head and put his hair into a severe topknot, with a blue button upon his hat, and now openly carried the pouch with the great red-sealed letter of his authority around his neck.

Temeraire knew Laurence had regarded this alteration of his costume coldly, as a reminder of injury—that Gong Su had deceived them all for so long, and spied, and passed on information. But in his own opinion, any injury could only be mitigated now by Gong Su's making amends and doing his best to make a good showing of himself; he was still, Temeraire considered, a member of his crew. And after all, why should Crown Prince Mianning not wish to send a messenger, a trusted servant, to accompany his brother? But Laurence had remained unconvinced by this argument, receiving it only with a snort.

In addition to digging up Wen Shen, Gong Su had spoken with the captains of the Chinese ships; all the vessels had subsequently weighed anchor and maneuvered, awkwardly, into places around the *Potentate,* evidently with the design of providing her some protection. Temeraire had heard this with some skepticism: the Chinese ships were so very much smaller, but Captain Blaise was very well pleased.

"At least it may give us some notice, if a monster like the one you knocked heads with decides to come up from under us," he said to Captain Berkley. "How we will come off in such an encounter, I am damned if I know, but we will give him a taste of hot iron down his gullet if only he gives us a chance, and see what he thinks of that," and he gave orders that men should be at some of the guns all hours of day and night.

Temeraire could not really disapprove of any measures for the egg's security; the sea-dragon had been so very unfriendly, even when there did not seem to Temeraire to be any excuse for such a cold reception. But he was not in the least pleased that Gong Su had also inflicted Wen Shen upon him, whatever any of them liked to say about the improvement in his condition since they had begun dosing him with the physician's recipe.

"For I am not well enough to go, yet," Temeraire said miserably to Lily, putting his head down again—somehow he had eaten up all the rice porridge, after all. "If I must be drinking medicine, at least it ought to work."

"Well, you are better already than you were," Lily said, consoling. "It was a great deal of time before I felt properly myself again, you know, after that nasty cough we all had a few years ago."

"You had better eat something more, and here: if you cannot go, in a few days, I will have a word with Berkley and we will go and have a look around for you, I dare say," Maximus said, which was very kind, but Temeraire did not believe it in the least: Berkley was like all the rest of them, quite insistent that Laurence was dead, and Temeraire was sure he would not be rigorous in any search.

"I only wish I knew where he was now," Temeraire said, low, and shut his eyes again.

"Kanpai!" the dragon cried, when Laurence had finished muddling through another passage, and dipped her own head into the silver bowl. Laurence was forced to at least moisten his lips in a show of accompaniment, and hope that he had indeed buried Caesar and not praised him, or for that matter raised him from the dead one act too soon; he was not perfectly sure. He did not think he had been this appallingly drunk since he had been a boy of twelve, trying to make good on every toast at his captain's table.

Junichiro had fallen asleep perhaps an hour ago, overcome with the liquor and the exertion of their night. He had by slow degrees eased to the floor, until his head had fallen onto Laurence's bundle and his eyes had closed, almost at the same time.

"I am delighted with it," the dragon continued, and hiccoughed. "*Neither wit, nor words, nor worth,*" this repeated unslurred and with a startlingly good accent, despite the truly remarkable quantity of liquor which the beast had consumed, "—that has a very pleasing rhythm. This is part of your funerary rites?"

"In the theater, when they have killed him," Laurence said, confusedly, trying to explain; he was beginning to find it difficult to make his tongue work in Chinese. "There is a dragon when he gives the speech," he added, with some vague sense that this might be of interest to another beast, trying with movements of his hands to convey some sense of the usual staging, which he had seen once as a boy of thirteen.

"I would be glad to see it," the dragon said. "I have lately seen a splendid performance by a troupe, who came by upon the road. I will give you a little of it."

She began to recite in a low melodious voice, rising and falling in the unfamiliar language. Laurence was not proof against so much inducement added to his own weariness, and before she had completed the third line he had fallen to sleep beside Junichiro. When he woke, the dragon was gone; Junichiro was stirring beside him, and the sun was going down. His head ached like the very devil.

"The guardian must have gone to the water," Junichiro said. "We should go onwards."

"Yes," Laurence said, wearily, "but we had better wait until the sun has gone, and eat," the bowl holding still a handsome share of leftovers, "and in the meanwhile, I will have a few answers: I am not ungrateful, but I would know what you are about. Did you—seek to escape Kaneko's service, yourself?" He spoke dubiously; he could scarcely imagine that to be Junichiro's motive. The boy's affection for his master had been too visible and sincere for that, and yet it seemed equally unlikely he had been motivated by any sense of injustice done to Laurence himself; there was certainly no personal attachment between them.

"Of course not,"Junichiro said, bitterly; he was brushing his own garments clean as best he could. "I heard my master tell Lady Arikawa you were too much of a coward to take an honorable death. There was no course of honor left for him. If he gave you up for torture to the magistrate, he would have failed in his vow; and he could not disobey the bakufu to protect you. What else was there to do?"

"What *was* this vow?" Laurence demanded. "Why would he have sworn an oath to aid a perfect stranger?"

"He made the vow to Jizo," Junichiro said shortly, "who guards travelers, to ask him to look after his wife and son."

His manner did not invite further inquiry. But Laurence recalled the silence of the house, the absence of a chatelaine, Kaneko's black clothing, and thought he might understand: a wife lost in childbirth, and the child with her. Enough cause, surely, for a man to seek the consolation of religion, and to hold the oath he had made for their sake more dear than a mere promise to be put aside when inconvenient.

"So I will keep you alive, and get you away," Junichiro went on. "My master will not have disobeyed the law; he will not have brought shame on Lady Arikawa and his own family: the guilt will be on my own head."

Laurence shook his head in dismay: it was a solution which he felt could only have appealed to the excessive optimism of a young man, a wish to be the hero of the piece. "Unless that magistrate is a fool, he will hold your master accountable for your actions, and you will have only gained a crime to your account and his," he said.

"He cannot," Junichiro said. "Kaneko is my teacher, not my lord. I am not yet sworn to service. My family were—ronin." Laurence did not recognize the word, but Junichiro looked away and spoke as though ashamed. "He took me in. When my training was complete, he meant to present me to Lady Arikawa, to see if she would—" His voice died away, and he swallowed visibly: a dream plainly now lost. He straightened. "My family are dead. The shame of my behavior falls only on myself, not on him," he said. "Why do you think Lady Arikawa let us escape?"

Laurence paused and looked at him doubtfully. He had credited good fortune for the improbable success of their flight, but he could scarcely deny that a deliberate impulse on the part of their deadly pursuer was compellingly more plausible. "If so," he said slowly, "then you have achieved your aim. Listen: let me bind you here. That dragon will free you. You can tell them that I forced you to assist me—"

"And shame myself twice over, lying, and saying I yielded to you to preserve my life?" Junichiro said, with perfect scorn. "In any case," he added, "you will never get to Nagasaki alone; and there will be no use in my having aided you this far, if I do not get you away," he added, and there was enough likely truth to that, to force Laurence to silence.

He could not like taking a clear advantage of the boy, even if Junichiro had chosen his own course: he was too much a young enthusiast to be trusted to make that choice clear-headedly. Even granting that the maneuver would spare Kaneko, Laurence could well imagine that gentleman's feelings on finding his young student had thus immolated himself to spare him; he knew what his own would have been, under similar circumstances.

But there was no answer to be made to Junichiro's refusing to lie: Laurence indeed could hardly encourage him to do so, when answered in such terms. The only saving grace was knowing the boy an orphan: at least he had not riven him away from family as well as home. Laurence could give him a place aboard ship—if they could either of them get to the ship, which was certainly more likely with Junichiro's guidance than without it. And if they could not, Laurence knew what his own fate would be; he could hardly imagine that Junichiro's would be any more merciful.

A low bubbling roar came from the river below, and Laurence looked down the hill from the temple to see the dragon emerge—at least, he thought it was the same dragon, but she had swelled out to nearly thrice her size, so wide that her very hide was stretched to a paler greenish silver. Laurence watched in astonishment as she spouted a great fountaining of water like a cascade that took illumination from the descending sun. The torrent of water continued a long time, the dragon reducing by degrees to her smaller size as she brought it forth.

"What sort of a dragon is she?" Laurence asked Junichiro.

"A river-dragon," Junichiro said, his tone implying strongly Laurence was a fool who required having the simplest of matters explained. "Like Lord Jinai!" the boy added pointedly, seeing Laurence had not followed.

"She is the same breed as that monster?" Laurence said, incredulous: the scale was so very different he could scarcely credit it.

"She cannot get big until she goes down to the ocean, of course," Junichiro said.

The water-dragon padded back up the hill towards them, stopping by the temple doorway to shake herself free of droplets again in a fine spray. "Now then," she said, stepping inside and ducking her great head beneath the lintel: Laurence recognized now the kinship between her appearance and the sea-dragon's, where her lines would spread out, as she grew in size. "I have refreshed myself, and I am ready to hear more of this Shakespeare."

Junichiro seated himself at once, as though this remark had the force of a command; Laurence hesitated, then said, "Madam, I beg your pardon: we cannot stay."

The dragon paused in the act of settling herself and regarded him with blank astonishment; Junichiro stared at him so appalled that Laurence supposed he had committed some enormous solecism. The sensation was discomfiting, but not so far, he was grimly certain, as would be their discovery and inevitable pursuit.

"We are bound for Nagasaki," he said firmly, "and cannot delay in our journey. I beg your pardon most sincerely if I do not express myself in the accepted mode, from unfamiliarity," he added. "I assure you I mean no offense."

The dragon sat for a moment, blinking; she seemed less offended than perplexed. "The river flows to the sea, whatever the wind says about it," she said, and reached up and rubbed a talon over some of the great swinging tendrils from her forehead, thoughtfully. "You have a long journey ahead," she said eventually. "Stay the night! In the morning we will go together, down to the Ariake Sea. You will not have so far to go from there."

Laurence had no notion of the geography, but he could well imagine that a dragon-back ride would speed their journey. He glanced at Junichiro, who wore a peculiar expression of mortification and longing mingled; as though Laurence had brazenly committed a crime, and been rewarded for it instead of condemned. He at least showed no disposition to reject the offer; and to be fair, Laurence did not see how it was to be refused. "Ma'am, I am honored by your condescension," Laurence said, bowing, and seated himself reluctantly again.

Hammond's boat rowed back three hours later, swiftly crossing from the harbor. Despite his avowed distrust, Temeraire could not help but watch her approach anxiously. The *Potentate* was very far from land, for the sake of her draught, and there were a great many small boats going to and fro in the harbor before them, betwixt which Temeraire could make no distinction. Captain Blaise came to the dragondeck and stood watching them for some time with his glass as Hammond's boat came nearer, and he said to Granby, "Well, it will be hot work, if they do try for us."

"Whatever do you mean?" Temeraire said, peering down.

"They have loaded up those boats there with tinder," Granby answered him, shading his eyes to peer at the shore. "They may come out and have a go at setting us afire, we think."

"What?" Iskierka said, rearing up her head abruptly, her eyes going very wide. "What? How dare they! I will go and fire *them*, at once!"

"Oh, no, you shan't," Granby said firmly. "Not until we have seen what they mean to do; you cannot blame them for having a lookout, when a transport loaded to the brim comes creeping into their harbor."

When Hammond had been put back aboard—he was so unhandy about coming up the side that Churki would no longer have it, pronouncing it a ludicrous and unnecessary risk, and insisted on reaching down to lift him up herself out of the launch—he did not say anything at all of Laurence, and nothing to reassure about the egg, either.

"The worst news imaginable," he said. "I had private conversation of Mr. Doeff, who is the commissioner here, and good God! Do you know a ship called the *Phaeton*?"

"Lost in the Pacific, two years ago," Captain Blaise said, automatically.

Laurence had thought well of Blaise—had called him a respectable and a sensible man, but in Temeraire's private opinion he was only a block: not the least imagination or interest as far as Temeraire had been able to discover in nearly the full year of their acquaintance. He was not afraid of dragons, which was the best Temeraire could say of him, and indeed he made a point of taking the air upon the dragondeck every day—after making a punctilious request of the most senior aviator on deck for the liberty—as a sort of gesture to reassure the hands. But his head was full of nothing but the *Naval Chronicle;* he had no other conversation but the weather, and that was not very much use as he insisted on always saying the prospect was very fair, even when it was plainly coming on to a three-days' blow.

"Pellew's second boy had her, if I recall aright, and she was looking in at the Dutch trade last anyone heard of her," Blaise added now. "Likely she went down in a gale—" and stopped as Hammond shook his head.

"She was sunk here," he said, "—*here,* after coming in under false colors, taking hostage two of the Dutch officials who went out to greet her, and threatening to fire the shipping in the harbor if the Japanese did not supply them. Her captain must have been a lunatic," he added bitterly.

The uproar this produced, Hammond had evidently not expected. He had meant to convey that the Japanese were not in the least pleased with the British, and that they naturally thought the *Potentate* had come to make a fuss over the sinking of the *Phaeton*. In this he had succeeded, but was dismayed to discover that Captain Blaise would have liked to confirm all the worst fears the Japanese might have entertained. When Hammond had finished, Blaise walked to and fro along the deck for an hour altogether in great fury, repeating that it was more than a dog could bear, that they should have sunk a British ship and receive no answer, even in the face of all Hammond's increasingly anxious remonstrations.

He was only at last persuaded to go inside to write a report of it to the Admiralty; Hammond turned at once to the dragondeck, so he might corner Captain Harcourt, who was senior, and try to make repairs by urgently pressing her in turn to disavow any possibility of action.

"Hammond, I haven't the least wish to start us another war in some hasty fashion," she said at last, in some irritation, "but no-one can blame Blaise for being distressed, and I am so myself. It is all very well to say her captain was provoking: whose word do you have for that, but this Dutch fellow, whose trade he would have gone after?"

She walked away from his importunities, and at last Temeraire could pin Hammond down with a clawed foot laid down in his path, when he would have dashed away from the dragondeck at once again. "Oh—no, no, they do not know anything of Laurence," Hammond said, distracted. "Pray will you move, I must go down and speak with Blaise again—"

"It is just as I thought," Temeraire said savagely, without giving way, "you have done nothing at all and it was all falsehoods, your promises to look for Laurence: did you even ask them about him? And what is he to do, now, when you tell us they all hate the British here, and he is all alone, and we are hundreds of miles away? I ought have let this wretched ship sink," he added, "and left you on it."

"I hope to God I will not wish as much, soon enough!" Hammond cried, taken aback by his violence. "But I *have* asked, I give you my word, and Mr. Doeff has promised me he should inquire among the Japanese. But you must see under these circumstances I was forced to proceed with the greatest caution. Imagine if they should know his value as a hostage against us? So I have only said we had a shipwreck, and we would be glad to have any news at all of our sailors, if any sign had come up on the shore of any of them. I will bring you any word at once, I assure you: and pray consider that any opening of hostilities between us should certainly make his rescue a thousand times more difficult."

He added this last urgently, and though of course Temeraire saw straight through this transparent piece of manipulation, he could not argue with it; neither could he do anything, for good or ill, to forward the matter. "Maximus," he said, feeling quite desperate, when he had let Hammond go dashing away again towards the stern cabin, "I do not suppose *you* would go and look for Laurence? That sea-dragon cannot come out of the water. If you should keep away from the coast—"

But, "Enough of that," Churki said, overhearing. "Maximus had much better stay where he is, and you had much better eat another bowl of soup and take your medicine, so that when we *do* hear some word worth acting upon, you will then be able to do so. Do you suppose Laurence would be grateful if you have made yourself ill or lost one of our company, in the meantime, just to feel as though you were doing something when anyone can see there is nothing sensible to be done?"

This shot went uncomfortably home: Temeraire knew Laurence by no means approved of any rash or hasty action, and had spoken with him on several occasions about the need for sober reflection. "Particularly," Laurence had said, "when you must know the others will often heed your advice and attend your requests: how much more should that trust increase your obligation to serve them well in such circumstances, by the exercise of restraint? You must be careful not to abuse it, in trying to persuade them into a course against their own interest or that of the nation, for your own benefit."

And how eagerly Temeraire had agreed with him! He sank his head upon his forelegs. The truth was he did not know where to fly, even if he had been well enough to go himself; and besides that, Maximus was not the fellow anyone would have sent on a search mission. He would have to spend half of every day only hunting, and likely making all the people very angry for the quantity of food which he should be taking from them.

"But I *cannot* only lie here!" he burst out. "And do not tell me," he added, "—do not dare to tell me that Laurence is dead, so I might as well do so. If he *is* dead, then I cannot see any reason I should not go to the devil any way I like."

The water-dragon's name was Lady Kiyomizu, although much to Junichiro's horror she breezily told Laurence to call her Kiyo, and not to stand on formality. "You have no manners anyway," she said, "and there is no sense your trying to put out *sakura* blossoms, when you are a bamboo."

Laurence ruefully swallowed this friendly condemnation as the price of his rudeness: he was more than willing to accept it, in any case, to gain such assistance as she was ready to offer in exchange for the scraps of poetry and drama which he could dredge up out of his memory. Fortunately he had always cultivated literary entertainments on his ships, to improve both the education and conversation of his young gentlemen, and the spirit of his hands. They had only just concluded the performance of *A Midsummer Night's Dream,* and on the King's birthday last, Lieutenant Riley had given the officers a stirring rendition of the St. Crispin's Day speech, which Laurence did his best to repeat now. Fortunately his cabin abutted Riley's, and so he had heard the speech said over and over in the evenings for nearly a month beforehand.

"But I beg you will pardon me if you later learn I have mistaken any of the phrases," he said. "I have not heard it since—" and stopped, for of course, he had not heard it in eight years gone and more.

Indeed the *Reliant* herself was surely no longer his at all. It would have been a peculiar career which after such a period should have left him in a prime frigate, and yet not seen him advanced to the command of a ship-of-the-line. Either an unlikely disgrace or promotion must inevitably have been his lot—and then he wondered suddenly if the transport herself was his, something in between the two.

He found it hard to sleep that night, searching for some scrap of memory to be a rope-line which he might have climbed to get a look at himself, past horizons which seemed empty all around. But nothing came to hand, and he felt ever more strongly the anxious sense of something lost; he put his hand into the bundle beneath his head and closed it around the hilt of the sword, the ray-skin familiar and not at once. He slept at last fitfully, ill-at-ease, and startled awake when footsteps came into the temple: an old woman carrying a steaming pot, and she screamed when she saw his face and dropped it, fleeing into the early dawn.

"Why, that is a pity," Kiyo said, yawning tremendously: she seemed able to almost open her jaws in a straight line. "You have made her spill half the sake. Pour the rest in the bowl! It is a little early, but the morning is nice and wet. I do not mind getting up."

She put them on her back again, when they had eaten the rest of the rice dish, and she had drunk the rest of the wine, and she tramped down the hill through a faint cold drizzle towards the river. "Put the baskets on," she said, stopping on the shore, "and let us get under way! It's a long way to Ariake, and we will have to stop and get something to eat along the way."

There was a sort of harness resting upside-down underneath a little lean-to by the shore: two tightly woven baskets, watertight, lined thickly with straw and a final lining of fabric. These were joined to each other with straps which went about her body; each was big enough for a man to climb inside, and when Laurence and Junichiro had strapped it upon her and ensconced themselves so, Kiyo plunged into the river and swam out into the deep part of the current, very like a horse bearing saddlebags.

Almost directly they had left the curve of the river leading to the temple, they were in settled countryside: women and children on the banks, washing clothing and carrying water, waved to them with enthusiasm as they passed, and fishermen poled small vessels out of their way, yielding precedence. Laurence had bundled his hair beneath a scrap of his old shirt, and he hunched his shoulders and looked down as they sailed onwards to avoid any comment on his features: he was increasingly conscious that any journey overland would have offered scarcely any hope of success.

Junichiro for his part also kept his head down; from what Laurence could see of his expressions, he seemed to be caught in a confused welter of pleasure and misery. His delight in the dragon's company, and in the condescension she had shown them, was very plain; it was equally plain he did not feel himself deserving of it, and Laurence would not have been surprised to have him burst out in confession of his crime at the least encouragement.

Fortunately this was not immediately forthcoming. The two of them might have been traveling alone, for Kiyo's head was nearly always submerged beneath the surface as she carried on against the current, her long tendrils streaming away to either side around her like trailers of seaweed caught on a ship's hull. Her speed was indeed remarkable: better than six knots, Laurence judged.

"Will you tell me about the course we are on?" Laurence asked Junichiro, when they were on an isolate curve of the river, hoping as much to distract him as to learn more of his circumstances: they seemed to have been swept up beyond his control for the moment.

"You must have done something notable in a past life," Junichiro said, half to himself, as though trying to explain to his own satisfaction what had brought them so much undeservedly good fortune. Laurence, for his part, should have liked to know what he had done either evil or good so as to produce all the ills of his present situation, but as he did not accept Junichiro's explanation, he could only attribute it to some forgotten act of his lost eight years. "And we are on the Chikugo River, following it to the Ariake Sea," Junichiro added. "That is between Chikugo Province and Hizen Province—"

"Hold, you leap too far ahead," Laurence said, and made Junichiro explain a little more of the geography of the nation, a small country like his own; they were upon the island of Kyushu, which after a little description Laurence mentally classed with Scotland: it was not the largest, nor the site of the capital, but the home of considerable wealth and industry; and this divided into several provinces.

"Nagasaki is in Hizen Province, on the western side of Kyushu—and Hizen is on the Ariake Sea, like Chikugo, so it will be much easier to get to there," Junichiro added, and with a finger dipped in river water sketched him a very rough shape on the dry part of the dragon's back, which shortly evaporated but left Laurence with the comfort, not inconsiderable for a man who was used to knowing his precise latitude and longitude at nearly every moment, of having some approximation of his bearings.

Junichiro said it should require the entire course of the day, to see them to the shore of the inland sea; Laurence settled himself low in his basket and prepared only to wait: the rocking motion of their journey was familiar, and he was ready to yield himself to sleep when cries from the bank started him up. He looked and saw a small crowd of people urgently waving a banner bearing several large-painted characters in red, which they had been in the process of rigging out on the riverbank from a signpost.

"Oh," Junichiro said, taken aback, and Laurence, looking over, wondered if this were to their account—couriers, he supposed, might have carried around a warning to be posted to try to capture them. But after a brief hesitation, Junichiro reached down into the water and tugged on one of Kiyo's tendrils.

Her head burst from the surface, rivulets streaming away, and the people on the riverbank renewed all their clamor; she did not hesitate for an instant herself, but immediately shifted her course out of the river's current towards them, and as they neared Laurence could see the chief of the delegation, as he supposed, bowing deeply before they had even come to shore.

Kiyo climbed out partway onto the shore to speak with this man, balancing herself on forelegs in a pose reminscent of the great sea-dragon which Laurence had seen. The conversation, naturally, proceeded entirely in Japanese. Laurence crouched in his basket and tried as best he could to avoid any notice, which effort met with success only because no-one present showed the least interest in Junichiro or himself; all their attention was fixed on the dragon.

It struck him abruptly that Kiyo also had no captain, no master; as neither had Lady Arikawa nor Lord Jinai, nor even the lightweight who had ferried about the magistrate and his servants. Laurence was startled, and startled even more that he had not even noticed it before this moment; he had thought nothing of it at all.

It ought to have been certain proof of an untamed ferocity. Dragons required a captain, harness, crew, all the forms of control, to be tolerated anywhere near settled country, or they would rampage and destroy; any beast not so restrained could only be penned in breeding grounds and bribed with cattle to remain there. So Laurence had always supposed—so he had always known. But even as he articulated to himself this commonplace understanding, it rang false. Proof to the contrary was before him, of course—but that should have seemed peculiar, disconcerting, and did not.

He had not managed to explain it to himself when the discussion concluded and Kiyo turned her head over towards them and said, "Down you get!"

Junichiro obeyed at once, and leapt to unbuckle the baskets; Laurence had scarcely any alternative but to follow his example, and hide his face from the expectant delegation by keeping it turned towards her side. They at least did not immediately seize him. Unburdened, Kiyo plunged back into the river and opened her jaws: she began at once to swell up into that wide immensity which Laurence had witnessed the previous evening. This time when she had reached her full size she did not bring the water forth again, but swaying and ponderous dragged herself up onto the shore, and in a strangely gargled voice gave direction. The delegation all turned and set out along a track that led away from the river, carrying their banner with them.

"What is happening?" Laurence asked Junichiro quietly, as they trailed in Kiyo's wake; but he might have reserved his questions. The path turned quickly out of the trees and opened onto a truly splendid wide-open vista: a series of very wide terraces falling away from them down a sloping hillside, each full of water and faintly green with the earliest sprouting of rice plants, though surely the season was too early. There was yet a sharp chill of frost in the air, which Laurence thought must be inimical to any farming, although only to be expected at this time of year.

At the summit stood a great stone basin with a wide irrigation channel running away from it down the hill: peering over, Laurence could see more channels leading to either side into each terrace. The delegation here broke up, and most of the number went running swiftly down narrow pathways along the hillside, calling notice: workers in the fields, who were mostly busy staggering under yokes of water-buckets, raised their heads from beneath wide-brimmed hats and, seeing the dragon, hurried to take themselves out of the terraces until they were lining the hillside paths.

From a village visible at the base of the hill, a neat hamlet of thatch-roofed houses, more people were streaming to join the welcoming party, children running with a cheerful clamoring; more banners were being carried out of a larger house, perhaps ceremonial, and set at the foot of the hill in bright array.

Kiyo was leaning forward into the basin and dipping her face into it, shaking her head so the tendrils made a great cloud around her. Laurence could hear a peculiar gurgling and hissing from her side, an internal noise like a man digesting an excessive meal. She raised her head up and shook off the droplets, and then nodded to the anxiously waiting delegation. Two of the great banners had by now reached the summit and were fixed to either side of the basin, cracking in the wind. All were standing silent, in attitudes of tense expectation.

Kiyo adjusted her position, and then she opened her jaws wide and began to expel the water into the basin: not in any massive quantity at first, a thin stream like the jet of a small fountain, but Laurence was astonished to see the water so hot that it was steaming in the open air. Shortly the rime of white ice, half-an-inch wide, which edged the pool in the stone basin had melted entirely away, and water was running softly away down the channels. Kiyo paused in her work and put her face into the basin again—perhaps working out in some way the desirable degree of heat—and then she sat up again and began once more, in earnest.

The gush of water came out of her jaws as from a kettle, steaming-hot, and went running down to water all the fields—likely saving them from that very frost which Laurence had noticed. As he watched the process, he realized that the Japanese might well receive from this influence an entirely additional growing-season: if they might rely on such a rescue, when a frost threatened the crop, they might begin the first planting earlier, and take the second harvest later, and get two crops instead of one. Their urgency was easily explained, now; having drawn the attentions of a water-dragon so soon likely had saved more of the crop.

When Kiyo had reduced herself back to her original dimensions and closed her jaws again, and the men along the hillside had tried each shallow terrace and waved one after another their banners in signal of success, the general relief was nearly palpable. More bowing and ceremonial thanks ensued, and though there were no effusions, no broad beaming expressions, even so shoulders had straightened; anxiety had lifted. Laurence could not fail to interest himself in proceedings so foreign to his experience, and yet so familiar: he had ridden the estate with his father on occasion as a boy, and there was not so great a difference between the expressions of the tenants receiving relief in the case of some disaster to their crops or homes, and the present—though his father had not nearly so dramatic a support to offer.

Nor so general: the entire village had benefited, here, and it was at once apparent they meant to show their appreciation in proper form: an ox was led up the hill, lowing in anxiety as it came nearer the dragon, and was shortly butchered before them. The tender offal was flung immediately into a hot pan over coals: sweetbreads and heart and liver and brains, and these having been quickly seared were presented to Kiyo, who devoured them delicately while the great sides of beef were carried away to prepare some more elaborate offering. Other preparations were already in train—cooking-steam was issuing from many of the houses below and baskets of cooked rice beginning to emerge; the leaders of the delegation were seating themselves formally on mats placed around Kiyo's head.

"Well, we will be a little late getting you to the sea," she said cheerfully, looking around to Laurence at last, as she settled herself down to eat, "but at least we do not need to worry about eating. How delicious good, fresh beef is!"

The remark fell, unfortunate, loud. Whether they merely had more leisure now for interest, or her addressing him drew attention, several heads turned: the village chief, some other of the older men and women, and Laurence found himself regarded with dawning astonishment, in a widening circle of silence.

Chapter 5

TEMERAIRE'S SPIRITS HAD BEEN equal to the challenge of thinking Laurence swept overboard and flung onto the shore, even in the face of general doubt and disagreement; but he began to find it difficult to sustain his confidence, knowing Laurence in such dreadful circumstances: not merely a shipwreck in a strange country, alone, but with every hand against him—every man his enemy, every dragon.

Temeraire could not bring himself to choke down more than a few swallows of soup and rice to share room in his belly with the lump of anxiety, nor could he take any pleasure even in the egg, though Granby and Roland had spoken to him several times that afternoon, anxiously, and remarked upon how nicely it came along. Ferris also had complimented it, very prettily, while Forthing scowled at him and then only stammered out his own attempt—which no-one wanted, anyway; but in neither case could Temeraire raise much of either satisfaction or irritation. He lay unhappy upon the dragon-deck, watching the harbor traffic more from a dull consciousness of duty than from any real interest.

The Japanese boats which crowded the harbor, though not large, were well-handled: fishermen and porters and barges. Besides these and the Chinese ships, the Dutch ship stood out in the harbor: a clipper, with a long and narrow draught for her three masts; she would be a fast sailor, Temeraire thought vaguely. He did not much care about her; she was no danger, as she was all alone, and would scarcely have made a threat to the *Potentate* even without aerial support. He could not see that she had any guns at all.

She did have a dragon: at least, she had put out a pontoon-platform for one to rest upon, and he wore harness, so he was a Western dragon, surely, although his harness was a little strange and looked like nothing so much as a waistcoat, at this distance. But he was only a light-weight, a little bigger than Dulcia, and not very dangerous-looking: a very ordinary sort of brown speckled with cream, with a long and narrow snout and broad forehead. Certainly he did not look anything like the sea-dragon; if anything he looked more like Churki in the conformation of his body, though he was not feathered, of course.

He did not stay at the ship for very long at any one time, but flew busily back and forth to the shore several times over the course of the afternoon carrying substantial parcels away from the ship, which the crew delivered to him over the side with pulleys, and taking them to the shore, where he held several conversations with some party, whom Temeraire could not make out at the distance, before returning to his own ship.

On the fourth pass, Temeraire suddenly picked up his head. "Roland," he said, "that ship there, that is Dutch; she is lawful prize, is she not?"

"Oh?" Iskierka said interrogatively, waiting with interest for the answer.

"Oh," Roland said, looking sidelong, "well, I suppose she is, as she is under Dutch colors; but—"

"No, no," Temeraire said, "I do not mean to take her—"

"Whyever not!" Iskierka interrupted.

Temeraire snorted at her. "Because we have more important matters to consider than prize-taking, at present! But if she is lawful prize, then I suppose she is quite afraid of us; they are taking those parcels to shore, so we should not get them if we decide to demand she strike. Nitidus," he said, twisting his neck around and over Iskierka, to peer awkwardly at him, "would you be so kind as to go over to that dragon there, and invite him to come and have a cup of tea with us, if you please?"

"But," Nitidus said, "but you don't suppose they will shoot at me?"

"Of course they will not shoot at you," Temeraire said. "We are all here, quite ready to come over and answer anything they like to try against you; but if you like," he added, "you may hang out a flag of truce, so they are not worried when you come."

Roland looked a little anxious, and ventured that she might go and speak to Captain Warren before Nitidus should go; but Captain Warren and the others were at dinner: Hammond had in great haste arranged that all the captains should eat together that evening, as his guests. He only wanted to better argue with them all at once more conveniently, but that did not give anyone an excuse for refusing when Hammond was the King's envoy, no matter how rude his own behavior or late the invitation.

"Besides, I am not going to do anything: we are only going to have a conversation," Temeraire said, "so pray do go over, Nitidus," and he was persuaded to go, carrying a scrap of white sailcloth streaming away.

Temeraire watched the encounter anxiously: he *was* quite sure they would not fire on Nitidus, he hoped; but even so, perhaps the other dragon would not like to come; or perhaps he would not speak either English or French, which was all that Nitidus could do, although in such a case he hoped there might be a translator aboard the ship. But Nitidus was received, if not with visible pleasure, at least with no hostility; the brown dragon politely made room for him to land on the platform, and listened with attention to his message, as did several men leaning over the ship's side straining with ear-trumpets to overhear.

Temeraire nudged the others beside him, when he saw the brown dragon look over, to make an inviting open place for him to land on the deck. That was no easy feat—Captain Blaise did not like to put out their own pontoons when their position was so uncertain, and so they were very sadly crowded yet—but with a great deal of squirming and writhing it was accomplished, just as the brown dragon leapt aloft, following Nitidus, and came towards them.

"Oh, Gong Su," Temeraire said, turning as he came climbing up to the dragondeck, with Roland and Forthing and Ferris, "we are to have a guest: pray tell me, do you suppose is there any chance of our offering him a proper bowl of tea? And something to eat? I should be happy to see us offer that last goat, which I believe is marked out for me, if I might beg you to put a word in the ears of the cook," he added. Of course it was not really suitable, to Gong Su's proper rank, to ask him to cook anymore; but it was a sad fact that none of the British cooks seemed at all able to make a respectable meal for a dragon other than the plainest roasted meat, and Gong Su had hinted to Temeraire that so long as he should put the matter on the footing of a personal favor, no shame could attach to the act on his own side.

Gong Su bowed deeply. "I will make inquiries, and see what can be done, of course," he said, and instantly went; meanwhile Forthing could think of nothing better to do than to stamp up to the dragondeck and say, "Look, Temeraire, whatever are you about? We cannot be gabbing away with the enemy."

"How absurd," Temeraire said with scorn, "only look how small he is! An enemy of mine: I should say not. Anyway, I am only going to have a conversation with him. Hammond was closeted for hours with the Dutch commissioner, so I do not see why I should not have a chat with this fellow."

Ferris was trying to catch Forthing by the arm, murmuring to him, "Look, if it should bring up his spirits at all—"

Forthing shook him off and said, in cutting tones, "I know very well *your* motive to allow any degree of license whatsoever—" and Ferris flushed angrily, but Temeraire could not pay attention to them further, as he had to turn to meet their guest as he came in to land.

The brown dragon's harness was odd indeed, as it came into closer view: it was indeed made up of almost pouches of some ordinary fabric, brown wool perhaps, and these were overlaid upon and attached to a fine mesh which covered him nearly from the base of his neck to his tail almost like a shirt, made up of many thin chains—chains of *gold,* Temeraire realized with a real start, as the sun caught upon them, and so many! although almost entirely concealed by the dull fabric.

"But why would anyone wear gold chains in such a way, where you can hardly tell they *are* golden," he whispered doubtfully to Iskierka; they certainly would not be very handy, in a fight.

They could not discuss it: the dragon landed with an easy flip upon the deck before them, and settled himself in the waiting opened place, while Nitidus landed on Temeraire's back and made himself comfortable.

"Hello," Temeraire said, inclining his head. "How do you do? I am Temeraire, and also Lung Tien Xiang; and I am very pleased to make your acquaintance: thank you very much for coming."

"Well, it's kind of you to ask me," the brown dragon said, in perfectly good English although broadly accented. "And I am John Wampanoag, of Salem, Massachusetts, at your service," and he bowed his own head politely as well.

Temeraire said, a little uncertainly, "But surely that is not in Holland?" He was not perfectly sure of the geography of that nation, but there had been a great many places around Capetown, which had possessed Dutch names, and that did not sound in the least like any of them.

"Why, no," the dragon said, "I am American, you know. That is my ship, the *Lacewing,*" and gave a flip of his tail in the direction of the Dutch vessel. "She is only under Dutch colors because we have been hired to bring in a cargo, since you have that Bonaparte fellow making hay of things in Europe."

"Oh, I see," Temeraire said, although he did not, at all: Bonaparte had conquered the Dutch, he was quite sure. "But is he not their emperor?" he inquired.

The American dragon shrugged. "The fellow in charge here

don't like to think him so," he said, "and he is the one who can sell my cargo for me and get me my copper for the return road, so I guess what he says is good enough for me."

"Your cargo," Temeraire said, a little perplexed, "and your ship—do you mean to say, she is your prize?"

"Prize?" Wampanoag said. "No; I paid to have her built, and I bought the wool cloth and the other trade goods in her belly. Well," he amended, "if you like to be precise, my firm did so: she is a venture of Devereux, Pickman, and Wampanoag: but as Devereux is in India, at present, and Pickman is back at Salem minding the store, you may as well call her mine."

Temeraire was staggered, and looked at the rather small and nondescript dragon with new respect: he was well aware that to outfit a ship, even quite a little one, was a very serious undertaking—thousands and thousands of pounds, at the least, and Wampanoag spoke of laying out the money for it as a matter-of-course, and buying cargo besides. "I do not suppose," he ventured, "—would it be quite rude of me to inquire, where you got the funds?"

"From other ventures," Wampanoag said. "I have been to the South Seas half-a-dozen times, and to India; we do a pretty brisk business in tea, I can tell you."

"Yes, but where did you get the money for the *first* one," Temeraire clarified, rather urgently. "—your capital, I suppose I mean."

He did not wish to be distracted from his original purpose for long, but he felt he could scarcely overlook such an opportunity as Wampanoag had just unexpectedly presented, of finding a way to restore Laurence's fortunes. A gauzy and splendid vision hung before him: Laurence rescued, Laurence back aboard the ship with him, on the way to China again, and very offhand, very casually, when they were alone on deck with the ocean slipping by Temeraire would say, "By the way, Laurence: I have brought you back your ten thousand pounds which I lost you, and I hope you will put them into the Funds, straightaway."

Of course it could be done with prize-taking—Temeraire knew

that, and Iskierka was forever nagging after finding some, but Laurence did not really approve of that. A prize taken legitimately, in the course of one's duty, he thought was very well; hunting after prizes for their own sake he frowned upon. Laurence would not be satisfied, if he were to ask where Temeraire had got the funds—and he *would* ask, Temeraire was glumly certain—should he hear, as answer, by taking prizes. And Temeraire had forfeited his own share of the perfectly correct prizes which he and his company had taken during the invasion of Britain, when he had been transported away with Laurence; those had all gone to building pavilions, back in Britain.

"I had a good bit from the tribe, when we formed the firm, which I have since bought out; but of course they would not go in with me until I showed I could raise some funds of my own," Wampanoag said. "I began with doing some cross-country carrier work, for other firms, and when I had shown I was a steady fellow and was not going to go haring off with someone's cargo, good old Devereux gave me my chance and hired me to be agent on one of his Indiamen, with two points of interest. When I had realized my share from that journey, the tribe went in with me, and Devereux's third son, and Pickman, to outfit our first ship; and we have done pretty well for ourselves since."

"Cross-country," Temeraire said, latching on to the first part of this nearly incomprehensible narrative, "—across your own country?"

"From Boston to the Kwaikiutl, on the West Coast," Wampanoag confirmed. "It's a good deal cheaper, you know, to carry things dragon-back instead of sailing all the way round." Then he sat back and looked at Temeraire with a tipped head. "I beg your pardon, am I being a dullard? Are you looking for work? There's not quite so much call for heavy-weights in shipping, as the cost of your feed is difficult to make back; but there is a particularly fine timber, on the West Coast, which I have been thinking might make it profitable to get a big fellow aboard."

"Why," Temeraire said, brightening, "that is very kind of you: how long a flight is it?"

"Not above a month," Wampanoag said, "once you are in Kwaikutl lands: that is three months' sailing, from here."

"Oh," Temeraire said, "I do not suppose I can: we cannot leave the war for four months. And then we should have to get *back,*" he added, and sighed a small sigh; he ought have known that it could be no easy matter to build up a fortune, or else everyone would have done it already before now.

"But *anyone* can do this?" Dulcia ventured, from Maximus's back: they had all been listening raptly.

"If you know your book-keeping, so you cannot be cheated; and will do steady work," Wampanoag said, "and if you don't mind an empty belly now and again, and you are steady about avoiding fights and trouble and fuss, and showing away," rapidly diminishing the luster of the enterprise as he went on.

"An empty belly?" Maximus said, and snorted. "That is not for me: anyway we do very well, Temeraire. We *do* have pay now, you know, and it stacks up quite agreeably, when you ask to see it in coin."

"No—yes—I suppose," Temeraire said, though regretfully. "Still it is very generous of you to offer," he added to Wampanoag, "and I am very flattered, I am sure: will you stay to tea, if you please?" He saw with great relief that Gong Su was coming back up to the dragondeck with several of the galley cooks, the ship's boys carrying handsome brass bowls polished to a shine and steaming cauldrons of food, and upon a rack dripping over porridge the roasted goat, with what smelled like some fish liver in sauce to give it some interest.

"Thank'ee, I don't mind if I do," Wampanoag said. "If I am not putting you out: I can see you are crowded a bit," a sad understatement: Maximus was curled over all of the deck where Temeraire was not, and all the others heaped atop them both, whenever they were not aloft or swimming.

"We do very well, pray do not think anything of it," Temeraire said, of course.

"I suppose you fellows have come from England? Have you the latest news of the war?" Wampanoag asked, when they had settled themselves and begun to eat: there was of course fish and rice, to eke out the goat, but Temeraire had made sure—frowning down both Maximus and Kulingile—that Wampanoag received a haunch entirely for himself, as the courtsey due a guest.

"We have come from Brazil," Temeraire said, "and we have only a little news from there: the Incan Empress has married Napoleon, and we suppose gone to France with him." He hurried through this part of the story, and added, "But far more importantly, the Tswana have quite cast him off—they have made peace, in Brazil, and they do not mean to help him make war there any longer."

He finished on this, as the best note of triumph available; although the situation in Brazil had by no means been quite so settled as all that at their departure. The Portuguese owners had been as laggard as they could in freeing many of their slaves, and those released had not all been perfectly happy to find themselves subsequently claimed as the family of the Tswana dragons, however much cherished by the same. But so far the arrangement had held, at least in name; they had remained in Brazil several months to see it established, despite all their urgent wish to be on the way to China, and Temeraire counted it yet as a success.

"Why, that is very interesting, there," Wampanoag said, thoughtfully, though not as impressed as Temeraire might have liked by the news from Brazil, and rather more interested in the Incan side of things, asking, "Do they have so much gold and silver as they are supposed to do?"

"*Heaps,*" Iskierka said, with a resentful and significant eye on Temeraire: she had not ceased to mutter quietly, where Granby could not hear, how much better everything should have been if he *had* married the Incan Empress instead, as she had busily tried to arrange. Temeraire paid her no mind. Granby had not wanted to marry the Empress at all.

"I must try and lay in some stock of silk, then, and pottery," Wampanoag said, which Temeraire did not follow at all, though he was too polite to say so; but Kulingile was not so shy of asking, and Wampanoag willingly explained, "Why, cotton will be cheaper soon, with this peace with the Tswana: the South shan't be looking to the sea-lanes and fearing to send out any ships, and gold and silver won't buy as much, if there is more to be had floating around. I will buy ten thousand dollars' worth of silk now, if I can get the Japanese to give it to me, and sell it for a hundred then: see if I don't." He gave a very decided nod.

"That," said Churki, when Wampanoag had flown back to his own ship, after tea, "is a highly respectable dragon, I am sure. And you see how many people he has, all his own! I wish you had asked him more about this tribe of his," she added, with a slightly censorious note, "instead of thinking only of his money. Money is very well and one must have enough, but it is not all that matters."

"That is not why I asked him, at all," Temeraire said, loftily, and well-pleased with the success of his opening gambit, swallowed his medicine in better spirits, and put himself to sleep with his new and private hope: if *he* could not go and find Laurence, and his friends could not, perhaps someone else might.

"He is just an Englishman going to Nagasaki," Kiyo said, eating a quarter of beef. "I am taking him as far as Seto. Pass that hot sake, if you please," she added to the headman, or something along those lines, Laurence gathered, picking out a few words and seeing the village chief looking between him and her helplessly and then turning to have the bowl of hot wine before her refreshed from a heated kettle.

There was very plainly an extraordinary degree of deference paid to the river-dragons, and Kiyo evidently considered herself—and likely was—above any considerations of the law. But the headman was not so, and his suspicions were not to be so easily allayed. He did not challenge Kiyo directly, but Laurence saw him speak to one of the other men, and shortly a few messengers slipped away from the celebration. He watched them go, grimly, and exchanged a look with Junichiro, who himself had been keeping back.

The headman came towards him shortly, to press him with smiling firmness to come down to the village and be housed there for the night. Laurence had not the least doubt there would be a guard on the house, and he did not mean to carve his way out of another prison through innocent farmers.

"Pray thank him for his kindness," Laurence said, casting for some way of deferring the entanglement, "and tell him I am honored to accept his invitation: we will come down very shortly, if Kiyo does not wish to get back on the water."

"Oh, I do not mind staying the night," Kiyo said, unhelpfully, without looking up from her gnawed bones. "We will not get to Ariake to-day, anyway, and there is not much moon to-night. We had much better sleep here, and get on the way in the morning."

By the morning, Laurence was sure, he would have no opportunity; but he bowed to the headman, and determined to wait for some small chance to get into the trees and out of sight. Kiyo abruptly compensated for her indiscretion by sitting up and belching enormously and noxiously, emitting a large diffuse cloud of greyish smoke that stung in the nostrils and left those near-by coughing and gasping: perhaps some aftereffect of her labors in heating the water, and the stink of it not unlike burning tar.

Many of the guests were wiping streaming eyes; the headman was distracted. Laurence seized his bundle in one arm and caught Junichiro with the other; they did not exchange a word, but together hurried as discreetly as they could back into the trees.

They ran as soon as they were out of sight, until they reached the banks of the river and pulled up again: there were a few small fishing-boats pulled up on the shore, with serviceable-enough oars. Junichiro balked. "We cannot steal from peasants," he said, but Laurence had already reached into the bundle and twisted off one of the gold buttons upon his coat.

He pressed it into the soft dirt of the bank. "Let us hope that will make adequate answer," he said. "I will tell you again, you may go back: it is not too late—"

"You know my course is decided," Junichiro said flatly, already climbing in.

"Very well," Laurence said, pushing off, and he bent his back to the oars with a will.

The river ran at a good pace, the boat was light; Laurence had labored harder, for less cause, and arms that took a regular turn at the pumps were not overly tasked by the steady pull. The day had been already long, even with Kiyo's assistance earlier, but Laurence thought it better to row through the night and seek some concealment for the day; the countryside would surely be roused after them, now. "How much further, to this Ariake Sea?" he asked Junichiro, as he rowed onwards.

"Another night after this one," Junichiro said, dully. He sat huddled low in the bottom of the boat: their narrow escape had been a fresh reminder to him of his crime, and there was no longer the pleasure of a dragon's company to distract him. He watched as Laurence rowed on and on; when at last they came to a quicker eddy, and Laurence shipped the oars to give himself a rest, he asked abruptly, "Are you truly a—nobleman?"

"What, because I can row?" Laurence said, half-amused. "Yes; my father is Lord Allendale. But I have been aboard ship since I was twelve years old. I dare say there is not a shipboard task I have not set my hand to."

The river was empty, for the most part, in the advancing night; only fishermen seeking a last piece of luck were out, and not many of those, mere shadows; one they passed was singing softly to himself, and raised a hand to them as they glided on past. Laurence felt the deep peacefulness of the countryside, its stillness, and the loneliness of being outside that quiet.

"Are we likely to meet anyone along the river?" Laurence asked quietly.

"Only at the fords," Junichiro said, "if we are unlucky." He paused and then said a little too quickly, as though he at once wanted very much to ask, and was conscious he should not desire it, "Have you been in a battle, at sea?"

"Three fleet actions," Laurence said, "and perhaps a dozen ship-to-ship. There is nothing very pretty in it. Have you never seen a battle?"

"The bakufu has kept the peace in Japan for two hundred years," Junichiro answered, with not-unmerited pride. "There are pirates and bandits, of course, but not near my mas—not near the honorable Kaneko's home." For all his satisfaction, there was a small wistful note in his voice.

"They are to be congratulated, then," Laurence said. "I do not think we have had peace in Europe for ten years together, in living memory: nor are like to have, with Napoleon roosting in France."

They fell silent together: there were a few huts approaching, and a lantern hung with a gleam of light. Laurence took up the oars again and fell into the easy rhythm of the work, no sound but the faint dripping patter of the water upon the river surface with each oar-stroke, the hush of the wind going by. The moon rose, gibbous and pale on the black water, and he drifted. He might have been on the broad deck of his ship at the prow, facing into the wind and the sails making a low *clap-clap* behind, the hands singing at the stern and a lantern throwing light in a circle on a book before him as he read aloud, looking up to speak to—

He started and looked over his shoulder: there *was* a light, and music, up ahead. A road came to cross the river at a ford, and on the left bank stood several houses lit up and festooned with lamps, women in long gowns at their doors calling out in a great noise to a party of travelers on the road, and several porters and two ferry-men perched upon both sides of the crossing, watching the approach of their small boat with interest and suspicion.

. . .

Temeraire had meant to send Wampanoag another invitation, the next day, but he did not need to; instead in the morning, when the hands had just finished holystoning down the dragondeck, the American dragon flew over of his own volition with a white scrap waving. Kulingile grumbled: it was his turn to sleep, after staying aloft during all Maximus's turn—as Temeraire could not presently take a turn aloft himself—and he disliked having to move.

"I am sorry to come shoving in amongst you," Wampanoag said, as he came down, "but as I can't ask you over to *Lacewing,* in turn, I hope you'll forgive me for making this answer instead for all your hospitality," and he lay down a large package wrapped in oilcloth, tied up with string.

"Oh!" Temeraire said, astonished but by no means displeased; Iskierka sat up and took notice. Maximus had been taking a swim, in lieu of going aloft, but he put his forelegs on the railing and peered over, and all the other dragons raised their heads to have a look; even Kulingile cracked an eye. "Roland, will you open it, if you please?"

She cut open the strings, and folding back the sheets revealed a glory of blaze, beautiful glass beads strung on silver chain, with pearls and gold beads scattered along the length, and how immensely long indeed—it might have made an anchor-chain for the *Potentate,* and a little more to spare.

"If you have a smith aboard, as I suppose you must," Wampanoag said, while they all gazed upon it in mute delight, "he can parcel it out for you all into lengths: I thought that might be better than my trying to cut it up beforehand. We wear it like so, in Salem," he added, and sitting up on his heels showed how a similar chain hung from one woolen pouch to another across his breast.

"Now that," Temeraire said, "I must call very handsome." No-one at all was inclined to disagree, and Temeraire considered it all the evidence which he required, of Wampanoag's being a very good sort of dragon, and to be trusted with important business. He knew perfectly well that Hammond might have a different view of the matter, of course—Hammond had complained a great deal of Temeraire's having spoken with Wampanoag yesterday at all—but Hammond had certainly forfeited any right to consideration after his shameful attempt to leave Laurence behind, and Temeraire did not mean to waste any time in useless quarreling with him where his own mind was made up.

It was too early to eat again, but Wampanoag was very ready to be persuaded to sit with them just for company, awhile, and when they had settled themselves as conveniently as possible, Temeraire delayed no longer in broaching the topic, very delicately. "For you see," he said, "I am afraid that Mr. Hammond may not quite have pursued the matter properly: it does not seem to me that any real search can have been put into train. And," he added, "I consider all the sailors of the ship to be our responsibility. I do not think it at all the thing for us to leave any of them here. We cannot sail away until we have found him: our lost sailor, I mean."

He was not entirely insensible to all Hammond's cautions: there was no need for anyone to know that Laurence should be a valuable hostage, so they might try to put him in prison; Temeraire much preferred for them only to know that if Laurence were returned, they would leave, and otherwise not.

"Are you sure he isn't only dead?" Wampanoag said, greatly diminishing Temeraire's opinion of his intelligence. "They usually are, if they get washed overboard."

Temeraire with an effort restrained himself from mantling. "I am *quite* sure," he said, repressively. "And I intend to remain so until I am offered *proof* otherwise."

Wampanoag had a trick of tilting his head a little to one side, as though he were looking you over from another angle to see if you seemed different, which Temeraire now found had the effect of making him feel under a too-sharp observation. But Wampanoag only said, "So you are only lingering to find him, this fellow you lost?"

"Yes," Temeraire said, eagerly. "And we should be *very* glad of any assistance in recovering him."

"But I beg your pardon," Wampanoag said, "aren't you here over the *Phaeton*?"

"No, for we hadn't any notion what had happened to her," Temeraire said. "We were only on our way to China: we have been invited to the court, you see."

Wampanoag was quite gratifyingly surprised to hear of their destination; he expressed himself very prettily on the matter indeed, calling it a remarkable honor. "And I will not scruple to say, that puts a very different shade on things here, it seems to me," he added, "if you are *not* here to quarrel."

"We are not, in the least," Temeraire said, although a stab of guilt, when he thought of what Laurence should say when he heard of the *Phaeton,* forced him to add, "although I do say we think it very hard that the *Phaeton* should have been sunk, so far from home with all her hands, and all because, we suppose, of some misunderstanding."

"Let us certainly call it that, for the moment," Wampanoag said. "That is a very good name for it, I must say."

He declared himself delighted to be of service in any way he could, promised to speak with the chief of the Dutch, a gentleman called Doeff, to forward the search, and even with the Japanese directly. "I have a bit of Dutch myself, you know," he said, "from the shell: my tribe adopted a good many of them back during the quarreling over New Amsterdam that was. So I can have a jaw with their translators, myself: that is why I hired us on here."

He was so ready to be obliging that Temeraire could not even be too angry with him for adding, "but pray do understand that it is more than I undertake, to return you your sailor. I don't mean to distress you, but my firm have lost a few ships entire ourselves, all hands, too. It is a dreadful sad wrench, I can tell you, to hear that a neat clipper with her hold packed full and three dozen men aboard has gone to the bottom of the ocean, to be gnawed by serpents, and a clear loss of twenty thousand pounds sterling."

Temeraire shuddered in real horror, his ruff flattening involuntarily down against his neck, and Churki exclaimed in passionate dismay; but Wampanoag made a prosaic flip of his wing in the air. "I don't complain: it is a hard business," he said, "and a necessary risk to run, if you mean to make your fortune at it. But what I mean to say is, not a scrap of sail or bit of timber do we have to show for any ship we have lost: we only know they are lost because they left the one port and never came in at any other, and after we had sat hoping after them a couple of years it was time to leave off saying, 'She will come in tomorrow.' So I cannot promise you we will find a trace to say, one way or another, what has happened to your sailor. But whatever I *can* do, I will, sure enough."

"I cannot hope for more than that," Temeraire said as politely as he could manage, rather wishing that Wampanoag would leave now before sharing any other ghoulish stories, and seeing before him a long empty stretch of days, waiting and waiting, while Laurence did not come.

The party about to ford the river was evidently the train of a lord on his way home from the capital, amongst them several armed retainers wearing two swords and more serviceable armor as well. Laurence kept his head bent down and rowed industriously but not, he hoped, too fast; Junichiro was silent in the boat's belly. Laurence thought for a moment they would manage it. The ferrymen and the porters lost interest when they saw that Laurence showed no intention to compete with their business, of which in any case there bade fair to be as much as they could manage with the sheer size of the lord's retinue, and the confusion and noise of the welcoming inns might have overwhelmed any interest in Laurence and Junichiro's quiet passage.

But luck turned against them: one of the lord's servants on the far bank, evidently in charge of getting the entire assembly across the river and looking exasperated and hot, with a few strands of hair straggled loose from his neatly swept-back arrangement, caught sight of the boat. He called out to them peremptorily, beckoning—*you there, you, the boat*—plainly wishing them to come and assist in the ferrying, despite the scowls of the ferrymen.

Laurence pretended not to hear, not to see; he rowed onwards with more vigor, trying to evade the clumsy-handled ferries, crammed too full of men. But an eddy pushed one of the waddling boats towards their little fishing-boat and bumped her, and a disapproving older woman in the prow took the opportunity to reach over and swat him reprovingly, gesturing back at the crowded bank as she chided him.

The swat dislodged the rag covering his hair; one of the samurai aboard the ship glanced over, and, after a moment of confusion, a recognition dawned. The samurai leaned over, and sought to grab him; Laurence shipped one oar and seized the other mid-stem, jabbing the handle hard into the man's belly, and tipped him over the side. Another was standing up in the ferry, trying to draw his sword, which he would have needed to practice a good deal more on the water before trying to accomplish it on a wallowing tub of the sort. Before he could get it out, Laurence swung up the flat of the oar and struck the man a hard and ringing clout across the head, knocking him down to the floor of the ferry.

The two boats were yet entangled. "Ma'am, I beg your pardon," Laurence said to the old woman, who was still sitting ramrod-straight in the ferry over the side from him and regarding him with a flat expression of utter disapproval and not the least evidence of fear; he put out a boot over the side and shoved the ferry off with a heave, and they were loose.

But the entire retinue were now alive to his presence, swarming out upon the banks, and a couple of the samurai wading out towards them with blades drawn: the ford was shallow enough to make attack practical, the river not waist-high on a man. "Take the oars!" Laurence said to Junichiro, who was hesitating with his hand on the hilt of his blade—he could scarcely have been eager to strike men of rank, of his own nation.

Junichiro looked even more torn; but he seized the oars and

began awkwardly to pull. One of the samurai had reached them, catching at the boat's side: Laurence gripped the man's wrist to hold away the blade, and with his other hand closed hard struck him across the face and away from the boat. Another was struggling furiously through the current, almost there, but Junichiro had mastered the boat, and they were moving into deeper water.

Laurence ducked a last wild desperate swing of blade, and then he sat again and took the oars—pulled as urgently as ever he had pulled in his life: no longer the easy strokes he had used to move them along, but deep cupping sweeps, legs and back and shoulders all gone into every stroke. He had put a hundred yards between them and the ford before the first ferry could be emptied of her passengers, and a pursuit began to organize. Then he was further on, around a bend of the river, and they had vanished from sight.

He did not slacken his pace; he thought at first he might hope to escape the pursuit—the boats at the ford had by no means been very serviceable, and any rowers they had were like to be unhandy. But as he pulled them onwards, a blue flare went shooting up, back from the ford, and burst with a great thunderclap noise and a shining light on the water. A signal, and faintly he heard an answering roar—a dragon, alerted.

"They will set the patrols on us now," Junichiro said. "We will be taken," with a calm certainty, given almost in a conversational tone. He had straightened up in the boat, and looked as though he were already preparing himself to meet his fate.

"I do not propose to be quite so dull a fox as that," Laurence said. "Pick up that bundle, and jump for the shore when we are near enough." He turned them towards the left, where the bank came low to the water, with trees close together but not impassable.

Chapter 6

LAURENCE PUSHED THE FISHING-BOAT off, water already rising inside from the hole he had stove in her hull, and saw her go away downriver not without a qualm: even if remaining aboard would have been certain doom, she was still the quickest road to the sea, and the only one at all familiar. He had left the remains of his already-tattered old shirt wrapped around a bundle of branches to make a sort of scare-crow, standing up in the prow and fluttering out white; if only the boat evaded capture long enough to get some distance away before she sank, he hoped it might prove some source of confusion, if not long defer the pursuit.

At least it would conceal where they had gone, for a little while. Junichiro was already doing his best to obscure the marks their landing had made in the bank with more dead leaves and branches.

The going was slow among the trees, and slower still for lack of clear destination. Laurence could look up and catch a glimpse of the stars, now and again, which pointed him south-west generally, but besides this his progress was wholly blind. "Do you have any notion what is in the countryside near-by here?" he asked Junichiro, as they struggled onwards through the rough terrain.

"We are in Chikugo Province by now," Junichiro said. He paused and looked up over his shoulder: a sound of leathery wings, faint but carrying over the water, not far distant.

Laurence caught sight of a large old pine, gnarled and twisted, roots erupting from the ground in low arches. They squirmed between two of these and pressed themselves back into the meager shelter their intersection offered. The night was not bitterly cold, but enough; they were wet, in thin cotton robes, and it would be a long while for the hollow to have warmed with their bodies. The dragon swept overhead a few times, with no particular direction, merely having a general look, or so it seemed to Laurence; but they huddled beneath the predatory search in silence, hearing the distant noise of search parties.

A clamor was raised somewhere off, in the direction of the river, and the dragon turned away towards it: perhaps the boat. Laurence breathed, but did not yet live and move; too soon for that. The sun was barely up, but had not yet penetrated the trees; he only saw the sky lightened overhead. The voices left off, after a while, and the dragon's searching resumed, but more distant—it was looking somewhere on the other side of the river, Laurence thought. In any case, this was the best chance which was likely to come; a search would close in upon them soon enough if they merely remained in hiding.

He stood, not very quickly or easily; all his muscles protested the cavalier treatment he had served them, going from hot work to a cold, crouching bed, and he could only ruefully envy Junichiro, who bounded out of the hollow behind him as easily as a deer with the limberness of youth. "Have you any notion of the best direction?" he asked.

"We should continue southward and make for the coast of the Ariake Sea," Junichiro said, "and follow its shore around to Nagasaki." Laurence nodded, and followed him into the thicket.

They walked in silence most of the time, speaking only in low voices; the woods were deep and hushed about them, and every word seemed to ring out like a bell, inviting capture. But Laurence asked Junichiro the distance to the sea when they made a brief halt by a spring and they gave their feet a rest; blisters were already raising white upon his skin. The number meant nothing at first, as he did not know how long a *ri* was, but when they began walking again, Junichiro did his best to tell Laurence when they had crossed the distance, and he made it something near two and a half miles. Ten miles to the coast and sixty around, if they could not find another boat and cut across: three days' forced march, for an infantry company—a company with boots and supply.

Laurence marched on after him and grimly did not make any close inspection of his feet: they would be worse before they were better.

"They are busy enough over *something*, there," Granby said, peering through his spyglass, which was rigged out with a loop into which he might slip his hook, and thereby use his hand to steady the front. Temeraire would have liked a spyglass himself; he could not see why one might not be made in dragon-size.

"Why would anyone bother?" Iskierka said, dismissively. "If I want to see what is happening, I will just go fly over and take a look; should you like me to do so, Granby?"

"Stay where you are, if you please," Granby said, "—or if you don't please, for that matter," he added. "The last thing I need is Hammond yowling at me some more; he leapt out at Berkley this morning directly he had put his head out of doors, before he had even swallowed a bite of breakfast: I think the fellow don't sleep."

Several dragons had come into the Japanese port. This alone was not unusual: they had seen several coming and going and in the town beyond, in the past several days, but those had been nearly all of them courier-beasts, or a few light-weights evidently engaged in the trade in some way. This party was led by a middle-weight, a grey dragon wearing an elaborate drapery of green, which had some sort of jeweled border that sparkled in the sunlight; Temeraire could not tell if it was diamonds, or beads, or something else, but it certainly looked very attractive. John Wampanoag had flown over a little while ago, evidently to meet the new party.

Temeraire observed it all with anxious hope: if only Wampanoag was right this moment explaining that they would leave should Laurence be found; if only the dragon were a person of substance, who might push things forward; if only she would listen to Wampanoag; if—if—if.

"Whyever has Hammond not been useful," he said, in rising impatience, "and got us aboard a translator? I might have begun to learn a little Japanese, and be able to speak with them directly. Can you see, is she speaking with Wampanoag?"

"I don't see, at all," Granby said, and Temeraire began to wonder if perhaps he had not ought to go ashore after all, just briefly, to speak with them. He felt a great deal better, indeed. He had drunk up all the medicine and eaten all the porridge resolutely, every day; and he had gone for a very long swim just this past evening, with not the least ill-effects.

"I am sure I could manage it without any trouble," he said, "and it only seems courteous that I should pay a call, while we are guests here—"

"Will you not ever have any sense?" Hammond said, when he had come running; Temeraire narrowed his eyes at Churki, whom he suspected of having made him some signal—perhaps they had agreed upon it in some way.

"They condemn us all as little better than pirates," Hammond continued, "and they must look upon this ship as the most rank provocation—a vessel of this size, this strength! Our armament! Bearing an entire formation's worth of beasts, and," he added, "you will note they do not have heavy-weights among them, so far as we have seen."

"That is perfect nonsense," Temeraire said. "I have never seen a dragon half as big as that sea-dragon."

"But he is confined only to the water!" Hammond said. "That is nothing to what a dragon of Kulingile's size could do, in the air, anywhere in the country he liked, if they have no heavy-weights of their own to check him: he might run rampant over them."

"I might, too," Maximus said, raising his head with a jealous gleam—he was not so inclined to quarrel with Kulingile as he had been, but he could scarcely be blamed when Hammond insisted on being so outright provoking.

"Good God, I hope I do not mean *that* in the nature of a compliment, I assure you," Hammond said, entirely missing the point, as usual.

"So much the better, then," Temeraire said. "I am very content for them to be worried, and to wish us gone: let them only find Laurence, and bring him to me, and we shall go."

"If they should even believe such a promise, and find it possible to fulfill your demands," Hammond said, "they will not fear us the less for going out of their sight, on such an endeavor. What do you imagine such a nation must think, with a vast neighbor so near-by, which has on previous occasions attempted their conquest, making alliance with another nation equipped with vessels of a size that might ferry a dozen dragons in a week across the China Sea? They cannot help but fear it."

"Then they must *be* afraid," Temeraire said, outraged. "You desire that alliance, you have said so again and again—"

"That does not mean I must be in a great hurry for the Japanese to *learn* of it," Hammond said, "and particularly not to think that more has been accomplished than has; it is better not to announce the wedding before the proposal has been accepted."

In Temeraire's opinion, this was quite absurd; if the Japanese wished to be anxious and imagine dreadful things happening, when no-one had done anything to them at all—bar taking a few trees which they had not been busy to use anyway—that was their affair. "Mine," he said, "is to see Laurence brought safe back to me, and if flying across and having a few words with that other dragon will persuade them, or our making some show of strength, I am happy to see it done: I would not hesitate in the least.

"Indeed," he added, with a sudden kindling impulse, and looked down to where Captain Blaise was consulting with Granby,

"Captain Blaise! Will you listen to me, if you please? I do not suppose we have exercised the great guns, in over a month—surely you ought to do it, do you think? If we cannot make answer for the *Phaeton* straightaway, at least we should like them to know we *might*—that we are not only sitting here because we cannot."

Captain Blaise did not look up at Temeraire directly, but he said after a moment, "Do you know, Captain Granby, I do believe we ought to exercise the great guns. And then at least those ruddy blighters will know we *might* answer them properly, if we liked."

Temeraire did not see why Blaise needed parrot what he had said, as though he had thought of it himself, but he did not very much care; Hammond's protests, swift to come, were not in the least heeded, and Temeraire had the pleasure, only a little while later, of hearing the drumroll as the ship beat to quarters, and every hand went to his rope or gun.

The eruption of flame and smoke and thunder was everything which he could have desired: the great dreadful roar of the broadside, the gouts of red and blue flame, the thick clouds of black powder smoke rolling away over the water before the wind, carrying towards the harbor. And then Captain Harcourt said, "Do you know, fellows, I think we will go up and have a bit of exercise, ourselves," and to compound Temeraire's satisfaction he could watch Lily and all her formation aloft, weaving through the intricate patterns of battle-maneuver. Even Iskierka took an interest, and capped the entire production by going aloft at the very end, and blazing a great circle of fire like a wreath around the ship. Ordinarily Temeraire by no means approved her rampant showing away, but in this case he forgave it. "*That* has shown them," he said with real joy.

"Yes," Hammond said, low and grim: he had not left the dragondeck all the while, but yet stood by Churki's side, his thin narrow hands clenched upon each other as though he wished to wring them out. "And now we must wait for what they will choose to show *us*."

. . .

A host of fiddler crabs, too small to be worth the attention of fishermen, scuttled away rapidly along the empty seashore at Laurence's approach: numerous enough that he and Junichiro were able to rake together a pile of them, with branches, onto a rock and away from their escape into the mud. They ate them raw, cracking the shells and sucking the large claw indecorously clean, without the least hesitation.

They went a little way towards easing the bite of hunger, and a small rivulet emptying into the sea near-by, running quickly over rocks, was fresh enough to drink. Laurence soaked his feet again in the salt water without removing the sandals, if he could even have done so without a knife at this point: the cords had sunk into his swollen flesh. He looked across the sea. The sun was setting at the far end, throwing an orange beam across a flat and level plain of water placid as glass, with scarcely a wave to be seen: broad gentle ripples only coming in to shore, nearly silent.

"I would undertake to cross it on a log, paddling with my hands," Laurence said to Junichiro. "It is not twenty miles across, here?"

Junichiro thought as much, when they had made some more calculations, and refreshed by their crab supper they plunged back into the forest and hunted out a few sturdy fallen branches, to be latticed together with saplings and the interstices stuffed with leaves. Three hours of work, by the fading light, gave them a raft serviceable enough for the distance—or so Laurence hoped.

"Can you swim?" he belatedly thought to ask, and was glad for Junichiro's nod; if she came apart beneath them, halfway across, the distance would not be insurmountable, if they could only hold on to a few of the larger limbs.

The moon had risen, brilliant full. "I will try her," Junichiro said, and carried the raft out upon the water and lay himself upon it flat, cautiously. She did not come apart at once; Laurence looked up from shore at his shout of triumph, and was very satisfied. The wind was in the west, gentle, a mere breath; he finished the last of the work, two branches crossed and tied with some strips of fabric cut, with a sharp rock, from the robe he wore; the rest of it he rigged on her as a sail, and striding out into the water he pushed the foot of the makeshift mast through the raft while Junichiro steadied her, and secured it beneath with another knotted length of fabric, filled with sand and pebbles.

He cautiously got himself upon her, braced his hip against the mast with Junichiro doing the same on the other side, slipped his finger into the loop of the cord he had tied around the end of the cross-yard, and drew her into the wind. The irregular sail stirred, and belled, and lifted; she began to move slowly but surely out upon the water.

"Well," Laurence said, after they had glided a dozen yards, and not yet sunk, "I would not like to meet even a strong breeze with this rig, but if we can contrive not to move very much, I suppose we may make it into sight of the opposite shore."

The sea was peculiarly still beneath them, broken more by the eddy of their passage than any waves. Laurence slept in fits and starts, rousing at the tug of the cord upon his finger to adjust the sail. Occasionally he glanced over the side and even saw fish moving, moonlight on dark scales through clear water, and watching them felt a curious sense of familiarity, something just out of reach.

"Have you any family?" Junichiro asked drowsy, drifting. "Any children of your own?"

"No," Laurence said; the lack of a ring upon his hand told him that much, enough that he could give the answer in confidence. "But I have my young gentlemen to look after, which is, as responsibility goes, not unlike: midshipmen, and some lieutenants, not your age," and as he said it he felt a name upon his lips—Roland, he thought, and was nearly sure of it; Roland. Hope filled him: that was not a name eight years old; that was something emerged from the lost depths.

They drowsed again and woke; they were nearing shore: the

moon had been caught in the frame of the open volcanic cone of a high mountain: "Mount Tara," Junichiro said. "We should try and land to the south." He did not need to say why: directly ahead over the water, a cluster of bobbing lights shone in the distance, marking a fishing village or a settlement.

Laurence adjusted their direction. The mast gave them another few miles, but the wind changed a little, likely as they emerged from the sheltering bulk of the mountain: it came suddenly into their faces with more strength, and the sail was taken aback. Mast and sail both tipped; branches cracked; abruptly Laurence was in the water. He put his hand out blindly, trying to get his bearings, and touched sand, groped, straightened: he and Junichiro were standing, only knee-deep in water, and there were trees visible against the horizon perhaps a mile distant through the shallows.

They slogged through the remaining distance slowly, with the longest branches as walking-sticks. The thin cotton of the under-robe was soaked and plastered to Laurence's skin, chilling-cold, and broad sheets of dark seaweed tangled clammy about their ankles, but the stand of trees ahead was all the encouragement he might have wanted. He undid his bundle again and put on the green coat, the good wool staving off some cold. They staggered out through thick sheaves of sea grass, crawled up onto the sandy shore, and onwards just into the trees without getting up off their hands and feet.

There were dry leaves, rough branches, a large stone—this time, Laurence prodded it first with his stick to be sure it was nothing more. The sun was rising. They dug into the leaves, and Laurence shut his eyes; hunger gnawed, and thirst; his feet complained in earnest; but none of these proved able to stave off sleep. He slept as long as nature let him: the sun rising across the water warmed their resting place, and eased both ache and chill. He woke warm, and with only a tolerable amount of pain was able to get himself halfway up and knee-walk awkwardly a sufficient distance away to relieve himself.

Junichiro still slept, and Laurence let him continue; he crawled down to the shore again and put his feet back into the cold water to numb awhile before he tried them. There were some fishing-boats out on the water, but at a long distance that made the men aboard them only stick-figures, in straw hats; when one waved, Laurence raised a hand in answer without fear. Sitting on the shore he worked out a loose thread from the green coat still in his bundle, to tie around the pin of one of the gold bars: bent in half, it made a serviceable hook, and he thought there might be a chance of some biting even so near the shore.

He took a mudskipper, by sitting still until they forgot to fear him, and with it as bait took a few better, and roused Junichiro to eat before they set out again. They had cut across a good deal of the distance: twenty miles left. Laurence counted it in quarter-miles and ignored his feet and the increasing heat of the day. He had bundled the coat back up around the sword, and wrapped the tatters of the sail around his head.

Junichiro said nothing, but eyed him sidelong, repeatedly; Laurence looked down at his bare chest, and realized Junichiro was looking at the many scars of pistol-shot and blade; mute testimony to Laurence's experience in battle. He did not recognize them all. He touched one long stroke along his shoulder, the white smooth long-healed line of it, then shook his head and let his hand drop.

When he had finished, Junichiro tried to press his own outer robe on him. "We look like beggars," he said urgently, in his persuasion.

"That," Laurence said, "I dare say we cannot avoid in any case; and it must be your task to approach anyone we must bespeak, while mine shall be to keep far out of sight. Keep it."

They struggled on through brush and trees, following a very awkward course well away from the road: but Laurence wanted only to find some coast, anywhere not settled, where they might approach Nagasaki cautiously. Any pursuit must expect the port to be his destination—the net would surely be waiting for him there, and his only hope should be to espy some European ship, or the

Dutch commission, and strike out for it in some roundabout way. An improbable goal perhaps, but he had come nearer than he had looked to do, in cold rational consideration.

And then—and then—but there was no sense in contemplating that future, and all its blank impenetrability, until he had come to it.

They found a little brackish pool, and drank, in the late afternoon. Junichiro dug up some wild radish, which he recognized as edible, and they gnawed its woody toughness as they walked. A few times they had to hide a little while crouching in brush, to avoid notice from other foragers; once they came upon a well-traveled road, and scurried across it like rabbits making a dash for safety, in a brief empty gap between walking travelers and sedan-chairs and ox-carts. A dragon went by overhead once, but flying fast, not searching; they listened huddled under concealing branches until its wingbeats faded.

The sun was sinking again, beginning to throw long shadows and wink at them through the branches. Laurence was trudging onwards, mind full of counting and steps, when Junichiro put out a hand to stop him. He lifted his face into the wind; he breathed in salt, and recognized belatedly the distant low crash of waves and voices both, not far off.

The trees were thinning ahead, approaching a road: a busy road, crowded with travelers and cargo. They crept up to a curve and looking down it saw before them the harbor laid out in a neat half-curve: a small island full of Dutch houses sat divided from the town by a narrow canal, and a great many boats filled the harbor together.

"Oh," Junichiro said, stifled, and Laurence followed the line of his gaze: there was a company of men standing off to the side of the road by a sort of tall signpost carved with characters, looking out upon the harbor. He at first did not understand Junichiro's exclamation, and then he recognized abruptly one of the party, standing to the side, armed: it was Kaneko, and down in a cleared field beside the port he saw Lady Arikawa resting, a grey-green curve of dragon.

"I thought she would have liked to let us go," Laurence said to Junichiro.

Junichiro made an impatient gesture: why would Laurence never understand? "Of course she wishes us to escape," he said. "But she cannot openly allow it, and my—and the honorable Kaneko would not merely stand by, either: it ought to have been the duty of the magistrate to secure you, but you were held in his house."

"Well, we must get around them, somehow," Laurence said, "and try to get there," indicating the tiny Dutch settlement. "They will hide us, I hope, even if they choose to ship me back to Europe a prisoner of war. Let us go south a distance, and see if we can get across the road: I would like a better look at the harbor."

Junichiro followed him back into the trees, not without a lingering look, regretful, back at his former master.

Temeraire looked dully down at the sodden scrap: white linen, very fine, with Laurence's mark plainly upon it; he had bought a dozen shirts like it, in Brazil, to repair his shipwrecked wardrobe, before they set out for China.

"I am sorry to give you bad news," Wampanoag was saying, "but I don't mind saying it is more than I hoped to turn up, whether bad or good. It must have washed up on the shore, I guess."

Maximus nudged at his shoulder, gently, a warm butting of his nose; Temeraire was aware of it, he supposed, and grateful distantly. "Did they tell you where they found it?" he asked, formally; he would pursue all inquiry—he would—

"You'll forgive my saying so," Wampanoag said, "but they weren't inclined to be talkative, after that show you lot put on. No-one could help but take it the wrong way: this whole city is full to the brim of warehouses, every last one of them built of nicely seasoned wood. I suppose if you just turned out this lady here," he dipped his head towards Iskierka, "the whole place would be burnt to the waterline in a couple of hours, even if you didn't care to lob over a few cannon-balls at the same time."

"Oh," Temeraire said, after a moment, "I am sorry to have occasioned them any concern. I hope—" He trailed off. He did not hope anything, really; he was only trying to be polite, since there was nothing else to do but try to behave in a civilized fashion, but he could not quite contrive something to say.

"*We* hope," Hammond said, jumping in at once into the breach of silence, when he saw that Temeraire had nothing more, "that you will be so kind as to convey our deepest apologies, to the governor, and to the shogun, for any action on our part which might have given rise to intimations—to false intimations—of hostility, and make plain to his Excellency that the Government of Britain desires nothing more than peace and future tranquility in the relations between our nations. And pray assure them," he added, "that we will at the *earliest possible moment,*" and he threw a hard look at Captain Blaise, "be taking our leave of them, with many thanks for their consideration in allowing us to remain so long in pursuit of our repairs, and our lost friend."

He carried on the conversation from there, for some time; Wampanoag seemed perfectly willing to listen to him, and to agree to carry more messages back and forth; Temeraire did not pay much attention.

The rest of the day passed away in useful, numbing minutiae. They had a wind already, as favorable as anyone could want; they had only to wait for the tide. There were the decks to be holystoned again, the sails to be slushed. Temeraire swallowed the medicine when it was brought him, and the physician looked him over again closely. He organized three of the stronger hands to pull down the lower edge of Temeraire's eye so he might inspect the dark flesh there, a particularly uncomfortable operation, but Temeraire made no objection.

Wen Shen sniffed, after prodding Temeraire a few more times, and said to Gong Su for translation, to Granby, "All right, he is well enough to fly; so do not let him sit there too long while you are sailing—he must fly a little every day, now, and swimming also cannot do him any harm."

So he was better, too, as though that mattered now. He might have been dreadfully ill for all the use he could hope to be, to Laurence. Temeraire felt the stirrings of resentment rising, suddenly, as he lay mute after the inspection—what had Laurence been about, after all, losing himself in such a stupid way? Anyone—anyone at all—might have cut apart the storm-chains. Anyone might have saved them, and the ship, if they had cared to do so—it had not been Laurence's duty alone, to do it. Laurence ought have let the ship sink, if no-one else had decided to cut the chains, and stayed with Temeraire. They had not been so far from shore. It would have been the work of a few hours to get them to land, and they might have saved all their crew and any number of sailors as well.

"I would rather have him back, than this whole ship and everything upon it," he burst out, without caring who heard him; and then Forthing, who was sitting by him, said, "I am very sorry, Temeraire, that he should have been lost—"

Temeraire snarled at him outright. "You are *not* sorry," he spat. "You think you may have your chance, now."

Forthing flushed alternately red and very pale, and then said, "I don't: you've made plain enough you've no use for me; and I *am* sorry, because he gave me my first lieutenant's step, when he might have left me on shore in New South Wales, and most men would have. If I live to get back to a covert, now I am like to have a chance for my own beast; and if I don't, my son will, when he is older."

Temeraire paused: "You have a son?"

"He is eight now," Forthing said, "and at Kinloch Laggan."

"Oh," Temeraire said. "Well," he added, "it does not make me like you any better; having a son is no excuse for looking like a shag-bag, and I dare say it is the opposite—you might consider you are reflecting on *him,* too, and not just upon *me.*"

Forthing stared at him and said, "What?" and looked down at himself.

"Why will you not buy a shirt?" Temeraire said. "Even if you do not buy a particularly decent one, you might buy something *clean;* and that coat is nothing like green: not at *all*. Whoever could wish to acknowledge you as a connection in any way when you look like an untended scare-crow? The hands before the mast have a neater appearance, and I *know* that Laurence has given you a hint, now and again—"

He stopped: *Laurence* rang in his ears, and the hot glow of temper died away beneath his spirits; he sank back low and put his head beneath his wing, as the bosun's bellowing cry went up, "Make sail! All hands to make sail!"

Laurence and Junichiro struggled away from the harbor, paralleling the course of the road for a short distance. The sun was lowering, and the traffic thinning out; at last it seemed worth the risk, and they came out of the trees and scrambled to the other side, heads down and shoulders hunched, between parties of travelers nearly lost in twilight; Laurence hoped they would see nothing more than a pair of lumpen beggars.

They climbed up the far side of the road, through the last thin ranks of trees to the shore: the narrow harbor still stretched out a long way southward to the open sea, and there at her mouth Laurence saw with a shocking, nearly painful sensation, the tremendous immensity of a dragon transport: four masts, the British colors flying stained to red with a last sun-beam, and a great horde of beasts upon her dragondeck tangled in a riot of serpentine colors.

She was making sail.

"Oh, God," Laurence said. "Fire—I must have some fire, at once—gather some kindling!"

He sprang back down through the trees to the road, all concern for disguise or concealment shed. An ox-cart was trundling along towards him, a lit lantern hung swinging from the seat, and ignoring the outraged bellow of the driver and the cut of his whip, Laurence seized the edge and snatched it away. Another lash stung his back as he threw himself back up the hill, but Laurence cared nothing for that: the light was failing.

Junichiro had already begun to scrape together a heap of branches and dry leaves, though with an anxious look, and when Laurence bent to set them alight he snatched up another branch and began to turn up the earth in a wide channel around the fire, to keep it from spreading. Laurence worked in nearly a frenzy: the wind was fair to the east, and the tide was going out. She would be gone in half-an-hour, if he did not raise her.

The fire was climbing, making a pretty blaze; Laurence undid his bundle and stood before the fire with his coat, and flashed the signals desperately: *assistance required—assistance required—*

He made them a dozen times over, and then heard an outcry coming from the road; he wheeled and found Junichiro standing pale and stricken before Kaneko, who was regarding him with an expression utterly flat, but for a thin shine of tears standing in his eyes.

"Kaneko-sama—sensei—" Junichiro said, nearly inaudible, and something else in the tongue, reaching out a pleading hand, and half putting himself between Kaneko and Laurence.

Kaneko shook his head once, sharply, and simply drew his swords both: answer enough, and Laurence bent and seized his own from the ground, before catching Junichiro by the arm and drawing him gently away. "All that you could do," he said, "you have done. Go and keep making the signal there. The ship will send an answer, or they will not."

"You may surrender," Kaneko said, over the crackling fire, "if you wish. The shogun has directed you are to be brought to the court. You will be made prisoner, but permitted to live."

Laurence looked back at the ocean. The ship was under sail: the lanterns lit, beginning to move away over the water. They thought him lost, surely, and the Japanese could have informed them otherwise: they meant to make him prisoner, not ransom him. He would be held the rest of his days, perhaps, in a foreign prison.

He turned to Kaneko. "I am under an obligation to Junichiro," he said, quietly, "who you must know has aided me for love of you. If I surrender myself and am made prisoner in this way, will your honor be satisfied?"

Kaneko did not look at Junichiro, despite the faint suggestion of a flinch. He shook his head briefly. Laurence nodded and pulled off the thin and badly rent white cotton of his under-robe to free his limbs for movement. Kaneko waited poised and still, the fire now leaping and throwing his shadow up against the trees behind him, until Laurence was ready; then he struck.

They exchanged the first few blows, testing, and disengaged to circle. Kaneko had an unfamiliar and an elegant style, slashing: a kind of fencing. Laurence watched the two blades warily. He had six inches of reach on Kaneko, and could give him fifty pounds at least: advantages which, Laurence hoped, would be enough to give him a chance despite the handicap of his present condition, half-lame and spent. At least he had no need to husband whatever remained of his strength—in ten minutes, surely, assistance would come for Kaneko, and Laurence would be overwhelmed if not slain. Laurence could only hope to gain those minutes, a little more time for a rescue whose likelihood was diminishing with every moment—and which, if it did not come, would strand him here forever.

There was not the least hesitation in Kaneko's attack when it came again, flashing, though his victory meant his own death. Laurence met the long blade with his own, steel cracking sparks off steel, and grappled the shorter, gripping Kaneko's wrist and squeezing with all the force he could exert. His hands were hardened by rope and leather, and Kaneko's hand purpled; then they were falling—Kaneko had thrown them somehow to the ground. Laurence found his legs tangled, Kaneko nearly pinning him; only through sheer brute force did he manage to break the incomplete hold, and threw them over.

He had not lost his clenched grip; he smashed Kaneko's hand against the ground, and the short blade sprang loose. Still half-entrapped, Laurence caught it and flung it away into the trees, and barely managed to deflect Kaneko's elbow when it came with crushing force towards his throat.

They broke apart and rolled back to their feet. Laurence had diverted the blow from his throat to his jaw, instead, which ached badly; broken, perhaps. Kaneko did not pause but came at him swiftly, both hands now on the hilt of his blade, with a series of rapid slashing cuts. Laurence parried and retreated, his pains fading into the queer, brief distance which so often accompanied battle. No opening was offered, no chance to shift the direction; Kaneko drove him around the leaping fire until Laurence, in grim desperation, forced the issue: he met Kaneko's sword with his own and stayed with it as he pushed it back, risking the chance of overbalancing, and threw his full weight against the blade.

For a moment both swords groaned, held; and then Kaneko's snapped with a loud crack like musket-fire, and he and Laurence fell to the ground heavily together. Kaneko rolled away swiftly and leapt back to his feet, still holding the jagged remnant of the blade, broken some six inches above the hilt. Laurence staggered up himself. A fine tremor ran up his arms, and he raised his sword only with difficulty; but now he had the advantage. Kaneko could not come into range of a blow without running himself into Laurence's blade.

They looked at each other, and Laurence knew Kaneko would in a moment do just as much: he would throw himself across the distance, and attempt another attack, though it meant his certain death. Laurence looked at Junichiro's despairing face, the boy standing with his own sword drawn and useless: whichever side he might have assisted, he condemned the master he loved.

And then a sudden roaring above, and Laurence flung himself to one side as Lady Arikawa came down upon the hill, her green drapes flaring and belling about her grey wings, talons coming down to strike: he barely evaded the blow and fetched up against the trees. "Wretched barbarian!" she said, furiously. "Will you cause no end of sorrow and misery? Kaneko, you are not hurt?"

Kaneko had taken already the first steps in his rush, and himself been nearly knocked flat by the force of her descent; he regained his feet and bowed. "I am not, Lady Arikawa, and the Englishman has fought only honorably—"

"I do not care!" she said. "Oh! Why did you ever make that dreadful vow; I should tear him to pieces!" She shook out her wings and glared the brilliant green of her eyes at Laurence. "You could not even manage to escape properly," she said bitterly, "and now what am I to do?"

"Lady Arikawa, we must deliver him to the governor," Kaneko said quietly, "and accompany him to the court in Edo, for the judgment of the shogun. The safety of the nation demands it." He hesitated and said, reluctantly, "It may be he will be exchanged back to his country-men, after all."

He spoke as one who did not believe what he was himself saying, offering a mere sop to feeling; and Lady Arikawa only shook her head and looked away in despair. She was silent a moment, but then she straightened, neck arched proudly over them, and looking coldly down. "I will do my duty," she said. "I will take you to Edo for judgment; and may the shogun sentence you to a traitor's death for the evil you have brought on my house!"

Yelling voices were nearing, through the trees, many men coming into the courtyard; Laurence, rising to his feet, looked around himself bleakly. There was no chance of resistance against so many, and Lady Arikawa reached out a taloned claw towards him.

Then: a noise too large to call roaring, a great tumult of rage above their heads. The trees upon the hillside behind Laurence were shattering like matchsticks, earth flying up in clouds, and a dragon came down upon that horrifying wreckage: thrice Lady Arikawa's size, pitch-black and with blue eyes. The noise stopped, and its absence left a dazed and muffling silence; in that hush the dragon bent over them with a savagery of bared teeth and said, in the clearest King's English, "How dare you! How dare any of you! Oh! I will kill all of you if you have done anything to Laurence!"

Even Lady Arikawa had drawn back, protective talons curled about Kaneko; and though she might not understand what the dragon had said, his wrath was by no means subtle, nor the threat implicit in his mantling. But she was not lacking in spirit, and drawing herself up said in Chinese, "Those who come as thieves and invaders to our country, and make threats, deserve no considerations of honor."

"Laurence is only here because he was lost overboard, saving our ship," the dragon said, answering her in that tongue, "and if you knew he was here, all along, it is a perfect outrage for you to call *us* thieves. We have taken but a few trees, and if you want us to pay you for them, we *shall:* that is nothing in the least to Laurence, whom you have tried to keep from me. I dare say we ought to have gone to war with you. If I had known of it, I should have, and I dare say the Emperor of China would have, too: it is too much to be borne!"

Lady Arikawa looked at Laurence with some doubt in her expression, which Laurence was inclined to share, at this particular piece of hyperbole. "And you need not look like that," the black dragon added, very coldly, "only because Laurence has been shipwrecked, and does not look his best at present. The Emperor adopted him, five years ago, and we are on our way to make a filial visit. He is a prince of China, and my captain."

"The devil I am," said Laurence.

Chapter 7

"I BEG YOUR PARDON," LAURENCE said, interrupting, "but if you please, Captain, I would be grateful if you would begin earlier: the last—" He paused, not liking to give it voice, and then forced his way onwards. "The last I recall very clearly is in the year four."

"Oh, Lord," Captain Granby said. He was the captain of the fire-breather, an officer of twenty-and-nine years; tall and somewhat battered, short one arm, and a pleasant, likable fellow, if almost shockingly informal in his manners and his dress of peculiar ostentation: Laurence had not seen so much gold on an admiral of the fleet. "Well, I know you took the *Amitié,* and Temeraire's egg was on it—that news was all over the Corps; but as for the rest of that year, or how you came to be there, I haven't the faintest notion. I suppose Riley could have told us—"

"Riley?" Laurence said, with relief for a name he recognized: his second lieutenant. "Tom Riley? Do you know his direction? I might write him—" and then Granby's look of startled regret halted him, even before Granby spoke.

So Riley was dead—his ship the *Allegiance* lost. Laurence rose and went to stand by the stern windows, to breathe in the sea-air in great gulps. Granby was silent where he sat at the table, but Laurence felt his eyes upon his back.

There was a dreadful strangeness to sit across from a man who called him *Will,* a man who had been his first lieutenant, and yet have his face mean nothing; it was worse, somehow, than having been all alone and adrift. Granby had been all that was kind—they had all been so, and visibly gladdened by his return. Deposited on the deck, Laurence had been embraced with enthusiasm by a dozen strangers before he had been able to make his confusion known; since then, there had been nothing but the most generous anxiety for his health—an anxiety, however, which reminded him at every turn that he *was* ill, wounded, and in such a manner that he might never recover from it.

Outside the window, near the harbor mouth, he could see the curves of the sea-dragon's body where it dozed nearly hidden beneath the waves, its presence a warning. Their own dragons were on the deck, and on a few pontoon-rafts floating about the ship; he did not, at the moment, see the black dragon—his dragon. Temeraire. Granby was speaking in low voices with the ship's surgeon, a Mr. Pettiforth, behind his back. "I must insist we halt this interview, Captain Granby," Pettiforth said. "You can see for yourself the inimical effects of only this one shock. There can be no question that any further strain on an already-weakened mind must be dangerous. You must withdraw. I must insist; I do insist."

The surgeon had vociferously argued from the beginning against any attempt to repair the omissions in Laurence's memory by recounting the events of the intervening years, as more likely to do harm than good. "I consider it a most unique species of brain-fever," Pettiforth had said. "I have heard of only a few similar instances described; indeed, I am sure the Royal Society will be deeply interested, should I have an opportunity to set down the facts of the case—"

But Laurence had dismissed his advice: he longed for every scrap of intelligence, of knowledge. His feet had been bathed and bandaged; a night's rest had seen him back on them; he could scarcely imagine delaying any further. He turned back. "Sir, I cannot deny this news is an unpleasant shock, but I am by no means prepared to halt. Captain Granby, if you please—"

"I beg your pardon," Mr. Hammond broke in, anxiously. "I beg your pardon most extremely, Captain, but I think we must abide by Mr. Pettiforth's advice for the moment, and ask you to consider—I hope you will forgive my saying so—consider it the course most consistent with your duty."

"I can scarcely perform the least duty," Laurence said, "when I do not know what that duty is, sir: so far as I knew before yesterday evening, I was a sea-captain, not an aviator."

"At present," Hammond said, "our most pressing need is for your continued health. You can do nothing if you have been prostrated by an aggravation of your—your injury, and your presence is vital—utterly vital—to all the hopes of our mission."

Laurence hesitated. Hammond was the King's envoy, and evidently in charge of their mission to China; his urgency could not help but carry great weight. "Thank Heavens that you have not lost your facility with the Chinese language—I must credit," Hammond added, "the extent of our practice, the several months of our voyage—your dedication there, Captain, has been very commendable, and I consider this the reward; everything else can be managed. I assure you, we will manage. We will begin at once to review the likely ceremonies of welcome: our arrival at Tien-sing, the forms of your greeting to the crown prince, and to the Emperor—"

If anything had been likely to give him a relapse of brain-fever, Laurence thought it would be the programme of etiquette study which Hammond laid out, which would have been a punishment even if spread over the course of three years. How he intended to touch upon all its parts in the space of time required to sail from Nagasaki to Tien-sing harbor, Laurence had not the least notion.

"All the more need, sir," Mr. Pettiforth interjected, "not to add any additional strain upon your nerves. Avoiding any particular, any notable shock," he looked at Granby with a hard, meaningful look, which Laurence could not interpret, "must be of the utmost importance."

Granby looked at Laurence helplessly; Laurence drew and released a deep breath. "Very well," he said, grimly. "I will be guided by you, gentlemen."

He would rather have forgone the study, and closeted himself with Granby until he knew every detail that could be obtained of the last eight years from one who had been his close companion in nearly all of that time, from what he understood. But he could not refuse Hammond's request. His weakness of brain had already endangered their cause—it was incumbent upon him to do whatever he might to assist a mission whose urgency was evident.

Britain's situation, and that of all Europe, was more desperate than he had feared at the worst. Granby had, to his great comfort, been able to assure him of the health of his family, but little else of good could be said. The story of the invasion of Britain, of which he until now had received only the faintest outlines, had filled Laurence with horror: Nelson dead—Nelson, and fourteen ships-of-the-line sunk. Even so complete a victory over Napoleon as had been achieved could scarcely compensate for such a loss.

Indeed, Laurence was forced to give some credence to Pettiforth's concerns: if there had been more such disasters, in the years he had lost, he did wonder how well he might support the news. "But I must learn something of my duties," he said, "enough at least to carry them out: there is no telling but we may see battle, and at least the dragons must be exercised, surely? Captain Granby, who is the senior officer of our company?"

Granby rubbed his face with his good hand. "It has been all in the air, anyway—Harcourt has command of the formation, but you and I aren't formally assigned to her, or she to either of us, and—oh, damn it all," he muttered, at Laurence's bafflement—*her?*—and turning said, "look, Hammond, I must tell him *something*."

But even when Granby had explained, appallingly, that Longwings insisted on female captains, and that the slim young gentleman captaining that beast was indeed a woman, he had not much clarified their chain of command. "It goes by the beasts, you know," he said. "It's not much use our standing on ceremony, if they settle it otherwise amongst themselves; it don't matter if a Winchester's captain has twenty years on me when Iskierka gives a snort, you can be sure."

With four heavy-weights and a Longwing aboard, such a policy must surely have kept the command in a state of peculiar confusion: all the more so that the captain of the largest beast, an immense golden creature called Kulingile, was scarcely more than a boy, and not British at all but from Africa; Laurence could hardly imagine how he had been appointed to his post. "Well, he wasn't," Granby said, "Demane is from Capetown, you took him and his brother up when—" He halted abruptly, biting his lip. "You took them up," he continued awkwardly, leaving an ominous gap behind him, "as your runners, and he picked up the beast when no-one else would have it: came out of the shell deformed, and not the size of a lamb."

In any case, despite his size Kulingile did not seem inclined to assert his precedence particularly; and even after what little time Laurence had spent on deck amongst them so far, he could scarcely help noticing that the other beasts seemed inclined to give way to Temeraire, if to anyone. Laurence realized grimly he might well himself be the senior officer, by such a measure, and his injury all the more potentially disastrous: better in some way had he been wholly incapacitated, than presenting this peculiar mix of competence and confusion.

But he did not press Granby further for explanation. To have worked through an accounting of eight years all together would have been difficult enough, but it was still worse to acquire piecemeal details, and see the awkward hesitation on Granby's face as he tried to explain first one and then another chain of events, yet without conveying any information likely to cause distress, entangling the narrative at every turn. He faltered too often, and with a look almost pleading, as though he hoped Laurence would suddenly be recalled to himself: even while that same hope, privately but deeply held, quietly died away in Laurence's own breast.

"So far as the command is concerned, then, I will defer to you, Captain Granby, at present," he said, cutting short the attempt, "and I trust you will feel not the least hesitation at correcting me in any failure to carry out my necessary duties. For the rest, my health has scarcely had a chance to recover, after the exertions of my escape; let us hope that in returning, it may restore my memory with it."

It was an empty sop, which he did not himself believe, though Granby seized upon it with eager relief and Hammond chimed in with eager agreement, although Mr. Pettiforth murmured quietly to himself, "Not at all likely—I wonder whether further degeneration ought to be expected, if anything. I must keep a journal of the progression—"

Laurence saw them out. He was glad to be left alone again in his cabin, though housed amongst things he did not recognize: even his sea-chest was unfamiliar to him, new and rough-hewn, a cheap construction which must have been bought in desperation and which should shortly have to be replaced; a green creeping stain was already to be seen growing upon the underside. The chest was full of books, though he had never been a great reader: *Principia Mathematica* so well-worn the corners of the pages were smooth where he evidently liked to turn them. There were only two pieces of correspondence: one letter from his mother, another, with the direction very badly scribbled and nearly unreadable, from the Peninsula: from a fellow-officer, then.

"Well," he said aloud, "I might be dead, or in a prison," and threw them back into his writing-desk, next to the log-book, which he also had not opened. He was resolved not to succumb to despair. He had the use of his limbs, and his reason; he had lost less than many another man in the service.

He belted his sword back on, went up to the dragondeck, and found Temeraire rousing from an exhausted sleep and looking for him. Hammond was there before him, trying to keep Temeraire's attention, and explaining in a loud voice, which could surely be heard across all the ship, "It is of the utmost importance that Captain Laurence be spared any unnecessary shock, which might further injure his weakened mind—I beg you to attend me, Temeraire! I assure you that we have every reason to expect his memory to return shortly, if you will only have a care not to—"

"Yes, yes, of course," Temeraire said, looking at him not at all. "Laurence!" he called, a ringing eager note in his resonant voice, which might be felt even through the deck: his ruff was standing up in a manner which somehow suggested to Laurence his excitement. "Laurence, how much more yourself you look: you must be better, I am sure," he said, when Laurence had mounted to the deck. There was an anxious question in the words, however. Temeraire had been lately injured himself, Laurence gathered, by some mishap in the rescue of the ship; and his spirits had been badly beset by the belief of Laurence's own death.

It seemed absurd to think of so terrible a creature as fragile in any way. The head bending towards him was nearly the size of a horse, the teeth standing in the jaws larger than his hand, serrated along their back edges and hard ivory. Strangely Laurence felt no fear, no instinct of alarm, though it seemed to him any rational man ought to; he had seen, only last night, what appalling devastation might be wrought by this beast.

But even without fear, it was difficult to think of Temeraire as vulnerable—and yet perhaps not so difficult: a first-rate off a lee-shore, and his the duty to keep her off the rocks. Laurence still did not wholly understand how he had come to harness the beast, to become an aviator; he did not know what might have impelled him to do such a thing. But for the moment, it would have to be enough to know that he *had* done so: that he had given up his naval rank, his ship, and all his hard-won prospects. No need to wonder, either, what had become of Edith Galman. She had surely wed another, a man who could offer her a respectable home and name. Laurence was determined to be glad of it; she deserved as much and more.

Duty remained: his country's need stood above his own concerns. "I am much better, indeed," he said. "I beg you have no concern for me. How is your own health?"

"Oh!" Temeraire said, "I am perfectly well, *now;* I *have* been a little ill, but that is quite done with; I am quite recovered. Laurence," he added urgently, leaning his massive head down to the deck, and peering at him with one anxious slitted eye, "of course you know that I would have come for you at once—I would not have permitted anything to interfere—if it had not been for the egg. I am so dreadfully sorry."

The rest of the afternoon was consumed in displaying this prize for him: the dragon insisted on Laurence's being taken below, on the crate and all its careful packing being undone to display the egg. It might have been made of gold and diamonds for the degree of passionate interest which Temeraire gave it, and not only he: the fire-breather, evidently the dam, roused herself and watched with equal attention, so that Laurence could scarcely make out the unremarkable shell for having one enormous eye peering in at either porthole, blocking the light.

He was invited to touch the shell, with great care and an open palm: a tender softness not unlike the head of his nine-day-old nephew, when that child had been laid carefully in his hands by a watchful mother. Having returned to the dragondeck and being pressed for his opinion, he used very much the same expressions as on that occasion. "A remarkable egg," he said, "perfectly hearty, and the size prodigious: I congratulate you both extremely, and I am sure it will do very well; extraordinarily well." He meant his compliments wholeheartedly: he could well imagine the worth to England of such a cross-breed. His effusions could not have satisfied Temeraire, however, if they had been ten times as enthusiastic, until Laurence gradually came to realize that half of the dragon's anxiety was to be sure that Laurence did not blame him, for not having come to his rescue.

"You could scarcely have found me, if you had tried," Laurence said. "I do not think I had been on shore half-an-hour before I was taken up."

"I would have contrived, somehow," Temeraire said. "I found you in Africa, after all, when—oh; I am not meant to speak of that, am I? But in any case, Laurence, so long as you are satisfied—so long as you do not suppose I would have allowed any lesser cause to weigh with me."

Laurence was *not* entirely satisfied: the lesser causes had evidently included abandoning the ship, their mission, and perhaps even setting off a war with Japan: all for his sake, and here was Temeraire making apology to him for *not* doing any of these things. He began to feel there was an almost dreadful responsibility inherent in the rôle, a rôle for which nothing had prepared him, and which he felt wholly unsuited to carry out. The distance between this and a ship's command seemed a vast yawning gulf.

But he could not chide the dragon for his affection; particularly not when Temeraire had been under so great a strain, its evidence marked in the dull hide and the weary look in the dragon's eyes: his eyelids were heavy again already. Laurence lay his hand against Temeraire's warm breathing hide, its peculiar combination of resilience and softness at once familiar and not so. "I have been restored to you in defiance of all expectation and without, I hope, any evil consequence to our mission; we must both be satisfied with that outcome, and I beg you believe me so."

Temeraire sighed deeply, and lowered his head to his forelegs. "I am very glad to hear you say so," he said. "I was sure, Laurence, that you would not think it right of me to leave the egg—that you would tell me, if you were here, that it was my own responsibility, and I could not leave it to others no matter how much I might wish to go looking for you, not when the egg was not perfectly safe. I was quite sure, but oh! It was dreadful nonetheless, and I did fear that perhaps I had judged wrongly."

"You did not, at all," Laurence said, with a good deal of relief: so a dragon need not be insensate to duty at all. And then he was at a loss: what ought he do else, for the beast? Should he order aerial exercises? He did not see the other dragons engaged in such work, and indeed it might have been a provocation to the Japanese, to do so in harbor; besides this, he knew nothing of what his duties should be.

He looked for one of the ship's boys: a small creature was darting by him on the dragondeck, head full of yellow curls and in a patched green coat. When Laurence caught him by the shoulder, the boy looked up and said in a piping voice, "Aye, Captain?"

"Light along to my cabin and fetch my log-book, if you please," Laurence said, and pausing added, "And tell me your name again."

"Gerry, sir," the little boy said, giving him a peculiar look; Laurence sighed inwardly and made a note he should have to get all the names given him, at least. He thought he would read it over, and learn the daily routine thereby; perhaps he might thus advise himself.

"What a splendid notion," Temeraire said, unexpectedly, raising his head; his eyes had brightened. "Of course that must help your memory return more swiftly. Although I must tell you," the dragon added, "the log-book has not been very interesting at all. It has been nothing but fish and wind, these six months, before we ran into that storm. We have not seen a battle anywhere, since we had to run from the Inca, and that was ages ago."

He was regretful. Laurence's own thought: the Inca? And hard on that, it belatedly dawned upon him that the dragon himself, unlike a horse, or even a recalcitrant landsman pressed into service, might be relied upon to tell him of their work. "Temeraire," he said, "do you know the names of the rest of your crew?"

"Of course," Temeraire said. "You have always told me it is the duty of any good officer to know all the names of his officers and his crew."

"So it is," Laurence said grimly. "Pray will you tell me them, one after another?"

"He is already much better," Temeraire said to Maximus, anxiously, hoping for confirmation. "I know it is quite odd, when he does not remember someone's name, or a thing which happened in front of him, and quite lately; but you cannot say he is not better."

"Of course he is better," Maximus said reassuringly, lifting his dripping jaws from his share of the cod stew. "I dare say he will remember all the rest of it in a week or so, Temeraire; no need to fuss."

But Laurence was so very strange—so very stiff and awkward; it was not only that he had lost a great deal of his memory, which was bad enough and very inconvenient, but he did not seem to know Temeraire, either, or any of the other aviators, for that matter. He had spent nearly all the last two days closeted with Hammond, and had said very little to anyone. "But I am sure he will improve, once he has had a rest, and we are under way," Temeraire said to himself, uncertainly.

There was some little difficulty over their departure: Temeraire did not understand, himself; he saw no reason why they should not have sailed out directly they had Laurence again, and he would have liked to: what if the Japanese should have taken it into their heads to snatch Laurence back? And it was no use Hammond's trying to tell him they had no reason to do such a thing; they had kept him back in the first place, after all. And as for Lord Jinai—that was the name of the particularly rude sea-dragon—if he liked to stop them, he was very welcome to try. Temeraire felt himself quite equal to answering him, with Iskierka, and Kulingile, and all the formation at his backs; not to mention the guns of the *Potentate*.

But Hammond had objected to *that,* also; and so a great deal of communication had gone back and forth, passed through the Dutch commissioner, who evidently did not like Napoleon at all and persisted in considering himself a neutral party to the war. "And through us," said Wampanoag, having come over to share a bite, "which, I don't mind saying, has done some good: they have decided to give you a proper dinner, to say farewell politely, and see you on your way."

"That," said Temeraire somewhat baffled, "is quite absurd:

they would have been perfectly welcome to give us dinner, anytime they liked."

"They might give us more than one, too," Maximus put in somewhat wistfully: the cod had vanished.

"Why, it's not the dinner that matters, of course," Wampanoag said. "It is the timing of the thing: if you sail out before they have given you permission, then they will have lost face; if they should give permission and you shouldn't go, they will have lost face. And you shouldn't like it any better if they should try and stop you, or try and chase you, either way. This way, everything will be quite clear."

Temeraire still did not see very much sense in this: if all parties wished them gone, it seemed to him they might simply go: no-one was asking Lord Jinai to sit there in the harbor mouth, in their way. But Wampanoag seemed to think it entirely sensible.

"And I will say, I am pretty grateful to you," he said, "for opening the door, as it were. I like them very much, now they have decided to talk to me: very polite fellows, perfectly honest: easy to do business with. They don't like to say no, so you have to keep a sharp lookout to notice when they *mean* no, but that isn't so difficult: the older fellows of the tribe are like that."

"I do not understand," Temeraire said. "Why would they not have spoken to you before, when they do have these Dutch translators?"

"Well, their shogun wouldn't have it," Wampanoag said. "They aren't much for foreigners here, but I guess they have thought it over and decided, since the Chinese are throwing in with you lot, they had better start making some more friends." He snorted and waved his tail in the air. "They aren't wrong, either: those of us who don't want to get dragged into this mess you lot and Napoleon are brewing up all over the place had better stick together. I'll tell you, you ought to think better of it. Bad for business, that sort of thing."

That was not very fair, in Temeraire's opinion: *he* did not want war—he did not object to battles, of course, but war did seem a great trouble for everyone. "But we cannot very well just lie down before Napoleon: *he* is always provoking war, and trying to conquer his neighbors, and tell them how they are to go on; only someone very poor-spirited indeed could endure it."

Wampanoag shook his head doubtfully. "If you say so: it takes two to make a quarrel, in my experience." He shook out his wings. "But I cannot complain of the consequences for myself: they have given me license to buy more goods than they had meant to allow, on credit, and I suppose I will have a commission for Yankee ships to come in our own right before I go away again. I have promised them we will bring them a company of shipwrights straight from Salem, next season, if they will give us a treaty and let us trade, and I don't doubt the President will back me if I bring him terms for *that*."

"The President?" Temeraire said, and listened with mounting indignation as Wampanoag said, quite casually, "Yes: I have met him half-a-dozen times, and I am sure he will see the sense of a proper treaty with the Japanese for us. I should have rather had Hamilton in the job, of course, but there! You can't have everything, and for all that he isn't a Federalist, Tecumseh is a clever fellow."

He gave a final nod of his head, and leapt aloft, leaving Temeraire to simmer. "It is a good deal too much," he said to Maximus stormily, "that Napoleon sits in Lien's lap, and Wampanoag is off chatting with the President, and we must yell and make a great noise in Britain only to be seen by a general now and again. I have never met a minister in my life."

"Why would you wish to?" Maximus said, sleepily. "Berkley is always saying they are nothing but a lot of tiresome old windbags."

"Not to mention," Iskierka put in, as her own pontoon-raft drifted closer, "that if you hadn't interfered, Granby should have been a king himself: then you needn't have complained."

. . .

Laurence found the dinner, which he could not escape, a peculiarly constrained affair. It was held at the estate of the Japanese governor, in his gardens very near the shore, and the whole of it passed very nearly in silence. Hammond alone had anything to say to any member of the other company, having monopolized the conversation of the governor since the moment he had come ashore, through one of the translators; with an oblivious rudeness almost painful to witness, he had taken the seat at that gentleman's right hand, although the servants had made a very valiant effort to reserve it for Laurence himself. Laurence had then been established on the governor's other hand, making him unwilling witness to the rest of Hammond's performance: a mortifying experience, as all Hammond's too-anxious entreaties and half-apologies were met alike with silence, or responses brief and noncommittal: the governor betrayed by not the flicker of an eyelid his opinions on any of Hammond's remarks, and offered no encouragement whatsoever to his proposals for an exchange of envoys, or an opening of diplomatic communications.

The governor's safety was secured by the looming bulk of Lord Jinai, who hovered ominously overhead in the shallow waters just off the coast, and a dozen Japanese dragons also in attendance, most of them in polished armor. There were not very many friendly looks exchanged between them and the British dragons: Temeraire had come ashore, and Iskierka, to keep close watch on Jinai; she in particular kept a gimlet and suspicious eye upon the sea-dragon, and occasionally remarked audibly of her perfect willingness to set the entire city ablaze if he should make any motion towards the ship and its precious cargo.

Only Kiyo, who had hauled herself out of the nearby river mouth to attend the feasting, was in good humor. She had greeted Laurence cheerfully: no-one had dared to challenge her on the matter of the assistance she had given him. "No, why would anyone mind that?" she said, with perfect unconcern, when he had asked if she had been put to any distress. "I have been meaning to have a good look at one of these Western ships, anyway, that I have been hearing about the last century, and I am glad especially to have seen such a prodigious one, because I suppose most people would not have believed in it, otherwise. How large it is! I have swum all around it," she added, a piece of intelligence which would not have failed to horrify Captain Blaise, or for that matter any of their party, "and we must certainly have some like it.

"I petitioned the bakufu on the subject myself, and they have agreed we must let these Americans show us how to build them. And that good little fellow Wampanoag has promised that his crew will perform your *Julius Caesar* for me, before they sail away," she added, with great satisfaction. "So you see, it has all worked out splendidly. And there will be fireworks, after dinner!"

She put her head back into her wine-bowl and glugged away; but Laurence grimly realized she was by no means a mere carefree fool, pleasing herself, as he might have supposed before. He did not think Hammond would consider it a splendid outcome, to have the Japanese allied with the colonials, and busy at building a navy of their own.

The fireworks, set off above the harbor and splendid, were a relief to all present, as preventing any further need of conversation: all rose and stood gathered near the shore to watch the blooms of glittering light. Laurence took the opportunity however of speaking with Kaneko, who had been seated some distance down the table from him, at Lady Arikawa's side.

He bowed deeply, when Laurence approached him, and addressed him as a prince; Laurence received the title with dismay. "I beg your pardon," he said, "but I assure you I cannot consider myself deserving of the mode of address: I am not a prince, whatever fiction may have been invented for political necessity."

Kaneko said quietly, "A thing cannot be at once true and fiction: and this, I think, must be considered true, when it is the foundation of an alliance of two great nations."

He made no outward reproach, but Laurence could not help

but feel one: he *had* lied to Kaneko, even if not deliberately. He awkwardly made his apology, on that score, and hoped rather than thought he was believed: Kaneko received it only politely. "I wished also to promise you," Laurence said, "that I will do whatever is in my power to secure Junichiro's future. His familiarity with dragons—"

"The fate of the criminal you mention is none of my concern," Kaneko said with an unanswerable finality, although when he turned back towards the fireworks the spray of the lights shone wetly in his raised eyes.

Laurence did not press him. "May I ask you, sir," he said, "if honor is satisfied?"

Kaneko was silent, and then said, "Lady Arikawa insists it must be so," somewhat reluctantly. He paused and added, "She has honored me with an invitation to take up residence upon her estate."

Laurence wondered at the significance, and still more at Kaneko's evident doubts. Kaneko glanced at him and said, "The honor of dragons can only with great difficulty endure conflict with their affections. The authorities hold that their best and wisest course is to retain a proper distance from any particular individual. I fear I have been the instrument of diminishing her standing."

Laurence was silent, thinking of Temeraire's willingness to spring out a cause for war and all for his sake. "Perhaps I take your point," he said, soberly, and then had to raise a hand: as if knowing himself spoken of, Temeraire had broken off his own rapt contemplation of the fireworks, and looked over anxiously towards him, until Laurence went to his side.

"I do not see why you must be speaking with that fellow who tried to kill you," Temeraire said, putting out a foreleg, as if he would have liked to gather Laurence in close.

Laurence thought, with black humor, that there was every reason: he knew Kaneko better than any other man present. "That was merely his duty," he said, "and nothing ungentleman-like in his behavior: I have no reason to think he means me the slightest ill, as a personal matter. I can scarcely condemn him for trying to uphold the law of his nation, or its interest."

"*I* can," Temeraire said, "when he thought he would do so by putting a sword through you." He gave Kaneko, and Lady Arikawa behind him, a cold glare: Laurence shook his head and let Temeraire put him up. The sooner they were gone, the better; there was too much wrath still simmering, nearly palpable when he lay his hand upon Temeraire's neck. Laurence felt again unequal to the strength of Temeraire's affection: like a gift handed to him unexpectedly, and which he did not recall having earned.

He woke in his cabin early on the morning, to the welcome hurrying thunder of many feet on the ladderways, the bosun's shouts. Hammond was meant to breakfast with him—they were to review the order in which the presents carried aboard were to be delivered to the harbormaster, in Tien-sing; after that it would be on the order of the presents for the Imperial envoy, and how those should differ depending on the rank of the individual sent. Laurence struggled with temptation; temptation carried the day: he rose from his cot, dressed quickly, and called in O'Dea.

"Aye, Captain, it's a fine morning, and the wind and tide bid fair to get us under way," O'Dea said gloomily, as he helped Laurence into his coat. "Properly into the kraken's mouth: that sea-monster is lurking ready there at the mouth of the harbor like Jonah's own whale, and it's sure enough the beast will try and have us down to the bottom if only it can."

Laurence swallowed down a cup of hot coffee, very bitter, and took himself to the dragondeck. There was no opportunity for conversation amid the cacophony, with every hand turned to clearing the dragondeck and making way for all the beasts to land. The dragons carried on their own negotiations, as to which should take a first turn in the air, to make the quarters more comfortable for all:

Iskierka and Kulingile leapt aloft, circling the ship; the rest arranged themselves in a complicated tangle on the deck, and the hands began to haul in the pontoons to be deflated and secured beneath the dragondeck.

Somehow it was managed in under an hour, and the massive anchors brought up by the beasts themselves while the men merely wound the chain back around the capstan. "Make sail!" the bosun cried, and they were under way: a cautious progress out of the harbor, past the raised and suspicious head of the sea-dragon, who paced the ship ominously while they crept past the harbor mouth and out to the open ocean, his great pallid eyes watching. But the wind held all the while, and they were in the clear before the sun had even reached its zenith. Blaise nodded to his first lieutenant, and the ship opened her own wings: "Make sail, make sail," the cry going up, the loud rumbling and snap of sailcloth unfurled, belling out with wind: coast and sea-dragon fell away behind them almost abruptly.

Laurence stood watching the whole from the railing of the dragondeck, at once glad and disquieted, feeling himself out of place. He had nothing to do, and no-one to speak with. Captain Blaise he recalled very vaguely, having met him some ten years before at an assembly in Mallorca: a sensible man and a proper sailor by reputation and who knew his work; not a blazing light by any means, but to be relied upon. There was not another soul aboard he knew even so distantly.

Save one: Junichiro stood by the taffrail, looking back at the shore. He ought not have been there, in the midst of the activity; it was a solecism, and several of the sailors cast him sour looks as they went past almost elbow-close, though on a transport there was no shortage of room, and he did not even understand their pointed muttering. He stood with hands clasped behind his back, and expression stoic, peculiarly isolated and standing out sorely despite his Western dress: a borrowed aviator's coat, and trousers.

"Gerry," Laurence said, catching that young boy where he

leaned over the rail into the rising wind of their passage, his tow hair blown up into a cloud, "light along to Mr. Junichiro, there, and invite him to the dragondeck, if you please; and be sure you bring him back along the port side."

The sea-dragon was vanished beneath the waves, a handful of fishing-boats on the water receding, the low mountains of the coast rapidly diminishing. Junichiro lingered for one final uncertain and lonely look back at his native shore before he turned and followed. His steps dragged. In the morning, Laurence intended to find some work for him—surely there could be no shortage of it, on a ship so heavily burdened with dragons—and see him worked to exhaustion for a few weeks. It would strengthen his appetite and dull his capacity for imagination: both ends much to be desired, at present, where his health was concerned. A ship's ration did not suit the palate of most landsmen, even ones not so gently reared; thankfully Junichiro was still young enough to adapt. And of an age with some few of the aviators, including one young sandy-haired fellow whom Temeraire had named Roland, in Laurence's own crew, who according to Hammond spoke the Chinese tongue: Laurence would have his young gentlemen to dinner, to-night, and introduce Junichiro around.

He turned his face back to the prow, and tried to persuade himself to be content. A transport was no graceful sailor, but the *Potentate* was answering beautifully to the wind so directly at her back, nearly her one good point of sailing. Surely no heart could fail to rise beneath so vast and brilliant a spread of sailcloth: four great masts rigged out from mainsail to topgallants. They might well be going twelve knots, a glorious rushing of wind upon his face and everything calculated to delight.

The dragons were still chattering amongst themselves behind him, speaking with pleasure of the entertainment they had lately seen, and their dinner: the equal of any party of drunken officers after a revelry, with two bottles of port in their bellies. Laurence was hard-put not to laugh. It ought have occurred to him, he supposed, that creatures gifted with speech would of a certainty proceed to gossip. He was an old hand at not eavesdropping upon shipboard conversations, but the flow of their strange, resonating voices, which seemed somehow to issue from the base of their throats and not their lips, was a comfortable rumble in the back of his mind, until gradually he became aware that there was an absence. Temeraire was scarcely speaking, and when he did answer some inquiry put to him directly, his voice was quiet and subdued; he lay facing the prow, looking ahead, and apart from the others.

Laurence slowly went to him; he felt uncertain—what could one say, to a dragon? He had no orders to give. But Temeraire's head lifted and turned to meet him, something half-hopeful and wary in his looks; Laurence said, "If you are not otherwise occupied, may I bear you company?"

"Oh!" Temeraire said, "as though you had to ask, Laurence. Would you—perhaps would you care to have out the dear old *Principia Mathematica,* and have a look into that? If you have forgotten it, you may at least have the pleasure of reading it afresh."

Laurence was taken aback: it had not occurred to him a dragon might be a great reader, although belatedly he recalled Kiyo's fascination with poetry. Gerry was sent for the book, and returned quickly; Temeraire dragged a foreleg forward, out from beneath the heap of dragons, and held it forth. He plainly meant it as a couch, and when Laurence put his hands to it, he found he knew how to climb up, and his body remembered the seat in the elbow's crook as though he were going blindfold up into the rigging. Laurence sat still a moment with the book open upon his lap, struggling with a kind of horror between bone-deep familiarity and endless strangeness.

"Laurence?" the dragon asked, anxiously. "Are you well? Shall I send for the ship's surgeon?"

"I am well," Laurence said, drawing his breath deep; for what alternative was there? "Where should you like me to begin?"

Part II

Chapter 8

DESPITE A DISQUIETING LACK of any shipboard duties, Laurence had very little leisure on their journey: every hour was consumed by Hammond urgently cramming a thousand details of a foreign court into his head, with the assistance of the Chinese nobleman who was the envoy of the crown prince, Gong Su. Laurence felt himself dragged unwilling back to schoolboy days, with two tutors far more zealous than his own had been—and he had fled the schoolroom for the sea.

Worse yet, the tutoring only increased his impatience with himself. The most absurd sorts of minutiae came to him easily: he could navigate a formal dinner of nine courses, walk without a stumble in the elaborate formal dress, incline his head in the correct degree, all as though he had known these things from childhood; he could repeat over long and flowery phrases in the foreign tongue as though he had been their author, and meanwhile his own history remained unfathomable.

Three days dragged by before he had so much as an hour to himself, on the occasion of Mr. Hammond's having been asked to dine by Captain Blaise. Laurence was in turn asked to Captain Harcourt's table and found that anticipated relief worse than the endless study: he could take no pleasure in being surrounded by those who so frequently checked their anecdotes, and hushed one another, and looked at him anxiously, lest he should have heard anything to distress him. Nor was it any comfort when Dulcia's Captain Chenery said heartily, "Do you know, Laurence, I knew a fellow who was knocked off his beast at the Nile—landed on his head on the deck of the *Tonnant,* and could not speak a word at all for three years; but then one day he woke up and asked for coffee," as on further inquiry, it turned out that this was the extent of the gentleman's recovery, and he had died in a sudden fit two years later on.

Laurence excused himself as soon as he could, and sought the solitude of his cabin as preferable; there in a kind of rebellion against the coddling he took out his writing-desk and opened it to read his letters. But he was only disturbed further by his mother's strange and half-stilted letter, and when he found amongst its general awkwardness a wholly incomprehensible passage:

> *And I trust that Miss Emily Roland is in good Health, and pray that you will assure her of my Interest in her Progress; I have enclosed a set of Ear-Rings, which she might enjoy, when not Impractical in the course of her Duties . . .*

Laurence read these words some four times over before he was perfectly convinced of having them correctly, though he could read his mother's hand as easily as print, and then laying the letter down sat back in his chair, very blank. He did not know what to make of it in the least.

He had been surprised enough himself to discover that Mr. Roland was in fact *Miss* Roland: Temeraire had not seen fit to make note of the fact while giving him the names of his officers, and so Laurence had suffered several uncomfortable moments on finding a young lady so unexpectedly at his dinner table that first evening. He could not think how she should be addressed, much less treated; whether she ought to be given precedence at the table, as the only lady present, or left halfway down the side as her midwingman's rank would have her. He had in some confusion resolved on treating her as an officer: she had come in uniform, wearing trousers, and was evidently destined for command of a Longwing, from what Granby had told him. But Laurence had not been easy with the decision, though Roland herself had shown not the least consciousness of any peculiarity.

She seemed, indeed, a perfectly respectable officer, from what little he had seen of her since then. But Laurence could not imagine he would have confided such a peculiar aspect of the service to his mother; and if he had done so, he would scarcely have made Roland personally known to her; and having done *that,* he could still not reconcile his mother's taking so particular and forthright an interest in a junior officer under his command, and sending her gifts of so personal a nature.

The ear-rings were gone, evidently having been delivered when the letter was first opened. Laurence looked into the writing-desk again, and drew out the other letter, which when he studied the direction more closely was revealed to be from an *Admiral* Roland: perhaps a close friend, he wondered, whom he had forgotten entirely? Eight years might have made enough intimacy to offer some explanation—if this Admiral Roland were of a family distantly related to his own, somehow? He could not remember any such connection, but as he read the letter through, he grew convinced: the letter, quite short and written in an unlovely hand, was generally not that of a superior to a subordinate, save in a few lines surely intended jokingly, that directed him by no means to run Britain into another war or two, or undertake a fresh Crusade. It was a frank note, and it quickly formed in Laurence's mind a decided portrait of its author: an officer not very much older than himself, confident in his own judgment, secure in his position and influence; a gentleman of perhaps forty-and-five, writing him a brief note amid the consuming routine of his duties, a serving-officer and not some mere retired admiral, and Emily's father, this last confirmed by the mention of a dragon named Excidium, who sent Emily his affection.

All seemed plain, easy to understand, until Laurence came to the end of the letter and this comforting portrait was entirely exploded by the scribbled signature, "Yours, etc., Jane."

Laurence could scarcely avoid the only, the obvious conclusion, about Miss Emily Roland's origins: a conclusion made all the more certain when he had looked in at the rest of his papers, and found in his brief accounts the salary of Mrs. Pemberton, Miss Roland's chaperone, paid directly from his personal funds. Badly staggered, he went up to the dragondeck: Miss Roland was returned from her own dinner and at the moment engaged, at his own request, in trying to teach English to a silent and largely unresponsive Junichiro. Mrs. Pemberton, a composed lady of not quite thirty years of age, her dark hair tucked neatly beneath a cap, was sitting on a coiled cable and sewing as she supervised; she nodded as he came up the stairs. "Captain," she said, politely: Laurence touched his hat and said a few words to her while he watched her charge: *could* the girl be his own natural-born child?

He saw no great similarity of feature: Roland's face was round and she was stocky rather than tall. But to counterbalance this, she did have rather a look of his aunt Stourland in the chin, a stubborn determination; and there was very little difference between her fair hair and his own, if one made allowances for the effects of sun-bleaching. Roland certainly had not treated him as a father, but as her commanding officer; however, as this was how he would have expected any son of his to behave in similar circumstances, whether illegitimate or no, he could not argue himself out of it on those grounds alone.

He crossed over to her and Junichiro. "How do your studies go?" he asked, to be answered only by a half-bow and silence, on Junichiro's part, while Emily said, "I am sure he will soon have the trick of it, sir," rather doubtfully.

Junichiro too plainly did not care to learn; he had a dull look of resignation. "I intend," Laurence had told him, "to seek you a commission with the Aerial Corps; you have no fear of dragons, I know, and I think you will do very well: there is no reason you should not be assigned to serve dragon-back, and advance through the ranks; you might aspire to a beast of your own, at length. Or I will buy your commission in the army, if you prefer: once you have learnt English."

Junichiro had expressed no preference, no enthusiasm at all; he had said only, briefly, "It does not matter." He had carried out any small task he was put to, silently and quickly, and took no initiative; he otherwise remained a solitary fixture on the deck.

Laurence shook his head privately; sensible of his own debt, he still did not know what else to do. "Carry on," he said to Roland, and went to the forward railing, near where Temeraire dozed after his own meal.

"Why yes, of course Admiral Roland is Emily's mother," Temeraire said sleepily, when Laurence could not resist quietly inquiring of him, "and whyever would she be married? She has Excidium, of course. There is not the least reason for her to be married."

Laurence could not conceive how Emily should have been got: she was sixteen, so her birth ought not have been lost from his memory, and he did not remember any incident for which he should have had to reproach himself, involving a Jane Roland. But the weight of evidence was too damning, and he now wondered with alarm whether he could not trust his memory of earlier dates any better than that of the later. He ran a hand through his hair: he could feel no trace of the injury; what swelling there had been, had vanished quite, without bringing any relief of his condition. The ocean streamed away before the ship to either side, very familiar and home-like—if only he stood in the bow and did not look behind him to see the dragons, the vast decks of the transport, the crew that were not his own.

He turned and found Temeraire grown more wakeful, and regarding him with an anxiety as great as that of his fellow-officers. Laurence meant to summon up a more cheerful expression, but Temeraire said abruptly, before he could put on a better face, "Laurence, shall we not go up together? I suppose that fellow Pettiforth knows what he is about," this said with as much doubt as Laurence felt, "but there is nothing which could be distressing about *flying;* and we needn't talk about the past at all. We might practice some more of those maneuvers Churki has taught me, that the Inca squadrons use: we might try some which I do not know very well, and work out our own counters for them, together."

Laurence surprised himself by finding this offer, though from so unexpected a quarter, intensely appealing; Gerry went running for his harness, which Laurence found himself able to sling on as easily as an old favorite coat, and Temeraire put him up to his neck. The carabiner clasps were comfortable in his hands. Laurence harnessed himself to the heavy and well-secured chain of the breastplate Temeraire wore, and felt the enormous leap that took them off the deck like a springing away from care: wind tearing by and the curving vastness of the world opening wide beneath them, even the massive *Potentate* diminishing into toy-like insignificance as Temeraire circled higher; they seemed almost level with the enormous cloudbanks that broke up the sky a little way north.

Laurence drew a deep breath of the thin cold air, gladly, and Temeraire turned his head at the end of his long neck, looking back at him, and called, "Is this not splendid, Laurence? Shall we try a first pass?"

"I am ready whenever you should care to make the attempt," Laurence answered him, and held on with real delight as Temeraire flung himself into a spiraling course.

He was all the happier to find that he could offer some thoughts—tentative, but he hoped not foolish—on the subject of the maneuvers: several points at which Temeraire's head had been concealed from him, by the contortions of his body, which he thought might open a dragon to being taken by surprise with an attack aimed at the vulnerable back. Temeraire agreed with his conclusions, and after some further exercise, they settled it they should ask Churki to practice, on the morrow—"If Hammond can spare me," Laurence was forced to add.

"We might invite him to come aloft also," Temeraire said, a

notion which Laurence privately could not very much imagine that gentleman appreciating: Hammond spoke rather dismally of Churki, whose affections had evidently been bestowed upon a very unwilling subject, and he was regularly to be found chewing enormous wads of coca leaves, which he evidently considered a sovereign remedy for sea-sickness, even when the swell was not above ten feet.

"I will have a word with Churki on the subject," Temeraire continued. "I am sure it cannot be healthy for him to be always closeted inside that stuffy ship, any more than for you: there is a much better color in your face now. And perhaps you will stay on deck with me to-night, Laurence? I have heard the ship's officers saying the hands would be turned up to sing, and a couple of the fellows exchanged books with Wampanoag's officers, which they might be asked to lend us: I believe Immortalis's Lieutenant Totenham has a new novel called *Zastrozzi,* which he has already finished, and pronounced remarkably good."

"By all means," Laurence said, and though he found the novel, a dreadful gothic with an appalling villain, wholly distasteful, he was more than content with his company: if Temeraire had no great quarrel with the novel's moral turpitude, which he seemed to find less shocking than peculiar, he roundly condemned its construction and what seemed to be several omitted chapters, so they had the pleasure of disliking it together, for their several reasons; and Temeraire did not treat him as an invalid, and shut his mouth on every other word. By the time they had finished out the novel, Laurence stealing an hour here and there from his studies as he might, he found he preferred Temeraire's society above anyone else's, dragon or no.

"I am glad to have had something quite new," Temeraire said, "even if it was not really satisfactory," when they went aloft for exercise again: a morning flight had already become their settled routine, "and now we are sure to have something better to read soon: I think those are the Changshan Islands, over there."

Laurence put his glass up to his eye and looked out along the line of Temeraire's gaze: a scattered archipelago of green and white islands, dotting the sea. Two days to Tien-sing harbor, if the wind stayed fair.

The flooring of the palace was constructed peculiarly on two levels: the lower of hard smooth-polished stone, great flags of green marble shot with deep veins of gold, joined by the thinnest mortar, on which the dragons walked, and above this a network of slightly raised platforms of dark amber-colored wood and gold, for the people. Laurence had been given ample opportunity to examine it, in performing his reluctant obeisances before Crown Prince Mianning, who sat upon a great throne of gold on a dais set at the very end of the great hall. A great host of scarlet dragons and dark blue were gathered on either side of the aisle approaching the dais, with a pair of sleek beasts of pitch-black coloration one to either side of the throne.

The value of the wooden floor, to those kneeling, was certainly very great, particularly those poor souls of rank so lowly they evidently were not permitted to raise their heads while royalty remained within the room. It had an echoing quality from the gap and the stone beneath, not unlike that of the hollow deck of a ship. Laurence found it comforting: the jewel-encrusted silken robes weighed on his shoulders enough to have made him feel a king in truth and not merely in play-act; he was grateful to have anything to remind him of his true and proper place.

When he saw the round incendiary rolling across the planks beside him with its fuse smoking, that same habit came to his service: he recognized the rumbling clatter of its progress, and automatically put down the thick, low-hanging sleeve of the robe in the path of the ball, and snatched it hot from the ground.

And there he was forced to stop an instant: the nearest windows, behind the throne, were latticed over with heavy wooden shutters. "Temeraire!" he called, without thinking: and indeed

Temeraire was already in motion, reaching forward to hook with a talon a pair of the shutters and tearing them away. Laurence leapt forward upon the dais and flung the incendiary outside as though heaving a rock. Even as it flew, the charge took fire and erupted, flame licking in at the frame of the window; long splinters from the wood, smoldering, scattered upon the floor.

Laurence ducked away from that furious hail, and only belatedly realized his shelter was none other than the throne. "What was that?" Temeraire said, and added, "ow!" in protest: the explosion had ceased, and Laurence looked around to see the dragon's side sprouting half-a-dozen red-enameled splinters the size of rapiers, dug in between the scales.

The first moments of blank surprise gone, abruptly the guards sprang into action: they surrounded the crown prince bodily, and Laurence found himself enveloped in their protective ranks as well. A deep-voiced man somewhere beyond them was shouting orders to get the prince away, to hide him—

"Laurence!" he heard Granby shout, but Laurence had no opportunity to answer over the noise: the enormous orange-red dragons in their armored plates, who had been arrayed at the back of the room, were running forward to make formation around the throne: smashing to pieces the wooden floor, bowling men and dragons to either side in their haste: there were twelve of them, heavy-weights all. Four of the beasts seized the elaborate carved borders of the dais, which Laurence had thought mere decoration, but now seemed to be intended almost as handles. A shout came; that deep voice—one of the dragons, Laurence belatedly realized—counted three, and they heaved; the entire dais swayed up into the air and they were moving, the dragons' heavy four-taloned feet thumping upon the ground as they began to run.

Laurence, holding on to the throne for very life, had only time to throw one startled look back at Temeraire, who had been shouldered out of the way by the pack and was only just righting himself. The back wall of the palace fell before the red dragons as they bulled forward; it went down not smashed but in a single piece, as though by design; then there were wings everywhere blotting out the sky, the translucent skin glowing orange-red with the sun above them, and with another heave they were aloft. The palace grounds fell away: off the side of the dais, Laurence could see the yellow roofs glowing in the late-morning sun, and the silver-grey brick of the vast plazas, rapidly dwindling away below.

Laurence said to Prince Mianning, "Where are they taking us?" He supposed it was a violation of all etiquette, but at present there was no-one to object to that: they were quite alone upon the dais. The platform was carried low, beneath the dragons' sides; each one clutched a handle, and their wings beat wildly overhead. Laurence could not even catch sight of a single officer, nor see the dragons' heads.

Mianning's face was composed, despite the assassination attempt and his having been swept pell-mell away in such a fashion. "To the Summer Palace," he answered, as calmly as though he had only gone for a pleasant stroll, but then he paused: he leaned forward from the throne and looked down at the ground that spilled away beneath them, and then towards the position of the sun.

Laurence caught sight of his look, of the frown that suddenly touched the crown prince's forehead. Mianning put his hand on the hilt of his long blade: though the sheath was adorned with jewels and gold, when Mianning drew a few inches of the blade to loosen it, they gleamed good serviceable steel. Laurence watched him: he missed his own sword painfully at the moment. "What is it?" he asked grimly.

"We are being taken in the wrong direction," Mianning said.

He fell silent, and Laurence could think of nothing to propose. He glanced over the side: they were already past the city limits, and the pale green fields of spring spilling away below were so far distant they were merely squares upon a chessboard. There was nothing to be done but wait. Laurence looked back: was there a small speck that might have been a dragon, to their rear? He could not be sure: it might as easily have been a bird. Temeraire would surely have followed them as soon as he was able, but he might have been held back somehow, or misdirected.

"Did you see the assassin?" Laurence said to Mianning, who regarded him thoughtfully a long moment; Laurence did not know what to make of his expression, until Mianning said, "He was of your own party: he wore Western clothes."

"What?" Laurence said. "That is impossible. Hammond, myself, your own servant Gong Su—Captain Granby, Captain Berkley—that was the sum of our party. It is perfectly impossible any one of them should have done such a thing. We were searched, in any case, before we came into the room, and required to leave our swords."

"And yet six of you entered," Mianning said. He raised a hand, when Laurence would have protested. "You misunderstand me. The sixth man was surely introduced to your party as you entered the pavilion. If his attack had succeeded, and I had been slain, your party would surely have been blamed."

Laurence paused. "And *will* be blamed, if, for instance, we should be found to have died of wounds taken in the attempt?" he asked grimly. Mianning inclined his head in answer.

Hammond had been deeply anxious over the preparations for this mission not least because its outcome was by no means certain: a substantial conservative faction of the Imperial court passionately opposed anything they called foreign adventures, and had made an attempt to unseat Mianning as the Imperial heir on the occasion of their last visit. It had not occurred to Laurence that this passion might extend so far as to openly murder their crown prince, but he could imagine no-one else who might have arranged such an incident. Napoleon might have a long arm, but not so long as this.

"Lord Bayan was given the right to oversee the preparations for our meeting," Mianning said. "The conservative party raised a great protest at your coming at all within the walls of the Forbidden City, and suggested I am excessively partial towards your nation, and might be inclined to allow you too much license." He looked towards the sun, which lay ahead of their flight. "His estate lies west of the city."

The dragons carried them towards the lowering sun for nearly an hour. At last they began a descent over what seemed to Laurence a sprawling country estate: a great wilderness of gardens in the Chinese style—meandering paths and great pitted boulders amidst running streams crossed by graceful arched bridges, and a large pavilion which might have accommodated a horde of dragons beside the house.

Their dais was set down in a wide courtyard with great care, and a gentleman dressed in embroidered robes of great magnificence came out of the house to meet them, prostrating himself with all correct formality. "Lord Bayan," Mianning said, calm but watchful; there were a dozen blank-faced guards on either side, besides of course the dragons.

"My humble abode is honored beyond measure by your visit, Your Highness," Lord Bayan said. "I am full of desolation that the peace and tranquility of your days should have been profaned by so desperate an attack upon you by the Westerners, whom I am told have infested the palace grounds like so many evil termites gnawing away at live wood." If this speech were not enough to make his position plain, the look he gave Laurence, sidelong, would have sufficed alone: a mingling of disgust and disdain. And beneath that, something of terror; there was a dew of sweat scattered upon the top of his broad shaven forehead, and he had the look of a man who knows he has gone too far.

"My poor home will be your shelter," Bayan continued, "and I pledge my own life to your safety from attack. I have three most beautiful young concubines, all virgin, who will attend you, and a troupe of actors are in attendance for your entertainment."

"We are indebted to you for your concern for our well-being, and our brother's," Mianning said. "We must at once however write to our father, who even now shall have heard such news as will make him concerned for our health."

"You shall be given pen and ink at once, Your Highness," Bayan said; after a few more stilted pleasantries and fencing exchanges they were with inexorable courtesy escorted inside the house with the guards trailing, deep within to a spacious chamber, nobly appointed, with a great writing-desk. Brushes and ink and paper were already laid out waiting. Mianning seated himself as easily as though he were in his own house and favorite chair, and taking up the brush began to write.

Lord Bayan hesitated, but after a moment kowtowed again and left them, the practiced smile already falling from his face as he went out the door. They were left alone.

Laurence himself remained standing by the desk. Mianning had given him the shorter of his blades; it was hidden yet beneath his robes, thrust into the waist of his trousers—for what use a single blade might be.

Mianning tapped his brush against the inkwell, noisily; Laurence glanced down and saw upon the sheet a message written in clear simple characters: *Having gone to such lengths, they likely cannot let me leave alive.*

Laurence inclined his chin halfway to his collarbone slowly, only once, to show he had heard and seen. Any act so overt as this would put the conspirators far beyond the pale, and surely demand reprisals. Except of course, if their plot succeeded. Laurence met Mianning's eyes, in defiance of all Hammond's laborious tutelage on the subject: in the moment they were no longer marionetting the forms of Imperial etiquette, representatives of states, but mortal prisoners together, and in that exchanged look shared the understanding of their likely fate.

Too many witnesses had seen them carried away alive, surely not all of them suborned, and the bomb had not wreaked much damage inside the building; Bayan could not easily claim they had been brought to him already dead, victims of the assassin. But some other deadly outcome might now be engineered: perhaps Mianning murdered by Laurence's own hand, the supposed culmination of a British plot to slay the crown prince, and Laurence slain in reprisal and wrath by Bayan's guards.

That would be a good story, and the Emperor would have little alternative but to accept such an explanation on its face to keep the peace in his own court, to gain the time for the laborious process of grooming another heir. And in doing so, he would be forced as well to treat the British as the murderers of his son and heir, despite their having come under pretense of seeking friendship: betrayers of the worst kind. There would be no alliance; instead the reverse entirely, all the wrath of the Imperial armies flung upon their party and on the *Potentate* in Tien-sing harbor, and every last man of their company put to torture and death for so outrageous a crime.

Laurence went to the door and looked out of the room. Two dozen guards were lined against the walls to either side. Too many to fight: if they wished, they could put a knife in Laurence's fist, close their hands around his arm, and force him to thrust the blade into Mianning's breast. They did not meet his eyes, nor even turn their heads to look at him. He closed the door again.

Mianning was taking his scribbled note off the scroll-handles and putting it to the lamp to burn; Laurence looked at it catching the flames, at the oil, at the jug of rice wine standing; and then he took up another of the blank scrolls from the table and unrolled it into a long sheet at his feet. Mianning watched him, and then silently joined him: soon they had laid all the scrolls down in rows stretching from one end of the long chamber to the other. There were two lamps burning in the room. They each took one and poured the oil out, spilling it in a glossy line across the parchment, and after that splashed on the contents of the jug of wine, and dropped the first burning sheet down. Blue flame went leaping across the wooden floor.

They took scraps of flame, burning pieces of paper, and spread the fire to the delicate scrolls hanging on the walls, to the silken draperies and furnishings. Smoke began to fill the room; the furniture, beneath its enamel, was catching. Laurence covered his mouth with a fold of his robe and kept to the work; the fire was climbing to a steady yellow-red crackling in a few corners of the room as the seasoned wood took light. His face was streaming sweat already, and Mianning's was made distant and blurred by the smoke: Laurence had the strange unpleasant itching of a memory he could not quite grasp, something he should have remembered—flame and smoke, voices shouting, a crammed struggling belowdecks. A ship in flames, a ship burning; but he could not remember her name, or what had happened, or when.

He pushed the sensation aside and flung cushions down into the building blaze, and then at last the door opened: the nearest guard looked in and cried out. Others came running to the doorway: Laurence leapt for the narrow entry with the short sword in his hand and stabbed the first man coming through in one eye, and got away his longer sword. Mianning took the other side of the door, his own blade drawn. They took the first three easily and backed the rest away from the door for a moment's hesitation: realizing the opposition that faced them, the guards began to group themselves together for a united rush, to bull through the door.

But the smoke was thickening now, and the sickening charred smell of human flesh rose as corpses fell amid the kindling: the opened door had fed the fire with a rush of air, and flames were now climbing the walls, leaping for the rafters. The house had caught, well and truly. Laurence drew a gulp of air from the doorway and then, catching Mianning by the arm, pointed to the fallen guards. Together they stripped off swiftly the slain guards' helms and retreated into the grey haze of smoke even as more guards came pouring through the door.

Laurence threw off his elaborate robes behind the veil of smoke, dropping them into another corner of the fire. The milling guards were shouting to one another as they swiftly organized a defense: already buckets of water slopping were being brought from the kitchens. The disorder was great. Laurence was dizzy and ill with smoke and struggling not to breathe; stinging burning cinders were falling into his hair, onto his bare chest and shoulders. He jammed on his helm, saw Mianning doing so as well beside him; Mianning caught his arm and they pushed out into the hallway together through the din of shouting and panic, and snatched empty buckets from the serving-boys who carried them.

They ran through the hallway towards the back of the house, where more servants came staggering under tubs and buckets; shouts pursued them almost at once. Laurence knocked down a burly cook's assistant who tried to thrust an arm in his path, and reaching for the pots and deep-bowled skillets standing on the stoves flung them behind him, leaving a greasy slick of steaming water and cooking-oil upon the floor. They burst out through the back door of the kitchens and were in the courtyard in back of the house, looking out upon the grounds; more guards were running towards them. Laurence did not suppose they could defeat so many; together he and Mianning drew their swords, however, and ran towards the stables. If they could but get horses—

Laurence stopped and caught Mianning's arm to halt him; he flung off his helm and bellowed aloft, "Temeraire!" waving his hand; and the guards slowed hastily and backed away as Temeraire landed in a rush of thundering wings, in the courtyard.

"Whatever is happening?" Temeraire said. "Why is that house on fire? Laurence, you see I did *not* let them keep me from coming after you, this time: although they tried; some fellow of the guards even had the gall to say that one of our friends threw that bomb, if you can credit it. But you may be sure I quite silenced him: I caught the fellow who threw it, though he was trying to put off his clothes, and he was not from our ship at all."

"'Ware above you!" Laurence cried out: the four scarlet dragons who had abducted himself and Mianning were descending towards him, claws outstretched, bulkier than Temeraire himself and plainly bent on his destruction.

Temeraire, startled, sat up on his haunches, fanning back his wings. "What do you mean by this?" he demanded, and then had to make a writhing leap, twisting himself away from their talons and teeth as he got himself aloft again, eeling between two of them. "Oh," he said indignantly, "I do not know in the least what you are doing, but if you mean to get between me and Laurence—!"

He beat up and away, drew breath, and roared at the foremost beast coming towards him: that terrible earth-shattering resonance again, which Laurence heard yet lingering in his dreams from the moment upon that hill in Japan, familiar and dreadful at once, and the scarlet beast's eyes quite literally burst in their sockets, blood erupting in a sickening rush. The dragon plummeted from the sky. It was already dead when its corpse smashed into the roof of the house and in its sprawl tore down half the north wall: smoke and flame leapt out around it like a massive pyre, and other rooms left gaping open to the air, cries of horror and men and women looking out in astonished dismay.

The three other dragons fell back in dismay and horror, and dropped to the ground cowering: they flattened themselves before Temeraire as he came down, and remained there with their wings nearly covering their heads.

Temeraire still did not quite understand what had happened. First that wretched assassin had nearly slain Laurence, and then the Imperial guards had flown off with him—Temeraire had tried to be understanding; Hammond had shouted urgently to him that they meant only to protect Laurence, to protect Mianning, and take them to a place of safety. That sounded well enough, until several of the courtiers had begun to cry out that the British had tried to kill the crown prince; fortunately Temeraire had already snatched up the bomb-thrower, as that fellow tried to creep out a side door, and he could see that it was only a fellow dressed in Western clothes, which were anyway not quite right: his too-long wool coat dyed royal blue, instead of navy or bottle-green, and no waistcoat, and his hair lightened somehow; he had been wearing a dented hat drawn low down his face.

Temeraire had been forced to knock down several guards, who had tried to advance on Mr. Hammond and the rest of his party with swords, to make them all listen to him; he had even been forced to roar—awkwardly; it had brought down a portion of the roof—and it had required the better part of an hour to straighten out the matter, and persuade the Imperial dragons to take charge of the scene. "Mr. Hammond," Temeraire had said, at that point, having handed over the assassin to Mianning's guards with what he considered was extraordinary restraint; he had not killed him straightaway, "I perfectly understand those fellows did not mean anything terrible by carrying Laurence away, and I will try not to be *very* short with them, but they certainly ought to have consulted my opinion on the subject of his protection, and you may be sure I will make that quite plain to them: I do not mean to have any repetition of such a misunderstanding. Now, someone had better tell me which way they have gone."

To the Summer Palace, someone had told him; but Temeraire remembered the Summer Palace quite well, and it was not due west of the city at all; they had *not* gone to the Summer Palace, so it was no use his flying that way. So he had been forced to chase them down directly, even though his flying strength was not entirely recovered; when he had gone out of the city limits, he had at last been able to distinguish them from the ordinary traffic, a cluster of specks in the distance, but he fell further and further behind. Once he had even lost sight of them entirely, and panic had clutched his breast a little while, driving him to a speed greater than he could comfortably maintain, until he had passed a small porter flying in the opposite direction who, chirping, had said, "Oh, they are going to Lord Bayan's estate, I am sure: he lives just over those hills. He is very rich," the porter added, "and a great servant of the Emperor."

"I am very grateful to you," Temeraire said, and, feeling relieved to hear that Laurence was in such good hands, he had flown onwards at an easier pace, though even more irritated at the guard-dragons: there was no call for them to have made such haste. They ought to have considered, it seemed to Temeraire, that in taking Laurence further away from him, they were *not* improving his safety: and where, he wondered, was Mianning's companion? Lung Tien Chuan certainly ought to have been there, at their meeting, and Temeraire would have felt a good deal happier to rely on *his* judgment, and not some soldier-dragons who had not even managed to stop an assassin getting into the room in the first place.

But still he had not been very anxious, and then he had sailed into the courtyard to find the house burning, the red dragons attacking *him* of all absurdities, and to cap everything Laurence fleeing the disaster stripped to the waist; his beautiful robes were gone. "Good God, that does not matter," Laurence said impatiently, when Temeraire anxiously inquired after them. "I imagine they have burnt by now; I dare say no-one has the least concern for my costume at present."

To his horror, Temeraire could hold out no hope for their rescue: even as he turned to look, bitter smoke and flames were boiling out of the windows, licking from under the eaves at the roof wherever the scarlet dragon had not smashed it to pieces. He leapt to action at once, and worked as quickly as he could, calling out instructions to the other dragons, who had cowered down now and were not behaving so stupidly: soon they were ferrying great loads of water back and forth from the nearby pond, while Temeraire himself tore down and stamped out the worst bits of the fire, and roared down other parts of it.

But it was no use. One wing of the house they managed to save; all else was a smoldering ruin, damp and stinking, the body of the scarlet dragon lying amid it blackened and surrounded by puddles. All the household stood huddled aside and watched it collapse, women with children in their arms and the servants still clutching dully at the small buckets they had been trying to use against the flames, and not even a scrap of silk left of Laurence's gown. Lord Bayan himself, the owner, did not do anything to help; he only stood surrounded by his guards watching his house burn, and when the flames had at last been conquered, Temeraire turned back and found the lord prostrating himself before Prince Mianning.

"I am desolate that my house should have been the scene of such events," Lord Bayan said, "when you ought to have been confident of safety here."

"Oh!" Temeraire said, glaring down upon him; his eyes were smarting from the smoke and ash flying through the air, "you may well apologize: how dare you have taken Laurence away from me, and the crown prince, too, when this is the consequence? And I should like to know what those dragons of yours meant, leaping upon me when I came in; it is absurd to say they did not know who I was, or thought I should be a danger."

Lord Bayan did not even answer, or rise from his kowtow; Prince Mianning only said to him, "Your service will be rewarded as it deserves." It was a small consolation to Temeraire that the crown prince himself was in no better state than Laurence: half-naked and smirched with a fine layer of black soot, except for the trickles of sweat and one pale smudged handprint across his back with the fingers stretched improbably long, as though someone had tried to grab hold of him and the grip had slid off.

Lord Bayan still kneeling said, "I would be honored to offer you escort and shelter—"

"Lung Tien Xiang will escort Prince Lao-ren-tse and myself," Mianning said and turning away gestured to Temeraire slightly, asking for a leg up. Temeraire was more than glad to provide it: he wanted nothing more than to get Laurence, and Mianning, too, well away from here; there was certainly no reason to stay. Laurence hesitated oddly, looking at Bayan as the lord rose up again; then he turned and climbed aboard as well.

As glad as Temeraire was to leave, questions pressed in upon him as soon as he was aloft again and Laurence securely with him; he turned his head to ask Laurence and only then received the full and appalling explanation. "What?" Temeraire cried, halting midair. "Whyever did you not say so! I should have torn him to pieces, at once; why did you not say he was a traitor and a murderer? I only thought he was a fool who had made a great mess of things."

He felt truly indignant: indignant, and wounded, and all the more by hearing that Laurence had set the dreadful fire himself. Why had Laurence not relied upon him? Surely Laurence should have expected Temeraire to follow, to come to his rescue—or perhaps not. Temeraire was painfully conscious he had not saved Laurence in Japan; he had not found Laurence and brought him safe away.

But on this occasion, Temeraire thought, he might at least avenge Laurence's ill-usage: he almost turned back at once, but Mianning said, "No: I can use Bayan's life better than his death, at present."

"Do you truly mean to allow a man who has failed once to slay you to get another chance at the prize?" Laurence said to Mianning, echoing Temeraire's own feelings on the subject: Temeraire did not see that Bayan's life was any use to anyone at all. "There can be no question of guilt, here—Bayan suborned your guard, abducted you, held you against your will. That the assassin came from him, at the first, can scarcely be in doubt.

"I beg you will forgive my frankness, Your Highness," Laurence added, "but this matter affects our own mission as much as you yourself. We both know how Bayan would have chosen to use this: not merely to destroy us personally, but to destroy all hope of alliance between our nations."

Laurence spoke very soberly; Temeraire knew Hammond had spared no efforts to impress upon him the urgent necessity of the alliance, and that Laurence felt very anxious for his part in achieving it, very doubtful of his own efforts. Temeraire had tried to assure Laurence that he would do splendidly, that there could be nothing wanting in his performance, but of course, Temeraire had not suspected that there would be assassins throwing bombs at him, and treacherous dragons abducting him; he had not expected such things in China, of all places.

He did not see any reason not to kill Bayan at once, as the author of these calamities, but Mianning answered Laurence, "And so, too, must I use his failure: to ensure that alliance, and the future of my nation and my reign. I have had no certain evidence, no sword to hold above their heads, until now, but they have overreached at last." He leaned forward. "Lung Tien Xiang, take us back to the Forbidden City: I will return to my own palace."

"With so many of your nearest guard turned traitor?" Laurence said.

"Those were not my nearest guard," Mianning said. "I did not have free choice of my attendants at our meeting, as I told you; I have others whom I can better trust. But in any case, there is no alternative. One who yields, always yields; I will not come to the throne in the minds of my enemies as one who may be moved by threats or danger. I have withstood worse than this, at their hands; far worse. Better if I die than permit them to hold my leash."

Temeraire thought this an appalling choice of alternatives, and one he scarcely imagined Mianning's own dragon Chuan would approve. "I cannot think my brother would permit you to go into such danger," he said. "Why was he not there, to-day? If only he had been by your side, I am sure together we should not have allowed those treacherous lizards to snatch the two of you away: I would certainly have done no such thing," he added, for Laurence's benefit, trying not to let his tone convey too plainly his sense of injury, "if only I had had the least notion, before now, that someone should be trying to kill you. I do not think I can be blamed, when we have just arrived, and no-one told me: but Chuan should have known; he should have been on his guard."

"Lung Tien Chuan is dead," Mianning said.

Chapter 9

MIANNING EVIDENTLY DID NOT care to discuss the matter further. It fell to Gong Su to convey the details: he seemed high in the councils of the crown prince, and spent nearly all the day closeted with his own associates within the government; later that evening he rejoined their small and wary party in Laurence's chambers, and quietly told them, "Lung Tien Chuan was slain six months ago. He was served with poison in his tea."

Laurence was appalled by the act: a dreadful waste, and it seemed to him pure cruelty, to punish the dragon for merely loving his master, and over a political quarrel with the latter, which the former should have had very little to say to, he imagined. "There are only eight Celestials in full, are there not?" Laurence said.

"Yes," Gong Su said. "There is no other to be the prince's companion."

Laurence only belatedly took the deeper meaning of this intelligence that evening, when he was alone again: he had been quartered in another part of the Imperial palace grounds under Mianning's control and surrounded by watchful guards loyal to him.

Laurence had closeted himself to write his report of the strange and convoluted events of the day, which yet he preferred to struggling through more of the letter he had not yet sent to his mother to acquaint her with his condition. But he set his pen down abruptly and, sitting up, looked out the window into the courtyard where

Temeraire slept, in arm's reach—in a dragon's arm's reach at least—recovering from his exertions.

Hammond had conveyed to him from the other side the necessity of Laurence's adoption: a Celestial might only be companion to a member of the Imperial family; and Temeraire's egg had been sent away from China in the first place only to avoid setting up a rival to Mianning. Therefore—the heir to the throne required a Celestial? Perhaps *required* was too strong: many things might be bent at the will of the Emperor. But tradition had its own power. If Mianning had no Celestial companion—if he had lost his own dragon—

Shipboard, Temeraire had spoken censoriously to him of Hammond. "I do not say he is not clever, in his own way," Temeraire had said, "but I am very sorry to say, Laurence, that he is not to be relied upon. When last we were here, he wished to insist upon your giving me back to the Chinese only so they would open another port to us."

Surely that request would come again, now, Laurence realized, and was disturbed by his own reaction to the possibility—a reaction which owed more to the viscera than clear rational thinking. Sensibly considered, he ought to be grateful for such an excuse to be restored to his respectable Navy career and a ship of his own; and if he were not grateful, if he had not wished to do it, nevertheless it would be no less than his duty. And yet—and yet he discovered he had begun to think of Temeraire as his own man, as it were. Such persuasion, coming from one trusted as a friend, would only be honorable if meant sincerely, if given from the heart and in expectation of its advancing Temeraire's real happiness.

Laurence did not think he could, even at the direct request of the King's envoy, consent to deceive a friend. To lie in such a cause would be contemptible, a kind of personal treachery. But Laurence felt himself on unsteady ground. It was surely his duty as a captain in the Aerial Corps to use the bond between himself and Temeraire to be both a check and a goad upon the beast, and that bond was one which many another aviator would willingly have taken on in his stead. Perhaps it was a kind of folly to think of a dragon as a friend, as a companion-in-arms; would he skate perilously close to treason to refuse such a demand?

Granby listened willingly enough as Laurence began to outline the situation for him, but Laurence did not reach the question: no sooner had he explained Mianning's need than Granby broke in, snorting, and said, "Oh, Lord! Yes, Hammond will be after you straightaway, I am sure; I dare say their Lordships would give him a peerage if he managed anything so neat as giving them a treaty and being shot of Temeraire all at once."

Laurence stared: shocked, silenced; Granby caught his eye, and a slow crimson flush overspread his cheeks. "Well—" Granby said after a moment. "Well—he is too independent by half; he's thought too clever for his own good—a little troublesome, perhaps—but you see," he added hurriedly, "you must see I've no room to criticize. Iskierka is a demon and a half, and it's not as though Temeraire hadn't any provocation, for that matter, you know—"

Laurence made him no reply; he could not conceive of any reply which should be fitting. He did not know: he did not know at all, that he was the captain of a troublesome beast; he did not know that the Admiralty should have been glad to see the back of his dragon, though Britain was desperately short on heavy-weight beasts, even ones of less remarkable capability.

Granby made a hasty and threadbare excuse of having to go see to Iskierka; Laurence mechanically said, "Of course," and rising left Granby's quarters. A fine thin rain was presently falling. Granby and the rest of the formation were quartered in one of the guest palaces to the south of Mianning's personal quarters, where Laurence had been invited to stay; the dragon-wide pathway between the buildings was grey and misty, blurred, and deserted but for a handful of servants, errand-boys, dashing quickly through. Laurence stood beneath the eaves; across the path another great palace stood, with a dragon's-head as gutterspout giving out a steady clear stream of water washing over the paving-stones.

The guards behind him, Mianning's chosen escort, shifted their weight behind him; he heard the creak of their armor, their boots on the stone, the nearly stifled sighs. The scene was wholly unfamiliar, wholly strange; in the distance was the great blue bulk of a dragon crossing the pathway, its wings half-furled to its back. It was something from a fairy-tale, nothing he would ever have imagined into his life. It gave his mind no purchase. He did *not* know, he did not remember, what could have made Granby ever say such things.

Laurence had never studied—to his recollection—to know much of aerial combat or of dragons, beyond learning the signals to bespeak them from his ship, but this much he remembered from the battle of the Nile: the formations wheeling, like flocks of birds, above them in the sky. In modern warfare, dragons fought in formation; and yet Temeraire did not seem to have a place in one. Laurence had not thought on it before: but a dragon so gifted, so powerful, so agile—he must have been placed in formation, if it could be done. If the dragon were not—were not a recalcitrant, mismanaged beast.

He had always prided himself on being a reliable captain, one who did his duty with honor, neither haring off after prizes or unreasonable glory nor guarding his ship too jealously from danger; he had prided himself on a well-run crew. It now bore in on him with sudden force that his crew was strangely depleted, and of a peculiar nature; he had paid little mind to that, struggling as he did merely to learn all the names of those men he did have, but by comparison to the complement Maximus bore, Temeraire had not half so many. His ground crew consisted entirely in a dozen men—several of them, Laurence now realized, former sailors. His officers were a motley and an awkward lot: Forthing, his first officer, was not a gentleman, nor of any particular brilliance which should excuse the same.

Laurence could scarcely imagine whom he might approach on the subject; Granby had certainly been most unwilling to speak. His subordinates he could hardly insult in such a manner, either, as to ask them whether they served on an inferior crew, and why.

Finally he strode out into the rain and returned to his own quarters, to speak with Temeraire himself: if he could not ask for a direct answer, he could ask where they stood with the Admiralty, together, he and the dragon. If Temeraire had some memory of chastisement, some punishment—

Temeraire was awake, in his courtyard, awake and spangled a little by the rain, which he shook off with a rippling shiver of the scales. "Laurence!" he exclaimed with relief. "I wish you had not gone away when there are assassins about: I was on the point of going to look for you. Wherever have you been? Surely you might have stayed here with me, and waited until I woke?"

He sounded an anxious mistress more than anything else, an odd mixture of plaintive and accusatory. "I left word," Laurence said, a little surprised. "I have been speaking with Captain Granby—"

"Granby had much better come and visit you," Temeraire said, "than the reverse: no-one is trying to assassinate Granby."

"No-one is trying to assassinate me, either," Laurence said dryly. "I had merely the misfortune of being near the crown prince."

"If they want to kill the prince, I dare say they may want to kill you just as well," Temeraire said. "After all, you are his brother and the Emperor's son as well; and if they do not like his being a friend to Britain, how much less must they like your being British, to begin with. But," he added, in tones which implied he was making a handsome gesture, "I do not mean to fuss: come and let us have a bowl of tea, and then you can read to me; that would be much better than wandering all over this palace."

"Temeraire," Laurence said, while the servants leapt without further instruction into a rush about them, bringing out a great porcelain bowl of deep red for Temeraire, and a small ironwork table and chair for himself, with a cup and saucer to match, and kettles full of steaming and fragrant tea. "—Temeraire," he repeated, unsure how to broach the subject: would a dragon even care anything for the Admiralty, for what men and government should think of him?

"No, of course I do not give two sous for the Admiralty, or the Government," Temeraire said, straightaway answering all Laurence's worst fears. "How could anyone, who has known anything of their folly? Why, Laurence, you know that perfectly well.

"I suppose you do not remember this," he added, "but Perscitia writes me they have still not made all the pavilions, which Wellington promised us during the war; but they are also upset if ever a dragon should chance to sleep by the road, on the way from London to Edinburgh, and perhaps eat a pig left wandering loose. But that is perfectly stupid: if there is no pavilion, and no provender, then how else is one to make a long flight? And nevertheless they complain.

"As far as I can tell, there is no-one in it who is worth two pins; well, except for you, Hammond," Temeraire added, as that gentleman entered in haste. "You are not a bad sort of fellow; but if you should attempt to do anything scaly underhand, such as tell me I ought to remain here to replace Chuan, I shall be very cross with you."

Laurence was thwarted in pressing his inquiry by Hammond's arrival, that gentleman in some disarray, his formal robes far from neatly pressed and showing sharp folded creases in the silk; his hair was disordered. "No, no, not at all," Hammond said. "I assure you, nothing could be further from my wishes. We cannot afford to lose you. The tie is too valuable to sacrifice, save of course in utter extremis. Without your connection, Captain Laurence's adoption may be too easily disavowed, and it is that bond which forms the foundation of all our negotiations.

"Naturally we must make some gesture, some effort; but I have had a hint, I believe, from Gong Su; with your permission, of course, I should propose Temeraire's favoring them with an egg. As I understand it," Hammond added, "your engaging in relations with an Imperial dragon would be the ordinary way of arranging such things."

. . .

"I should like to know," Iskierka said, with a hiss of steam and a roiling eye, "what is wrong with *our* egg. If an egg of yours were wanted, why should anyone look further than that?"

They were being served their dinner in Temeraire's courtyard: a truly splendid dinner, of stewed oxheads and bowls of live eels, seasoned expertly with pepper and vinegar, which unfortunately Maximus did not seem to much enjoy, nor Immortalis and Messoria; they poked a little anxiously at the squirming masses and then nudged the bowls aside, although they were pleased enough with the oxheads, so tender the meat fell off the bones and with the skull cracked open so one might take them into one's mouth and suck upon them for the excellent brains.

"I am afraid," Temeraire said, a little loftily, "that they do not think much of fire-breathers, here in China—and in any case," he added, "it is a matter of certain particular superior qualities, which belong to the Celestial breed only, and distinguish us from all others, which must be present in the next Emperor's dragon."

"Dear one," Granby said to her, "we don't at all want to give them your egg: we want to take it back with us, to Britain, and see it in the hands of some proper captain of the Corps."

"I do not see any reason why it should not stay here and belong to the Emperor of China," Iskierka said stormily. "No reason at all; it is ten thousand miles back to Britain, and who is to say we will not run into some trouble along the way—someone might steal the egg, or it might be cracked. Of course my egg would be very valuable, in the war," she added, "but I do not believe in taking foolhardy risks—"

Granby choked heavily upon his own dinner, coughing, and had to be rescued with a steady thumping upon his back, and several glasses of wine.

Iskierka was in no better mood even after their meal had ended with a marvelous shaved ice, flavored with a syrup of plums and studded with the same, imparting delightful tiny bursts of flavor upon the tongue when one happened across them in a swallow. However, she did not hesitate to eat all her share and then some.

"That is something like, I will admit," Maximus said, licking out his enormous silver bowl, "but I don't suppose you could ask them for us, Temeraire, what they have done with the rest of those cows? I haven't any objection to those cow's heads, very tasty, but I would be glad of a side of beef, or perhaps two," he added, with a slantwise look at Kulingile—who had at last stopped getting longer, but had only just yesterday sprouted the beginnings of a pair of horns, much to everyone's bafflement: neither the Chequered Nettle nor the Parnassian, his progenitors, possessed any similar adornments.

"I wouldn't mind one, either, if they are just lying about somewhere," Kulingile said, raising his own head; and stifling his own remonstrations, Temeraire addressed the servants and conveyed the request. It was met with some confusion and a great deal of delay; when the beef was at last delivered two hours later, it was presented in the form of a false cow, the meat having been roasted, stuffed with grains and dried fruit, tied up with string, put into a wrapping of dough, and propped up on legs made of sticks; the head was a separate lump of meat, adorned with horns made of bread. Maximus sighed but ate it anyway, particularly after Kulingile had devoured his own share in a few bites.

As the servants began to bring out the bowls for tea, one came to Temeraire's side and murmured that a visitor had come and sought admittance. "Oh!" Temeraire cried. "Lung Qin Mei! Pray ask her to join us at once: how delighted I shall be to see her again," and he looked himself over anxiously. If only there were time to send Roland for his talon-sheaths, and if only they had a little black enamel paint—

Mei landed gracefully in the courtyard, though they were crowded and there was little space—but then, she did everything gracefully. Temeraire straightened himself up to meet her, abruptly conscious that he was now more cut-about than when last she had seen him; there was that very nasty scar upon his breast, where the barbed ball had taken him, before the sinking of the *Valérie,* and he had not filled back out from the long dismay of the sea-voyage and Laurence's disappearance. He had not had much appetite, of late, and it was difficult to be always competing shipboard with Maximus and Kulingile; one felt a little awkward taking anything more than one urgently needed, with the two of them casting mournful looks at their own share.

Iskierka said rudely, "I do not see why she is come; who wants her, anyway?" when Temeraire presented Mei to the company, but naturally Temeraire did not translate this remark. Iskierka drew herself up and raked Mei with a cold eye. "So that is an Imperial? Skinny, if you ask me; I dare say *she* could not go eye-to-eye with a Copacati. I don't see she has any scars at all."

"Mei," Temeraire said coldly, "is a great scholar, and took highest honors in the Imperial examinations."

"Oh!" Iskierka said, dismissive, "say nothing more! She does not fight at all; I see. I hope you have a splendid time talking over books together while you are making this egg of yours: I hope it don't leave you any more out of frame than you already are. Granby, I should like a flight before bed: pray let us go aloft, and then we shall go have a look in at *my* egg," she added, "and I take your point entirely; we shouldn't want to leave it in this country, where they don't value courage as they ought."

Temeraire was ruffled to indignation by this speech, and would surely have made a particularly sharp rejoinder if Iskierka had not gone away directly. The others were more polite to Mei, and looked with respectful interest on her jewels—this evening a collar-like delicate netting of pearls and silver wire, brilliant in the lamp-light against her dark blue scales. Although Temeraire writhed a little inwardly to see Maximus look up from the indelicate gnawing of a leg bone between two teeth and greet her with a mere joggle of the head, scarcely even a nod, saying jocularly, "How d'ye do," before going back to rattling the bone around in his mouth in what seemed to Temeraire a particularly noisy way.

And then Berkley *would* say, coarsely, "Put down that leg, you mannerless gobbler: we had better be going along and let the two of them have at their business. Laurence, will you come and have a hand of whist?" which even if Temeraire did not translate it for Mei had too obvious an effect: the dragons and all their captains getting hurriedly up and leaving the tea-bowls half-full, rudely. Even Laurence rose and, speaking softly with Berkley, made to climb aboard Maximus's back.

Temeraire would rather Laurence had not left, either; he did not see why Laurence should go anywhere. He caught Lily as they departed and whispered, "Lily, you will keep a lookout for Laurence, will you not? Pray do not let him wander off, or be assassinated; or lose any more of his memory."

"Of course," Lily answered, stoutly. "I will make sure he stays with Catherine and Berkley, and do not let Iskierka trouble you. I am sure you will make a perfectly splendid egg with this Imperial."

"Lily, I do not look too wretchedly scarred, do I?" Temeraire asked.

"No," Lily said, with a quick critical look. "—no; and you will fill out again very soon, with good eating. She must know you have come from a long way."

This was not terribly reassuring, but there was nothing to be done for it; the others were all leaping into the air: it was only Temeraire and Mei left in the courtyard. The servants laid out fresh bowls and poured the tea again.

Then they withdrew as well, to the hallway where they might hear a call; with a desperate leap into the ensuing silence Temeraire said to Mei, "How well you look—those jewels are particularly becoming."

"You are very kind," Mei said, and then to his horror and dismay added, in quite respectable English, "I am glad to see you so well, Lung Tien Xiang: too many times has the moon turned since we last saw one another beneath the boughs of the peach-trees, in the Summer Palace."

"Why," Temeraire said, wretchedly, "you have learnt English."

"Yes," Mei said, and with her usual tact added, "but I still cannot follow it very well, if someone speaks quickly: I have not had enough chance to practice."

"I must have words with Iskierka," Temeraire said. "I *will* have words with her; oh! I am so very sorry, Mei, that she should have been so rude. I only wish you hadn't known of it."

Mei ruffled out her wings a little, but did not pretend any longer that she did not know exactly what he meant. "I do not take any notice of it," she said. "She must be very attached to you, I suppose: I do not fault her for that. One cannot expect civilized manners from barbarians."

"She is not very attached to me, in the least," Temeraire said. "She is only attached to showing away, and annoyed she cannot do it so well as usually." He fell silent; he was not sure how to approach the matter. Diffidently he added, "I imagine—I expect Hammond has told you—" and then paused helplessly; this was not the breeding grounds of Pen y Fan in Wales, where everyone treated the matter with an easy coarseness, and everyone understood what they were about and merely wished to have the matter over with as quickly and easily as they might.

He had never expected to regret anything of those conditions, anything of being treated as a dumb bestial creature good for nothing else, but at the moment, if old Lloyd had appeared from nowhere to say, "Here now, why don't the two of you share a nice cow, and then have yourselves a splendid time," and Mei had acquiesced, Temeraire might almost have managed gratitude. If only Laurence had stayed: Temeraire might have introduced him to Mei, and they might have conversed awhile; they might have been quite comfortable and easy, and the subject of eggs might have been allowed to rise naturally, in the flow of conversation. But that seemed quite impossible now: Temeraire found himself adrift and speechless.

Mei took pity upon him, and said gently, "I have not spoken to Mr. Hammond; I have come at the request of the crown prince. But

I will be frank with you, dear friend: your minister's thoughts have run along behind his, it seems, for I have come to ask if you would consider doing me the very great honor of permitting me to attempt to bear a Celestial egg to you."

Temeraire felt rather heaped with coals of fire by this gracious speech, and made haste to convey to Mei his own willingness, and gratitude. He hesitated to go too far, in expressing the latter; after all, though he might be cut-about, he had come by his wounds honorably; and he was a Celestial: he did not want to abandon his dignity. Nothing could be less pleasing, he thought, to Mei; he did not want her to feel that she condescended. But he felt he could say, and did, "Nothing should give me greater pleasure than to make the attempt, if you were willing. I am very honored that His Imperial Highness would look to myself, to sire a companion for his reign."

And then he heaved a sigh of relief, to have escaped the rocky shoals and come safe to harbor; now they could be easy together. He asked her if she had read any English books. "I hope you will let me make you a present of some," he added, "if you haven't many here: I do not suppose you have had a chance of seeing the *Principia Mathematica*? It is of all books my favorite," and they passed a very pleasant hour discussing the poetry which Temeraire's mother, Qian, had lately sent him.

"Mei," Temeraire ventured, "pray tell me, if I might ask—is there not—is there a reason that Qian should not have had another egg?"

Mei said quietly, "The physicians think it inadvisable: she suffered greatly in bearing the twin eggs, last time, and in Imperials, where such a birth has happened once, it oft occurs a second time; the Empress does not wish Qian to risk her health."

"Oh," Temeraire said, sadly. "I am very sorry, I am sure; and my uncle?"

Mei shook her head. "A dozen attempts have come to nothing," she said. "We have been breeding a great deal amongst ourselves," she added, "—we Imperials, that is, in hopes of another Celestial arising, but without success. I assure you, Xiang, no-one will think any less of you, should we fail: it is well known that Celestials often cannot produce issue."

Temeraire was glad of an excuse to preen a little; he coughed, and gave Mei to understand he was not in the least concerned, at all. "For Iskierka, you see, has had my egg," he said. "That is why she is making such a fuss: she does not care to see it passed over, for yours."

He trailed off, a little puzzled, by the expression of open surprise upon Mei's face: she stared at him unblinking a moment and then said, in cautious tones, "Is it—perhaps the egg is yet in the shell?"

"Yes," Temeraire said. "It is in our quarters, under guard, of course."

Mei hesitated even longer and then said, "Is it not possible the egg should be—the gold dragon's, perhaps, the very large one? There are many young males in your company—"

"What?" Temeraire said, taken aback. "Why, no; Iskierka particularly wanted *my* egg; it is not as though just anyone's would have done for her. She followed me to New South Wales to get it, and threw over an Incan royal dragon for me," he added, a little wounded that Mei should not think him worthy of such dedicated effort.

"I beg your pardon very much," Mei said, bowing her head deeply in a courtesy, her wings spread a little. "I would not for the world give offense; only it is not to be heard of, that a Celestial might get an egg on anyone but an Imperial. I have always heard it described as impossible. The divine wind is a great burden, which often defies the powers of the body to support it."

A little mollified by this explanation, Temeraire forbore to stay offended, and when they had finished their tea, he and Mei repaired to the gardens, to walk awhile, and at length to enjoy a little sport before going on with the breeding: Mei might not be a fighting-dragon, Temeraire silently told Iskierka in his head, with some hauteur, but she was certainly very lithe and agile, and no-one could have complained of the experience.

Afterwards, a little out of breath, they ambled together to the courtyard again and had a refreshing second helping of shaved ice. "We must see the crown prince safely to the throne," Mei said soberly, when the servants had retreated again. "I know your heart is divided, Xiang, and I am grateful already for what you have given; but I will not conceal from you that I fear deeply for the sake of the nation. The death of Chuan was a grievious crime against the throne, and yet those responsible dare name themselves defenders of the law and of right thinking. What can it portend if such twisted people should gain control over the Celestial Throne? And they will let nothing stand in their way; they have shown as much time and time again."

"Mei, surely the Emperor must do something to Lord Bayan," Temeraire said. "Why, I would have slain him myself, if only Laurence and the prince had told me what mischief he had been about; and I would not have let anyone stop me, either."

"It is not enough to cut off the serpent's head," Mei answered. "This one grows another, and another after that. There are too many now who refuse to think of the future. They think only of what will enrich them—what will make them comfortable—what will guard their precedence and their estates. They wish to keep China preserved in glass, and if it could be done, they would not be wrong! I have seen a little of the rest of the world, through your eyes, and I do not think there is anything to compare.

"But so of course the world will be envious, and come knocking at our door. I have seen your monstrous ship in Tien-sing harbor; I have seen men felled by guns. We also must have ships, and more guns, and cannon. Our army must be renewed in strength, and the banners must be brought back to their old strength and discipline."

She spoke passionately, the tips of her wings nearly trembling with urgency, and leaning towards him rested her neck across his shoulders, coiling loosely about him. "I fear greatly, Xiang," she said, low, "even if I should bear this egg, if that will be enough. So many things can happen to an egg! They may persuade the Emperor to grant it to one of the other princes; or they may try—they may try—"

She shuddered, silently, and Temeraire bent his own head and nosed at her comfortingly. "I do not blame you in the least for worrying," he said. "If they are mad enough to try and kill Laurence, and the crown prince, and to murder Chuan, they might do anything at all."

"That is my own thought as well," Mei said unhappily. "Xiang, will you forgive me: would you not stay? Let the alliance be made, let China send legions to this war; might you not remain here in their stead, where you alone can act? I do not ask you to forsake your companion," she added swiftly, "but you might stay to keep watch over your own egg, quite reasonably; you might demand that it go only to the crown prince, and perhaps even—"

She faltered, and then said, low, "I have thought that perhaps the egg might even be bound to him at hatching; though it is not the proper way."

"Well, I have never found anything to complain of in it," Temeraire said. "I am very glad indeed to have had Laurence all my life, from the beginning; even if he did not know much about dragons, and nothing at all of China. I see nothing against it, provided that one ensures the captain is quite the right sort of person, which of course Laurence is, and not some wretched fellow like Rankin; that is where it goes all wrong."

Mei flew away not long afterwards, and Temeraire had just been deciding to go and find Laurence, when he came back into the courtyard: the captains had seen Mei go. "I hope," Laurence said to him, "—I hope you have had—a pleasant evening."

"Oh! A splendid evening," Temeraire said, reassuringly as he could: Laurence sounded so doubtful. "Mei is a magnificent lover," he added, "whatever Iskierka likes to say about her, and I dare say we may already have made a very handsome egg."

"Ah," Laurence said, in a slightly stifled voice. "I—Temeraire,

I beg your pardon; I do understand that this is—ordinarily considered in the normal course of your—your duty, but I should hope—that is to say, I should have been certain—"

Temeraire listened a little puzzled, but he soon worked out that Laurence only feared he might not like making the egg. "Oh, I certainly do not mind obliging Mei," Temeraire said. "I only minded in Wales, when they would set me to every female dragon in the Corps, it seemed, and only the meekest ones at that: some of them only middle-weight, for that matter. It was not what was due to me, I felt; I only obliged them for your sake," for at the time, of course, Laurence had been a prisoner aboard the ship *Goliath:* a prisoner, convicted for treason, and sentenced to die.

Temeraire shivered a little; he did not like to remember that dreadful time of separation. He hurried on. "But pray do not think this anything like: after all, this is quite an especial compliment to me, that the crown prince should want my own egg—even if he hasn't any other choice," he added.

"Very—very well," Laurence said, still awkwardly, and then said, "Pray shall I read something to you, this evening?"

"Shall I not read to you, Laurence, instead?" Temeraire said. "Mei has brought me a new book of poetry, which we read into only a little way; I should be glad to read it with you."

He felt a little craven in making the suggestion: it was merely a delaying tactic. Temeraire could scarcely imagine that Laurence would be willing to stay here in China, with the war in Europe from all reports going badly and Britain in such dire straits; even if an alliance was formed, Laurence would wish to be there. And yet, if they remained, and so protected Mianning and saw him to the throne, *that* would serve Britain and China both.

He marshaled his arguments in one corner of his mind while they read several of the lovely poems together, and Temeraire explained to Laurence his sense of the meaning; and then as the moon climbed overhead and bathed the courtyard stream in white, Temeraire drew a deep breath and broached the subject at last.

Laurence was silent a long while afterwards, as silent and grave as Temeraire had feared. His ruff drooped against his neck. He could not press Laurence; he was still painfully conscious of the great debt between them yet to be repaid: the loss of Laurence's reputation, of his countenance, and most sharply and terribly of his fortune of ten thousand pounds. At least Temeraire had seen him restored to his rank—with seniority—but that did not make up for all the rest. Temeraire still woke occasionally with a start from dreams in which he heard Roland saying again, "He has lost his fortune," and found the eyes of all his friends upon him accusingly, horrified, as they all repeated in unison, "*Ten thousand pounds.*"

He felt still low and guilty, and so he said hurriedly, "Laurence, I would not for the world distress you—"

"No," Laurence said, rousing, "no; I was only considering—but no. I beg your pardon. You must consult your sense of what is right, not my feelings. God forbid I should lean upon friendship to stand between you and your duty: it could not be borne. I would not for the world act in so false a character, towards any man—towards anyone. All feeling revolts at the idea."

"That is just how I feel myself," Temeraire said, a little puzzled, but relieved: Laurence was not angry. Perhaps Laurence *would* consider their remaining? It occurred to Temeraire belatedly that if they should remain, then perhaps the Emperor would grant Laurence an estate, and at least surely some finer clothing and jewels might be arranged.

Relief, gladness surged; he meant to add this handsome suggestion to his persuasions, to expand upon them, and then all was shattered—all turned at once dreadfully wrong, for Laurence added, "I hope having said as much, I may add I should most deeply regret the parting," and Temeraire realized, in slow-rising horror, that Laurence meant he would not stay himself. Laurence would leave him.

. . .

Laurence was taken aback by the violence of Temeraire's response; and only after a sharp recrimination did he understand that Temeraire had meant to propose not a separation but their remaining in China together, as though Laurence had anything to do here but make a cake of himself, prancing about in false honors bestowed for mere politics and luxuriating in a wealthy foreign court, while on the other side of the world, his country-men fought and died to defend their country against an encroaching tyrant.

It had not occurred to him even as a possibility that he should remain. Failing that, he had therefore made the only answer he felt endurable: and he had felt only ashamed of the reluctance which had slowed it coming from his lips—a reluctance which had not even the excuse that he had thought of his duty and Hammond's wishes. His reluctance had been wholly selfish and irrational: a disquieting pang at the thought of losing Temeraire. But such sentiments had even less place, in a question of duty, than the political considerations which Hammond had put forward.

"But you must see," Laurence said bewildered, "I cannot contemplate remaining. While Britain stands on the brink of subjugation, my remaining behind, to serve no purpose, could be nothing better than rank cowardice. *Your* remaining may indeed have some beneficent effect; mine, none. I should be a mere supernumerary, and useless here, just when every able-bodied man in Britain ought beat to quarters, as it were."

"You said once before we should remain if I liked," Temeraire said, accusatory, to Laurence's broad astonishment, "and you needn't look at me that way, as though you did not believe it, only because your memory is all ahoo; so I do not think I am in the least foolish for having *asked*. I did not propose keeping you from *your* duty, which properly considered ought be *our* duty. Of course I did not. Only, I thought you might have felt as I did, that our duty might lie here. *I* did not propose we should be parted—that you should go back to those wretched fools at the Admiralty, who do not want us, anyway; not really. And I dare say if I *did* let you go back without me, they would only hang you."

So concluding his wild outburst—the most singularly irrational thing Laurence had heard Temeraire say—the dragon flung himself aloft and vanished into the night sky with a rattle of black wings, leaving Laurence calling, "Temeraire—!" after him into the air.

Disheartened and impatient all at once, Laurence turned to his quarters; a cup of tea was offered but he rejected it to pace instead. That he had misstepped, and badly, was plain; but he had no idea how he had gone wrong, and where the fault lay. Temeraire's final words rankled, as well: that the Admiralty should not want them echoed yet again all Laurence's worst fears, and hinted at an almost mutinous disposition.

And the absurdity, to talk of the Admiralty hanging him—or perhaps not, if one treated the loss of a dragon like a captain's loss of his ship; Laurence supposed that he might be court-martialed over it, and yet he could not envision any reasonable jury finding against him in such a case. A ship had not her own mind, and could not decide to run herself onto rocks, or be captured and go over to the enemy, or be sunk in battle or by incompetence. A dragon, possessing its own will, who chose to remain behind, could scarcely be compelled by any man.

He sat down upon the bed, troubled suddenly: and yet that seemed untrue. Temeraire's anger and their misunderstanding had this real and understandable root: where Laurence had not contemplated remaining, Temeraire had for his part not contemplated separation; he had viewed their connection as indissoluble. In such a case, Laurence realized, he indeed did have the power to compel—he had the power to say, I will go, whether you will or no; and it seemed perforce would Temeraire go as well.

That was a strange and even disturbing power to possess over so great a creature: one which demanded a respect that Laurence was unhappily conscious he had not shown, just now. When in an hour's time he heard wingbeats returning, and Temeraire settled himself into the courtyard again, Laurence went out to him, ignoring the head curled pointedly beneath its wing. "I hope you will forgive me," he said, to the dark grey translucence of the membrane, which hid the great blue eye from his view.

"I hope you will forgive me," he said, "and accept my assurances that I would not for the world have wounded you: I see I have not understood how matters stood between us, and that we may only be stationed together, as it were. I can only beg your pardon and assure you that I stand ready to be persuaded, on the subject."

Temeraire made him no answer, but there was a shift of the wing-joint, and beneath the membrane as it spread out, Laurence could dimly make out a large narrow-slitted eye watching him.

"I cannot—I cannot pretend," he added, "that I feel I ought easily be swayed to see it our joint duty to remain here, taken all in all, in the present circumstances. I do not doubt you in the least that, on a prior occasion, I should have been willing to remain; I can only suppose that the circumstances of the war must have been considerably different, at the time. But I will do my best to consider the matter, if you wish to—"

The wing lifted away. "No," Temeraire said, shortly, "no; I do not see any sense in it. Pray forget I mentioned it," and he thrust his head back beneath the wing, and was silent again.

Laurence hesitated, torn, and at last gave way and went inside the house again. He did not immediately attempt to sleep: his mind was in an excess of disorder. The guilt of having caused pain to one deserving only consideration at his hands mingled with unanswered disquiet. He wondered if he had been wrong now; or if he had been wrong before: had he spoilt Temeraire? Temeraire was a high-spirited creature, with a remarkable intellect; Laurence could not deny that he took great pleasure in his company, and in the camaraderie that had endured even his loss of memory. Had he indulged that pleasure, and Temeraire's spirits, at the cost of discipline—at the cost, perhaps, of character?

A dreadful notion, and yet—Temeraire was so certain they should not be missed by the Admiralty; Granby also. It seemed a settled matter with them, scarcely to be questioned. If that were simply a matter of old men preferring more docile breeds, the sort of political caution that saw dull and predictable officers advanced over brilliant ones, Laurence might not have cause to blame himself: God knew he did not find the Admiralty faultless. But if there were something else—

Laurence looked out at Temeraire, who had not stirred out from under his wing. He could not think how he might question Temeraire on the subject, not after this unhappy misunderstanding; he could not make Temeraire feel still more wretched, perhaps without just cause. So he said nothing, while he thought what he might say; and he had still said nothing when a knock upon the door of his chamber interrupted his considerations, and Hammond without invitation thrust his head within, most anxiously. "Captain, I beg your pardon, we must intrude," he said, and opened the door for a messenger in pale green livery who followed him into the courtyard, and prostrating himself with a quick efficiency presented a letter bearing elaborate seals. Laurence took it up and opened it, and found therein a brief missive from the Emperor himself—a piece of enormous condescension which he supposed had been merited by the assassination attempt.

It contained wishes for his good health, an expression of outrage at the recent events, and concluded with a mild hope of seeing him, at some time. "His Majesty is most generous," Laurence said to the still-prostrate and waiting messenger, who seemed to be waiting for some immediate answer; but this did not satisfy him: or, at least, it did not make him rise. "Hammond, will you pray tell me how I am to answer this?" He held out the note.

Hammond read the letter through more swiftly than Laurence had managed to puzzle it out, and paled. "Good Heavens," he said, "we must go at once: and I suppose we have not the first thing for you to wear."

. . .

The Emperor did not look well: a heavy-set man and jowled, fatigue was writ upon his face; he breathed stentoriously and sweat gathered upon his thin mustaches and glistened to the sides of his chin and upon his forehead. Laurence began to realize what particular urgency had driven the conservative party to strike at Prince Mianning so blatantly: they foresaw him coming shortly to the throne. But the Emperor's ill-health did not place bounds on his temper; his expression was set in grim lines and a glitter of anger that revealed itself plainly when the formalities had been quickly dispensed with.

He was not enthroned in state, but received Laurence in a courtyard with his own Celestial, Temeraire's uncle Chu, coiled watchful and heavy along a raised dais behind a chair that was a simple and comfortable affair of wood. Temeraire had been permitted to accompany them only so far as the outer court of the pavilion; Laurence had been conscious of that anxious gaze upon his back as they had been ushered away into the inner halls of the palace, and thence to the great central court.

Laurence was not the sole guest; Mianning and Lord Bayan both had preceded him and were seated before the throne. Mianning was the nearer; Laurence followed Hammond's hissed whisper to seat himself at a distance between the two, and they all three faced the Emperor as if defendants at a trial. Nor was the simile inapt: with the flick of a hand the Emperor dismissed nearly all his attendants, save the well-armed and watchful guards; Hammond, too, was forced to go trailing reluctantly away, leaving Laurence to rely upon nothing but his own uninformed and lately doubtful wits. There was at first no difficulty, however, no call for decision; he had merely to sit and be thundered at in company.

"I scarcely know who to blame the more," the Emperor said, "for this upheaval of the Imperial court and therefore of the state, its mirror; for whatsoever evil begins here, it will show itself reflected tenfold throughout the nation! What madness should have permitted any man to lay a plot within their hearts upon my chosen heir and my adopted son? What reckless actions, in pursuing foreign involvement and disregarding the sage wisdom of centuries and respect for tradition, should have driven otherwise loyal servants of the court into such madness?"

Laurence wished badly for Hammond, adrift and struggling to pierce the veil of the Emperor's terms; but despite his inexperience he felt he understood this much: whatever the Emperor might choose to say officially, he knew in private all that had transpired. He surely knew: the cold rage in his eyes, beneath which Bayan flattened his head, was not merely that of a ruler jealous of disruption in his palace, but that of a father. He knew Mianning's intentions; he knew of Bayan's assault; what power struggle here transpired, he permitted, to some extent.

But only to some extent: and evidently that extent had been exceeded; he meant to rope them in one and all. Laurence felt cold anxiety settle stone-like in his belly: he did not need Hammond to tell him deadly shoals lurked beneath these waters, and he had neither pilot nor chart nor even soundings to tell him where they lay. One misstep and he might ruin all their hopes as effectively as Bayan might have wished to do. Laurence resolved to shut his mouth and say nothing, so far as he might; he would offer nothing but the meekest response. Mianning should have to speak for their side, if at all.

"I will hear your explanations," the Emperor said, concluding his tirade, and slumping angry back into his throne; he held a hand out and a cup bedewed with cold was placed within it. He drank heavily and put it aside.

Mianning prostrated himself, and quietly said, "My honored Imperial father, my trespasses against the wisdom of my elders would be unforgivable, save if by respecting that wisdom I should neglect my greater duty to the nation: surely it is my obligation to plant and tend the seed for a future harvest of peace and prosperity, that the fortune of Heaven will continue to smile upon our land. Though in summer the winter storms seem far away to those who must labor on the present harvest, they are coming nonetheless; and one whose shoulders do not yet bow over the sweep of his scythe may look towards the West, and see them approaching from afar."

Bayan said, "And in looking afar, mislead himself that the distant clouds he sees, which soon will disperse of their own accord, are grave dangers; and worse yet, in chasing a defense against them will forget what nearer danger threatens, and let the crow plunder his fields."

"This can only be the argument of all men who will not raise up their eyes at all," Mianning said. "For these clouds have lingered now long years, and the storm grows ever larger."

He made a quick gesture, and two servants scurrying unrolled a great map of the world over the floor: not entirely accurate as to shape, with China outsize and the other continents somewhat awry, but plain enough to recognize. "My father, already the Emperor of France, Napoleon, has stretched forth his hand to make alliance with mighty nations across the sea." France itself and all Europe were stained a dark green color; so, too, the Incan Empire and Africa: they stood like dark blots against the pale canvas. "His appetite knows no bounds, and already once have the evils of this foreign conflict crossed our borders, bringing the pestilence which struck at the ranks of our dragons, the breath of our nation. If not for your own foresight in having secured my brother's service with the bonds of filial devotion, and his courage on that occasion," he gestured to Laurence, who could only wonder what he had done to merit such an encomium, "who can say how many would have perished?"

"And yet what worse sickness, what worse miasma," Bayan said, "could enter our nation but the poison which their ships carry unchecked into Guangzhou? How many lives and souls have they destroyed with the crushed seed of the poppy, which makes men drown themselves by their own hand? Thrice have you commanded a reduction in this evil trade; thrice have they obeyed only with sullen reluctance, like disobedient children, and then stealthily permitted it to resurge. And it is the British, those to whom you have in your generous love given most license, who do the most evil in this regard by far. They are poisoners, and liars, and should all be banished from our shores.

"And, Dread Lord," he added, and Laurence glancing saw him press his forehead to the ground again, "I pray you forgive my humble words: I wish to offer no disrespect to the crown prince—"

Mianning's shoulders were stiffening, and the Emperor's eyes narrowed; Laurence had one moment to realize, *Now we come to it,* and then Bayan concluded, "—but I have received a report of General Fela, whom you charged with repressing the remnants of the White Lotus rebellion, and ensuring they did not flourish to regrow, that he has seen the British bringing those evil traitors aid, in the form of this evil drug."

"By God," Laurence said, too outraged to restrain himself, "—that is an outright lie."

He at once regretted having uttered a word, however justified; Mianning threw him a short unreadable glance, and the Emperor's eyes turned towards him. Laurence only at the final moment remembered to drop his own gaze, but he was caught: plainly he was now expected to speak. He saw from his lowered eyes Mianning flick his fingers towards the ground, and belatedly made another prostration himself, however reluctant. As he had dug himself a hole, he could only jump into it without complaining.

"Your Majesty," Laurence said, speaking to the ground, "I must beg to be excused from speaking on behalf of His Majesty's Government, for which I have insufficient authority; but I have not the least hesitation in most heartily repudiating the scurrilous accusation which Lord Bayan has made against my country which, if true, would be injurious not merely to her honor but to her sense, and which should defy all rational consideration. We have come here for no lesser cause than alliance against Napoleon. How could it profit us in any manner to create turmoil and distress within your borders, which should make you less able to aid us, even were we not the guilty culprits?"

He halted there, hoping at least he had not made matters worse; neither Mianning nor Bayan spoke immediately, which, Laurence rather dismally suspected, meant that he had spoken so far out of turn they had neither of them been prepared to respond to an outburst of the sort. The Emperor gave no sign of his own thoughts yet; but he left the field to them, and after a moment Lord Bayan bent forward and said, "Your Majesty's adopted son, who to do him credit has shown all the instinct of proper filial respect—"

The instinct only: Laurence supposed this was meant to hint at the deficiencies of his training and education in the same. "—all the instinct of proper filial respect," Bayan went on, "would scarcely be the confidant of those of his country-men intent upon such dishonorable behavior: even within a band of thieves one man of good character may be found."

"But not to deceive himself that his fellows are themselves honest men," Mianning said, "unless we are to believe him a fool."

They feinted back and forth a little further along these lines, it seemed to Laurence very much like two fencers feeling out their way onto unfamiliar ground, trying to ascertain which of them should take the better advantage from it, in which direction and what manner they wished to press the attack. And then abruptly Bayan made his lunge, adding, "And if nothing else, what he has said is surely true: China can ill afford to involve herself in the disputes of a foreign nation while strife rends the state from within."

"I am surprised to hear that you have so little confidence in General Fela's ability to put down the White Lotus resurgence," Mianning said.

"When a hidden hand props the foe from behind, and he is forbidden to strike at the true source of danger, even the greatest general cannot be expected to easily find success," Bayan said. "Perhaps," he added, with a false air of having been suddenly struck with a new idea, "the foreigners should be tasked to go to his aid, under the command of the Emperor's son and Lung Tien Xiang. If the British are responsible, they may correct their own wrongdoing. If they are not, they may do a singular service to the nation, and thereby properly merit some acknowledgment."

Laurence heard this proposal with dismay: he could well imagine what Hammond should say to their entire party being sent away from the heart of Imperial power to the hinterlands of China, silenced and expected to clear away a provincial rebellion that might be as much whisper and legend as armed force, and nearly incapable of defeat. Let a man be robbed on the road, and the conservatives might claim rebels had done it. And if the rebellion were real, were some truly dangerous insurgency against the throne, Laurence could scarcely imagine that their own party would be of particular use, stumbling over themselves in a foreign land. They might well merely be in the way, and in so being might make Bayan's accusations almost true.

He was all the more dismayed, then, to hear Mianning slowly say, "While rising from questionable suppositions, nevertheless Lord Bayan's proposal has merit."

Laurence could not help but stare at him, while Mianning serenely continued, "Though the remnants of the White Lotus may not yet have become truly dangerous, the creeping vine is best pruned back early, and with greater zeal than necessary. To send my brother—with a force appropriate to his rank—to see them put down and restore harmony, would be a wise course and a duty befitting his dignities."

It was little comfort to Laurence to see Bayan as taken aback as himself by Mianning's unexpected yielding. "What escort could the prince require other than his own company?" Bayan said at once, urgently. "General Fela and the army are there already—"

"And yet have so far been insufficient to halt this insurgency, by your own report," Mianning said. "Surely you would not propose that such a risk be taken with my brother, nor the honorable Lung Tien Xiang, who have not had the blessings of proper military training. When I myself first led men into battle, I was arrayed not only in armor, but with the wisdom of the senior officers who advised me."

Laurence could not like the proposal any better for Bayan's evident dismay; but neither he nor Bayan had any opportunity to object further: the Emperor had straightened in his seat, and it was plain the audience had reached its conclusion.

"My son Laurence," the Emperor said, "taking General Lung Shao Chu, and consulting at all times his advice and wisdom, you will gather three *jalan* of dragon bannermen and go south with them, to deal with the rebellion and uncover the source of these strange and evil rumors about your country-men, proving them false if you can. Return swiftly and victorious home."

He had scarcely finished speaking when one of the half-a-dozen scribes working busily by his side, the one nearest the throne, rose and kneeling before the throne presented him a clean copy of the orders upon a writing-desk. The Emperor took up a brush and signed, swiftly, and taking up the red seal pressed it down; the sheet was folded over thrice by the scribe's skillful hands even as he turned to offer it to Laurence, who with a sense of numb disaster bowed his head before it.

Chapter 10

"HM," SAID GENERAL CHU, deep in his throat, when he had been presented to the rest of the formation, and to Iskierka and Kulingile. Temeraire eyed him uneasily. His yellow crest had evidently with age sprouted a great golden-colored mane, which framed his broad flat jaws and the curving horns which bent away from his forehead, and the edges of his vermilion scales were tipped with translucence. He was not quite so large as Temeraire himself, smaller considerably than Maximus and Kulingile, and he was not a Celestial, of course; but somehow that did not seem to matter very much.

He had been very polite, of course—very gracious—on their introduction; he had bowed quite formally and correctly to Laurence and to Temeraire himself, with all the respect due to the Imperial connection. No-one could possibly have faulted his manners, only Temeraire could not quite help but feel that the general did not think very much of their company.

"Hm," General Chu said again, after a moment's silence in which they all stared at one another. "Well, we will not get to Xian any sooner. Let us be going."

"Oh," Temeraire said, a little taken aback. "Do you mean, now?"

Chu peered at him from under the bristling fringe of his mane, with an air of raised eyebrows. "Are you ill?" he said, with a hint of waspishness. "Is the chill of the day too great?" The day was in fact not in the least cold, an early-spring pleasantness in the air.

"No, only," Temeraire said, "are we not to take a great many soldiers with us?"

"Three *jalan,*" General Chu said, and paused as if waiting for Temeraire to go on; but since Temeraire did not know in the least what to say, after a moment Chu added, "Of course you would not expect them to gather all here and fly along the entire way with us," in heavy, pointed tones.

Temeraire had expected just that. He had been on fire, in fact, to see a proper Chinese aerial company assembled; and he knew Laurence and the other aviators were as deeply interested as he was himself. "Of course not," he said, a little abashed, and turning his head down murmured to Laurence, "Can we be ready to leave very quickly, Laurence, do you think?"

"He means us to leave on the moment?" Laurence looked at Hammond, and at the other captains; no-one spoke a moment in their confusion. Laurence had only returned two hours before, and had scarcely even had enough time to explain to everyone the Emperor's command.

Then Captain Harcourt said, "I suppose there's no reason to wait, if we *are* going. Have we any better notion of what to do?"

She looked around, and no-one answered her: they had all been debating just that, vigorously, before General Chu's abrupt arrival; but while disliking the orders, no-one could work out an alternative. Hammond had just been saying, "We *cannot* refuse this direct Imperial command—at least, Captain Laurence cannot, not and maintain any thin fiction of familial connection: and having lost that tenuous connection, they will assuredly not merely refuse our requests for alliance, but order us out of the capital forthwith, and revoke all those particular and unusual trading privileges which have so benefitted our nation, in the last five years—"

Temeraire, for his part, had no objection to taking Laurence away from here, where assassins lurked around every corner and he was not even to be permitted to deal with Lord Bayan as that treacherous coward deseved. Temeraire was sure that they should certainly be able to quash this rebellion handily, and it seemed to him as good a means as any for ensuring they should gain the alliance they required.

"Well," Harcourt said, when no-one had anything else to offer, "let us call it settled: I don't say we shall *stay,* but I don't suppose it will hurt us to *go*. Mr. Hammond, you would oblige me greatly if you would dash a few words to Captain Blaise in the *Potentate,* so he knows where we have got ourselves off to; and I dare say we can be off in a trice."

She turned and called to her first lieutenant, "Richards, we must get aloft: and there is not a moment to lose, if you please."

The aviators went into the tremendous scrambling rush of getting away: gear tumbled pell-mell into chests, the ground crewmen hauling up the belly-netting to the shouts of, "Heave! Heave!" and the officers leaping aboard. Temeraire watched with a little disgruntlement as his own crew went aboard Kulingile. Of course he understood that, according to the Chinese way of thinking, there was a loss of dignity in carrying so many men and going under harness, and for a Celestial to be so burdened was unthinkable; as a consequence, they had devised this arrangement for their journey to the capital from Tien-sing harbor. And while certainly Temeraire did not want to look undignified, he still could not like it in the least; he sighed.

"Will I come with you?" Junichiro was asking Laurence. Temeraire did not quite know what to think of him: he had been very ready to take Junichiro to his heart, when he had learnt everything that young man had done, to see Laurence safely back; but Junichiro had been so very standoffish; he had spurned Temeraire's thanks, saying, "I did nothing for *his* sake," and when Temeraire had asked him for lessons in Japanese, shipboard, he had refused with a flat, unfriendly, "Of what use could such instruction be to you? We will never return there again," and he had walked clear away across the dragondeck. He did nothing all the day but sit and stare across the ocean, or, since they disembarked, at a wall, it seemed to Temeraire; and though Laurence had asked Emily Roland to teach him English, Junichiro did not seem to be making any progress at all: he scarcely answered when she tried to make him repeat the most basic words.

Even now, he did not ask with any interest, only a cold question, as though he did not care either way, and did not very much *want* to come; but Laurence said only, "We are all going; stay with Midwingman Roland, if you please," and sent him up to Kulingile's back after her.

"Have a little patience: he has been a great deal bereft," Laurence said, as he climbed into Temeraire's cupped talons to be put up. "And I cannot give him any real work to do, until he has learnt English; we must let time work on him, and isolation. He is a young man: I dare say he will lose his taste for solitude, soon enough, and want some more society than he can get speaking only Chinese."

Laurence latched his carabiners on: Temeraire did not even need to shake himself and settle his own harness, as he had none but his polished breastplate, which O'Dea had looked over for him. "It is sure to tarnish sooner or late, with all this sea-air and flying," O'Dea had said, alarmingly, but when pressed had added, "though not yet: the rot lies far off in wait, for another day."

Leaning over to speak to General Chu, Laurence asked, "Sir, may I inquire, are there arrangements we ought make for our supply?"

"No particular arrangements will be necessary until we are closer to Xian," Chu answered, without even looking up. He had sighed heavily, watching their preparations, and had shut his eyes and lay his head down upon his forelegs to rest.

Those preparations were accomplished in under half-an-hour; he cracked one enormous green eye and peered out. "Are you ready at last?" he said, and heaved back up to his feet. "Very well, then," and coiling himself up on his hindquarters launched himself into the air. His wings were short, the veins and ribbing in green, and his body long and sinuous, so he went undulating as he flew.

"I do not see in the least what he has to object to; we went very quickly indeed," Temeraire said to Laurence, grumbling, and leapt after the general's dwindling figure.

A quartet of Jade Dragons, the tiny light-weight couriers scarcely much larger than a man, rose from outside the Imperial grounds to join them: the four of them bore long fluttering banners, red emblazoned with golden characters, and preceded General Chu in the air in a straight line. They led the way southward out of the city, the broad avenues and teeming marketplaces falling away to narrower streets thronged with men broken with the occasional great pavilion crammed with dragons sleeping or amusing themselves. Temeraire saw from aloft, as they passed an immense complex upon the outskirts of Peking, a handful of the most common sort of blue dragons playing some sort of game with stones, which he made a note to inquire about when he had anyone more sympathetic to ask than Chu.

The city yielded to settled sparse towns and then all at once to farmland and fields. Temeraire noticed large square markers set at regular intervals beneath them, dark grey stone engraved with white-enameled characters: they all bore the name of Peking, the direction to that city, and the distance. He pointed them out to Laurence. "That is very convenient," he said, "and I wonder we do not have them in England; it is much less trouble than having to follow a road, only to know where you are; I can see these from quite far away without the least difficulty."

"It is a clever notion," Laurence said, peering down over Temeraire's shoulder with his glass, "although I suppose it is no use at night."

But that proved not to be the case: as the evening fell, the letters still came onwards, taking on a pallid glow, faint but enough to make them legible for a little while as they swam out of the dark. "I cannot imagine how they are arranging it," Laurence said, trying to look through his glass. "Perhaps when we land we may have an opportunity to examine them. Temeraire, we must ask him for a halt in any case, not long from now; those fellows in the belly-netting must be allowed to stretch their legs. We are not flying to a battle."

They had gone nearly ten hours straight, without a pause; but even as Laurence spoke, abruptly General Chu and the Jade Dragons turned their course and began to descend gradually from the sky towards a pavilion, its eaves hanging with shining white lanterns and a thin trailing column of smoke rising from the roof, and they came to ground in a broad hard-packed courtyard before it.

There was a splendidly appetizing smell of roasted pig coming from within. The Jade Dragons stepped aside and bowed their heads, and Chu also stepped to one side waiting for Temeraire to precede him in, which was as satisfying as anyone could wish, and when he had gone in he found a high-roofed hall, splendidly formed of what looked to be entire tree-trunks bound at intervals with polished bronze, and a handsome dinner laid on for them already.

At the head of the table, waiting, was Prince Mianning; and to his either side several dragons, both Imperials and the scarlet war-dragons, but that was not the important, the very important point: one of the dragons was Mei.

"The dangers of your charge are many, I am aware," Mianning said, "and the chance of failure is great; but the rewards of victory will be commensurate."

His servant was pouring the tea with great carelessness; it slopped freely to every side, leaves and liquid spattering hot across the table and even to the ground. The dragons had sated themselves all upon roasted pork, and most of the aviators as well, and fallen into a stuporous sleep well-earned by their day's long exertions; it was surely almost the middle of the night. Laurence alone had been invited to join Mianning within the inner chamber, for this final leavetaking, although he half-suspected Hammond of sitting by the door outside with his ear pressed to a crack.

"My intention is to send Lung Qin Mei with you," Mianning

went on as the servant with ceremony handed him and then Laurence a cup, of a brew which had a peculiarly smoky and strong flavor, bitter on the tongue. "This will ensure further opportunities for conception; and should we be fortunate and an egg produced, will also enable you to keep the news concealed from the capital as long as possible. With your company, sheltered amongst foreign dragons and away from the Imperial household who are ever-watchful for such signs as mark the coming of an egg, she may conceal her state a long while. You and your fellows may then hide away the egg, and perhaps bring it back to the palace in secret.

"For the rest, I hope you have seen the advantages of the situation. You will travel under our banners, and with a company of three *jalan*. Should you succeed in your mission, nothing will be more natural than to send a similar force westward with you, to your war against Napoleon."

Laurence did appreciate that advantage, but not in the least the high-handed way in which the situation had been thrust upon them. Hammond's endless strictures still rang in his ears, but he and Mianning had gone through fire together, quite literally, and though the crown prince could not at all be said to have a manner which encouraged license, Laurence determined to take the bull by the horns. "Your Highness, I beg your pardon for speaking plainly, but I cannot undertake to commit even myself, much less my country-men, to this mission: not for any length of time and certainly not for the time required to produce an egg. We are certainly *not* responsible for the resurgence of this native rebellion; we cannot contribute materially to its end. Mr. Hammond has urged our going, rather than defy the Emperor's will openly; but I cannot conceive our long remaining, kicking our heels in your back-country. There is open war in Europe, and if our party seems to you insignificant to that effort, I assure you by the standards of our own nation it is not. If you desire this alliance as much as we do, then I must tell you that we will require some excuse for our returning, sooner rather than late, if you do not mean us to give it up."

Laurence had no idea how this was received: Mianning heard

him out with no evidence of either impatience or sympathy. "We must permit events to unfold," Mianning said only. "The situation of your army in the West is naturally of great concern to you." Polite enough, but making no promises. "I suggest that you take this opportunity to observe the work of General Chu, and of our *jalan:* this will afford you opportunity to gain a better understanding of the management of aerial warfare as its principles are understood by our nation." He did not say outright that he felt their understanding of those principles was far superior to the British, but he hardly needed to.

"When we have actually seen scale or tooth of any other dragon in this so-called company," Captain Warren said, with some asperity, when Laurence had recounted his conversation, "it will be soon enough for us to be amazed. I suppose we have managed well enough against Boney, even with that Chinese worm of his whispering advice in his ear. If these fellows will only give us a few dozen beasts, I will thank them well enough, and they can keep their principles."

"Pray not so loud," Hammond said, glancing worried over his shoulder: he had nearly suffered an apoplexy at Laurence's account. Mianning and his escort had already departed, but Chu droned in sleep in a warm forward corner of the pavilion, and the Jade Dragons lay in a neat row against the entry wall. Laurence did not think they were in any state to overhear, despite the thin gleaming slits of their eyes still cracked ajar, but the impression of being observed lingered, and he could understand Hammond saying, "Perhaps we ought to retire, gentlemen; we will surely have a long flight ahead of us again on the morrow."

They parted, the captains each joining their own beasts; Laurence went first to see how his crew were settled. A folding screen, pilfered in haste from their quarters in the Imperial palace, made at least the illusion of a private space for Mrs. Pemberton and Emily in the corner, although when Laurence tapped and was invited to look in, he discovered that rather in defiance of their respective rôles, Emily had placed herself nearer the open floor, and her hand rested in her sleep upon her unsheathed sword.

Mrs. Pemberton yet sewed by the light of a candle. "Yes," she said ruefully, "I am afraid she insisted, and asked what I would do if someone did choose to come in. As I had no answer to give but that I would certainly raise a cry, she told me I could do that perfectly well from behind her, while she taught the fellow a sharper lesson."

"I am sorry to subject you to such a journey," Laurence said; she had been swept along in their general pell-mell departure, but now he wondered if he ought send her by some escort back to the *Potentate*. He made the offer, but she avowed herself quite willing to endure the hardship.

"Emily has offered to teach me how to shoot her pistols, and to reload them," she said, "and I believe I will take her up on the offer if you have no objections, Captain. Not that I am truly concerned at present, but as I understand it, we expect to be joined by a large force of soldiers?"

"How large," Laurence said dryly, "remains to be seen."

He bowed and took his leave of her, making note to speak to Forthing about arranging some guard of steady and respectable men for the ladies. He had not yet decided what to think of his first officer: it was perhaps the worst of his loss of memory, to have no measure, no sense, of those on whose judgment he had to rely; and he was the more disturbed to have some cause to doubt them. At least Forthing so far seemed steady enough—he was no gentleman, it was true, but that was a charge which many a good officer of the Navy could not answer. But Laurence knew nothing of him in any difficult circumstances, under exigency.

The rest of his men were sleeping on the other side of the folding screen, bundled into rough blankets and bedrolls. O'Dea and a few of the ground crewmen were engaged in a muttered game of cards, their legs stretched out around them and their deck so worn that the faces could scarcely be distinguished.

Baggy was sitting with them; Laurence silently caught him by the ear and drew him up and away, the boy scrambling to his feet wincing and stifling a yelp. "Take his cards, will you, O'Dea?" Laurence said. "Sleep well, men; we will do what we can tomorrow to see you do not have so cramped a time of it."

"Ah," O'Dea said, scooping up the cards, "and two queen in his hand; well, 'tis the wages of sin." He tossed them into the discards. "No call to go to great lengths, Captain, when we are flying into a hive of very iniquitous rebels: the Old Nick can make us dance even if our legs are stiff when we get to him."

The other ground crewmen did not look very enthusiastic about this description of their prospects; Laurence sighed inwardly, but only nodded them good night and hauled Baggy away. "Sir, I didn't think there were no—any harm in it; they're only playing for pence," Baggy said, tipping his head sideways to ease his ear, and trying to peer at Laurence out of the corner of his eye at once.

Laurence let him go at his empty bedroll, near the other officers. "You have been advanced before the mast, as it were," he said, "so I will make allowances this time, Mr.—" He stumbled; he realized he did not even know Baggy's real name. "—sir," he substituted. "But you are an officer now: you cannot sit to cards with the ground crew at night, with men twice and more your age, and then make them give you precedence in the morning. Nothing could be less respectful." He paused, glancing over: Junichiro, who shared quarters with the junior officers, was sitting yet awake on his own bedroll; he was looking steadfastly down at his hands, and pretending not to observe the lecture.

"You will show Mr. Junichiro the ropes," Laurence said abruptly to Baggy, "beginning tomorrow. We will put a little more harness on Temeraire, and you will come aboard, as my servants; I dare say the Chinese cannot object to that. You will take him above and below while we are aloft."

"How am I to learn from *him*?" Junichiro said, with at least some sort of a spark, even if it was of dismay, when Laurence had conveyed this programme to him in Chinese. "He does not know any civilized language, and he is—" Junichiro hesitated, for lack of the word, but Laurence did not require it said aloud: Baggy was indeed not very prepossessing, and no-one could have called him gentleman-like.

"As you must learn English, however uncivilized, before I can seek a commission for you," Laurence said, "that must not be a bar; and Baggy is an officer of the Corps, regardless of his manners. You will sit together on the left shoulder, and inquire of me if you require a translation now and again: you will have to climb over to my position to do so, but it will be as well for you to have that practice." He left them staring at each other, satisfied himself if they were not. At the very least Junichiro would be diverted some more from his desolation, and Baggy from seeking inappropriate society; and Laurence relied on the power of boredom to make them learn to talk to each other eventually, trapped aloft for ten hours at a time: Baggy was a sociable creature, and might with his very lack of sensibility wear down Junichiro's resistance.

A separate inner chamber of the pavilion had been set aside for Temeraire's use; but as he had withdrawn to it with Mei after their dinner, Laurence was far from wishing to interrupt them. He had delayed as long as he might, however, so tentatively he looked inside. To his relief, the two dragons slept already, with their noses only touching; and he found a separate sleeping alcove set aside where his own things had been laid out, the archway leading to it closed off by heavy drapes.

He roused early and found the main chamber empty: going outside he saw Temeraire at some distance from the pavilion, an enormous bulk in the midst of a bare field peering intently at something on the ground; he looked up when Laurence called his name and came towards him. "Pray come and see," he said, "I admire it very much." It was one of the carved numbers, and at this close range Laurence could see the white paint lining the sides of each carved channel had in it a great many silvery flecks, polished to a mirror-shine, which evidently caught whatever starlight or moonlight offered and brightened the characters thereby.

Everyone was awake when they returned to the pavilion, and rousing for the day. "Is there more of that pork, anywhere?" Maximus asked, yawning, his eyes half-open.

"Pork!" General Chu said, when Temeraire ventured to ask him, and snorted disapprovingly. He bounded across the chamber to Maximus and, seizing in his jaws one of the tall reeds from the wall, which carried a banner, thwacked him soundly on the hindquarters.

"Oi!" Maximus said, rousing up, "what does he mean by that? Temeraire, tell that fellow to stop, or I will pin him down."

"Hah! Will he!" General Chu said. "Well, if he is awake, then, tell him to get aloft and stop looking for more food: we will eat to-night, not weight our bellies down for a long day of flying, and if he is sleepy and hungry in the air, perhaps that will remind him to eat more porridge to-night, instead of only gulping meat as though he were a dog. We are on campaign!"

With this rejoinder he put down the reed and stalked outside to make ablutions: a large fountain stood outside gushing from a tall stone pillar, fed somehow from underground; he drank thirstily and deeply from the gush, then thrust his head into the deep pool which it fed, and flinging it back let the water pour off his mane and cascade down his back to the ground. Then he flew some short distance to the nearby midden.

"It don't make any sense to me; we've always stuffed them full as they could hold, when we were going to be doing any long flying, if there was food to be had," Granby said doubtfully, when Laurence asked him his opinion. "But we can't drum them up some pigs from thin air, and I don't see any here, so we must lump it for now whether it's good advice or no."

They followed Chu's example at the fountain, and got themselves aboard again, not without some stifled sighs from the ground crewmen, who could see ahead another day of endless crammed-in flying. "Pray forgive us, Larring," Harcourt said, to her own ground-crew master. "I don't mean to use you all so unkind. While we fly to-day, piece out the spare leather into belt-harnesses for you all, and beginning tomorrow we'll have you take it in turn to latch on to the back harness yourselves. It will be good for the officers to have some exercise climbing about, anyway; it's been too long since we had maneuvers."

She added to Laurence and Granby afterwards, before they themselves mounted, "But it will slow us down, if they have to be clambering all over creation while we fly, with only belt-harness. Will there be any more dragons, any time soon, so we could let the fellows ride?"

That question was answered late that afternoon: beneath them the markers changed, and instead of Peking the name of another city was shown, unfamiliar to them all; General Chu glancing down saw it, and said something to one of the Jade Dragons. The green dragon nodded, with three quick efficient jerks rolled up her banner, handed it on to the second, and wheeling shot away into the upper air and south-easterly, vanishing with almost unbelievable speed.

She returned scarcely an hour later, dropping back into place, and took up her banner again. They flew on another two hours, and as the sun descended Laurence saw in the distance four dragons, three red and a blue, gathered at a marker up ahead. Even as their own company approached, the party leapt aloft to meet them and fell into place off their left flank and slightly above, in a simple arrow-head formation, the blue dragon at the rear and center. The leader, who wore a thin flat band of silver about his neck, bobbed his head respectfully to Temeraire and to Chu, but not a word was said: they all flew onwards together.

Laurence could crane about to peer at them more closely, at least at their underbellies, and could see the other aviators doing so all amongst their company. The three red dragons wore a kind of light armoring, thin hammered plates sewn together and bound very near the skin; it was heaviest at the pockets where the legs met the body, padded a little there. They carried not a single man amongst them; Laurence had seen a few upon their backs, but those were not visible from below, and did not at any time come climbing into view.

The blue dragon, on the other hand, wore no armor but bore a silken carrying-harness, some thirty men aboard in rows down its sides, and long nets between those rows bulged with supplies. It flew a little below the red dragons, and Laurence realized after a time observing that where the three red beat their wings in time, the blue beat his at a pace off-set and quicker, three to each stroke of the larger beasts. "I wonder if it improves his speed," Laurence said.

The next day two more such groups joined them; the day after, another. By the end of the first week, as they crossed the border into the neighboring province, they flew with forty dragons at their back.

Chapter 11

CHU CALLED HALTS NOW two hours earlier, and these occurred in staggered fashion: first he landed, and the formation with him, accompanied by one of the four-dragon clusters; the rest of the body flew onwards, and might be observed for some distance ahead landing two groups at a time in sequence, spreading themselves out across a wide territory.

No sooner did these land but the crew were leaping off the blue dragons, bringing with them the packed nets, then the blue dragons all went aloft again and flew off to either side of the course of their flight, returning an hour later with motley supply acquired, Laurence could only guess, at storehouses and villages around them, which all of it went into cooking-vats already prepared by the crew and full of boiling water. Bags of grain formed the largest part of this supply, with only a few oxen or sheep or pigs to leaven the porridge, and there was now no opportunity to pick out the meat: all went into the pot and was cooked an hour, then served out.

"It does not seem right they should all have to work so hard when we only sit and wait," Temeraire said, observing their labors, but Chu, overhearing him, shook his head.

"We are too big to spend our time on supply," he said. "We must save our energies for the heat of battle."

"But it is far more pleasant to do the fighting, and have someone else bring your dinner," Temeraire said. "I do not understand why anyone should agree to do it."

Chu shrugged. "They are paid twice, of course."

"Oh," Temeraire said, with a nearly longing sigh. "Twice?"

"General," Laurence said, listening to their exchange in some surprise; it had not occurred to him that dragons might be paid at all, "might it be possible to bring on a few more such dragons to aid with our own company's supply?"

Chu immediately bowed to him formally and said, "It will be done at once," and vanished off issuing orders before a startled Laurence could even say he had only meant to ask, and not to command. By dawn the next day three more blue dragons had joined their own party, bringing carrying-harnesses, and the much-relieved ground crewmen were given leave to be carried on their backs.

Laurence began to suspect that he had merely given Chu an excuse for what the general must have longed to do: the blue dragons and their crews managed to snatch away all the supply meant to go in the belly-netting while the British dragons were refreshing themselves at the fountain, and they were already packed and waiting expectantly for boarding before anyone had seen what they were about. Harcourt uncertainly said, "Well, I suppose it would be churlish of us to insist they give us back our baggage," and the dragons went aloft with only their officers, with a marked increase in speed.

"I would be glad to be enlightened," Chu said to Temeraire as they flew that day, "why the rest of those men may not go and ride aboard the porters also."

"Well," Temeraire said, "the officers are needed in battle, of course: if we should be attacked by surprise, we would not like to be taken aback."

"Ah," Chu said. "And may I inquire why we are to expect an ambush under the present circumstances?"

This was a fair-enough question. Their company had ceased to grow day by day, but it did not need to grow any further; it was difficult to envision so massive a force meeting with any kind of truly unexpected attack. Laurence had not known what three *jalan* would be, neither had any of them: it was staggering to think that a company of this size might be so casually assembled, and sent to deal with a mere provincial unrest. He did not think he had heard of forty dragons being brought together in England since the Armada.

"We had sixty at Shoeburyness," Granby said that night, over their own helpings of porridge, "during the invasion; and Napoleon brought over a hundred, though he had to send a good number of them back. So it's been done, but not at the drop of a handkerchief, I will say."

It was plainly the substitution of porridge for raw cattle which made so vast a difference in what force could be fielded, Laurence supposed: he would have expected it to take more of a toll on the size and strength of the beasts, but though none of the Chinese soldier-dragons approached the sheer massive bulk of Kulingile or Maximus, they were by no means undersized.

"For my part, I should not mind sending our men onto those porters," Sutton said: Messoria's captain, the oldest of them, and a fellow of much seniority. "I expect Chu would like us all to fly lighter, and I cannot blame him; we are bounding their speed."

Captain Berkley grunted his own agreement, setting down his mug of beer. "I will tell the fellows to strip Maximus bare," he said, "and have them go aboard those blue dragons: I can cling on to a neck-strap well enough by my own solitary self. Do you suppose they will really let us take these beasts, after this rebellion of theirs is put down, only because we've pranced about and waved a sword with them?"

"If so, I would call the help cheap at the price," Sutton said, and all the aviators murmured in agreement. "I would be glad to see Boney's face if we show up on his eastern doorstep with these forty fellows at our backs: a nasty shock for him, I would say, and all the more so with the Army in the Peninsula nipping at him from that side. He won't be looking for us to have so many beasts, not after—"

He halted; the conversation fell into an awkward silence; all eyes turned towards Laurence. Laurence had meant to ask how matters stood in the Peninsula. "You will excuse me, gentlemen; good night," he said instead, and went away from the fireside; shortly their conversation resumed at a louder and a happier pitch behind his back.

He could not blame his fellow-aviators for preferring his absence; their situation was a complex and a precarious one, and they could not be glad for any reminder of the disordered state of his mind when he made so crucial a member of their company. He was uneasy himself; about too many things. He stood in the cool night air, looking out past the fires. They were sheltering this night in an open field, dotted with their handful of tents and the great lumps of the sleeping dragons. At the center of the camp stood the one enormous and—to his mind—absurd silk-draped pavilion erected for Temeraire: a cleverly contrived sheet of wooden shingles sewn together, which could be rolled for carrying; unfolded and stiffened with poles, and mounted on tall shafts, it formed a high roof from which enormous drapes of red silk hung billowing in the wind. It was wreathed also in thin wispy trailers of fog: Iskierka lay not far away, upwind of it, glaring at the elaborate structure and emitting envy and steam together.

Laurence's own tent, a gaudy but more prosaic affair, stood directly beside. At the moment, though, Temeraire and Mei lay entwined within the pavilion still; Laurence could not immediately seek his bed without intruding. He turned aside instead, and went slowly through the avenues of their small encampment, until he saw Hammond's tent on the lee side of a small rise, with Churki sleeping half-curled about it.

"A moment, please, I beg your pardon," Hammond said, rummaging urgently in his packs, which had only just now been delivered him from their luggage; he did not enjoy flying, and had still less enjoyed the last strenuous stretch. "Ah, there." He took out a sheaf of folded and mostly dry leaves, which he moistened with water and put into his mouth to chew. "I ought never have left them with the baggage; those porters took it away, and I have not had a leaf all day. Thank Heavens," he said, lowering himself to sit upon one of the camp-stools. "Forgive me, Captain: what did you say?"

"That I cannot account for it, sir," Laurence said, remaining himself standing. "The size of this force is nothing short of extraordinary. Lord Bayan ought have moved Heaven and earth to keep them from being assigned to my command. He ought have retracted his accusations, and protested, sooner than promoting this expedition in any way.

"I should not like to think he or this General Fela had any cause to believe such a thing," Laurence added, "—that we should be offering aid to these rebels; much less any proof."

"He can have none, none at all," Hammond said, with a firm nod, "and indeed I scarcely know how we are supposed to have managed it: that we should have somehow supplied the wants of a gang of rebels from so distant a position."

"By the sale of opium, as I understand it," Laurence said, watching his face, "shipped to their shores, the profit of which is also meant to be our motive, as little as that ought to answer for any honest man. Mr. Hammond, do our factors in Guangzhou knowingly disregard the prohibition on the importation of this drug?"

He asked it abruptly, half-ashamed to ask; his suspicions, as inchoate and confused as his memories, troubled him. He did not wish to accuse, he did not think any accusation merited.

But, "Oh," said Hammond, with an easy shrug, "no more than you might expect. There is scarcely any market here in China for most of our goods, and enormous markets for their goods in the West: the deficit was quite unmanageable, until opium was introduced. His Majesty's Government was very alarmed by the quantity of specie flowing out at the time, very alarmed indeed; the drug quite reversed the situation.

"Naturally," he said hastily, glancing at Laurence's expression, "naturally, that does not mean—that is, I do not mean at all to say that we are promoting any evasion of the official regulations. Only, there is a certain ebb and flow, in these matters. A limit is established which is excessively severe—it drives prices higher—we make our best efforts to impress it upon the merchantmen—but Captain, you must know it is difficult to make men restrain themselves when they have risked their lives to go around the world, and they can double the profit of their journey by smuggling in a chest or two—"

"Thank you, I have heard enough," Laurence said grimly. "I dare say it is difficult to make men restrain themselves, when you wink at them."

Hammond flushed. "I must reject such a characterization of the work of our factors," he said, "—utterly reject it, Captain; I wish you would not insist on reducing such tangled matters to angels and devils. And in any case," he added, "I do say categorically we have not the least interest in promoting this rebellion: I assure you I myself have scarcely heard of it, save as a piece of distant history; they were put down years before I ever came to my post.

"On that, I am happy to give you my word: and if that does not suffice, sir, I am afraid I cannot satisfy you," Hammond finished defiantly.

Laurence left him without courtesy; he thrust the drape of the tent out of his way and strode out angrily into the darkening camp, voices mostly fallen silent. He was *not* satisfied; he was by no means satisfied. He remembered his vigorous words in the Emperor's chambers, to Mianning himself: they now felt like more than half a lie. He would not have spoken so if Hammond had told him this much beforehand. It had not occurred to him that any representative of the King, or even the officials of the East India Company, would endorse maneuvers so deceitful; and if they would, what more else might they not do? It had not occurred to him—

But after all, it had. Laurence slowed his steps and halted. He had doubted, and felt that doubt gnawing at his belly, when he ought not have. Even now he was merely unhappy; he was not surprised.

He had reached Temeraire's pavilion. Temeraire lay within, Mei beside him, both of them heavily asleep after their dinner and their congress. Laurence stood silently by Temeraire's head, listening to the sighing breath with all its sussurations; he half-wished to wake him, to unburden himself. But Laurence did not feel he could confide in Temeraire with Mei mere paces away; he scarcely wished to speak any of it aloud at all. If Hammond were lying—

Laurence shook his head to himself; no, he would not think so, even in the back of his mind, of a man he had no right to believe vicious. Hammond had spoken to him frankly and then given him his word, when he might as easily have concealed all. But he need not be lying, merely himself unaware. What if there *were* some more vicious and less official plot under way?

Laurence could too-easily imagine opium smugglers, already subtly encouraged by their own government and eager for more profit, might well decide to fuel an internecine conflict to open fresh markets for their wares; and perhaps to undermine the Imperial authority which was too plainly their only real restraint, if they knew the British Government would applaud them so long as they brought back shiploads of silver and gold, regardless how obtained.

In three days' time, they would be in the mountains, hunting for whatever traces might be found of the rebellion. Laurence hoped that they would not find any condemning evidence of British involvement—a wretched, cowering thing to be forced to hope for. But if such a plot were under way, if any proof were to be found, that would destroy any chance of alliance—would condemn them all, and very likely bring Mianning down with them.

Laurence tried to persuade himself he was wrong, that he was unreasonable even to fear; and yet he was unsuccessful. "I would almost wonder if I am fevered," he said, low, "if this is some lingering consequence of the injury to my mind; that I now entertain thoughts of the darkest nature—"

"Captain, I cannot think it at all likely," Mrs. Pemberton said.

Laurence had unburdened himself to her only hesitantly, unsure what counsel she could give him; he could not disclose to her all his thoughts. He could not confide any particulars to her which should in any way tend to discredit their country. He had said nothing of opium, nothing of smugglers, nothing of the accusation that British plotters might support the rebellion; he spoke only in the most general terms, and of his own mind.

But he had begun lately to find her company a balm against his own confusion of mind and spirit: a relief from questions and from the anxious tension of his fellow-officers; her conversation a welcome change from the constrained silence that fell upon the others so often. Her cool and sensible nature was itself a worthy solace, but better than that, she was no close connection of his own; she had been employed for Emily's protection only a little more than a year, and they had not been intimates previously, his own time preoccupied by his duties and his fellow-officers his true companions.

She said, "I cannot speak with very much authority on your past; however, sir, I will speak for your present: you are a rational man, and if you have fears, they are founded on sensible causes. I do not mean to say you may not be mistaken: certainly you may, and you speak in such forboding terms to make me hope you are, whatever it is you fear; but you are not in the least given to building castles in the air.

"I am no physician," she continued, "but I have had to do a great deal of nursing in my life; and I have seen illness and injury alter a man's character or a woman's to no little extent. But not in such a wise that you would appear yourself in every other respect, act according to your former character at all times, and remain competent, save in this one particular instance. That, I must find too remarkable to believe—I am sorry if that opinion should distress you, in this circumstance, more than please you."

He was silent; she was not wrong, that was the heart of it. He would willingly have heard himself called a lunatic to find his fears unfounded. "I must always value your honest opinion," Laurence said, "whatever its conclusions; I thank you, sincerely, and for imposing on you in such a manner."

"There is no imposition felt, Captain Laurence, I assure you," she said, and looked up as footsteps came: a moment later, Emily had put her head around the corner of the folding-screen to see them sitting outside the tent, before the fire.

"Oh," she said, "Captain, I didn't know you were here; did you want me for something? I have just been over at the next fire over those rocks: and you needn't frown, Alice, they are all girls there."

"Oh, dear," Mrs. Pemberton said, with a sigh.

"Not that sort!" Emily said. "I mean soldiers: more than half of them on the dragons are girls. Not just the captains, though some of them, too; but nearly all those fellows who manage the baggage. I dare say we ought to just bunk in with them instead of perching out here away from everything."

For safety, their campfire had been established at the very edge of camp; their tent was of double thickness and sheltered further by the folding-screen: Laurence had solicited a pair of pistols, from the aviators, for Mrs. Pemberton, and had shown her how to send up a flare, if need be.

Laurence stared at Emily. "Do you mean to tell me half their army is women?" he demanded, to his dismay recalling he had without the least consciousness stripped and bathed at several of their previous nightly halts, in full view of Chinese companies. "Are the dragons so insistent upon it?"

"It's not the beasts at all," Emily said. "They tell me they can come instead of their brothers, if their families like, so they don't have to spare the boys from the fields."

"Well," Laurence said, helplessly. He found it difficult to accept, and yet he was no pot to be calling names for kettles: if not his daughter, then a young woman under his tutelage was in the service; he could scarcely condemn those families, if it were the accepted mode. But he should have to tell Forthing and also his fellow-captains at once: if the men should work out they were surrounded by an encampment full of young women, they would surely run riot and make nuisances of themselves, given half an opportunity.

"Are they willing," he began to ask, and then Emily leapt at him, in one straight bound across the small campfire, and knocked him to the ground as a sharp blade thrust down through the air towards him.

Emily rolled away from him, and came up drawing her sword; Mrs. Pemberton with a cry had fallen back upon the tent. Laurence drew his own sword: five men were descending upon them, drawn metal gleaming in firelight. Their sabers were peculiarly workmanlike: a wide blade at the tip and tapering to the hilt, and they wore black that made them almost invisible against the dark; one scattered the fire with the end of his sword, stamping out embers. Laurence swung a wide circle leaping forward to press them back, and seized one still-burning branch; he thrust it towards the nearest man's eyes and then fell back with Emily, putting the tent at their backs before the men closed in.

The steady rhythm of sword-strokes occupied his next moments to the exclusion of thought: no room for anything but answering to one strike and another. He and Emily had the reach of them, their own blades the longer and the better, but they were outnumbered. She fought well at his side, matching his pace. There was a brief opening; he shouted, "Ho, the camp!" at the top of his lungs, "Murder!" and they were fighting again.

Laurence bent to parry low, and only just in time brought his sword back up to catch a slash meant for his throat. Another did catch him in the shoulder, but he wrested himself away before he felt more than the tip scoring his flesh; he heard the thick wool ripping away around the blade, and dropping the burning brand managed to reach up and wrench the blade away from the man's grip.

But he was forced to pay for it: the third man, on his left flank, lunged for Laurence's exposed side with two knives in his hands, feinting one at his eyes. Laurence turned to slash back, but Emily was there, her sword flying upwards, and she sheared away the man's hand halfway to the elbow, blood spurting from the stump; she reversed her grip on the blade and jammed it brutally through his chest, and booted his corpse off with a shove of her foot into the other standing beside him.

Now there were four: Laurence whirling back struck one of the men upon the bridge of his nose with the pommel of the short sword he had taken, and then ripped the man's throat with the blade as his head tipped back.

A pistol-crack came jumping-loud from over his shoulder, deafening in his ear; Laurence felt a few hot flecks of burning powder on his chin, and saw a thin thread of smoke rise from his sleeve; a hole stood in the chest of the man on Emily's left. Mrs. Pemberton stood pale with the smoking pistol in her hands a moment, then she let it fall and reached to raise the other from the pocket of her skirt; Emily, turning, snatched it from her hands and shot another.

"Captain!" a shout came, "Captain Laurence—" and a young man, his personal servant Ferris, came scrambling over the rocks; Forthing was on his heels.

The last attacker looked at the corpses of his fellows and the approaching men; Laurence caught for his arm, but too late. The man turned his blade inwards and throwing himself away fell upon it; when Laurence turned him over with his foot, his eyes beneath the sooty mask were staring blind and dead.

"Good God," Ferris said panting, coming to a halt; he held a pistol, which he carefully uncocked and put back onto his waist. "You are not hurt, sir, I hope?"

"Nothing to signify," Laurence said, looking at Emily, who did not show blood anywhere. He was a little torn: surely it ought to have been his own duty to shield her from danger, and yet in the moment he had not the least difficulty classing her with himself as a combatant, and he could not help taking a degree of pride in her skill and courage; she had been as resolute a fighter as he could have wished at his side. "Ma'am, I trust you are well?"

"I must be," Mrs. Pemberton said, though she had not let a tight grip on Emily's arm. "I am perfectly untouched; only, very shaken. Emily—"

"It takes you so, the first time," Emily said to her, consolingly. "Pray don't give it a thought; that was a very pretty shot. What? Oh! No, I am fine; they didn't get a touch on me. They scarcely tried: I don't think they cared a lick about the two of us; they meant to kill the captain."

"And it will be wonderful, at this rate," Iskierka said with mean satisfaction, "if these assassins do not get their way, when you are always busy making up to this Imperial flirt of yours, and paying no attention."

Temeraire would have hissed her down, but he hardly could; wretched guilt silenced him. He ought have been there; no assassin ought ever have been able to get so close to Laurence. "Only," he said unhappily, "Laurence ought to have been asleep—or at least, safe within the camp; I do not understand how he ever came to be so exposed."

He clawed the dirt of the clearing; whyever had he gone to sleep without seeing Laurence properly settled? He thought Laurence had only gone to have supper with the other captains; Laurence had told him to rest and be comfortable—surely Temeraire ought have been able to rely on him. Laurence could not have imagined Temeraire would be in the least comfortable, knowing that Laurence was endangering himself.

Iskierka snorted. "It is easy to say, he *ought* to have been asleep: he wasn't, he was nearly being stuck with swords," she said. "I don't see that you should be blaming him, when you didn't take the trouble to look out for him properly. You may be sure, Granby," she added, "if you ever are a prince, I will not begin to neglect you; not that I am very sorry anymore that you are not, since all it would mean is that people were always trying to kill you."

"Come, dear one, pray don't stir up Temeraire," Granby said, coming from the tents. "Temeraire, there's no harm done: Laurence hasn't a scratch."

"He does too have a scratch," Temeraire said, "—upon his shoulder; and his coat has been ruined. Whatever was he doing so far from the pavilion?"

"You cannot go calling a mere pinprick a scratch," Granby said, "and I am sure we will put him in the way of a new coat, soon enough. He went out there to have a word with Roland, that's all."

But Laurence had *not* gone out to speak with Emily. "Why, I wasn't there," Emily said, when Temeraire asked her later, as they packed for resuming their flight, what had been so urgent as to induce Laurence to go so far upon the outskirts of camp. "I only came upon them later; I suppose he wanted to talk to Alice. Mrs. Pemberton, I mean," she added.

"What?" Churki said, lifting her head up abruptly from her sniffing over the packs, and ruffling up the feathers of her collar. "What is he doing with Mrs. Pemberton?"

"Lord, *I* don't know," Roland said. "He likes to talk to her, I suppose because she's a gentlewoman; you know he is ever such a stickler."

"Hrmmr," Churki said, frowning, but then she smoothed down her feathers. "Well," she said to Temeraire, "I do not have a *real* claim, and I suppose Laurence is older; although I *had* thought of her for Hammond. But I do not mean to interfere," she said, as though making a handsome concession.

"Interfere with what?" Temeraire said, in alarm. "Whatever do you mean? I am sure Laurence does not think of her like *that,* at all—"

"Why should he not?" Churki said. "She is a hearty young woman: she might bear him children for twenty years, if they begin quickly. Certainly they should neither of them wait any longer; a man should begin to have children at twenty, in *my* opinion, and a woman at sixteen."

Temeraire stalked away from them and back to the pavilion. "I do not see why she must always be on about Laurence marrying," he complained in some irritation to Mei, who very kindly put aside the poetry she was reading to comfort his distress. "Laurence has quite enough to do, as it is. He has his crew to oversee, and there is the war, which we must contrive to win; and when that is done, there will be our valley, and I dare say I will find him another fortune, sooner or later, which he will have to manage. I do not see that he at all ought to marry."

"Well," Mei said, "if he is not married already, certainly he ought not without the Emperor's approval, and the choice must be carefully made. There is no call for a prince to marry in haste; concubines may suffice him quite well."

"Aren't those a sort of whore?" Temeraire said, doubtfully. "I know Laurence does not hold with visiting those—"

"No, no," Mei said, "a concubine, bound to him and him alone; surely that woman who travels with you, who is under guard by your young soldier, is one of his?"

Temeraire flattened down his ruff. "No!" he said. "That is Mrs. Pemberton; she is Emily's chaperone, and why we must needs have brought her along, I am sure I do not in the least know! Laurence hasn't any concubine, at all."

"What, none?" Mei said, staring at him with her eyes widening.

"No," Temeraire said, suddenly wary.

"None!" Mei cried. "Prince Mianning has seven: one has borne him a promising boy of four already, with another child coming soon. However is he to have heirs?"

So Temeraire spent the day's flight in high dudgeon, speaking to no-one. Why would everyone see Laurence married? He did not see that it was anyone's concern, other than his own. "You are quite well, Laurence?" he asked, turning his head around. "Are you certain you are not feverish, and warm through?"

"I am perfectly comfortable, I thank you," Laurence said, tiredly, and fell silent again. They had searched the camp through and searched again, of course, all the rest of the night and in the early hours of the morning, looking for any trace of the assassins—whence they had come, what their purpose, but without a trace at all.

By the end, General Chu had shrugged and said he supposed the men were mere outlaws, having made the attempt only to get at Mrs. Pemberton and Emily. Which was perfect nonsense: Emily was quite a remarkable young officer, but Temeraire did not see that there was anything out of the ordinary about Mrs. Pemberton, nor why anyone should have gone to particular lengths to get at her.

"I must suppose," Laurence had said to him and to Hammond, after they had given up the futile search, when morning light at last coming had uncovered nothing more of use, "that this is another endeavour of the conservative faction."

"I will make the argument, sir, if I may," Hammond had said to Laurence with a somewhat stiff tone, "that *this* explains their willingness to permit this expedition. To separate you from the Imperial court, exposed to such blatant attempts as these upon your life which their partisans may nevertheless easily explain away, must be sufficient good in their eyes, and preclude the notion that they must have some *real* complaint to make.

"I suppose," he added, "that we may expect more of these assaults, when we have reached camp: General Fela is, we know already, one of their partisans; and they must rely on your death, in severing the one formally acknowledged tie between our nations, to remove the impulse to alliance."

"Then we ought not go any further," Temeraire had said, in high alarm. "We ought to return at once to the court; and then I *will* squash Lord Bayan, and that will put a stop to these assassination attempts."

But Hammond had protested at once, and Laurence shook his head as well. "Prince Mianning has had the right of it: the reward we seek is proportionate to the risk we run," he said. "An alliance between our nations might well change the course of the war and the fortunes of all Europe, if not the world entire: we cannot give up the chance of it merely for a personal fear. This force alone, if we can bring it to bear smartly, may well make the difference between victory and defeat."

He had gone to sleep then in his tent having been awake all the night; and now when Temeraire glanced back towards him, Laurence had drifted once more to sleep again. Temeraire wished he had made Laurence promise to keep close to him at all times henceforth, and in particular not to go speak with Mrs. Pemberton again: when Laurence woke, he would discuss it with him, perhaps. He was only not entirely certain how to open the conversation: he shied from the thought that Laurence might object, might dislike the request.

"Temeraire," Baggy said, calling out to him through cupped hands, "be a good fellow: will you tell me how to say 'spend the night with me'?"

Temeraire obliged him, but asked, "But why should you need to ask Junichiro that? You are already quartered together."

"No, no," Baggy said hurriedly, "I didn't mean to ask him; I don't mean to ask anyone; I was only curious."

"He means to ask one of those soldier-women, I suppose," Junichiro said, contemptuously, "in defiance of your captain's orders: a shameful lack of discipline."

"Oh!" Temeraire said. "I dare say he is right; what are you about?"

"What did he say?" Baggy said, eyeing Junichiro doubtfully.

"That you mean to pester the Chinese soldiers," Temeraire said, "even though you know very well Laurence has said not to."

"I don't!" Baggy said, with a quick furtive look over at Laurence, who yet slept. "Only we are coming up on a city, and I dare say there will be a girl or two about; that is all. And what business is it of *yours*," he hissed, to Junichiro.

Temeraire had been drifting himself, with more attention to the air currents than to the landscape; now he looked ahead. There was a blue smudged haze on the horizon, a long narrow blot. "That is Xian," General Chu said, peering ahead, "and we have all made good time, I see."

"We all?" Temeraire said, and squinted. There were five small clouds converging upon the city—clouds which might each of them have been a flock of birds. "Baggy, perhaps you might wake Laurence," he said uncertainly.

Baggy clambered carefully over to rouse Laurence; Junichiro was standing in his own straps, his eyes shaded with one hand, staring. Laurence came awake at once and opened his long spyglass; he gazed through it in silence. "Yes," Laurence said finally. "Those are dragons. Temeraire, will you ask Chu if those companies are coming to join us?"

They were all nearing the walls of Xian, at almost the same pace; already Temeraire could make out the long banners flying before each of them, and the steady rhythmic beat of the wings: each one a company the size of their own.

"Of course; did the Emperor not command three *jalan* attend to this task?" Chu answered over his shoulder, absently; he himself was eyeing the companies on their way, critically. "But Commander Li is a couple of *niru* short, I see. Well, we will recruit them from the city outpost here: it is good for fat guardsmen to get a little exercise."

That evening, Temeraire looked down from an enormous pavilion, established upon the fortified city wall: two hundred dragons and more sleeping beneath him, many in other pavilions, some draped over the walls, others on the open ground at their base; several of the companies had gone to encamp some distance from the city, and their fires might be seen dotting the low hills. Laurence stood beside him, a hand upon his foreleg, with Forthing near-by and Ferris also; scarcely any man of the aviators had said a word, since the company had assembled.

"I understand from General Chu that we leave early on the morrow, Mr. Forthing," Laurence said finally. "Pray encourage the men to go to their sleep, if you please, and let us get those camp-followers out of the pavilion; they will never get any rest otherwise."

"Yes, sir," Forthing said, touching his hat; he lingered looking for a moment more, and turned away.

"We cannot reach the mountains in less than another week, I suppose," Temeraire said to Laurence, trying for nonchalance: he felt a little daunted, though he did not like to admit it, by the size of their assembled force. "We must be a little slower, with so—so *very* many dragons."

"I imagine so," Laurence said, soberly. He gave Temeraire's flank a pat and sought his own bed, and Temeraire settled himself; the only one left awake was Junichiro, who was standing half-hidden against one of the pavilion columns, nearly at the edge, still looking down at the great crowd of dragons. "You had better go to sleep also," Temeraire said, yawning. "Not that you are doing anything much, but you will have to get up and go aloft, anyway."

Junichiro said, low, "I have never heard of so many dragons gathered."

"Well," Temeraire said, glad to exchange his own private surprise for authority, "of course China is a very large country, and they know dragon-breeding very well here, and dragon-husbandry. There is really nothing very unusual in the size of this force; it is nothing to be amazed at, after all, when there are so many dragons here. I dare say the Emperor could call together an army ten times the size, if he liked."

Junichiro was quiet again; Temeraire half-shut his eyes and had just begun to drift off comfortably, before Junichiro abruptly asked,

"That transport ship we came upon, the large one—how many are there, in Britain?"

"Well, we captured two French, only last year," Temeraire said, "so I think we are up to twenty; they take a good deal of building." He yawned again, pointedly, but Junichiro did not take the hint, and only kept standing there; and then Gong Su came climbing up the stairs from the ledge below, and bowed. "I hope I am not intruding, Lung Tien Xiang; I only wished to see that you and His Highness have everything you might require, and that you are satisfied with our preparations, and the humble force under your command."

Temeraire sighed; he could hear Maximus snoring away behind him, and he was very ready to go to sleep himself. "Yes, there is nothing wanting, thank you very much," he said politely, however. "I understand we will be leaving very early in the morning? It is very kind of you to look in on us, but I am sure you should be asleep as well: Laurence has already gone to bed.

"And if you have any questions," Temeraire said to Junichiro, hitting upon the notion to divert him, "I am sure Gong Su can tell you anything you would like to know, about the *jalan;* I was only just telling him," Temeraire added, "that of course, this is not an exceptionally large force: that China has so many dragons, that one cannot really be astonished."

Gong Su looked at Junichiro thoughtfully. "Indeed. If you are interested in such matters," he said to that young man, "perhaps I will speak with His Highness. There might be a place for you in the service of the crown prince: it may well be that relations with your nation will at some point assume a closer character than at present, and I do not believe we have very many officials with knowledge of your tongue."

Junichiro paused, then bowed. "I am honored by your consideration, but I cannot think of leaving the service of Captain Laurence."

"As you wish," Gong Su said, and made his good nights, retiring formally and disappearing again down the stairs; Temeraire meanwhile had roused up again to eye Junichiro doubtfully.

"I cannot see why you would say such a thing, when you have not the least interest in doing anything, or even learning English: it seems to me you would do very well to stay here and help the crown prince, if he means to make better friends with your country."

"China is no friend of my country," Junichiro said flatly, and looking one last time down at the immense dragon-horde below turned and vanished into the back of the pavilion, to bed down amongst the other officers.

They woke early and the aviators breakfasted only lightly; there was nothing but a bit of porridge for them, and water for the dragons. "I cannot conceive how such a force is to be supplied or maintained at all," Laurence said to Temeraire, as he went up again. "We must surely strip the countryside bare as we go."

But as they all began to go aloft, several dragons of varying colors in green-and-gold trappings took up positions throughout the flying armada, and raised a strident chant to which the larger dragons all matched their wingbeats: they began at once to set a grueling pace, greater by far than their speed before. Temeraire had not been hard-pressed so far, during all their journey. Even now, of course, he was not at all *struggling,* but he had to keep his head down and think about every stroke to keep up their speed.

Before the sun had reached its zenith, they had covered a hundred miles of distance, Laurence told him: they were flying nearly fifteen knots. Temeraire would not at all have minded a pause for rest or drink or food, but none was called, and he did not at all mean to be the one to propose it. General Chu himself did not seem to be having any difficulties, and he was a great deal older. Poor Maximus and Kulingile were both of them having a bad time of it, however, and late in the afternoon Berkley raised signal-flags to say he was dropping behind, and would catch them up shortly. He signaled Demane, too, to keep with him; the two huge dragons sank towards the ground. Temeraire privately would not have minded at all stopping to rest with them, if only he could have thought of a way to suggest it, between one wingbeat and the next.

The mountains grew before them all afternoon. In the foothills, as they drew near at last in the late evening, Temeraire glimpsed below a supply depot prepared for them, surely over weeks: pens holding cattle and swine, and enormous granaries; oh, how he would have delighted in a cow, that very moment. The very thought of the sweet gush of juicy blood upon his tongue made his ruff prick forward for a moment.

Their force, he abruptly realized, was breaking apart again into smaller parties, three or four groups splitting away from the main body at one time, the blue dragons diving to take up some supplies from the pens below, and each such company then vanishing into the craggy mountains, to some ledge or cavern or hidden valley. They overflew a few of them already busy making camp, and Temeraire was wondering how much further it would be to their own, when at last they came over a ridge and saw outspread below the bowl of a valley full of tents, and in the middle of an open landing ground several men in armor, one of them in the lead with a splendid cloak, and with them a large wooden chest.

The Jade Dragons with their banners had already landed, and disposed of themselves to either side of the landing grounds; General Chu was stooping towards them. Temeraire came to earth beside him, making a great effort to descend gracefully, easily, as though he were not in the least tired; but he *was* glad to fold his wings. And then General Chu said sharply, "What is that smoke coming from, there to the west?"

The man in the cloak bowed low and said, "Honored General Chu, we have this very morning destroyed a stronghold of the rebels: and if those in your company are British, we gladly await their explanation for *this*."

He turned and beckoned: the chest, nearly six feet long, was carried forward; Temeraire saw to his surprise it was a sea-chest, the front painted with a banner reading LYDIA. They flung the lid open, and inside to the very lip was loose sackcloth, and the chest was heaped with large round balls, wrapped in faded brown petals. "What is that?" Temeraire said over his shoulder, to Laurence, who was gazing down upon it with a hard and grim expression.

"Opium," Laurence said.

Chapter 12

GENERAL FELA WAS YOUNG for his rank, but his hands and his face were those of a man who had spent his life not in drawing rooms but in the field, hardened and sword-callused and leathery with sun; his mustaches and his queue were trimmed to an efficient length. His pistol-belt and swords all of them showed heavy use.

He led the way personally up through the silent ruins of the village: a small creeping terraced place, ancient and clinging to the mountain-side, grey stone mortared to make the walls and steps of the narrow lanes that wound between the houses. The door of the largest house stood thrust open, and blood spattered the floor; the bodies had been removed. Laurence followed Fela and his soldiers inside, grimly, and stood looking in the courtyard: two dozen chests and more, stacked upon one another to the height of a man's head.

"We followed a British dragon to this place," Fela said, coldly, "bearing more such chests. The guilty culprits fled before our approaching forces, however, and left their allies to their destruction."

Laurence looked at Hammond, who did not answer, but only stood in pallid silence.

They went back out through the village. The attack had evidently come in the early hours before dawn, and the town had been brutally punished for its support of the rebels: cattle and goods stripped, citizenry put to the sword. The streets echoed emptily beneath their boot-heels, and the doors stood open, ruined.

A poor mountain village, worth nothing to anyone but its citizens; and now all of those were dead. Laurence could see the marks of talons and jaws, where roofs had been ripped away, walls torn down; and through one gaping hole as he walked along the dusty, smooth-cobblestoned lane he saw a cradle, empty and overturned, blackened with smoke. Laurence was not unused to blood nor to brutality; God knew he had seen more than enough men dead, falling corpses into the ocean or hacked apart with saber and cannon-fire. And yet when he stood looking over the empty and ruined village, his stomach twisted wrenchingly with disgust: a passionate horror.

"Was there more opium there?" Temeraire asked, from where he stood nearly upon the outskirts of the village, leaning anxiously over the roofs.

"Yes," Laurence said shortly. "Twenty thousand pounds' worth, or near to it; a monstrous amount."

"Oh?" Iskierka suddenly raised her head. "Is opium worth so much? I have never heard that, before. What do they mean to do with it, now that they have taken it?"

"Burn it," Laurence said.

"*That* seems a great waste," she said, in disgruntled tones.

"I cannot—I cannot by any means account for it," Hammond said, in much agitation, when they had returned to the encampment.

The British party had been directed to establish themselves on the western side of the valley, separated pointedly from the rest of the forces by a wide furrowed line of open dirt, with sentries posted along it and a dozen of the red dragons encamped surrounding them. "To do honor to the prince, and to Lung Tien Xiang, and ensure none should trouble them," Fela had said, coldly, paying lip service to the fiction of Laurence's command.

"I thank you," Laurence had said, and did not argue; he was himself savagely angry. Across the camp, Chu was directing that his own pavilion be raised up at the farthest point from theirs, beside Fela's tent.

Their baggage had been heaped carelessly at the boundary, and the cauldrons of porridge: not a generous allotment of the last, particularly when Maximus and Kulingile dragged at last into the camp; the dragons were snappish and sharp at one another over the pots. Spent from their long and arduous flight, however, they were too weary to quarrel long; the porridge was eaten quickly, and they all collapsed into sleep almost at once.

Hammond's tent had been put up near the center of their encampment, surrounded for privacy by the tents and pavilions of their own men; Churki slept now half-circled round it, the steady heaving of her side gently swelling the back panel of the tent.

"It will be a wretched mess, if we have to fight our way out of this," Catherine Harcourt said to Laurence, low, as they ducked inside Hammond's tent together, with the other captains. "If those twelve can hold us long enough for any reinforcements to come up, which I suppose is what they are thinking, we will be sunk. Our only chance will be to bull out through them as quickly as we can—Lily in the middle, Temeraire and Iskierka on her either flank, one pass to clear out anyone before us, and then they give way to Maximus and Kulingile, and we all fall in behind the two of them and make due west. How we are to contrive to win home, with no supply—"

"Pray keep your voice down!" Hammond said. "There can be no call to begin planning so disastrous a course. I grant you the circumstances are awkward—"

"Awkward!" Harcourt said. "Hammond, we are landed in the middle of the largest aerial army of which I have ever heard tell, and now they are only waiting for word that they may put us to the sword and claw."

"Word that will not come," Hammond said. "It is preposterous, the idea that we should have provided opium to these rebels—that we should have somehow delivered it here." He blotted his forehead with the back of his hand and looked around his tent, anxiously. "Where are—ah." He dug after his pouch of leaves. "I assure you," he said, folding over a hunk of crumbling leaves with hands that shook, "there must be a misunderstanding. In the morning, I will consult with Lung Qin Mei—we will draft a reply. There are any number of possible explanations. Perhaps these rebels meant to sell opium in order to fund their efforts; it does not follow that *we* must have been involved in their crimes."

"And I suppose," Laurence said, reaching the end of his temper, "that this ragged band of rebels have somehow contrived in their small and impoverished territory to acquire the funds to purchase so enormous a supply?"

He rose to his feet; Hammond stepped back from him, warily. "What use do you imagine it will be to defend ourselves against other charges, when we have already been proven so demonstrably false?" Laurence said. "Twenty chests of Indian opium, of the same make, packed together and certainly from a single British ship. This is no private, no individual endeavor; this was not concealed from the eyes of our factors. This is no secret winking. This is deliberate, orchestrated defiance of the law, and our guilt *there* is undeniable."

Laurence was grimly aware that a courier had already flown for the Imperial City with the news of this latest discovery. He would be obliged to follow it with his own; he would have to make excuses, to scrape and connive at justification. He would have to let Hammond put falsehoods into his mouth, or see his men and fellow-officers condemned, his country-men in Guangzhou chased out, all hope of alliance ruined. And he could scarcely see any hope for averting that fate even if he did all this.

"You have made me a liar, and yourself," he said, bitterly, and stalked from the tent.

Outside the last of the tents had gone up, and the night had gone quiet: the quiet of a prison camp. The ground crewmen and the junior officers were sitting wearily at their fires, supping on the remnants of the provided food. Several knots of officers stood looking across the boundary line at the rest of the camp and the twelve red dragons drowsing along it: not with more caution than was deserved.

Granby ducked out of the tent and joined him, watching them. "Laurence, I don't mean to tell you not to be angry: this is a rotten hole for us to have been put into, all because some fellows in Guangzhou want to line their pockets," he said, after a moment. "But there's a stink to this all around. Fela hasn't told all the truth, either."

Laurence looked at him. Granby said, "Where is this British dragon supposed to have come from, that he says was lugging these chests? It's the sort of thing he might imagine: I dare say all their merchants ship goods dragon-back, here. *We* don't; we haven't any merchant dragons. Even our courier-beasts don't come to China: we can scarcely get one to India four times a year."

"And yet those chests *are* from Guangzhou, and from a British ship," Laurence said slowly. "They were conveyed here somehow."

"I suppose so," Granby said, "but they weren't brought by a British dragon, and if Fela says they were, he's a bare-faced liar."

"I beg your pardon; I am distracted," Laurence said, to Mrs. Pemberton: she had spoken to him, and he had not attended, for the lingering turmoil in his mind. "Thank you, tea would be most welcome."

He had not slept easily or well. The ruined village lingered in his mind, in his dreams; he saw again and again the cracked stone houses, the mill fallen silent, the walls blackened with smoke and the claw-marks standing pale against them. Again and again he had walked through the street, hearing somewhere distantly the roar of dragons, with a strange and dreadful sense of familiarity: perhaps because it might almost have been an English village, a village of Nottinghamshire on his own father's estates, pillaged so and broken. He had woken unsettled, cloudy.

The day stood before him without direction. He had still the charge, in theory, of finding this rebellion and putting it down, but it was hard to imagine how he ought to carry that out. His command had never been more than a nominal fiction, and if Chu's sympathies had not been with Lord Bayan and the conservative faction from the beginning, they were surely fixed in that direction now.

He had contemplated crossing the camp to Chu's pavilion and speaking with him. "I hope you will pardon me, Captain," Hammond had said, cool and formal with him after the previous day's reproof, "but I must urge against it. Let us not forget the attempts upon your life. In the present—difficulties—your death would surely be the cap to the efforts to sever relations between our nations. I must ask you to remain within the camp."

Hammond had spent the rest of the morning in Temeraire's pavilion, drafting the letter to the Emperor, with Mei offering him advice on the choice of argument and phrase. Mei had regarded the chests of opium with a stony expression as they were brought out of the ruined village, and afterwards had curled herself to sleep without any word to Temeraire, or any of them; but at least she had remained in his pavilion. She had met Hammond's request for assistance that morning without pleasure, but with a nod of her head.

She had as little choice as he did, Laurence supposed: the conservative faction would surely try to use this to topple the crown prince, if they could, and certainly to undermine his plans for modernization. But to her, the British could be now nothing more than a gang of ruffians, smuggling poison into her nation and conniving at treason; she could scarcely have liked any better than Laurence did, to attempt to defend their acts.

But Hammond had written the letter; she had helped him; Laurence had signed his name to it, and one of the Jade Dragons had borne it away. Then they had all three of them retired, separately: Hammond, with a short bow, to his tent; Mei curled into a corner of the pavilion in pointed silence. Laurence had gone to see Mrs. Pemberton settled: he had ordered that her tent be pitched as near Temeraire's pavilion and his own as possible, and had begged the most reliable men from the other captains' crews to stand guard.

She gave him a cup of tea: to his surprise, with milk. "There are some sheep down there below," she said, with a ghost of a smile, "and Emily has made several acquaintances amongst the young women. They were kind enough to find us a milch one and liberate her. The ewe is picketed down that crevasse, over there, so she needn't be troubled by seeing the dragons, poor creature. The flavor is not quite right, but at least it is something."

She had also somehow assembled and kept a service, though a small and motley one: her two cups were now the handle-less Chinese sort, and the saucers wide and smooth; the sugar bowl was of Portuguese make, evidently acquired in Brazil; the teapot, plain earthenware, had been given her by the American merchant in Nagasaki. She stirred her cup with a chop-stick inverted, and her hands did not shake, though she looked still drawn: it had been only three days since the attack, and those full of wearisome travel.

"I find nothing wanting, I assure you," Laurence said. "I hope you are recovered?"

"I would be ashamed to be anything else," she said, "when I was of so little use, and in less danger. I hope I am not so poor-spirited as that."

"More than a little, of both danger and use, ma'am, I must protest," Laurence said. "But I am glad if you are well."

She drew a breath and sighed, then looked away across the camp. "May I confess something to you, Captain?" she said. "I hope it will not make you very angry, but I should like to clear the air, on my side—I should like to be quite frank."

Laurence paused and set down his cup upon his knee. "By all means; I hope you need never even ask, to speak so," he said.

"I was shocked, very shocked, when I first understood Emily's position," Mrs. Pemberton said, "when I first knew she was an officer. I thought it the most outrageous thing I had ever heard, to see a mere girl imposed upon in such a manner, from childhood; and I must admit, sir, I thought—I assumed—she was surely imposed upon in the other manner, as well."

"I cannot reproach you," Laurence said grimly. "What else is anyone to imagine, who knows a little of the world?"

She nodded. "If she had given me the least encouragement, I should have taken her away with me at the first opportunity—the first ship we met—and laid suit in court to see her respectably established," she said. "I was quite ready to name you a villain, and all the Corps with you."

Laurence looked at her in surprise, and some respect; he could not fault her impulse, even if he knew it could hardly have found a less willing object. "*That* encouragement," he said, "I know very well you did not receive."

"No," she said. "She quite abused me for an idiot."

She laughed and exchanged a rueful glance with Laurence, who could well imagine the nature of Emily's reaction, and her scornful answer; she had griped to him often enough, in only the last month, about being saddled with a chaperone at all.

"And now instead I must say I do increasingly see the justice of her complaint," Mrs. Pemberton said, "though I would be sorry to lose my post; I cannot see that I am of the least use to her."

She fell silent, and after a pause quietly added, "I dare say I would not at all like to be an aviator. But there is nothing quite so unpleasant as to find oneself so wholly dependent on another's protection, in such dreadfully visceral circumstances. I would cheerfully have exchanged a life of hard service to be able in that moment to defend myself."

Laurence offered her his handkerchief; she waved it away, and drew out her own to press to her eyes briefly. "I beg your pardon," she said, "and I am done with being a watering-pot. I will have Emily teach me to fence, if I can learn; and oh! I am sorry now I sold my husband's guns after he died, for I would be happy indeed to have a pair of pistols of my own."

"I should be happy to be of service to you in the matter," Laurence said, "when we next have the opportunity."

"Thank you, Captain," she said. "I would be grateful."

He took his leave of her to return to his own tent, pausing when he saw Temeraire standing watching him, his tail lashing in so uncontrolled a manner as to threaten the supports of his pavilion. "Is there something wrong?" Laurence asked him, in some concern; Granby had given him to understand that the danger he had been under was likely to provoke some long repercussions of watchfulness and anxiety, but Temeraire could hardly suppose him to be in danger from a conversation with Mrs. Pemberton.

"Oh!" Temeraire burst out. "Do you *wish* me to stay in China, then, and let you go away from me, so you *may* be married, and have as many children as you like, and a house again?"

Laurence stared, astonished and bewildered. "What?" he said.

Temeraire was nearly trembling with resentment and indignation, which Laurence could scarcely understand. "*Her,*" Temeraire said. "Whyever are you always speaking with her, and going to her tent? And why has her tent been moved so close to your own?"

"Do you mean Mrs. Pemberton?" Laurence said, in no diminished confusion. "She is under my protection, and was lately abused by ruffians—" He stopped, helplessly: he had not expected to find jealousy in a dragon, and still less so much imagination. "Do you—I beg your pardon, have you any reason for supposing I mean to marry her?" he asked, in sudden alarm. "Had I—before my loss of memory, had I—had I made her any promises, or expressed to you any intentions, in that quarter—"

"Oh! None at all," Temeraire said, "but what does that signify, when you are so dreadfully altered, and everyone thinks you should marry; even Mei does, even if she does not call it marriage. She thinks you ought take a concubine, and *ten* of them at that."

"I may confidently promise you to do no such thing," Laurence said, much relieved and beginning to be half-amused, "and I have not the least notion why anyone should concern themselves with my marriage, save myself and my nearest relations."

Temeraire calmed a little; at least his tail settled slowly to the ground. "And you do *not* want to marry her?" he said.

Laurence looked round; it was an outrageous subject for conversation, and Temeraire's voice could not be called discreet. "Pray let us go inside," he said, "if you wish to speak any further on the subject," and went as far to the back of the pavilion as he could, and seated himself on the cushions there. Temeraire sat before him coiled tightly, and curled his tail around his limbs, still radiating wary distress.

"I should begin," Laurence said cautiously, unsure *how* to begin, "by asking you whether you object to the lady in particular, or to the—to the event, in a general way?"

"I do not see anything particularly remarkable about Mrs. Pemberton at all," Temeraire answered, "which should make her in the least suitable for you. After all, you are a prince of China, and my captain, and you have been in a great many battles. Whatever has *she* done, to brag of? But I do not at all mean to be rude," he said, in succession to this piece of outrageous rudeness. "I should not like it in the least if you were to marry anyone else, either."

"Pray explain to me a little further," Laurence said, wondering if it would console Temeraire to be assured of his own ineligibility; few gentlewomen would contemplate throwing themselves away upon an aviator. "I would by no means distress you, but I had not been aware of any objections you might have, nor that my marriage—not that I contemplate any such step at present—should be any bar to my continuing to serve. So far as I knew, while aviators make poor material for an eligible woman, we are not barred from establishing a home, and—and I beg your pardon, but Roland has given me to understand that providing you an heir is rather in the nature of my duty."

"Well, *I* have never wanted an heir," Temeraire said, snorting. "I should certainly never wish to replace you with another, no matter the circumstances. I understand Excidium feels differently about the matter, and I do not at all mean to criticize, but that is *his* business. For my part, I do not see why I ought to be expected to like it if you should be married, only because it means that someday, if you should die, there might be another person I might like. It is all very airy and unreasonable, it seems to me, and I do not care for it at all."

"Well," Laurence said, "if it will relieve your mind, I will promise you not to marry without seeking your consent: I must consider your feelings as engaged in the matter as those of my family, and I can conceive of few circumstances in which I would proceed over any objections you might express."

He hesitated, then; he could conceive of one: namely, an obligation which could not be escaped. "Temeraire," he said, "before I can make you such a promise, however, I must ask you whether I should be obliged by decency to—that is—" He drew a deep breath and bluntly asked, "Do I owe Admiral Roland an offer? Is she—is Miss Roland my daughter?"

"Why no, she is not, at all," Temeraire said, in surprise. "Her father is some aviator in the North: we have never met him, and I do not think Emily has seen him over three times in her life. Whyever would you suppose she were your daughter?"

"You have relieved me greatly," Laurence said, but the relief was short-lived. Temeraire went on, "After all, Admiral Roland has only been your lover since the year five, and Emily was nine when you met; how could the two of you have made her? But it doesn't signify," Temeraire added in tones of reproach, "for you have already asked her, and she wouldn't have you, because she was your commander."

So Laurence hardly knew whether to laugh or be mortified: it seemed his life the last eight years had been a succession of scandals and outrages, which he ought have blushed to think of. To have intrigued with an unmarried gentlewoman, and a fellow-officer no less—

But Temeraire, perceiving his distress, misread the cause; he said in a small voice, "Why, Laurence—do you *wish* so to be married? I knew that you were quite unhappy that Miss Galman would not have you, after—after I was hatched."

"Did I offer for her, then?" Laurence said, glad that at least he had been decent enough to give *her* the opportunity to refuse him.

"—yes," Temeraire said, with a hitch. "So—so I suppose you do wish to be married, whatever you have said." He fell silent, and then with a very evident summoning of all his resources said in determined tones, "Well, then I suppose, if Mrs. Pemberton will be sensible and not wish you always to be leaving me to go and be with her, and will not expect you *always* to be having children, and if she will not mind coming back to live in our valley, in New South Wales, after we have won the war—"

"I beg your pardon!" Laurence said, raising his voice to stem this torrent of conditions. "Temeraire, I have not the least desire to be married to Mrs. Pemberton, I assure you. And when should we have been living in New South Wales? There can hardly be any call for dragons, there."

"—when we were transported," Temeraire said in surprise, "Oh," he added, "I suppose you do not remember *that,* either? Laurence, it is very inconvenient you should recall nothing at all."

Chapter 13

LAURENCE COULD SEE GRANBY speaking softly with Harcourt and Berkley; they had trailed him to the edge of the escarpment and stood now at a distance together, all of them looking at him warily as though they imagined he might fling himself over, and as though they would have been sorry for it if he had. Even though he was a traitor—a convicted traitor. Even though he had carried aid and comfort to the French, deliberately, of his own free will, and undermined thereby a stroke which might have averted the invasion of Britain.

An appalling stroke, one which would have meant the slow and dreadful death of a thousand dragons or more, a deliberate plague-bearing—but notwithstanding this, a stroke which had been commanded by his officers, by his Government, and through them by his King. He had betrayed them all, and the invasion of his country might be laid at his door.

"Laurence," Granby said, low, coming to his side, "—pray will you come back to my tent? Temeraire is frayed like a torn rag already, and he'll be worse the longer you stand out here. He is watching you."

Laurence did not answer; he could scarcely yet form thoughts in his own head. The worst of the matter was to be unable to recall what should have shaped his choice: he had committed no mere act of passion. He had acted with deliberation. He had also been pardoned, Temeraire had urgently told him, pardoned and even restored to the list of officers; but Laurence felt that he would have given up that pardon, given anything, only to *feel* again the sentiments that had driven him to such an extremity.

But he did not; he did not remember, and only now understood that he did not know himself any longer. He did not know how he ought to feel. Temeraire had evidently driven him to the act; a court-martial had condemned him; the Government had pardoned him. But none of these facts could tell Laurence whether he had condemned himself, or ought to, and whether he should long since have separated himself from Temeraire as ought a sailor shut his ears to the Sirens.

Granby gently took his arm, and Laurence after a moment let himself be drawn away. They walked slowly back across the encampment, past the watchful, suspicious looks of the red dragons. Laurence did not look towards Temeraire's pavilion, but ducked into Granby's tent; there he took the glass of strong rice liquor Granby offered him and swallowed it straightaway.

"I'm damned sorry," Granby said, sitting on a chest. "We ought have found some other way to break the news to you, whatever Pettiforth and Hammond said; we must have known you could not go forever, not learning of it. I suppose we have all been telling ourselves you would remember, surely, any day now." He leaned over with the bottle, and filled Laurence's glass again.

Laurence took another hot, too-bitter swallow. "I think I can scarcely blame myself," he said, low, "if having forgotten, I did not wish to remember *this.*" He downed the rest of the glass and asked abruptly, "I beg your pardon: may I ask your opinion of the act; of the—" He stopped; he did not put a word to it. He did not know what name to give it; he did not know why Granby should consider his feelings, in the least, nor tolerate his company, in the face of it. But he desperately wished to know.

Granby hesitated a moment and then said, "I haven't anything to say, Laurence. I was damned glad the French had the cure, and so was any aviator worth his salt, in my opinion. They asked me, you know, if I'd had a part in it; they asked all of us, and all I could tell them was you wouldn't have taken any help, and I wouldn't have thought of it. And that's too paltry for words. Anyway," he added, "you wouldn't have, either; Temeraire came up with the notion."

"Yes," Laurence said.

"I don't deny it was ugly," Granby said, "and I dare say it has given you a sad turn now, but—but do recall, we have all come about. Boney would have got his hands on the cure sooner or later anyway, and he would have come over anyway. And he'd be in England still if Temeraire hadn't brought half the dragons out of the breeding grounds and to the war with him. You've your pardon, now, and you're restored to the list."

"A pardon cannot restore a man's reputation," Laurence said, "and still less his honor, if lost." He was silent, and then said, "I suppose I was pardoned for Temeraire—that the Corps should continue to have the use of him."

"Well," Granby said.

Laurence nodded. He wondered bleakly if such a motive had kept him by Temeraire's side; if he had clung to his post to save himself from hanging. But even as he had the thought, some instinct rejected it. He finished the glass and put it aside. "I beg your pardon," he said quietly, "I cannot suppose I concealed my feelings from Temeraire at all well, and he was distressed already. I must go and speak with him."

Temeraire huddled in his pavilion, as wretched as ever he had been; it seemed to him disaster followed directly on disaster. First their shipwreck; Laurence's peculiar brain-fever; the assassination attempts which so nearly had succeeded; then the discovery of the opium, which might ruin everything—might prevent an alliance and leave them at a standstill. Mei had been very stiff and withdrawn, since then. She said she had accepted Temeraire's assurances that *he* had known nothing of the smuggling, and neither had Laurence, but she had not wanted to try again for the egg since then; and all the other dragons in the encampment kept a cold distance.

But all that paled before this. Temeraire could not conceive how Laurence had forgotten the treason—the treason, which had so deeply wounded him. It seemed wretchedly unfair. If only Temeraire had known, he would never, never have said a word; how gladly he would have joined Laurence in forgetting, and Laurence need never have known anything about it ever again.

And if Laurence had forgotten the treason, surely he had forgotten everything else, as well. He had forgotten about the loss of his fortune. Temeraire would have to confess *that* to him, all over again; he would have to explain to Laurence that he had lost him ten thousand pounds, and that loss Temeraire had not repaired. Laurence would have all the pain of it afresh, and Temeraire should have to face all his justified blame. Temeraire huddled his head beneath his wing and tried not to think of it.

Forthing had tried to speak with him, half-an-hour ago; Temeraire had paid him no attention. He returned now with Ferris, who came by Temeraire's head and said quietly, "Come, Temeraire; it will come out all right, you will see. The captain will come round. Will you eat something, or would you like Sipho to read to you?" He turned his head and called out the pavilion's side, "Sipho! Will you bring that book over here, of poesy?" and added, "What you need is some distraction—"

"How can you speak of distraction to me?" Temeraire said, lifting his head up. "If I had paid better attention—if I had properly understood—oh! I am distracted, far worse than I ought to be. Where is Laurence?" He reared up his head, and tried to see him. Laurence had walked away across the camp, and his eyes—his eyes had looked half-blind—

"He is with Captain Granby," Forthing said. "He will be all right, Temeraire; it's all that knock on the head he took—"

"It is not!" Temeraire said. "I dare say he *wished* to forget, and whyever would he not wish to? I have lost him his fortune, and his rank, and his ship, and his wife—"

"What?" Ferris said. "Whenever was the captain married?"

"Never!" Temeraire said. "That is what I mean; and everyone *will* have it that nothing could be more splendid than marriage, and he has put it aside for my sake—that, and everything else, and he regrets it so that he has forgotten all of it, so he needn't think of it."

"Lord, Temeraire!" Forthing said. "You can't suppose he has chosen to drop a hand of years out of his head."

Temeraire turned his narrowed gaze sharp on Ferris. "Would *you* not, if you could?" he demanded. "Ferris! Would *you* not rather be shot of me? If you had anywhere else to go? It was my fault you were dismissed the service—"

Ferris flushed and said shortly, "I shouldn't reproach you or the captain for any of it, if only you had asked me to take a part. I should have been happier hanged for such a cause than dismissed for a cowardly liar."

"Oh," Temeraire said. "But—but I am very glad you are *not* hanged," he added awkwardly, "and I dare say if you had helped, you should have been, so I cannot be sorry for that." His ruff drooped against his neck.

They were all silent a moment; Forthing stared at the ground, and Ferris, his cheeks still hot, looked away from the pavilion. Sipho came trotting in with the large scroll of poetry, and paused to eye them all doubtfully.

"I do not want it," Temeraire said. "Pray take it away. I must *do* something," he added, and heaved himself to his feet. "I will go flying, over that burnt town—I will see if I cannot find some trace of the rebels—"

"Wait!" Forthing said. "There's no call for you to go venture yourself like that, and not in this mood, if you please. Let me go and fetch the captain—"

"*No,*" Temeraire said, fiercely; he could not bear to speak with Laurence at the moment, not when so many dreadful things might possibly be said. Whatever Ferris might feel, whatever Laurence himself *had* felt, before he had lost his memory, too plainly he did not feel those same things any longer. Laurence did not remember anything, and would be happier not remembering. What if Laurence were to come back and indeed tell him they should part? "No. I am going straightaway."

He walked out of the pavilion; Ferris caught with a desperate leap at his foreleg, and scrambling went up the side to get hold of the breastplate chain, which Laurence ordinarily used to latch himself upon Temeraire's back. "I am coming with you," Ferris said. "Sipho, will you go and—"

"Oh!" Temeraire said, and caught Sipho and Forthing and put them up onto his back as well. "You will *all* come with me, and not run tattling; I do not see any reason that anyone ought go and tell Laurence. If we do not find anything, there is no reason at all."

"A flight won't hurt him," Ferris said to Forthing in an undertone.

"I can't like it in the least," Forthing said, hissing back. "Half this camp is ready to leap on us and tear us to pieces for the least excuse, and if we did find some rebels, they'd like to do the same. We oughtn't let him go anywhere away, and without a word to anyone."

"These fellows are hunting the rebels, aren't they?" Ferris said. "If there were anything to be found at that town, they would have found it by now. We'll go for a flight there and back, and then likely enough he'll come down and let Sipho read to him awhile."

"I don't think they have been looking very hard," Sipho said unexpectedly, in his still-high voice, "when they think we are guilty, and want us to be," which gave Forthing and Ferris both pause; Sipho added, "I don't mind going to have a look, either, and seeing some more of this country. But I don't think Demane will like it if I go off without him for a long while," in rather cheerful tones: he did not have a very great distaste for upsetting his brother, who was somewhat given to a smothering and anxious degree of affection.

"Well, I am going, and so are you," Temeraire said, "so latch on your carabiners," and he delayed only a moment longer before he threw himself aloft. Privately, his thoughts were urgently turning, even as he beat up and turning flew away from the encampment. Surely it was not himself, but Laurence who required distraction; Laurence ought above all things be distracted from thinking of his losses. Perhaps General Fela's men had missed something, some sign—perhaps he *would* find some trace of the rebels. If only Temeraire returned in some victorious accomplishment, perhaps having smashed a rebel army or at least discovered one, Laurence could hardly reply to it with chiding, with a desire to part from him.

The destroyed village, when he reached it, no longer smoldered; the last of the fires had gone out. The opium had been taken away, and the streets cleared; now it was merely abandoned to time. There was no trace, so far as Temeraire could see, of rebels. There were no weapons scattered, and when he flew in widening circles around, the old worn road bore few signs of any traffic at all: the stones were overgrown with grass.

But Temeraire paid no mind to Ferris and Forthing already importuning him to go back to camp; he did not mean to swallow defeat so easily. "After all," he said, "the rebels would not keep their opium in a village they did not come to, now and again; and if they have not come by road, I suppose they must have dragons as well."

"If they have, all the more reason we ought go back to camp and not encounter them on our own," Ferris said.

"Well, we do not know for certain that they do," Temeraire said hastily. He was already aloft again and hovering, looking around at the nearby mountains, trying to decide where he might have liked to perch, if he had been coming to and from the village, or wished to observe it unseen. "What do you think of that mountain, over there—the one with the double ridge. I suppose anyone might have hidden between the two."

Ferris had a glass in his belt, and he took it out and looked as Temeraire flew towards the ridge. "He isn't wrong," he said to Forthing, and passed him the glass; but Sipho was the only one who was of any real use, for as Temeraire flew along the ridge he said, "Is that a trail, over there?" pointing downwards.

It *was* a trail: with at one end a clearing full of gnawed bones, and fresh claw-marks on the rock. "We must get back to camp," Forthing said. "Temeraire, you must see—"

"Why, those could be anyone's markings," Temeraire said, outwardly dismissive; inside his heart leapt with excitement. By the signs there had not been very many dragons, perhaps even only one, and not very large; he was sure he could win out over one, or even a few. "We cannot merely waste everyone's time. If you like, you may wait here, and I will go and have a look."

"Give over," Ferris said to Forthing, grimly. "He's looking for a fight. Have you anything to make a light with, or some noise? Blast this notion of not having Celestials in harness; we ought to have half-a-dozen flares to hand."

Forthing had his pistols. "Whatever are you doing?" Temeraire said in irritation, looking round, as he shot them off one after another into the air. "If there *is* anyone, you will warn them off."

"I hope I do, before you run yourself into their teeth," Forthing returned, and he fired again. He was sitting on Temeraire's back directly between his wing-blades, where Temeraire could not conveniently reach around to stop him.

Temeraire snorted in irritation, and beat on quicker following the trail, and coming round had to pull up hard as it descended abruptly between two jagged rising walls of stone. He caught an updraft and threw himself up along the wall and caught onto the summit so that he might take a quick look over, unsuspected from below—he did not at all mean to be foolishly reckless, whatever Forthing and Ferris might think.

And then "Oh," Temeraire said, in astonishment, and pulled himself up higher to peer over the ridge and into the valley below. "Arkady? Whatever are you doing here?"

. . .

Arkady stood in the midst of a small encampment otherwise hastily and very recently abandoned: tents left pitched and a fire-pit still smoking; ragged bundles of supplies everywhere and one bleating sheep staked out at the far end of a gully.

"Why am I here?" Arkady said. "I am looking for *you,* and see what it has got me." He did present an appearance very unlike himself, drooping and his grey hide dull and grimed with dust.

Temeraire landed beside him, baffled extremely. The last he had seen Arkady, they had parted on the shores of Britain, not long before Temeraire had embarked on his transportation and taken ship with Laurence for New South Wales. Arkady and his feral band of dragons had been persuaded to take up service with the Aerial Corps in exchange for a regular payment of cattle; but they were natives of the Pamirs, nearly two thousand miles west of China. If he had decided to throw over the Corps, Temeraire could not imagine why he would have come here; and in any case, he was still under harness.

Under harness, and something else: "Whatever is that thing upon your back?" Temeraire said, nosing at it cautiously. Temeraire had never seen its like: iron bars linked together in a long chain, the ends of two bars pierced through Arkady's wings, and others dangling down to Arkady's back—and then Temeraire drew his head back in horrified disgust: the ends were barbed spikes, and they had been planted into Arkady's flesh.

"They put it upon me," Arkady said, "so I cannot fly; it is dreadful if I even move my wings a little. Take it off me at once!" And he leaned against Temeraire miserably.

Forthing and Ferris had already leapt cautiously from Temeraire's back to his, to inspect the chains. "I don't dare touch that," Forthing said to Ferris, "do you? We want a surgeon, double-quick: I dare say we could spoil him for ever flying again, if we took it out wrong."

Ferris was looking with grim disgust at the bindings also. "We ought try and get the links open, if we can," he said. "Then at least he won't be forever pulling on it."

"But who put it on you?" Temeraire said, still bewildered, "and what did you want with me? And if you were looking for me, why would you be here? *I* was not here, until presently; are you saying you have just come from Peking?"

"Why do you say such ridiculous things?" Arkady said. "As though I meant to be here, in this dreadful condition! We were going to Peking: there was some letter you sent, that you meant to go there, or so Admiral Roland said. And as for what did I want with you, how dare you ask me such a thing. What has happened to *my egg*?"

"Your egg!" Temeraire said, with a guilty start of remembering.

Arkady was rousing up despite his miserable state, and he blazed on reproachfully. "I left it in your charge, on that great ship, to take to New South Wales; then I hear you are in Brazil instead, and going on to China. Why are you not there, keeping watch upon it?"

"Oh," Temeraire said, writhing a little in shame and discomfort; he did not know how to tell Arkady what had happened. His egg had been treated with the greatest of care; but that had not availed anything: it had hatched out Caesar, a most disagreeable dragon, who had taken as captain none other than the paltry Jeremy Rankin. "I did assure Caesar," Temeraire offered desperately in his own defense, "that he needn't take on anyone he didn't like; that I should not have permitted Rankin to force harness on him—only Caesar would have it, because he learnt that Rankin is the son of an earl, and, I believe, very rich—"

"Ah! Why did you not say so at once?" Arkady closed his eyes in relief. "Then all is well. I am sorry I doubted you," he said handsomely. And by way of heaping coals of fire on Temeraire's conscience went on, "Only some very strange stories came to us, that you had lost an egg—that someone had stolen it from under your nose—"

Temeraire squirmed even more wretchedly. He had indeed lost an egg to thieves, though not Arkady's, and it was not much excuse that he had found it safely hatched in the end; the egg had not hatched in British hands, and anything might have happened to it during the long dreadful chase across the desert. He seized upon the quickest excuse to change the subject. "Well, I did not lose *your* egg, at all," he said hastily, "and I am very happy to have been able to reassure you on the subject. So that is why you came from England?"

"Yes," Arkady said, "for Wringe is brooding again," triumphantly, "and you may be sure we were not going to let go another egg, when the first had not been properly looked after. But now that it seems there was right care taken, I suppose we will let the officers have it, after all."

"Well, I am sure they will look after it properly," Temeraire said, relieved to have escaped with so little of the scolding he guiltily felt he deserved, "but now pray tell me, *how* did you come here? I suppose you took transport to Guangzhou?"

He had already worked out the picture: surely General Fela's men had seen Arkady being taken prisoner by the rebels, and had misunderstood; they had thought *he* was bringing the opium, when instead he had been their helpless prisoner.

But Arkady said, "No, of course not! It is eight months at sea; there was no time for that! I suppose you would have gone somewhere else by the time we came, the way you have been running all over the world. We came by the Pamirs, and to Xian, because we thought this would be a quicker way to Peking. Instead here I am all chained up, and you *have* gone on somewhere else."

"I do not see that you have any business complaining about my having gone on," Temeraire said, a bit indignantly, "as I have gone on here, and otherwise I dare say the rebels would have kept you chained up here forever."

"Rebels?" Arkady said. "What rebels?"

"The White Lotus," Temeraire said, "who took you prisoner.

But it will all be all right now," he added, "for this proves you were not bringing them opium: if you were, they would certainly not have chained you up."

"I was not bringing opium to anyone, but I do not know anything about this White Lotus, or any rebels," Arkady said. "I was chained up by some great red dragons, a dozen at least. I fought them very bravely, but there were too many of them: they held me down for the men to put those chains on me, though we were only flying through and asking them the way to Peking."

"Red dragons?" Temeraire said, puzzling. "Like the dragons in the army?"

"Yes," Arkady said, "in jeweled collars, and their men shouted at us a long time, but I do not understand how they talk, nor do I want to."

"What is he saying?" Forthing said, looking up from his search of the camp, as Sipho came scrambling out of one of the tents with an odd blade in his hand, wide at the end and narrow at the hilt, and brought it over to them.

"Look what I found," Sipho said. "There are more of them, inside."

"That might do, to pry these open," Ferris said, reaching for it.

"That is not what I mean!" Sipho said. "These are the same kind of swords those fellows used when they tried to murder the captain."

"Oh!" Temeraire said, whipping his head around. "Oh, these are not the rebels; these are the assassins! Where did they go?" Temeraire demanded of Arkady. "How many of them were there—"

"How many of who?" Arkady said, opening his eyes again to slits and glaring sullenly: he had drooped weakly against Temeraire's side again. "I did not count them: there were enough to chain me up. Hundreds, I suppose! Why do you not get this thing off my back so I can fly again?"

A low rumbling of distant thunder came, and came, and came, growing louder and more near. Temeraire looked up in alarm, and saw the narrow shelf of rock above them crumbling. "Look out!" Ferris called out, but there was no time to get him aboard, to get any of them aboard: the rock was coming down in a roaring torrent. Temeraire lunged and put himself above Sipho and Ferris, and scraped Forthing in quickly beneath him as well with one foreleg; then the rockslide was upon them, boulders pounding Temeraire's hips and back painfully as a rain of pelting pebbles and sand roared down with them. Arkady pressed up against his side, taking less of the brunt though squalling furiously nonetheless.

The noise died away first; then the rocks settled, though the air was still full of choking, clouding dust. Temeraire sneezed and sneezed, and coughed, and said hoarsely to Arkady, "Do stop yowling; it does not make matters any better." He shook his head to cast off the worst of the dust; he would have liked to wipe his eyes against his forelegs, but the pebbles and stones had buried him up to his withers.

"*You* are not wearing this monstrosity," Arkady returned, "and you are half out of the rocks," with some justice, for the rocks cascading over Temeraire's back had covered Arkady to the base of his neck, so only his head and his wing-tips poked out. "Aren't you strong enough to heave out of them and get us loose? It hurts," he added plaintively.

"I am sure it does hurt; I am not at all comfortable myself," Temeraire said. "And I dare say I might get us out," he added, although he was not in the least certain; he felt very unpleasantly pinned, "but I cannot risk shifting these rocks. I am sure if I moved they would kill Ferris and Sipho, and Forthing, in a trice. There is nothing to do for it but wait until someone should find us," he finished glumly.

He did not in the least look forward to being found in such an absurd position, having done nothing whatsoever heroic, and found only Arkady, who was of no use to anyone; and Temeraire supposed that now the assassins would have fled to some new hiding place long before he should ever be dug out.

"I do not see why that mountain should have chosen now of all times to fall down on us," he added resentfully, and looking up saw some men peering down upon him from the ruined summit: men in soldiers' uniforms. "Oh!" he said. "You there," he called, raising his voice, "send word to the camp—"

"Why are you talking to them?" Arkady said. "Hurry and get loose, and never mind about your men, I am sure they will be all right! Those are them, those are the ones who put these chains on me!"

Temeraire jerked his head around to stare at Arkady. "What?" he said. "But those are soldiers from the army—" and broke off, in understanding and in swelling wrath. "I *will* kill General Fela, I *will,*" he vowed.

"You will not kill anyone if you are stuck under those rocks," Arkady said, "Quick, quick!" and looked with fear as the soldiers began to pick their way down the loosened slope, with long sharp pole-arms in their hands.

"And you have seen nothing of him since?" Laurence asked, frowning.

O'Dea shrugged. "Mr. Ferris was aboard, and Mr. Forthing, too," he said, "and that young black fellow. I suppose they may have run into a thunderstorm, or gone afoul of some mountain current; ah, it's sure there's many a dragon's bones littering these peaks, Captain. And those pernicious rebels out there somewhere, no doubt looking for a choice target."

"Yes, thank you, O'Dea," Laurence said. The more likely, and perhaps worse possibility, was that Temeraire had fled the camp in misery, and wished to avoid Laurence entirely; that Temeraire did not wish to return. Laurence stood a moment in the pavilion, worrying the straps of his well-worn harness in his hands, the carabiners hanging empty. He should not have cared so much as he did; his heart ought not have been bound up so completely, and yet he could not but recognize that it was. There, perhaps, was his answer: loving Temeraire, and seeing in him all dragonkind, he had not been able to take refuge behind some comforting fiction of their being mere beasts. He wondered now that he had ever thought them so. It had outweighed treason, in his heart; he was not sure he had been wrong.

He looked hesitantly over the camp. They were still under guard, the scarlet dragons watching from their posts, and the British dragons had not tried to go on maneuvers. Chu had evidently ordered patrols of the region, but only by the other dragons under his command. Laurence had seen them overhead, flying in small groups.

To take Iskierka up, or Lily, or one of the heavy-weights, would at once be provoking and leave their own party too bare. But one of the Yellow Reapers was sleeping near-by, Immortalis, and his captain, Little, was sitting beside the drowsing beast and sketching a little upon a writing-desk—an illustration of a Chinese pistol, which he had evidently got somehow from one of the soldiers, perhaps in exchange for his own. He had a neat hand; Laurence paused and Little looked up from his work and straightened.

"Captain Laurence," he said, formally.

"Captain," Laurence said, "I would not disturb you, but Temeraire has been gone some time, and I—I have some reason for believing him in some distress. May I presume so far as to ask you to take me up in search of him?"

"Ah," Little said, and was silent, obviously hesitant. Laurence recalled too late that Little had been awkward about him and had avoided conversation whenever conversation might be avoided. Easy to understand, now: Little of course had known of the treason which Laurence had committed, even when Laurence himself had not. Little had known the stain upon his character, and perhaps cared more than the other aviators; because Granby sympathized, and Harcourt, did not mean they all did so.

"I beg your pardon," Laurence said. "I have not the least desire to impose on you; pray consider the request withdrawn." He would have gone, at once, but Little rose hastily.

"No, no," Little said. "I do beg your pardon. Of course we ought to go and find him."

They had flown a couple of widening circuits of the camp when Immortalis turned his head over his shoulder and said to Little, "Augustine, what is that there, do you think?" A plume of smoke and dust was rising from a knot of mountains not far in the distance.

"That is no ordinary rockfall; that is black powder," Laurence said, when they had gone close enough for the sulfurous smell to reach them.

"The rebels, do you suppose?" Little said. "We had better have a quick look," he told his dragon, and came rounding over the smoke, cautiously, to find Temeraire buried in stones up to his collarbone with a small grey dragon by his side, its head marked with a bright crimson patch like a birthmark.

"Good God, is that Arkady?" Little said.

"Do you know that beast?" Laurence said, startled. "Is he is one of ours?"

"Yes, but what the devil he is doing in China, I should like to know," Little said. "Immortalis, take us down there. What they have been doing to get themselves buried like that—"

There were some soldiers already clambering over the stones towards the two imprisoned dragons; but Temeraire whipped his head around on his long neck and snapped at them, his jaws clashing on empty air: the men were beyond even his reach. "Temeraire!" Laurence called out surprised as he leapt from Immortalis's back.

"Laurence!" Temeraire cried, catching sight of them, "Laurence, look out! They are assassins, all of them."

"What?" Little said, himself just slid down from Immortalis's back.

A shadow was growing on the ground beneath them, and Laurence, seeing it, turned and shouted to Immortalis through cupped hands, "Aloft again, quick!" while he and Little both dived for safety. A great scarlet beast in armor came heavily down where Immortalis had just in time darted away, its claws digging furrows in the rock; the beast roared and swung its head narrow-eyed over them all.

Laurence scrambled away over the loose stones, towards Temeraire and Arkady. The red-patch dragon looked down at him and said in a strange tongue, which Laurence only a little followed, "Make Temeraire move! They will all be squashed anyway, if those men kill him."

"Laurence, be careful," Temeraire called anxiously. "Do not get anywhere near these fellows; and that is for you," he added, snapping again at one of the soldiers, who had lunged at him, a weapon a little like an old-fashioned halberd in his hand, a curved and wicked blade bound to the end of a long staff, which he jabbed at Temeraire's eyes. "Ow!" Temeraire added, and Laurence saw one of the other soldiers had climbed up onto his back and was stabbing the blade down towards Temeraire's spine.

Laurence realized then in sudden horror that Temeraire was not merely buried but helpless to free himself; Temeraire could not move, and the soldiers might carve him at their leisure like a side of slaughtered beef. He drew his sword and leapt for the would-be murderers. The ground was perilously uncertain, a loose slide of pebbles beneath his feet. Still, he scrambled for the top of Temeraire's back and charged the man jabbing at the great column of the spine.

There were several other men drawing close down the unsteady slope, but Laurence thought for the moment of nothing but the enemy immediately before him. He dived under the man's swing, that already-bloody blade shaving painfully along the back of his head, taking skin and hair with it; but Laurence came up inside the man's guard and, seizing his shoulder, drove his sword up between the loose plates of armor, through and through the man's body to his back. The soldier was a young man, only a scruff of beard yet grown; his eyes and open mouth stared and clouded, and the halberd fell away with a clatter to the rocks as Laurence heaved the body off his blade.

Laurence looked down at Temeraire's wound: the scales had resisted, but the flesh was hacked enough to let grey bone show through, stained with the dark dragon blood that ran away in rivulets down Temeraire's back. The enormous lump of the backbone, the size of Laurence's trunk nearly, had defied the halberd's strokes so far, but five men more were nearly upon him, and if unopposed they could hack away at it, like woodsmen together felling some great monster of the forest.

"Laurence!" Little called, and Laurence reached down to catch the end of the halberd, which Little had taken hold of, and was holding outstretched to him. Little used it to scramble more easily up the slope of rocks to Laurence's side; he drew a pistol from his belt, and his own sword.

Above them, Laurence saw Immortalis feinting bravely around the Chinese beast, which outweighed him so greatly. But the red dragon was not merely the stronger but the more maneuverable, its long lanky body snapping with great agility back upon itself almost, allowing it to turn sharp in mid-air, and its wings had something in common with the structure of Temeraire's own, which allowed him to hover. Immortalis could merely hold it off briefly, and not hope to defeat it.

"If Immortalis went back to camp, to raise the alarm?" Laurence said to Little.

Little looked up at Immortalis with a grim expression, and back at Laurence, shaking his head. "That last day of flying, those fellows could manage twenty knots," he said. "A Yellow Reaper can't get above sixteen. If he turns tail, he'll only be brought down by the hindquarters."

He spoke with a hard flat tone, as though he were not speaking of the death of his beast, but when one of the soldiers came down off the slope, Little leveled his pistol and fired with a look of very savagery, distorting his face which in ordinary repose bore almost a poet's half-dreamy look. He hurled the pistol into another man's face, and sprang forward to meet the halberd and cut him down.

Laurence leapt with him, to take advantage of the unsteady footing the men would have as they came off the slope. He felt all the same useless fury he saw in Little's face: to see Temeraire brought so low, so hideously, and by a pack of cowards and traitors—murderers indeed—burned through him with an intensity that came from no rational font. Laurence had seen his ship sink; he had suffered that—he was sure he had suffered it, though the name slid from his mind. He remembered sea-water pouring in waterfalls through the gunports; he remembered sitting in a boat rowing, rowing, while the masts slid in ragged tatters beneath the waves.

The *Goliath,* he suddenly thought, as his sword met the halberd-stave with a clanging; and he jerked his head in a shake to send away the false memory—he had not served on *Goliath* since the Nile; *Goliath* had not sunk there. But the feeling stayed on his tongue: black powder ash and the smell of burning sails, and the roaring torrent. And yet that pain, that sorrow, was distant and removed by comparison.

He set his teeth and flung his enemy's weapon wide by sheer brute force, heaving it up and clear, and risked the brief opening, overbalancing himself for an extra inch of reach, so that the tip of his sword tore open the man's throat. Blood spilled down his neck along a bloody line, but as Laurence completed the stroke and stumbled away, it suddenly spurted red with ferocious energy. The soldier clapped a hand up to the gush and then fell to knees and toppled away over the side.

Laurence caught himself on Temeraire's back with one hand and tried to twist himself up to his feet; but not quickly enough, and he felt another blade catch his sword-arm and bite into the meat of the muscle. He jerked away from the hot pain, falling, and rolled along Temeraire's back hearing Temeraire above roaring in fury.

"Laurence!" Temeraire cried, and did manage to heave himself a little despite the weight of stones, tumbling all of them off their feet together, and straining he brought his head around and snatched the soldier with the dripping pole-arm in his jaws.

There was something dreadful in watching a man broken between those enormous jaws; Temeraire cracked his body like walnut shells, and flung the wreck of him to the ground. He roared again, that terrible shattering roar, and the soldiers involuntarily cowered back from it.

But he could roar only to the sky. He could not turn that power upon them, not without breaking apart the unstable slope and burying them one and all in a shared tomb, and aloft, the red dragon was closing in on her tiring adversary. Immortalis darted low beneath her, and tried to claw at her belly, but with striking speed she reversed herself again and caught him, claws tearing into Immortalis's shoulders, driving him with a powerful thrust of her great body into the ground.

"Immortalis!" Little cried, anguished. The red dragon had seized him with her jaws by the back of the neck, just below his skull, and was shaking him like a rat terrier, a great clawed foot holding his thrashing body pinned. She would break his neck in a moment; then she would be free to do as she wished, and Temeraire and Arkady yet pinned into helplessness.

Then a roaring above, and a monstrous shadow falling: Kulingile came down with Demane and Junichiro and Baggy all three upon his back and his claws outstretched, the scarlet dragon an easy target for him. She gave an undignified squawk of alarm and let Immortalis go, but too late: Kulingile smashed her down into the ground. He closed his jaws midway down along her throat and wrenched her neck away from her body with brute force. Laurence heard the audible crack, and she collapsed into dead weight.

"Captain," Demane cried from Kulingile's back, his voice sharp and high with anxiety, "where is Sipho?"

"I have not the least idea," Laurence said, grimly anxious himself; there was no sign of the boy, nor of his officers, and the cascade of rock that had buried Temeraire and Arkady would have crushed them like insects.

The would-be assassins were trying to flee, too late. Laurence had heretofore thought Kulingile of a remarkably placid nature, but that was not in evidence now as the great golden beast turned towards them: having been roused to violence and with Demane's fear driving him, he hissed and swept the soldiers into a broken heap onto the ground with a few swipes of his massive talons, careless of them as a child with its toys; only a few of them groaned and moved a little, and soon they, too, were still. Junichiro leapt down from Kulingile's back and drawing his own sword stood over the bodies, while Baggy cautiously collected away their blades.

"Sipho is here," Temeraire said, "underneath me; I will keep him quite safe, only get Laurence back to the camp where he will be safe, at once; hurry!"

"I am certainly not leaving until I see you freed," Laurence said.

"Are you sure you hadn't better go, after all?" Little said to him, doubtfully, and Laurence, startled, looked at him. "Your head is all over blood."

Laurence reached up to wipe the grime from his face, and finding his hand come away red with gore felt back to where his scalp hung open and wet. "Help me fold it up again," he said. "A head wound is always a bloody nuisance; but unless my brains are out in the air, I suppose it will not kill me."

Little gave him his neckcloth, to tie it up with; and Laurence settled himself by Temeraire's side to wait out the slow, cautious labor. Kulingile scraped away the loose crumbling rock only a little at a time, so as to free Temeraire without risking the death of the trapped men below, if they had survived so long, buried alive; meanwhile Junichiro and Baggy wordlessly helped Little to get thick bandages from Immortalis's belly-netting, to pack into his sluggishly bleeding wounds; the poor dragon lay heavily and breathing in gulps.

Temeraire also was silent, his head resting awkwardly upon a heap of loose-piled rock, breath wheezing a little through his nostrils; the rocks pressed in upon his sides and drove them inwards, forcing him to struggle for his air. Laurence stroked the soft muzzle while he waited. He had longed for the feelings which might have driven him to treason, having only the stark barren knowledge of it; here, seeing Temeraire so vulnerable to murder and treachery, he had instead been roused to sentiments of great violence, unexplained by reason. He groped after the truth of himself like a prisoner in Plato's cave, watching shadows.

The grey dragon, Arkady, was rather the worse for wear; his eyes were drifting half-shut and groggy, and his breath came noisily: the weight of stone had pressed still more of the breath out of him. Laurence watched him with concern, seeing Temeraire's fate looming ahead if he was not quickly freed, and only with an effort held himself back from urging Kulingile to work faster. Demane had as much right to fear for his brother, and the dragons were not yet in truly dire straits.

"Laurence," Temeraire said, hoarsely, breaking the silence suddenly. "Laurence, I must beg your pardon."

"There is no cause, as far as I know," Laurence said. "I hope you know I do not hold *you* responsible for my own actions—where I have allowed myself to be persuaded, the decision must in the end have been my own. And where apologies between us may have been merited, in the past, and there made, I hope you do not imagine me so unreasonable as to expect you to repeat them."

"Oh! That is very easy to say," Temeraire said, unhappily, "when you do not know the half of it. You do not know—" He heaved a breath, which rolled a cascade of pebbles from his back. "Laurence, it is not only the treason; it is not only your rank: I lost you all your fortune," he said. "I lost you—ten thousand pounds. A court took it away from you, because you could not answer the charge."

Laurence waited, but this seemed the sum total of Temeraire's great confession. "I hope you do not think me so wretchedly mercenary as to weigh that in any wise with the rest," he said, more than half outraged.

"I suppose you have forgotten *that,* as well," Temeraire said. "But ten thousand pounds is an enormous sum! Why, Gentius said to me it should be worth a dozen eagles, like we took from Napoleon."

"I am perfectly aware of the size of the sum; and as it might be ten times the greater and still not buy me a thimbleful of honor, I must beg leave to continue to disdain it by comparison," Laurence said. "I suppose I have been in the way of twice that sum, in prize-money, if I had chosen to ask for a prize-cruise or to chase shipping, instead of harrying the enemy's forces if ever I could."

"But *that* is all the worse," Temeraire said, with a heaving gasp. "For you got it just so, honorably, and it was all your own. You had won it, by yourself, before ever I was hatched; it was not *our* fortune, at all; it was yours. I had not the shadow of a right to do such a dreadful thing, and after you had built me a pavilion as well. I did offer you my talon-sheaths," Temeraire added wretchedly, his voice sinking low, "but oh—you would not take them; as though I could not even repair the injury."

Laurence struggled to make sense of it. He had seen Temeraire gloating over the prized sheaths, to Laurence's mind a singularly absurd piece of adornment which made any sort of eating ten times the more awkward and battle impossible; and he thought Temeraire would have seen his wings clipped off his back before surrendering them. "I suppose if you imagine it a kind of theft," he said slowly, "I can better comprehend your misery; but if I have been plundered by a court, either it was unjustly, which cannot be your fault, or for some act of my own. In any case," he added, with as much energy as he could, "I do assure you I do not regard it; I am not made in the least wretched by *that* loss."

Temeraire was silent, and then said low, "Very well. Not by that, perhaps; but certainly by—" He halted, and then said even more softly, "Surely you would be happier, if you had—if you had never found my egg; if you had not harnessed me at all."

Laurence hardly knew how to answer; it seemed to him true as well. Temeraire dragged in a breath and added with a strange rasp like the hum of bee-wings beneath it, "If you would prefer—I will stay in China, alone; if you would like. You may go wherever you like. Or, or you may stay here, where no-one would call you a traitor, and I—I will—"

He halted, evidently fumbling for some alternative, but Laurence said, "No." It came easily to his mouth, as easily as anything: that itself would have to be answer enough. "I would not make the exchange," he said, "even now; what I have done, what I have chosen, I would not unmake, even if I could."

Chapter 14

ANOTHER HOUR PASSED; NIGHT had come. Enough of the rocks had been drawn away, by now, that Temeraire could breathe freely once more; but he scarcely noticed the relief, by comparison with the rest, although he was very glad when Arkady—who had begun by then to feel well enough to complain incessantly and fidget—was freed from his side and helped away. Immortalis had stolen back to the camp, under cover of dark, to tell the others what had happened; Nitidus had flown back carrying Maximus's surgeon Gaiters, who now was studying the dreadful chains and considering how they might best be removed.

Temeraire could not quarrel with his situation despite the discomfort. It was worth, oh, everything! to know that Laurence did not wish to leave him. Temeraire was with some difficulty trying to comprehend Laurence's disgust of his own lost fortune—he could scarcely call it anything else—only because it could not buy him honor. The fortune *could* have bought him a great many other things, all of them very splendid, so that did not really explain it to Temeraire's satisfaction. But he was not so determined to be unhappy that he would insist on Laurence's being so, having been given such assurances.

"Why is he taking so long about it?" Arkady demanded of Temeraire, breaking in on his thoughts. Temeraire jerked his head up, for he had been drifting in a half-doze, dull with fatigue even though he could breathe now more easily. "Tell him to finish and take it off me. I do not see why he is waiting."

Temeraire looked over. Gaiters had already drawn the hooks which had been driven through Arkady's wings, by cutting them and pulling them away; his point of concern seemed to be how to cut out the barbs in Arkady's shoulders so that the flesh would not be torn so badly that he could not fly.

"Well, I will have a go at it, at any rate. Horrocks, get me my knives," Gaiters said, calling down from Arkady's back to his assistant, and Kulingile was pressed from the work of digging to hold Arkady still for the operation. Arkady indeed shrilled loudly in protest and shuddered all over while the cruel knives dug around in his flesh; Horrocks pointed, now and again, and Gaiters, without taking his eyes off his work, grunted and nodded in answer, while the blood welled up continually around his hands. Horrocks mopped about them with a rag, and three of the midwingmen stood holding the bar of the barb steady.

Temeraire tried not to watch; it was gruesome, and he did not like surgery at all. But some fascination drew his eyes again and again to the spectacle, until at last Gaiters gave the word. "All right, fellows, lift away," and he and Horrocks together reached within the wound to guide the barb out as the midwingmen raised up the bar. It emerged little by little—a thing of horror with curling spikes and gobbets of flesh still clinging to them.

The second one was extracted more quickly: not five minutes, and then Horrocks was finishing the sewing while Gaiters washed his hands. "What a vicious piece of work," Gaiters said, looking it over laid out upon the ground. "I have never seen the like. I suppose they have so many dragons here they don't mind if they ruin a number of them."

Temeraire was very glad to have it bundled up and taken away, in any case; Arkady was coaxed limping away to a corner of the encampment, as he had been warned away from any exertion until the wounds had healed, where he collapsed almost at once into slumber, snoring loudly.

Kulingile turned back to help with the digging. Nitidus had been working industriously on the stones directly before Temeraire's chest, clearing a safe path; he suddenly exclaimed, "Oh! I hear them; I am sure I do," and in another quarter of an hour Sipho scrambled out of the first narrow opening, and a little while after Ferris and Forthing came staggering out over Temeraire's forearm, which was still pinned in place.

Then at last Temeraire could heave himself free, the last of the stones pouring away from his hindquarters as he lunged out, and he collapsed wearily with a sigh beside Arkady. "Oh! how tired I am," Temeraire said, closing his eyes, only for a moment, as Laurence came to his side and stroked his muzzle again. "But I am not going to wait an instant. We must get back to camp, and I *will* squash General Fela, and I do not mean to let Hammond or anyone else talk me out of it, either."

But somehow his eyes did droop shut; they closed, and he heard Laurence saying, "He must have some water, and something to eat. Can we get it out of the camp, without being observed?"

He woke again with Mei nosing at him anxiously, and an even more anxious cow lowing in his ear: fortunately this second might be dealt with in the most summary fashion, if somewhat indecorously. Temeraire swallowed down the last bite of the head, spat out the horns, and said, "I beg your pardon: I was extremely hungry."

Arkady himself was still sleeping, and Laurence was drowsing as well beneath the remains of one of the encampment's tents, ragged and much abused by the landslide. Immortalis and Kulingile had gone back to camp. "We do not at all want General Fela to know you have uncovered his treason," Mei said, much to Temeraire's outrage. "We must find proof of his treachery which can be demonstrated to the Emperor, first. You have killed everyone here, so we have no-one to obtain a confession from."

She sounded faintly reproachful about the last. "Well, they were trying to kill us, so I do not see how you can complain of that," Temeraire said. "It is the outside of enough to say that we must have *more* proof. They are soldiers, they are under Fela's command, and they were holding Arkady prisoner here, hidden away from all of us, and pretending that *he* brought the opium."

"But you must see that Fela can make any number of excuses," Mei said. "He will say that he did not know of these soldiers, that they are some small band of deserters; or he will say that Arkady *did* bring the opium, and is a false witness, and demand that he be put to torture."

"What is she saying about me?" Arkady said, pricking up his head, his eyes sliding open. "And what is there to eat? I smell blood: have you not left me anything?" he added accusingly.

Temeraire did not think it was very prudent to tell Arkady that there might be any question of torture. "She is saying we must have more proof that General Fela is guilty, and that you did not bring the opium here," he said. "And you needn't complain; there is a nice goat, right there." He also did not think it needed to be mentioned there had been a cow, too, just lately; anyway he was much bigger than Arkady, and needed a larger meal.

"Hm," Arkady said, and reaching out seized the tethered goat with a practiced blow, to break its neck. "I do not see that question is sensible at all," he said, around a mouthful. "Where would I have got any opium, and why would I have brought it here if I had? What good is it? Is it worth a lot of money?"

"Well, it is," Temeraire said, "but General Fela would have it that you brought it here to give to some rebels."

"He could scarcely have brought so many chests, alone," Laurence said, coming out of the tent and buckling on his sword as he did. "Temeraire, pray inquire where he was intercepted, and how long ago? Why did he not come through Guangzhou?"

Arkady was disinclined to be helpful; he was already sagging back into exhausted sleep, and complained that he was tired after his meal, but after a little prodding muttered fretfully, "A month, and all this while I have been alone, and in chains, and now you will not let me sleep. Why would we have come so roundabout a way as the ocean? We had to come quickly: we have an important message for you."

"Who does he mean by 'we'?" Laurence asked.

"Oh," Arkady said, lifting his head abruptly, looking more wide-awake and to Temeraire's instant suspicion guilty; then he said in feigned tones of great surprise, "Why, Tharkay was with me, of course; haven't you rescued him yet?"

"My God," Granby said, springing up with dismay, when he heard the name. "You don't remember," he added to Laurence, "but he is a damned good fellow; he has saved all our necks more than once. I suppose Roland must have asked him to play the courier. He knows those roads backwards and forwards; his people on his mother's side are in Nepal. He took us to Istanbul overland, the last time we were in this country."

Laurence briefly caught at an elusive twist of memory: running beside someone through dark half-deserted streets, and a great echoing vaulted chamber half-drowned in water, drops striking like bells; but it meant nothing, and slid from his grasp without leaving him a face or a voice, though from what Granby said they had known the man five years and more.

"It was some human thing, about the war," was all Arkady could tell them, maddeningly, of the message Tharkay had carried, "—something that fellow Napoleon means to do." This ominous news might have encompassed everything from another invasion to offering peace on terrible terms, but Arkady flipped one wing in a small shrug when they pressed him. "It did not seem very important to me; I had my *egg* to think about. You will have to ask Tharkay."

"If he is even alive," Granby said, "and we can find him: Fela and his crew have been torturing him, no doubt, to get a confession out of him to use against us."

"What we're to do about it is the question," Captain Harcourt said, later that night. They had gathered in her tent, as secretly as they might, to discuss the matter; Mei had smuggled Laurence back to the camp, under cover of dark, while Temeraire and Arkady remained hidden in another valley. "We haven't the faintest notion where they are keeping him, and if we challenge Fela, he will claim it is all a lie and he has no idea where Tharkay is; and like as not will kill him.

"I suppose Fela must be wary already," she added. "Those guard-dragons are his, that much is sure enough. They are watching everything we do: they will have noticed Temeraire has been gone more than a day, and have seen Immortalis and Kulingile and Mei flying back and forth as well. If anything, we are giving him all the cause he needs to accuse us of going about and giving more aid and comfort to the rebels, in the meantime."

"Rebels," Hammond said slowly, from the chest upon which he sat, "—rebels, of whom we have seen not the least sign, and have no evidence for, but General Fela's own reports," and they all regarded him in surprise. "Oh! It is the prettiest arrangement," he added, answering their growing astonishment, "I wonder I did not guess at it before. The conservative party required some excuse, some argument, to resist an alliance and to undermine Prince Mianning's growing influence at court. They trumped up this rebellion, General Fela sent in a few false reports—"

"The devil," Berkley said. "Are you saying there are no damned rebels at all?"

"I dare say there are some number of malcontents, and some quantity of small banditry here and there: enough to make reports plausible," Hammond said. "But we have not heard a peep of any kind of truly organized force—no rebel army, no real fighting."

They none of them spoke a moment; the implications hideous: "Good God, Hammond: if it is true, he put that village to the sword without cause," Laurence said.

"Pray consider the desperate nature of Fela's situation," Hammond said. "He might have expected to vanish away a false rebellion as easily as he had created it, with no such measures required. Yet quite unexpectedly, the crown prince proposed your superceding him in command, with a substantial force and an experienced senior officer to back you. From that moment, he has known the lie of the rebellion could not long be preserved. His only hope is to quickly discredit us, and have General Chu and his force recalled—and he has made excellent headway on that front. But if Prince Mianning had *not* made the suggestion, and we had been sent here alone as the conservatives wished, I am sure he would have been delighted to keep us traipsing about these mountains looking for mythical rebels until the end of days."

"Doing his best to arrange Laurence's murder in the meanwhile," Granby said. "But how are we to prove any of it?"

There was scarcely any hope of their finding Tharkay, or any other evidence, so unfamiliar with the territory as they were; General Fela and his own forces knew it far too well themselves, from having been stationed here for some time. "We must have help," Laurence said.

Temeraire could not but feel the most dreadful awkwardness, marching coolly past the guard-dragons to General Chu's tent, and summoning him out of it. Of course Laurence was nominally in command, and he himself as a Celestial technically took precedence over any other breed, but oh! What did that matter when everyone *knew* perfectly well that General Chu was a most senior dragon, a great general, and really meant to be in command; he could feel the outrage of the other dragons' eyes upon him, and writhed inwardly to be behaving so rudely.

General Chu came out of his pavilion, between the two scarlet dragons whom Fela had appointed his personal honor-guard, and very stiffly bowed his head. "How may I be of service?" he said shortly.

Temeraire did not know how he could have answered; but Laurence had not the least hesitation. He said in quite a calm voice, "General Chu, have you found any trace of the rebels that the Emperor has commanded us to destroy?"

Chu's mane bristled. "As yet we have not discovered their base of operations," he said, even more shortly. "The search continues."

"Then you would oblige me greatly by coming with us to discuss how we may improve that search," Laurence said, and nothing more—no explanation, no polite adornment. One of the guard-dragons flattened his own heavy brows, and Temeraire avoided their eyes.

Chu's eyes narrowed under the forward ridge of his mane. "If I may propose to Your Highness, there is no reason we cannot discuss the matter profitably here," and indicated with his claw the great maps laid out just inside his pavilion, with clustered markers of red upon them showing the maneuvers of the dragons.

"I prefer to be surveying the territory directly, with my own eyes," Laurence said. "We will seek out a higher vantage point, if you please. You there, you may keep your places," he added, when the honor-guard would have risen. "We do not need an escort." He touched Temeraire's side; Temeraire was desperately glad to leap aloft and escape the mortification and the cold glares. He hovered just out of ear-shot, pretending not to notice the outraged expressions on the other dragons, and their flattened wings and spines, as General Chu heaved himself into the air and followed.

Arkady was not yet well enough to fly, but that dawn they had loaded him onto Kulingile, who was good-natured enough not to mind his ongoing sighs and restless shifting. He had shown them the way to a pass through the mountains, not far from the encampment where he had been chained, and a valley at its end with a small and glacier-cold pond fed by a trickling cleft in the rock.

"Here," he had said, "this is where they took us. We saw them having a drink, so Tharkay thought we should ask them for direction; but after he climbed off my back, and spoke with them, suddenly they sprang on him."

"What did you do?" Temeraire said.

"Oh, well," Arkady said, "I thought it would be a very good thing if I could only get away, so I could come round and free him later, of course—so I tried to fly away as quick as I could; but those red fellows are fast, even if they do not look it much," he added disgruntled.

"As though he had any right to be," Temeraire had said indignantly to Laurence, after, "once he turned tail and left poor Tharkay, and I am sure would never have given him another thought."

Arkady and Kulingile were waiting for them there in the valley when they descended with Chu; Temeraire had been sure to fly on ahead as quickly as he could, without pausing for conversation. "What is this?" Chu demanded. "Who is that peculiar dragon, and why have we come here?"

"Sir," Laurence said, "I beg your pardon for the maneuver which has brought you here. We have reason to believe we have all been practiced upon, to an extent difficult to swallow; but we have not a hope of demonstrating it, without your assistance."

But Chu received the explanation of Arkady's presence, and of Fela's treachery, with enormous skepticism; Temeraire laid back his ruff to see it, and said angrily, "I suppose you would rather believe that we are all liars—that *I* am a liar, and Laurence as well, even though he is the Emperor's adopted son."

Chu snorted a little. "*That* does not disqualify anyone to be an emperor's son, or an emperor for that matter: what is an emperor but one who tells a lie that all the world believes?"

Temeraire was rather taken aback by this remark, which made an uncomfortable sort of sense, and did not quite know how to answer it. Chu waved a wing-tip dismissively and said, "But in any case, I do not think you liars; I think you want China to make alliance with this foreign nation of yours, and so you are willing to believe the lies of others. General Fela, to have committed such treachery? To have sent false reports, and connived at the attempted murder of the crown prince?"

"Sir," Laurence said, "*have* you seen any evidence at all, of the rebellion which he claimed was so greatly resurgent as to challenge his own forces?" General Chu was silent in answer, frowning; in the cold mountain air, the breath from his nostrils drifted forth in pale clouds.

"Then I ask you to indulge us this far," Laurence went on. "You yourself commanded the army which cleared away the last insurgency. You are well acquainted with these mountains, and whatever rebel fastnesses were taken and secured by the army at that time. Is there anywhere close-by, where they might have taken and concealed a prisoner? If we can find our man, we may find answers with him; his guards may be questioned, and other evidence found."

"Hm," Chu said, after a moment, and then he said, "Well, it will not hurt for us to take a look."

He leapt aloft, Temeraire after him, both dragons beating far up to where the air grew thin and cold. A thin clouding layer of haze reduced the mountains to faded blue, but the sharp and angular lines of their peaks might be clearly seen below. Temeraire heard Laurence's breath coming quickly; his own was laboring in his chest, and his wings working mightily to keep with Chu.

Chu did not keep them so high long, but soon dropped to a more comfortable height. There he flew in ruminative circles a while, and then beat up a second time, as though to confirm some conclusion; then he swung in easy circles back down to the clearing. He plunged his head into the cold pool and drank deep, then raising his head shook water from his mane vigorously.

"It is a long while since I hunted these mountains," he said, half-aside to himself, "but I have not forgotten all the bolt-holes of the rabbits yet. There was a White Lotus fortification, a cave, near Blue Crane mountain. And there is some smoke coming from the mountain-side now."

. . .

"Ha, this makes me feel like a young soldier again," Chu said, peering over the mountain's ridge, "flying over the northern plains looking for the enemy, under the great Kang-Xi Emperor! It is not at all respectable, of course," he added, "for either of us; but it can be excused in this case, I think."

There was some sort of activity at the cave, certainly: as Temeraire raised his head cautiously to peek over, alongside, he could see that the fortifications by the mouth of the large cavern had been rebuilt, and fresh traces of cart wheels tracked through the dust of the slope and into the entryway.

"Either we *have* found your nest of traitors, which I do not suppose in the least," Chu said, "or we have found the rebels. But we will soon find out. We will go back to camp, and send ten *niru* here to investigate thoroughly—"

"Temeraire!" Laurence said sharply, and Temeraire sprang for Chu and bowled him over the slope, only just in time as three dragons plunged towards them from a concealed height above, talons outstretched, and plowed dirt and stone into a cloud where they had been: three scarlet dragons, the very honor-guard which had been appointed to Chu by Fela.

Though flung off his feet, Chu nimbly rolled his entire body over itself and got up roaring. "What is this outrageous behavior?" Chu said, rearing up onto the slope and bellowing at them. "You *are* traitors! Lost to all decency and right thinking!"

The scarlet dragons half-cowered from him a moment, plainly hesitant, as well they ought to have been, but Temeraire could see that they did not mean to stop. He gathered his breath, his chest swelling, and as the red dragons steeled themselves to leap he roared, shaping the thunder of the divine wind into their path, and the slope crumbled away and left them tumbling down in a heap of stones and broken shale, falling trees entangling their limbs. That seemed poetic justice to him, after his own half-burial. "It serves them all very well," he said, dropping down to his own feet.

"Temeraire!" Laurence called to him. "We must away at once,

before they can call more assistance. If you and Chu only return to camp, with this evidence, Fela is undone; they must slay you at once, or face disaster."

"The disaster they have made for themselves!" Chu said angrily. "Come: your companion is right, we must get back to camp." But there was no chance; more of the scarlet dragons were spiraling down from the clouds, all the dozen dragons and more who had been guarding them in the camp: Fela's loyalists, and all too plainly a willing part of his conspiracy.

"Let me down!" Arkady was squawking, further down the slope, where he and Kulingile had waited for Temeraire and Chu to finish their spying.

"Well, hurry up then!" Demane said, as Arkady scrambled off Kulingile's back and crept hastily away into a narrow crevasse, peering out and up at them with only the tip of his grey nose showing.

Still they were three against a dozen, and Temeraire struggling to gather his breath again. Chu said, "Quickly, behind me!" and leapt aloft. Temeraire and Kulingile dropped in behind him. Chu darted into a gap between two mountain ridges, angling himself sharply to pass his wings through the space, and led them onwards through a dizzying rush of mountains: thick green slopes and grey stone flying past at such a speed that Temeraire could only blindly follow, twisting himself to meet every new gap and losing his sense of direction all over again at every third turning.

Kulingile was gasping, but at last they burst out between two peaks into the air over a valley, and beneath them, chasing through the very channel they had fled along, were the traitorous dragons. "Now!" Chu said, and Temeraire gathered his breath and roared out, and the peak before him shattered; boulders toppling. Kulingile flung himself down after them, and bore two of the red dragons to the ground beneath his wickedly long talons, drowning them in the rockslide before he sprang aloft again.

The enemy had split up their ranks, however, and still more beasts were coming; six and six from either side approaching, and another six descending from above. The odds were too great. "We must try and fight a way through for you," Chu said to Temeraire. "You must return to camp, with the Emperor's son," and while Temeraire could appreciate that sentiment, his heart recoiled at the idea that he should flee and leave others to fend off the enemy. He felt very sorry suddenly he had ever criticized Laurence for risking himself; he had never properly understood how dreadful it would be.

"We cannot on any account desert you, General," Laurence said. "Your own survival must be of paramount importance: if you can win back to camp, you will be trusted and obeyed, where we may be considered too partial, and your death somehow laid at our door by further machinations."

"Laurence," Temeraire said, "perhaps you ought to go with General Chu, and—"

The knot of dragons was closing in upon them; but shrieks and cries erupted, as a torrent of flame enveloped their hindquarters and Iskierka burst through their ranks behind it, her talons raking along their sides in either direction. "What are you all hovering about here and talking for?" she demanded, whipping about them mid-air. "Don't you see you are under attack? Hurry up and do some fighting! The others are coming as quick as they can."

She whipped away again, and Temeraire dived after her, indignant at her reproaches; he roared as she flamed, and together they broke apart the other side of the closing net just as the arrow-head formation massed behind Lily came diving towards them all. "Hah," Maximus called, as he swung by, "we thought you might have got yourselves into trouble, after those guard-dragons slunk off: we followed them here, and so you have."

"We did not get ourselves into trouble, at all," Temeraire said. "It came to us, without any effort on our parts."

Chu was falling in on his left flank, calling to Temeraire, "Hurry! Tell them to send up a signal! Blue lights and red, together!"

Temeraire was inclined to think, himself, that they were quite enough to manage the enemy; together their formation had dealt with quite more than a dozen dragons, and the red dragons were not as large as himself, much less Maximus and Kulingile. But Laurence shouted the word on to Granby, through his cupped hands, and in a moment the flares went up: blue lights bursting against the mountain-side, and Iskierka followed them with a torrent of red flame.

Dodging another pass from the red dragons, Temeraire noticed that the fighting had doubled back over the cave, and too late realized they had been neatly herded. Soldiers were coming out of the cave-mouth and hoisting into the air bundles which, when the scarlet dragons dived to seize them, proved to be enormous weighted nets.

Four of the scarlet dragons threw themselves in a tumbling pass through the narrow gaps in the formation, their crews lashing out with long barbed whips in either direction that threatened the British dragons' wings and managed to cut the formation apart, while others in groups of three pounced with the nets. Nitidus and Immortalis were falling off in one direction, a net catching at Nitidus's wing and leg, so that he would have plummeted into the jagged mountains but for Immortalis giving him support.

Another three of the dragons managed to entangle Lily and Messoria and flung nets over them both, carrying them to the ground, wings and limbs thrashing as they roared, men of their crews broken and bloody beneath them as they fell. Three of the scarlet dragons were feinting at Maximus, drawing him in one direction and another, their crews carving up his flanks with the long whips while the British riflemen fired volleys that the twisting and darting of the dragons sent astray.

The scarlet dragons were fighting too well together, Temeraire realized in dismay: being so nearly alike they all might take any position in the fighting, and exchange places, and alter their formations to suit any particular moment of the fighting. Meanwhile Maximus and Dulcia were the only ones left, and Dulcia could not do very much to help Maximus, outweighed by the scarlet beasts as she was.

He could not go and help; he and Iskierka were struggling to keep together as the enemy beasts came towards them, and even with her fire, it was proving dreadfully difficult: he could not build up enough force behind the divine wind to use it to proper effect over and over. Iskierka only just turned her head over his back and burnt up a net as it flew for his wings; he managed to dive beneath her belly and roar away three dragons coming from beneath with their crews aiming for her with stakes topped by pointed steel caps.

Below, he heard terrible screams, and smelled the acrid bite of Lily's poison: she had righted herself. The spray of her acid had gone through the net and spattered the defenders before the cave-mouth, and with a great heave, she and Messoria burst free, themselves bellowing as they brushed against a few lingering drops.

But Temeraire could see Kulingile being driven down: one of the scarlet dragons had flung herself at him in a sacrificial roll, hurtling into his chest heedless of his clawing talons. As he reeled back, three others seized on him with jaws and talons closing over his wings and his legs, tearing at the membranes. Temeraire wanted to fly to his rescue, but he could not gather the divine wind, or drag himself free: he was being dragged down as well. "Laurence!" he cried in alarm, thrashing, trying to see if Laurence was still on his back, still hooked on and safe, as three dragons pinned him to the mountain-slope.

Chu roared, coming down upon the back of one of the red dragons, and seized the younger beast by the neck and wrenched it expertly sidelong; the dragon shrieked and fell off Temeraire's shoulder. "Hah!" Chu said, and seizing one of the fallen trees from the slope flung it at the dragon on Temeraire's other legs, and Temeraire managed to heave up; the last of the three dragons fled aloft. "Come along!" Chu said. "It is time for us to get out of the fighting."

"What?" Temeraire said, gasping for breath, and then looked

up as a thrumming noise came sharply from overhead: more of the red dragons were wheeling into view, but these were not Fela's beasts; these were Chu's soldiers, their armor polished and fresh, gathered in two formations of six and nine.

"This way," Chu said, and led Temeraire to a flattened peak, broken earlier by the divine wind, high enough to let them see the wheeling, fighting dragons clearly.

"Come upon their left flank," Chu roared to the smaller formation, and "Zhao Lien, bar their escape," he shouted to the leading dragon of the other, then sat back on his haunches with satisfaction as the dragons moved skillfully and methodically to begin bringing down the traitor-beasts. "Where are you going?" he demanded, when Temeraire would have gone back aloft. "No, no: there is no excuse for that anymore. We have won the battle: it is only a matter of time, now."

Temeraire flattened his ruff to his neck in irritation, especially when he saw Iskierka dart by, flaming another two beasts. But he could not quarrel with it; they were winning, that was plain enough.

"Temeraire," Laurence said, and to his alarm Temeraire saw him unclasping his carabiners, and Forthing and Ferris with him. "We must get down and look into those caves: we must find Tharkay. When the traitors see the fighting going against them, they might well kill him rather than leave him to be witness against them and perhaps General Fela himself. General Chu," he added, "you would oblige me if you might send down some soldiers with us, from your beasts."

"Oh," Temeraire said unhappily as Chu roared the command to his dragons: the cave-mouth was indeed not at all large enough to let him or another dragon go inside. He had only just resolved not to condemn Laurence for wishing to go into fighting, but he had not thought that resolve would be put to the test quite so soon. "Pray be careful," he said, steeling himself to it, and watched in anxiety as Laurence plunged within the caves, Ferris and Forthing on his heels, and a number of Chu's soldiers with them.

And then he could do nothing but sit and watch the battle, and wait, while Iskierka and Lily and Maximus and Kulingile helped knock about the traitors, as they well deserved; Temeraire clawed the slope in frustration.

"Hm! I must have a better look at that fire-breather of yours," Chu said to Temeraire, adding insult to injury. "It is the accepted understanding that they cannot be bred without a grievous lack of balance, but I see she is a most skillful flier. Her temperament, I have observed, is not ideal, but one may make some allowances. Where was she hatched?"

"She is Turkish," Temeraire said, rather coldly, as Iskierka went showing away again with a great corkscrewing spiral turn, flame sweeping the air like a banner. "She is a Kazilik dragon. I suppose you are quite an expert, on these matters."

"I am indeed," Chu said, equably. "I am a minister of the breeding office, and I have served three terms as overseer of the Imperial breeding programme."

The ground before the cave-mouth still smoked with the Longwing acid, several crates burnt through: Laurence caught a glimpse, in one, of balls of opium charred through and wafting a thick rope of pale grey smoke into the air. He plunged between them and over the deserted fortifications, dead soldiers sprawled over the ground, one with a face half-eaten-away and stiffened hands still clutching at his own head stared as he went past and into the darkness of the cave-mouth.

Laurence's eyes took a moment to adjust: a few lanterns hung from a thin rope strung overhead, and a honeycomb of tunnels dividing away in front of him. "Sir," Forthing said, "we had better mark the way we've gone." He took down a lantern, and tearing it open fetched out the candle.

Laurence nodded, taking a piece of the candle. "Each of you take a side," he said, "and do not go down more than five branchings, for the moment." He spoke grimly; if the tunnels did go so deep into the mountains, they might search months without finding a concealed prisoner.

He shouted Tharkay's name, and called in English as he led the way down the first tunnel; distantly for a little while he heard Forthing and Ferris doing the same, until the rock swallowed their voices. He dragged the softened wax across the rough rock wall, at each division of the passage, choosing always the rightmost way; it left a smudge of pale yellow that showed clearly in the light of the torch one of the soldiers carried by his side. The wind currents brought other noises: he heard shouts and footsteps, echoing queerly along the hallways, and his mouth held the unpleasant taste of bitter smoke.

They looked into storerooms, mostly empty and disused. By any fourth or fifth branching, the tunnel would begin to take on more the character of what the place had once been, Laurence supposed: a mine, the tunnels rough-hewn and pickaxed; when they reached a dead end in one, the torch gleamed on a thin line of silver, the remnant of a vein pursued to its end.

In one chamber, somewhere near the third branching, they found a writing-table, with a handful of scattered letters and pen and ink: but old; the ink dried to a black crumbled clot. Laurence glanced at the topmost sheet, a work broken off mid-stream, and then held it to the soldier nearest him, an officer he thought; the man wore a mark of senior rank. "Can you make anything of it?"

The soldier studied it and said, "This is a letter written to Ran Tian Yuan: I believe he was a chief of the rebels," in a woman's clear voice. "He was executed ten years ago." Laurence with a start looked at her: deep lines about her eyes, her face not very old but leathered from sun and wind, and a peppered scar of burnt-in powder upon her cheek.

The woman took up the papers and held them out to one of the other soldiers, to be bundled up together; she fell in again with Laurence as they went through the tunnels. Laurence glanced back at the other soldiers behind them. Their hair was bound up beneath snug caps, with wrappings bound down beneath their chins, likely for warmth when aloft; in the dim light he could not tell whether they were men or women.

The tunnel died shortly after, and they retreated towards the entry, to take another branch; before they could go down this, footsteps came towards them running. Laurence was appalled to find the soldier thrust him behind her arm as they drew their swords, and another of the soldiers push through the hallway to take her side instead.

The enemy soldiers coming had a look of desperation, drawn blades wet with blood, and pulled up short to see them; then it was a sudden, close struggle in the passageway. Their numbers were even, Laurence thought, but he could not easily tell; the tunnel was too narrow to see clearly, and the soldiers at the front, of both parties, had dropped their torches to free their hands for fighting. He took a blow from a fist to his temple and shook his head to clear it; then thrust back high, his long blade coming over the other's guard. Then he caught another arm descending, and the woman soldier drove her own blade, a shorter one, into the man's arm-pit beneath his thick jerkin. She grunted abruptly with pain and fell: one of the enemy had thrust a sword into her thigh. Laurence stepped into the gap. He killed three more, and then a sword took him hot in the meat of his arm; he dropped back and let another step into his place.

Abruptly the enemy soldiers gave over the fight: they made one heaving push, and then withdrew hurrying down the hall. Laurence said, "Let them go." Twelve lay dead in the corridor, and five of their own party. The waste of it made him sorry, with the battle above already decided. They bound up their hurts as best they could. The woman officer was limping; another soldier, Laurence thought a man, looked dazed: his cap and its bindings were wet through with blood, and a trickle coming down his cheek. Two soldiers stood with him; he swayed between them and did not speak.

Laurence looked down the branching they had been on the

point of taking: he wished to get the wounded to safety, but the enemy soldiers had been coming this way. "Come with me, if you please," Laurence said, to two of the unwounded soldiers, one of them a torch-bearer, "and the rest stay here. We will have a quick look, then return to the entry."

The passageway smelled of smoke: burning wood, a torch, acrid. His head ached. Blood was wet and sticky upon his arm and on his fingers, and the orange glow of torchlight played from behind his back and over the corridor walls, leaping like a bonfire. There was a strange familiarity to it: the narrow walls in around him. And when he came to a wooden door set in the wall, he put his hand upon it and pushed it open.

There was a room, and a pallet inside it; a small torch burned low in a socket upon the wall. A man lay upon the cot, his face bruised and battered, his hands curled against his chest bloody: and Laurence knew him; knew him and knew himself. He remembered another door opening, in Bristol, three years before, and a voice asking him to come outside his prison, in a Britain under siege.

"Tenzing," Laurence said, and, as Tharkay opened feverish eyes, went to help him stand.

Chapter 15

"La Grande Armée, he is calling it," Tharkay had said, lying exhausted and thin against the cushions which propped him, in Laurence's own camp-bed: they had carried him gently and carefully dragon-back, in a hammock of netting, back from the caves. "They have been mustering all winter; he will march into Russia in three months—in two—" He stopped, breathing hard, and asked, "What is the day?"

"It is the third of May," Laurence said, quietly. The abuse had not marked Tharkay excessively: fortunately they had wished to preserve the appearance of a more honest confession, perhaps, when they had wrung one from him. But he had been lashed more than once, judging by the half-healed marks; there were burns upon his limbs as from a hot poker, and his hands were badly mangled.

"In a month," Tharkay said. "He will march in June; that was our latest intelligence."

"With near a million men?" Laurence said, low.

Tharkay nodded, minimally. "And some hundred dragons."

It was indeed a message terrible enough to bring a man racing flat-out halfway around the world. The largest army ever heard of, and with it Napoleon meant to crush the last embers of resistance out of Europe: first Russia, and then he would turn all his attention to the Peninsula. Hammond was already rising, pale. "I must go speak with General Chu at once, and with Qin Mei: we must—these events must require our immediate return to the capital. Oh! We must return at once." He left unceremoniously, and Tharkay closed his eyes.

Laurence sat silently with him in the growing dark of the tent, groping back through patchwork scenes of memory. He remembered the *Goliath* sinking more clearly now; he remembered the faces of the officers at his court-martial; he remembered the cold bleak desperation of the flight across the Channel, to take the plague-medicine to France.

"I hope you will forgive my mentioning it, Will," Tharkay said, eventually, rousing Laurence from his reverie. "—I recognize there is a certain pot-calling quality to my doing so under the circumstances, but have you noticed that the top of your head appears likely to come off?"

Laurence put up a hand: he had taken off his hat. The scalp-wound had crusted over, and the bandages had come loose in the fighting; he had not had an opportunity to repair them, and the scabbing made a gory line of dried blood around half his skull. "It is only an inconvenience," he answered. "Will you try and take a little wine?"

He eased Tharkay up, and gave him the glass; Tharkay held it awkwardly between his bruised and bloody hands, drank thirstily, and sank back again.

Temeraire peered in through the tent-opening, with one enormous platter-like eye. "I have seen to General Fela," he said, with an enormous and glittering satisfaction which made unnecessary any questions about that gentleman's fate, "—General Chu acknowledged I had every right to do it; but how is poor Tharkay?"

"Not yet expired," Tharkay said, dryly, without opening his eyes again. "Though I would be glad of some rest; and that, I think, I cannot rely upon."

"No," Laurence said, quietly. "We will have to leave at once; and, pray God, bring some of these legions with us."

. . .

"Be careful, there," Iskierka called, a hiss of steam escaping her spikes, and Temeraire craned his head over a little further, just to be sure there was not good cause for her concern. The egg was supported in a nest of furs, within a well-tried net, and there were three dozen handlers directly beneath it, their fingertips lightly touching the surface, in case the net should break, but still anything might happen; one could not be too careful. Temeraire was glad when the maneuver was complete, and the egg transferred at last from his back to the waiting, ceremonial dais where it would await its hatching.

He nosed at the dais again, to be sure it was just the right temperature. With his head close, he could hear the low gurgle of water running through it, which the head of the Imperial household had explained to him brought the heat, from a cistern below. It was indeed very pleasantly warm without being excessively hot, and a gentle breeze played through the hall in which the egg now stood: the central hall of Prince Mianning's palace, where they had first made their bows on arriving in China; but in attendance now there were only Mianning's trusted retainers, as well as Mei and a handful of Imperial dragons, and Temeraire's own mother, Qian.

Iskierka finished her own re-inspection of the dais, and drew her head back to snort with satisfaction. "That is well enough, I suppose," she said. "I hope you will make a point to those fellows, Temeraire, that they will answer for it, if anything should go badly. You may be sure *I* will not listen to anyone telling me that I cannot squash this fellow, or that fellow, if anyone should hurt the egg; I will certainly come back and answer it."

Temeraire had already expressed similar sentiments to the handlers, very delicately, a few dozen times; but he did agree, of course, that on this point he could not repeat himself too often. He had a final reminding word with Huang Li, the minister who would oversee the egg's protection and nurturing; that gentleman took it very kindly, and assured Temeraire that everything would go well.

"We will send you dispatches every week," Huang Li said, "with a report upon the egg's progress, until it is hatched."

"Oh!" Temeraire said, with delight. "That would be of all things wonderful. But do you suppose those will reach me, in Britain?"

"The Emperor has commanded it," Huang Li said, which was indeed heartening.

Iskierka nodded in satisfaction when Temeraire had translated this for her. "That is just as well," she said. "I want to be quite sure they are taking proper care of *my* egg," with a pointed stress on the possessive, and throwing a smugly superior look towards Mei before she pranced across the room to Granby's side.

Temeraire went to Mei to make his own farewells; they were leaving in the morning. "I am sorry we did not manage an egg together," he said, "but I am very glad to have seen you again, Mei. I hope you can forgive me," he added, "for the opium; I promise we will put a stop to it somehow, even if the Government does not like to. Laurence and I will make them give over."

Laurence and Mianning were speaking quietly together, near the dais. Laurence had been permitted to keep his sword, and a second one, a shorter blade, now sat upon his other hip; he wore a splendid set of new robes, in red satin, the gift of the Emperor himself. Temeraire rested his eyes upon him in tremendous satisfaction. If only he could persuade Laurence to wear them always, or at least on special occasions.

"I hope it will be so," Mei said, "and yes, I do believe you, Xiang, that you did not know. In any case," she added, "the crown prince means to send me there, in the company of the minister Ruan Yuan. We will soon begin to search the ships when they come in to Guangzhou, and burn the opium when we find it."

Temeraire was well aware this new policy would not be received with equanimity by the British Government, and the East India Company, but with a guilty glance over his shoulder, he decided he did not wish to spoil the parting, and he would just forbear to mention it to anyone else, except perhaps to Laurence once they were already on their way. After all, if the East India Company wished to complain, they might stop the opium coming, themselves. If there *were* no opium upon the ships, there would be nothing to burn.

Mei leaned out and rubbed her head against his, affectionately. "And perhaps you will return and we can try again, when you have won this war of yours. This egg might not breed true Celestial, after all, although we must hope for the best."

Temeraire flattened his ruff a little; he was quite sure the egg would hatch splendidly, regardless: one needed only look at its magnificently pearlescent shell and exquisitely proportional dimensions to see that it was something out of the ordinary. "I am sure that all will be well," he said, dignified, "and the egg will make a most notable companion for the prince."

"Oh! Yes, of course," Mei said hastily. "Only, one does not wish to see the true Celestial line disappear; another line may equal, but not surpass it."

Temeraire thawed; *that* he could accept. "If my honor and duty permit me, I would be very happy to return," he said, with only a little loftiness.

He would be, too, he thought, and sighed a little, looking around the gorgeously appointed hall, the comfortably high rafters, as he went back to Laurence. "You must admit, Laurence," he said, "that they do things very properly, here; no-one can complain of the hospitality, or the arrangements."

"I do not deny it in the least, my dear," Laurence said, resting a hand upon his flank. "And I will once again make you my promise we shall return, if fortune permits it; but you could not wish us to remain now, in these circumstances."

"No, certainly not," Temeraire said. "It is the outside of enough, for Napoleon to be beginning another war, and only just after he stole the Incan Empress, and caused so much trouble for us in Brazil."

. . .

They had undertaken the return to Peking in a blazing rush, as swiftly as dragons could go; but even so the weeks seemed to Laurence to melt away and run through their fingers. By now, they were all dreadfully aware, Napoleon might already have crossed the Niemen; if the Russians had chosen to give battle, the fate of Europe might already have been decided.

The speed of the Jade Dragon couriers, within China, depended on their intricate system of relays; traveling so far as Moscow was no easy matter, and they labored without intelligence. They could only muster with all possible speed and go, hoping. Laurence had wondered how swiftly the assembled *jalan* could be brought back north from the mountains, but Chu had shaken his head in some bemusement even to be asked. "There is no sense bringing those soldiers all that way," he said. "Those *niru* will go back to their usual stations; we will muster up fresh as we fly north. You Westerners seem to insist on thinking of dragons as though we were infantry. Telling ten thousand where to go is very difficult. Telling three hundred is not! Now, *feeding* them, that is another matter."

Tharkay had not wholly recovered, but he had preferred to come with them than to remain behind for his convalescence. Laurence now stopped into his bedchamber in the palace, returning from the ceremony of handing over the egg. They had made use of the sickroom, which gave out upon the courtyard, to spread a great many maps upon the floor and consult upon the quickest route towards Russia's borders.

Gong Su and General Chu had come three mornings ago to look these over, bringing with them a nondescript middle-weight dragon, one of the common blue sort, who was distinguished however by a silver headdress featuring two cabochon amethysts nearly the size of her own eyes, and who was introduced to them as Lung Shen Shi.

They looked over the maps, the dragons' heads thrust through the open wall; withdrawing, Shen Shi had shaken her head doubtfully as though casting off water; the movement set the silver jingling. "I suppose we cannot rely on them to have any proper depots?" she asked Chu. "We must rely entirely on forage?"

"I am sure the Tsar will be pleased to put his resources at your disposal," Hammond began.

"Herds of cattle, I suppose," Chu said, with a snort. "We cannot rely upon them."

She nodded her head. "In such circumstances as these, Honored General," she said to Chu, "I regret most deeply that supply will be somewhat difficult to assure."

Chu grunted. "How many dragons will this Napoleon have?"

"No more than a hundred?" Laurence said. "He can scarcely muster and supply a force larger than that which he brought across the Channel to England, so much nearer to home."

"That is something, at any rate." Chu said, not very enthusiastic. "Well, I hope he is not as clever as all of you seem to think."

"I had not thought, sir, that you thought so highly of our Western tactics," Laurence said, a little dryly, but wondering truly; he himself would not have given much for Napoleon's chances in the air against the Chinese legions, so outnumbered and in hostile territory.

"I am not worried about the fighting," Chu said, "when we have any. I am worried about time. I do not like to think what it will be if we have not defeated him before the harvest season. As the Emperor has commanded, however, so it must be." He heaved himself up. "There is no time to lose, but I suppose you will not want to go until you have seen the egg safely conveyed," he added to Temeraire. "We had better go the day after that, then. I will send on the word to the *jalan*-commanders, and we will rendezvous at Moscow."

"And I myself must leave at the earliest possible moment," Shen Shi said. "I ought to have been there six months ago, to assure proper supply."

Gong Su nodded and turning to Hammond said, "Mr. Hammond, will it be convenient for you to leave at once?"

"Oh," Hammond said, dismally. "I thought I—that is, I had expected, in the new circumstances of amity between our nations—surely I ought remain, as our standing ambassador—" He looked around as though for rescue. He had spoken with much enthusiasm of the opportunity of promoting the fragile new alliance, of cementing closer ties with Britain; and Laurence suspected he would be equally enthusiastic to be done with flying from one corner of the earth to another.

But Gong Su said gently and implacably, "The crown prince desires me to serve as the envoy of the court to His Imperial Majesty the Tsar, and relies upon you to provide the necessary introductions."

"Perhaps a letter—" Hammond said, half-desperately: he had already written three of these, in French and English both, and sent them on ahead by courier to Moscow, to inform the Tsar of the approaching windfall of dragons.

But he could scarcely deny that a single envoy appearing, in the company of several unharnessed dragons and claiming to be from the Emperor of China, should find it difficult to gain the confidence of the Tsar; and Gong Su pointed out he himself had not the advantage of the French language, nor could he rely upon finding an English interlocutor at the Russian court. "No, yes, of course, your point is well taken, only—" Hammond said, until at last with an unhappy look he had gone away to gather what few things he could assemble before being swept away: amongst these Churki, who shook her head disapprovingly at the prospect of the war herself.

"Three thousand miles to cross before we even come to the battle?" she said. "I do not deny the Chinese managed things very nicely on this last journey: I do not know that I have ever seen a neater job of supply. But that was in *their* country, with all the arrangements and storehouses they have laid up. It is unwise to fly so deep into a strange country without making arrangements in advance. But," she added, "in any case, Hammond, yes, it will be for the best if we go on ahead with this advance party. If I do not like the look of things, we will be closer to Britain, at least."

Her pleasure at the prospect of returning to Britain had very little to do with having absorbed Hammond's loyalties. He had in desperation, to prevent her trying to keep him back at her own mother's estate in the Incan Empire, explained his unwillingness to be severed from contact with his family. This being large and numerous, and by Incan tradition Churki's right to claim under her own protection, had changed her mind entirely; she spoke of them already in a possessive light at regular intervals, and had made Hammond teach her the names of all his nieces and nephews.

Hammond had given over trying to detach her, by now; he merely threw her a look of anxiety, and said to the rest of them as he made his hasty farewells, "Gentlemen, I trust I will see you in Moscow, not very long from now," a little grimly, as if he *hoped,* rather than promised, to be there.

"Hammond," Captain Harcourt said abruptly, "I beg your pardon, but I don't think you will see all of us." Laurence looked at her in surprise; he saw the other captains turn to look at her as well. "I have read over our orders, and they are clear enough: we are to get help to the Russians. But we have done that; I don't think our formation will make a particle of difference with three hundred Chinese dragons there, and we *will* make a good deal of difference in the Peninsula."

She turned to the other officers. "As soon as we have seen the egg safe delivered, gentlemen, I am taking the formation back to the *Potentate,* and we are going to make the best time we can for Portugal."

She spoke with decision; she was senior, as Lily headed the formation, and the right was hers. In any case Laurence could not quarrel with her judgment. In company with the Chinese legions, the formation could only be incidental, accompanying a force already more powerful than anything they would face in the air. In the Peninsula, they would represent very likely a substantial alteration in the balance of power. He could see at a glance, in Berkley's face and Sutton's, the immediate agreement, the eagerness almost at once to be gone where they might do so much good, and rejoin their own ranks; Laurence himself was hard-pressed to regard their prospects without envy.

"You must go with them," Laurence said to Demane, later that same evening, and found as he spoke that he knew Demane would not wish to go; that he knew, remembered, that Demane would not wish to be parted from Emily Roland. "I trust," he added, when Demane drew a breath, "that you do not propose to offer me an argument against your departure that would be as ungentlemanly as it would be ill-advised, when she has refused your offer."

Demane hesitated, and Laurence softened his tone a little. "No better chance is likely to offer itself to establish your career and see your rank confirmed properly: away from the Ministry and political concerns, on a battlefield, under Admiral Roland's command and Wellington's. Resolve to win their confidence, to behave as an officer and a gentleman, and you may hope to be treated as one: there are not so many heavy-weights on a scale as Kulingile that the Corps can easily let you go begging.

"And you could hardly hope for a better encomium in the eyes of the one whose good opinion you most desire," Laurence added, "than Admiral Roland's approval—nor should Excidium's feelings towards Kulingile be of small concern to you."

Demane was silenced by these last arguments more than the rest, Laurence was regretfully aware; but the point was won. Temeraire had then to be reconciled to being parted from Sipho, obstinately refusing to grant Demane's greater claim to his brother's company. "For after all," Temeraire objected, "it is not as though Demane is going anywhere that he should need someone who can read Chinese, and whatever else has he for Sipho to do, but hang aboard Kulingile's back, and perhaps be shot by some French soldier? I cannot like it in the least."

"What he can do," Laurence said, "if confirmed as a captain, is give Sipho his step to midwingman; and like as not to lieutenant. In any case, you must see that we cannot propose to separate them."

"I do not see whyever not," Temeraire said sulkily, though the two brothers had not spent a day apart from each other likely since the half-remembered occasion of their orphaning; Demane had been as much parent as sibling, since then. "I do not see why *either* of them must go," Temeraire added. "Demane can be confirmed as a captain very well here. If Kulingile considers him a captain, I do not see why anyone else ought to quarrel: you and Granby and the others have not in the least argued."

Laurence was well aware that *his* opinion on the matter should weigh with the Ministry not as much as a lofted feather; Granby himself was half-disgraced from their association and, unhappily, by Iskierka's general recalcitrance. As for Captain Harcourt, she had said nothing, but Laurence was well aware she and the other captains of the formation regarded Demane doubtfully: still too much a boy, still too much given to distempered brawling, and of foreign birth and race. They had not witnessed Demane's rescue of Kulingile as a misshapen hatchling when every other aviator would have seen the beast put to a quick death, nor the daily lengths to which the boy had gone to feed a ravenous young dragon in the midst of the Australian desert.

They had deferred to Laurence's judgment, and to the practical consideration that they none of them had the right to speak. Kulingile was unassigned to any formation, and too large to naturally acknowledge himself or his captain subordinate to any other beast of their company, for all his easy-going temper. But Laurence could not pretend to himself that they would not have been delighted to see Kulingile shift his affections, for instance to one of their own junior officers.

"He deserves the chance to show what he can do," Laurence said, "before the eyes of senior officers whose preferment can assure him the acquiesence of the Ministry. You cannot doubt that they, at least, *would* be full willing to quarrel with Kulingile's choice."

"Oh! I can believe anything of them, certainly," Temeraire said, "but I do not see why we must pay them any mind: after all, we have resolved *not* to do so, haven't we, when we think they are mistaken."

Temeraire was only at long slow length convinced that perhaps such a half-vagabond and uncertain existence as their own should not be the only nor yet the ideal course for a young man only beginning on his career to follow. "And one," Laurence added quietly, "who has not the advantages of family and name which both you and I possess, even if not in such measure as you might desire. Recollect he is an orphan, alone in the world, divided from the country of his birth and from his very tribe: even if he wished now to return, the port of Capetown is closed to our ships, and he is not of the Tswana; his own people have no dragons among them, and would scarcely welcome him and Kulingile back."

All now was nearly in readiness for the moment of parting, come upon them so swiftly and, Laurence only hoped, not too late to bring them to the aid of the Russian armies. The egg was now safely in Mianning's keeping; at dawn they would make their last farewells, the dragons of the formation taking wing for the harbor, Kulingile and Iskierka with them; and Temeraire and Arkady flying north with General Chu.

Laurence ducked into Tharkay's chamber again. The maps had been rolled into their cases and the meager baggage packed; Tharkay was lying in the bed, his eyes closed, dressed but for his sword-belt and his boots as though he meant to sleep in his clothing before waking for the journey. "It will be just as well not to be fumbling to dress in the dark, with these hands of mine," Tharkay said, dispassionately, working them gently open and shut as Laurence sat in the chair beside him: bruises still darkened the skin, and half the fingers were splinted.

Granby came into the room to join them and said, "You're

determined you won't take ship with us?" while perching upon the end of the bed. "It won't be an easy road. You'll be flying cold, Laurence, I'm afraid: I dare say the Chinese would have a fit if you tried to put up a tent on Temeraire's back. Have you got a new flying-coat, yet?"

"I have, thank you," Laurence said. Mianning had made him free of his own purse, towards repairing his wardrobe, and Laurence had swallowed his half-remembered irritation and begged Gong Su for assistance in navigating the etiquette of commissioning a garment from one of the local tailors in such a way that would not oblige the poor tradesman to proffer the item as a gift.

The coat had been delivered with sufficient alacrity to mean that the fellow had however stayed up night and day working upon it. But Laurence was grateful for the speed, which should let him take the coat with him; and more so that the garment did not make a guy of him. The leather was a supple black and the sleeves darted cleverly at shoulder and elbow with padded dark blue silk: a little outré, perhaps, but when Laurence had discovered how the contrivance served to ease the sweep of a sword, he had no objections to make. There were a few more ornate embossed decorations than he might have liked upon the sleeves, but these were subtle and easily to be missed at a distance.

His memory had begun more steadily to come back to him—flashes of recollection and emotion, conversations and actions: still with blank spaces full of surprise between them, but he felt no longer that strange sense of division from himself. Even that, he now recognized, was not so great a distance from the state of his mind these last several years. He *was* divided from the man he had once been, and by a gulf he could no longer cross.

"I fear there is something of cowardice in it," he admitted, meaning his loss of memory. "A retreat, and weak-minded at that, when I can no longer be what I was even if I wished; there is no pretense, no masquerade that could achieve it. I thought I had faced up to it; I had not thought to be so easily overcome."

"I am of the opinion," Tharkay said, "that you ought not assign to free will something more likely the consequence of a sharp blow to the skull."

Granby snorted. "You are the only fellow I can think of, Laurence, whose notion of a weak-minded retreat would be to cast your own head ahoo and slog onwards confused beyond everything, and nearly kill yourself thrice over."

He rose and gave Tharkay a bow in lieu of shaking hands: as he was short one, and Tharkay's still in sorry condition. Together they left him to his rest, closing the courtyard door behind them as they stepped out. The dragons of the formation were engaged in post-dinner ablutions—a final enjoyment of that pleasure which they would not so easily find after leaving the Imperial precincts, where enormous dragon's-head spouts were placed at the eaves of the buildings through which torrents of pleasantly hot water might be pumped over the dragons' backs.

"What an ungodly flood: we will be lucky if we are not all carried away," Captain Little said, as he sprang up onto one of the stone benches to save his boots, after Nitidus had grown too enthusiastic in his pumping: a broad gushing stream developed, running down Immortalis's back to the drain. "John, we will need Iskierka to toast their rumps before we get them back under harness, or we will all be flying wet," he said, offering a hand to pull Granby up by his good arm; and then, after a moment's hesitation, Laurence afterwards.

Laurence took it in an equally awkward spirit. The return of his memory had belatedly clarified all Little's avoidance: of course Little knew, for Granby had surely told him, that Laurence had by misfortune and Iskierka's indiscretion been brought into not only Granby's guilty secret, but his own.

And not, as one might learn of such a thing aboard a ship—not by whispered ship's gossip, and eavesdropping through her wooden walls, and one suspicious circumstance laid upon another like bricks to make a wall of certainty. Laurence could by that sort of testimony have denounced a score of men, in the Navy, and would nevertheless cheerfully and with a sense of perfect honesty have sworn, under oath, that he knew nothing of their predilections and personal habits, and denied any knowledge of a crime, even if Admiral D— had maintained an entire troop of particularly beautiful young men who could not reef a sail or pull upon a line, and Captain K— had so passionately greeted his first lieutenant of ten years, that man returning wounded from a boarding party, as to require all present to avert their eyes.

No: in this case, Granby had confessed it to him, outright, and thus made him complicit; and Iskierka had as plainly marked out Little's guilt. Laurence could not argue to himself that he did not know, and that he had no duty to speak.

The man he had been eight years before, Laurence realized, would have acknowledged that duty; perhaps would even however reluctantly and unhappily have denounced them to a superior, and set in motion all the machinery of the courts-martial to destroy them. That man would have put duty above not merely personal sentiment and attachment, but above the natural sense of justice which revolted at the idea of exposing to ruin and misery any man for such a crime.

He would have not valued his own feelings, on such a matter, higher than the law and the discipline of the service. If he *had* kept silent, either from affection or a sense of having received a confidence, or a more practical consideration of the damage the loss of two skilled captains and their beasts would do to the service, he would have felt a painful and bitter guilt at doing so. And so aside from an ordinary mortification at having his intimate concerns so exposed to a man not his close friend, Little had indeed a cause to fear; and especially a partial and stumbling return of Laurence's memory.

Laurence ruefully admitted to himself that he *had* been a great deal happier in this instance not to remember: it was wretchedly awkward to know that which he ought not know, and to know that Little and Granby should both know he knew it, while none of them might utter a word on the subject. But he felt no guilt; he was done with that subtle species of cowardice which hid behind the judgment of other men. He said to them, "I had better take my leave of you now, gentlemen; you will have a difficult time enough getting away, I think," and offered Little his hand. "My most sincere regards, and good fortune, to you both," he said, as close as he could come, he felt, to conveying a reassurance without being so plain as to embarrass them both. Granby he embraced, and added, more lightly, "And for Heaven's sake, John, have a care for that other arm."

"Trust me! Though I can't very well complain," Granby said. "I did say that I would have given an arm to have Iskierka a little more biddable, so if I have been taken at my word, that is not the fault of Fortune. So at least this time, you may indeed hope to be shot of me: I have Iskierka's word she will go quietly to the *Potentate,* and no more haring off madly."

"I am sorry for the pains she has put you to," Laurence said, "and I will refrain from expressing the sentiment to her, but for my own part, I must be grateful to her: I cannot think what we should have done, these last two years, without you both. Godspeed!"

He took his leave of them and navigated from one stone bench to another, making his farewells to the other captains as he passed them and their beasts in the flooded courtyard, until at last he was across, and stepped through the house and out to the palace lanes, returning to Temeraire's courtyard. "What is all that noise, over there?" Temeraire asked, raising his head from his book. The ground crewmen were bundling up their supplies, and the house servants were busily engaged in packing all Laurence's things under Temeraire's watchful eye, including the scarlet robes of silk and velvet. Laurence sighed inwardly to see them; he would gladly have left them behind by oversight.

"They are making something of a lake," Laurence said. The stones of Temeraire's court were still a little damp from his own bathing, and his hide still speckled with drops that had not run off him; Laurence took one of the large soft silken rags from their basket in the corner of the courtyard and dried a small pool which had accumulated in the crook of Temeraire's foreleg. Temeraire nudged him with pleasure and thanks, and Laurence seated himself upon the arm.

They sat together a little while without a word required, in silent contentment, a peace that would vanish soon enough; and yet would still be there to be found again, Laurence thought. How nearly he had lost it, entirely, without even knowing what he lost.

"Laurence," Temeraire said after a little while, "Napoleon will be quite outnumbered in the air, will he not?"

"So we hope," Laurence said. "And he will not be able to bring his full infantry and cavalry to bear against us, either. He will have to leave detachments behind to hold his lines open. Numerically, we should have the advantage, and the advantage of fighting on Russian soil."

"It does sound so very promising," Temeraire said. "Surely we shall have him this time. And you need not make that noise, either, O'Dea," he added. "We will have three hundred dragons with us: I am quite sure even Napoleon and Lien cannot have anything to say to them."

O'Dea, sitting on a rock and sewing links of mail back onto Temeraire's armor, had given a lugubrious snort. "Why, it's true enough we've a great many dragons *here;* I suppose we can hope that most of them will still be with us when we're *there*. We must hope for it, sure, seeing how Boney has sent the Russians scampering more than once before now. 'Tis a cold winter in that country, so I've heard: a cold winter to be out on the barren plain, haunted by wild beasts, without a fire to sit beside and all the French Army on our heels."

"I do not think you ought to speak so discouragingly," Temeraire said disapprovingly. "Why, Maximus and Lily and even Iskierka would not be going away if they thought there were any chance of our being beat: you see how sure they are we will win."

O'Dea wagged his head. "Ah, indeed; 'tis a pity, all those fellows going away by ship, and like as not to the bottom of the ocean."

Temeraire flattened his ruff, and maintained a dignified silence until O'Dea had gone back into the house, as the lanterns were dimmed; then he said to Laurence, "Laurence, what *will* we do, if Napoleon should defeat us?"

"Starve," Laurence said, dryly.

Part III

Chapter 16

THE ROOM WAS ABLAZE with candles, many standing before mirrors of gilt and shining on gold and silver; the guests an equal brilliance of jewels and silks and velvet, their voices rising and falling in steady rhythm over the delicate threads of music. There might be a hectic flush on some cheeks, a nervous edge to laughter too quickly suppressed, but no-one surveying the company would have imagined that four hundred miles away, St. Petersburg was occupied by Napoleon's army; nor from overhearing their conversation.

"They say that one could walk across the Seine on the backs of those foreign dragons, so closely were they crammed in upon one another outside Notre Dame," Countess Andreyevna said, in tones of solemn horror more appropriate to the discussion of a funeral than a baptism. "We see now where all this dreadful revolution leads, and what a monster has taken hold of France! He will not content himself with regicide and self-aggrandizement, but will tear down the Christian faith with everything else: he is a heathen, that is plain to see.

"And not seven months since the wedding," she added, with a flavor of spitefulness. "I hope that Bonaparte may be confident of his paternity."

The new *Roi de Cusco*, as he had been styled, was by now four months old and reportedly thriving: he had been christened Napoleon Joseph Pachacuti Yupanqui—by Cardinal Fesch, and quite in accordance with Catholic rites, despite the complaints of the countess.

Laurence had not held much hope of some event preventing the marriage. The Incan Empress had shown plainly she had as much quick decision in her nature as ever did Bonaparte, and having made her choice to accept his suit, she had already flung all the resources of her own vast Empire behind that course. Her dragons had driven the British out of the Incan Empire the very same day, and she had taken ship for France with Bonaparte not three months later, from the reports which had reached Laurence in Brazil.

Evidently, Anahuarque had also chosen to anticipate the rites, and thus had Napoleon so quickly gained the heir required to secure the loyalty of the Incan dragons and the future of his dynasty—the only thing which might have been wanting to further spur his relentless ambition. But however much the child's birth might be deplored, Laurence had not the least desire to engage in gossip about it. Napoleon's son could as yet do nothing; his army, everything.

Laurence quitted, without much ceremony, the company gathered around the countess in some impatience, and went seeking Hammond. He had been raised amid political dinners, gatherings of men either in power or soon to be, and his sense of such things was finely tuned: this was nothing of the sort—merely society, not politics, nor even the mingling of the two. There were a handful of aristocrats with some influence, each of them courted by a subtle band of hangers-on seeking personal advantage; a few staff officers and adjutants, none as high as a general. The rest of the company were merely the wealthy or titled or connected to the same, and of not the least significance.

"Hammond," Laurence said, having cut him out of his own conversation with an elderly dandy of a baron with a brusque swiftness of which he would have been ashamed under less dire circumstances, "why the devil are we here?"

He and Temeraire had arrived the previous evening, with Chu

and a couple of *niru,* and joined Shen Shi at the supply depot outside Moscow: enormous granaries piled high with wheat and cured meat, which she had displayed to them with an attitude of deep embarrassment. "I regret that my preparations have been so inadequate," she said.

They could not in justice be so called; but they were not, however, what one might have wished for a force of three hundred dragons: the Russians had been recalcitrant in providing assistance. "I am trying," Hammond said now, with some asperity, "to catch someone's ear: they will not listen to me; not even our own ambassador," he added bitterly, "the wretched old fool! There are a thousand adventurers all over the city, peddling miracles to anyone that will give them an audience; they have decided I am to be classed with these charlatans.

"My only hope," Hammond added, "was that your arrival would bring an end to their doubts—that they could scarcely deny the evidence when you had appeared—but I called at the department of state this morning, and a staff-officer told me that if you would fight, you might go westward down the New Smolensk Road and report for duty to whichever colonel you found first; but if I did not leave, he would lay hands on me and kick me all the way to the door. They have not received any report whatsoever, from the east, of any force of dragons approaching. Where *are* the rest of the beasts?"

"That is not a new question, to be asked of the British," a man said, approaching their corner, and Laurence looked at him startled: an extraordinary intrusion, and the note of rancor as palpable as the thick Prussian accent.

"I beg your pardon," Laurence said, grimly, wondering if he was on the point of facing a challenge, a wretched trap between honor and duty; and then there was something familiar about the man, the face. Laurence had a brief, vivid memory of gunpowder smoke in his nose amid a clear and brilliantly blue sky: of a vast army pouring over fields, tricolor flags billowing; a great dragon lapped in heavy scales almost like mail, a bellowing laugh; and he found he did know the man, despite his greying hair and his paunch. "Captain Dyhern, I believe?" he said, slowly.

They had fought together, briefly, in the disastrous campaign of the year six. Dyhern had been taken prisoner at Jena, he and his dragon Eroica, an impressive Prussian heavy-weight, both of them among the many victims of the revolution in aerial tactics which Lien had brought to Bonaparte's service.

Dyhern's face was hard and sour and scarred, thinner than last they had met and aged far more than the intervening years could account for; but they had been allies, once, and had done him no injury of which to be ashamed: Laurence and Temeraire had given what aid they could, even in the midst of that overwhelming rout. The anger was not personal, but general, then; Laurence looked steadily into his face, and Dyhern after a moment looked aside, as one who knows himself in the wrong and does not care to admit it.

"I am glad to see you at liberty, sir," Laurence said; he felt no obligation to press for any more satisfaction. "I hope it is not—I hope the cause is not an unhappy one." A captain would not ordinarily be paroled or released by the enemy, save if his dragon were slain; although in the legal sense Napoleon and Prussia had made peace, Napoleon had neither withdrawn his occupying troops nor released the dragons, nor his most valuable hostage: the crown prince of Prussia, who lived yet in Paris under his supposed guardianship.

"I escaped prison a year ago," Dyhern said, briefly for what could only have been a long and a dreadful tale. "As for Eroica—I know not. I have sought him in the breeding grounds. But they did not know of him. They sequestered many of our beasts deep in France—some we hear they have persuaded to turn coat and join their ranks: you may be sure he will never be seen among *those,*" he added, with a touch of fierce pride. "But of anything else—" His hand moved a little sideways, limply, as though to convey that the sum of his knowledge was insufficient even to be put into words.

So he was an aviator without a beast, grounded and unable to be of any use, and burdened by the wretched knowledge that if Eroica did live, he was yet kept a prisoner by his fear for Dyhern's own safety: a cause for bitterness Laurence had himself tasted, enough to make him sympathetic. But the twenty dragons that Britain had promised to the Prussian war effort, in the campaign of 1806, had only been held back due to the deadly plague which had descended so mercilessly on Britain's dragons, and would not even when healthy have made any material difference to the disaster.

"Yes, perhaps it is true," Dyhern said, with a snort. "But it is no wonder if the Tsar and his generals think very little of British promises now, and little of this story, this fantasy, of three hundred dragons from nowhere, from the hordes of the East. I have heard your story: you bring eight dragons, and call them three hundred."

Laurence shook his head: he did not himself know where the bulk of the Chinese forces were, nor why they had not yet arrived in Moscow, and in truth he would have felt doubtful himself if he had not already seen once with his own eyes the rapidity of their mustering. Dyhern was not wrong: with a few seeds of doubt sowed already, particularly if many other Prussian officers were also refugee among the Russians, and the British ambassador himself unconvinced, it was no wonder any longer if they could gain no ear.

"We had best go and speak with Chu," Laurence said to Hammond. "The remainder of the dragons cannot be far distant now: we might persuade the Russians to send a courier to confirm the approach of at least one cohort, if he can tell us their direction."

There could be no question of their merely departing for the front: the armies might be anywhere in a square five hundred miles across. An aerial force with no ground support, even one of their extraordinary size, would be perilously vulnerable to any encounter with a substantial French force mingling dragons and artillery; three hundred dragons was not so many that they could afford to lose half of them.

Laurence hesitated, on the point of departing, and then quietly said to Dyhern, "Captain, if you are not otherwise engaged in the war effort, I hope you will permit me to say that Temeraire and I would be glad of your assistance: we are short-handed, and my crew have many of them not seen aerial combat." Several of them indeed were former sailors, recruited from the survivors of the wreck of the *Allegiance;* his officers were a wretchedly scanty bunch, most of those having also perished in that disaster. Forthing was brave and competent enough, but not by any means a star in the firmament; Ferris could not be called a lieutenant, though he deserved the place; besides them Laurence had only a few ragged midwingmen and ensigns.

Dyhern was silent; the lines of resentment and misery stood out upon his face more strongly for a moment it seemed, in the candle-light of the room; then abruptly he said, "My God! I will not sit by the fire while there is a dragon to fly and fight; yes, I will come with you. Of course I will come. Do you go now?"

Laurence would have gladly made arrangements for his later joining them, but Dyhern refused: "I have with me my boots, my coat, and my sword. What else do I possess?" He accosted a servant to write a hasty note of apology to his host, begging for his things to be delivered to Hammond's care at the embassy when it should be convenient. "Baron Sarkovsky will understand: his mother was a Prussian, a cousin of my father," he said, "and he has been kind enough to give a home to a few of us who have not been able to stomach bending our necks beneath the Corsican's boot-heel: even those like myself for whom the army has had no use." The treaty which the King of Prussia had signed with Napoleon had been humiliating in the extreme.

The streets of Moscow were silent and humid, heat lingering in the late air of August, thick even at night, and the moon above them shone through an aureole of pale haze. "Napoleon is near Smolensk," Dyhern said, "or so they say; but he might be outside the gates of Moscow tomorrow, for all that damned coward Barclay has done to slow him down. He has not given a single battle.

He flees and flees, like a rat evading—Oh, it is Davout! Run to the east! Ah! Murat is there! Fly to the south! My God, Napoleon himself! And he faints away like a maiden," with a contemptuous sweep of his hand, his deep voice descending again from high-pitched mimicry. "It is enough to turn one's stomach. They let St. Petersburg fall without a shot fired; and still he flees. But Barclay must defend Smolensk; he cannot let it fall: so my friends say."

The streets had wound through a narrow and unpleasantly scented warren of crammed-in impoverished buildings, approaching the gates of the small main covert of the city. Hammond had at least gained them the use of the British embassy's courier Placet, a glum Winchester of middling years whose captain, a man named Terrance, contented himself with his isolate post through a good-humored drunkenness: they could not presently fly their usual routes with the French Army blocking them to east and north. Dragon and man were both snoring in harness, and were roused only with difficulty for the flight out to the encampment: this lying some ten miles and more beyond the city limits.

"*Three* of you, now?" Placet said with a sigh at Dyhern's addition to their party, though he outweighed an elephant handily and could have taken several more passengers without any real trouble. "Well, I suppose you had better lock yourselves on; we won't get there any sooner."

The encampment was barely respectable, by Chinese standards, though its appearance astonished Dyhern to silence. Shen Shi and her escort, eight of the common blue dragons and their numerous crews, had labored extensively: large cooking-pits were covered with rough-hewn stone lids, and over these enormous mats of wood and metal had been unrolled, on which dragons might sleep warm: more stood yet unused and waiting. Wells had been sunk up on a hill, near-by, and channels dug to bring the water rolling downstream, diverted into distinct pools for drinking and for bathing, and continuing on towards the cattle pens.

Above all this stood the great gauzy pavilion which had been erected once more for Temeraire, and beside this the one for Chu, where the general was napping; as they approached he raised his head, peering narrowly at Dyhern, and before Hammond could address him on the subject of the missing beasts demanded in tones of irritation, "Well, is *this* a Russian general, finally? Where are his maps? Will he tell me where the enemy is? My army cannot travel any slower than they already are."

Hammond, mouth half-opened, recalled himself and stammered, "Sir, no, this is Captain Dyhern, a Prussian officer, a friend of Captain Laur—that is, I mean, of His Imperial Highness. But so far as the army goes, we had come to ask you that very—that is to say, to inquire of you, where your army might be. I am afraid the Russians have had no reports, from the countryside, of any substantial forces approaching—"

He trailed off, in the face of Chu's stare, and fell silent. "Your remarks are very peculiar," Chu said. "Are you complaining because we are *not* spoiling the territory of our allies? My troops are not undisciplined yearlings."

"I beg your pardon," Hammond said, "but surely by now many of the—of the *niru* will have joined up, in preparation for the final muster? Even a quarter of a *jalan* could not escape notice—"

"No," Chu said, "nor travel more than twenty miles in a day, through this barren and unsettled countryside, before they had to stop to be sure they could feed themselves; certainly stripping the farmers bare to do so."

Laurence could not but recognize the plain sense of Chu's remarks: he realized in dismay he had unconsciously gone too far in assigning to the Chinese legions some fantastical power of supplying their wants, by the example he had seen within China itself, where undoubtedly there had been, unseen, supply depots and warehoused goods in the near distance available to the building force. "Sir," he said, "do you mean they are traveling in their individual *niru*? Keeping some substantial distance from one another?"

"Twenty miles, at least," Chu said, agreeing: indeed a sufficient separation to permit even many groups of dragons, traveling four at a time, to make themselves nearly invisible within the vastness of the Russian countryside. "It will require four days to muster the full force upon the battlefield: but that," he added in some heat, "must be presently!

"I have already sent the couriers to delay their pace, having seen the inadequacy of our supply here, but they cannot merely halt where they are, nor slow very much: the countryside is too poor. We must find the enemy, concentrate to defeat him, and disperse again to return."

Hammond cleared his throat and said, "Sir, I am—I entirely take your point, and—and I beg you do not suppose I in the least mean to question your arrangements; but perhaps if—perhaps if some fraction of the force might be assembled, and summoned hence—"

Chu lowered his head to stare at him. "Why?"

"The Russians think us liars," Laurence said bluntly, when Hammond would have continued to evade. "They do not believe that the force is coming."

Chu snorted and shook out his fringed mane with disgust. "They will certainly believe it when they have three hundred dragons eating every last scrap of wheat in twenty miles around this city, but they will not be very happy, and less so when I will have to send all my *jalan* away again before we have even seen any fighting!"

"I am very glad to see you, Captain Dyhern," Temeraire said, "and oh! It is the greatest shame, about Eroica: we must try and find out where he is, and I dare say then we can get word to him that you are at liberty. Perhaps we will take some French dragons prisoner, and I will ask them: I am sure no dragon could fail to be sympathetic to his situation, nor wish him to be denied a reunion with you."

"Temeraire," Laurence said, "you could not ask them to commit treason against their own nation."

"I do not see why it should be treason," Temeraire said, "when their nation has no business keeping Dyhern away from Eroica: you might as well say Moncey committed treason, because he told me you were on *Goliath,*" recalling with a shudder his own dark days in the breeding grounds of Wales; Moncey and his fellow feral Winchesters had been his only hope of himself being reunited with Laurence, then.

"But if they do not like to talk to me about it," he added, "I will speak to Moncey himself when we are back in England. I do not see any reason why one of the Winchesters mightn't nip across and have a word with some of the unharnessed French dragons, from their own breeding grounds. They did as much only to gossip; indeed, Captain, I am sure we will be able to find him for you."

Dyhern flushed red, when Temeraire had finished; he said, "I will thank you, if it can be done," very shortly, and then stepped away; Laurence said to Temeraire quietly, "My dear, pray do not raise false hopes: a thousand things may arise to prevent our being able to assist him."

"Well, I will not say anything more about it, at present," Temeraire said, but privately he did not see why it should be at all difficult: after all, Eroica must be somewhere, very likely with other dragons about, and it seemed very poor-spirited to be getting in the dumps without having at least asked properly. So far as Temeraire could see, Dyhern had only ever spoken to other men, and not tried to ask any dragons at all, much less the couriers or better yet the unharnessed dragons of the breeding grounds, and the ferals, who had the most chance of flying about as they liked.

"I don't suppose you know any of the unharnessed dragons in this country?" he asked Placet.

"You suppose rightly," Placet said. "I haven't seen hide or wing of a feral, and as for their couriers here, they are rudesbys; they speak some outlandish stuff and don't care to even nod their heads, in a friendly way, when they see you. They only go and take their pig, and sit in a corner and stare at you, as though they supposed you meant to come and steal it from them." He sighed heavily. "Not all of us get to go gallivanting about the world to charming places, with fancy dinners, and gewgaws; but one would think that perhaps the Admiralty might let a fellow come home, once in a while. But I don't complain, of course," he added.

"Well, there must be a breeding ground here, somewhere," Temeraire said, "and at the very least, they must have a bigger covert near-by for their own beasts: and," he added in sudden inspiration, "Laurence: surely we ought to go and speak to them in any case. I dare say the dragons will know all that Chu would like, about where the French Army is; they must be hearing of it from their officers every minute."

Dyhern could speak the Russian tongue, and direct them to the main covert of the Russian beasts, some twenty miles from the city, on the opposite side from their own encampment. It seemed a peculiarly inconvenient arrangement, in its relation to the encampment they had been allocated: when he drew it upon a map for them to see, there could hardly have been a greater distance, and yet keep both in an hour's flight of the city. Temeraire flattened his ruff at this discourtesy.

"Let us be a little more generous than that," Laurence said. "We have claimed the approach of three hundred beasts; even doubting us, they may well have wished to give us as much room as possible. I can conceive of no other reason that would place us at opposite ends. They can hardly imagine that we should seek a quarrel with their own dragons, when we are come as their allies."

"No, indeed," Temeraire said in some irritation, a state which only increased upon their arrival: the Russian covert was far better placed than the ground which they had been allocated, with better drainage, several small ponds and lakes sharing ground with a series of low craggy foothills, into which hollows had been dug and large roofs built out to make neat and comfortable dens, and from aloft many of these looked quite deserted but for small bands of men: Temeraire felt he and Chu might at least have been invited to take up residence, as a gesture of courtesy to the senior officers of their force, even if there were not enough room for all the dragons which were coming.

He descended through a brush of low straggly trees and scrub and nudged his way to the hollow nearest the border of the covert, and then he halted short, staggered, as the morning sun crept through behind him and broke like a stream upon the mass of a mighty and glittering hoard.

Gold—jewels—silver—Temeraire did not know where to look. Heaps of brass pieces, long chains of thick links of bright metal, dazzling great chunks of polished stone and glass, long carved sticks of polished ivory and mahogany and ebon, great cups and plates—dented and scratched from lying in a heap, but what did that matter when there were so many of them! so large!—and swords, and helms, and even huge bolts of cloth—velvet and silk, stained perhaps and torn, but still luxurious—enormous carved chests of wood heaped high with glinting shards of glass in colors, huge blocks of marble carved—

"Temeraire!" Laurence said, and Temeraire shook himself all over and jerked up his head. A low rumbling hiss of warning reached his ears, and he saw only then the huge dragon sprawled over the ground—she was lying upon the very heap itself, as though she had so much treasure she might make a bed of it.

She had a peculiar appearance: her body was sheathed in great plates of bony armor overlapping one another, not unlike the Prussian dragons Temeraire had met before, but to a far greater extent, and she seemed to bulge strangely underneath them: thick rolls swelled over her shoulders, and a large hump upon her back. Steel spikes and great steel rings had been bolted to her natural armor, silver over the natural green coloration of her hide, and were bristling all over her body; she was enormous, larger than himself and nearly as great as Maximus.

She reared herself up with a great heave; several other dragons scrambled away from between them. Temeraire had not noticed them before, either: small frightened-looking creatures, lightweights, mostly grey and white; they did not have the same armor plates, but the steel rings were planted in their bodies as well.

"Temeraire," Laurence said again, "she must fear you are here to quarrel over that treasure; we must reassure her at once."

"Oh," Temeraire said, "oh—yes. Of course. Of course I am not here to challenge her. Pray tell her so, Dyhern," a little wistfully: only look how much treasure there was! And he could surely have made a successful challenge, and perhaps won some of it for Laurence—"But we are allies," he said, mastering himself with an effort, "and we must think of our duty first. I am not at all going to challenge her, no matter how much treasure she has."

"We had better go away at once," Dyhern said to Laurence, low, in French. "The beast will pay no mind to us: why should she? We are not her captain, nor her officers; you will do your cause no good if you provoke a quarrel."

"Sir," Laurence said, "dragons cannot be blamed for not speaking to us, if we do not address ourselves to them. Pray translate for Temeraire, if you can, and let us make the attempt; we will certainly not engage. If she attacks, we must withdraw at once, Temeraire, without offering a blow in return."

Temeraire did not at all like the notion that if she should strike him, he should be obligated to run away; she would think him a terrific coward, and all those other dragons who were watching as well. "I do not see any reason she should attack me," Temeraire said. "I have done nothing to her, and I do not mean to; nothing at all."

Dyhern spoke to the dragon in Russian; Temeraire pricked his ears forward to listen to it: quite different from any tongue he had ever learned. But the enormous dragon did not pay him any attention, nor even look at him: instead she bared her teeth at Temeraire and hissed again, taking a step towards him that required no translation at all. He swelled up his chest, his ruff flaring: "I am not to be hissed at, if you please," he said coldly in French, "as I am perfectly able to manage you, if you *do* want to be quarrelsome."

"Temeraire—" Laurence began, but one of the small dragons, who had ducked behind the great one, put out his narrow white head, arrow-shaped, and said something timidly in a queerly accented French, "What do you want, please, if you are not here to fight?"

"Oh, you speak French, do you?" Temeraire said. "Well, we are here to find out where the French Army is: Napoleon, I mean. We are your allies," he added, "and might have expected a more polite welcome than this, I must say; I do not know what you are about, when someone cannot even land to pay a visit, without being hissed at and treated like a thief. And you may tell *her* so, anytime you like." There was a great deal of righteous satisfaction in making this speech, which a little consoled Temeraire for *not* being able to fight.

The little dragon turned and spoke to the larger in a tongue that was very much like Durzagh, the dragon language which Arkady and his ferals spoke, in the Pamirs. Temeraire could follow it better than not, and understood quite plainly when the large dragon snorted and said, "That is nonsense. Tell him to go away at once, or I will crush him, and take that breastplate of his for myself."

Temeraire flattened his ruff and snapped, "I should like to see you try—" But Laurence's hand upon his neck reminded him, so with a great effort he straightened his neck and with chilly condescension went on. "—but we are not here to pick a quarrel: so if you do want me to go away, you need merely answer my question, and we shall leave; I do not in the least wish to remain in the company of a dragon whose wealth is by no means sufficient to excuse her poor manners."

"And why would you ask me such a question?" the dragon said coldly.

"Well, I do not mean you must know where the *French* Army is, I suppose," Temeraire said, "but you can tell me where the Russian Army is, and that will be where the French are, soon enough; so that will do."

"What Russian Army?" the enormous dragon said. "What is this to me?"

Temeraire drew back his head upon his neck, in some confusion. "Laurence," he said, turning his head, speaking in French, "and Captain Dyhern, is there perhaps some mistake? This dragon is not in the army, at all."

"Of course she is," Dyhern said. "There is her regiment number, upon her shoulder," and indeed, Temeraire saw where he pointed to a large 26 painted in bright red that stood out upon one of the armor plates, and beside it the number 8.

"The captain is in a regiment," the little dragon interjected, a little uncertainly, "—I believe? I have heard him speak of the regiment."

The enormous dragon shrugged when this had been relayed to her, and said without moving her suspicious eye from Temeraire, "So this is some human matter. I do not care about that. If you want an army, you had better go find some humans and talk to them; and while you do it, you may go far away from me and *my* treasure."

She reached out her foreleg and jealously scraped a few spilled coins back into her heap: her talons were sheathed in bright caps of polished steel, which had been nailed on; she certainly *looked* as though she were a fighting-dragon. But Temeraire felt quite at an impasse: how could she not know if she were in the army, and not care about it in the least? Before he could ask her anything further, however, a man appeared in an officer's uniform: out of breath and red in the face, with several other younger officers running behind him, and shouted up at Laurence in French, "Who the devil are you? How dare you come stir up my beasts?"

"Sir—" Laurence said, and slid down from Temeraire's back,

to go and speak with the gentleman, who coldly deigned to give his name: Captain Ivan Rozhkov, of the Twenty-Sixth Regiment of the Air. He had a luxuriant mustache and beard, brown shot through a very little with silver, and a narrow face fixed presently in anger; he held in one hand a peculiar sort of short whip, with a heavy silver handle. The little white dragon had sidled over towards him, and was murmuring quietly to him; but he waved the dragon off. "As far as I am concerned," Rozhkov said, "you are a pack of spies: you will go, or I will set Vosyem upon you."

"If you mean that dragon there," Temeraire said, interjecting, "I have fought bigger dragons than her, without the least difficulty," although privately he did admit to himself that she would present a notable challenge: the armor might, he feared, stand up to the divine wind; and those spikes and her tipped claws would certainly be quite nasty at close quarters. "So you needn't be threatening. We are only asking so we can go and fight alongside you, after all."

Rozhkov only looked up at him halfway through this conversation, and then snorted and said to Laurence, "You English, you make your dragons into house-pets and parrots: keep your three hundred fairy tales, and take this trained dog of yours away to them, also! There are ten fighting-beasts in this covert all her size; I will rouse them all up if you are not on your way at once."

Temeraire reared up on his hind legs, to take a quick look around, and indeed he saw two more of the hollows in sight, and then he realized that in each of them a gleam might be spied out, through the treees—ten dragons! Ten dragons, all of them with so much treasure, it nearly could not be borne. "Oh," Temeraire said, longingly. "Oh; but how can they all be so rich?"

"If you think you will be pillaging here, you are very wrong," Rozhkov snapped to Laurence.

"That is enough," Laurence said shortly. "More than enough, sir; I am sorry to have distressed your beast, and to have disturbed your morning. I hope to God you will have no greater cause to regret the occasion. Temeraire, we will be on our way; there is nothing to be gained here. We must rely on Hammond to procure the intelligence for us."

"Certainly," Temeraire said, as haughtily as he could manage, dragging his eyes away; he reached out to put Laurence up. "It seems very peculiar to me, to find dragons so perfectly uninformed about the war they ought to be fighting in; but as their officers do not seem to be much better, one cannot blame *them,* I suppose."

He paused, with Laurence in his talons, and raised up on his haunches again: a heavy clanging bell had begun to ring, not far away, and cries were going up across the covert. Vosyem had lifted her own head in fresh suspicion. In the distance, approaching swiftly, a knot of five dragons were flying, unsteadily and on a wavering course. One was a beast on Vosyem's scale, enormous and armor-plated; the others were smaller, in motley colors, trying to support him as they went. He left a thin spattering trail of blood behind him.

Temeraire swung Laurence to his back and sprang aloft, even as Rozhkov shouted some commands, cracking the whip, and the small white and grey dragons all went up together alongside him. "Why is Vosyem not helping?" Temeraire demanded of the little one who spoke French, as they flew up. It would have been a great deal handier to have a beast or two that size, when there was one so large to manage landing; the poor fellow did not look as though he could come down properly on his own.

"But what if one of the others took her treasure?" the little dragon said, looking at Temeraire dubiously. "There are no guards posted, and it has not been locked up properly."

While that argument could be said to have a great deal of sense, it was also distinctly selfish, in Temeraire's opinion. At least there were a great many of the smaller dragons, and together they caught the huge beast from beneath and managed to get him landed safely in a vacant clearing. His head hung forward listlessly, and he seemed as though he only wished to lie down. But an officer aboard his back cracked his whip, and he continued to hold himself up while a rope ladder was flung down, and men scrambled off: he was carrying a crew of nearly thirty, and many of them officers.

They were met by the officers of the covert, running to help; several men in bandages stained badly with blood, some being let down from the belly-netting strapped down to flat cots; they were all carried away. A man in a captain's uniform staggered off, took a rag from a colleague and mopped his bloody brow, said in French, "Give me a drink, for the love of the Holy Mother," and took a cup from another and drank it down. He wiped his mouth and said, "I must get back aloft and to the city. Rozhkov, will you get Tri settled and get that belly-wound stitched up? By God! I didn't think we would make it in the end, even though I swore to General Tutchkov we would manage."

He took another gulp; his crew were already busily re-harnessing one of the smaller dragons, a white creature stippled with spots of grey and black, for him to ride, while dragon-surgeons scrambled for the beast. "For God's sake, Vasya," cried a younger officer, "don't keep us all holding our breath: what has happened? Has there been fighting?"

"Fighting!" the captain laughed, a harsh noise, hoarse. "If you want to call it that. We have been run out of Smolensk. We are falling back on Valutino, and if not there on Usvyatye, and if not there, on Tsarevo Zaimische—and if not there, God help the Tsar!"

Chapter 17

HALF-A-DAY'S FLIGHT, AND A pillar of smoke rising in the distance: another Russian town burning. As Temeraire beat towards it, Laurence saw the Russian Army straggling by, the small dragons flying past scarcely to be made out beneath the infantry soldiers clinging all over their bodies, being borne back with the retreat more swiftly than their feet could carry them. Officers were astride at the neck or in some cases being dangled beneath from a sort of swinging chair.

"Too much for their weight," Chu said, observing the flocks of smaller beasts, "although they are performing well, but infantry-dragons ought to be one hundred and fifty *picul,*" this measure being roughly on the order of nine tons; the white dragons were not more than six or seven, to Laurence's eye: barely light-weights. In the far distance, he could see a melee of courier-weight dragons skirmishing: Cossack troops, he supposed, tangling with the French scouts; the pursuit was not far behind. It was the thirtieth of August.

The army was in disarray; beneath them, Laurence saw the men marching in long columns, bedraggled, dusty; heads bowed with exhaustion, sullen. Endless numbers of men; Chu himself fell increasingly silent and astonished by the numbers, the further they flew; when they had come to rest upon a hill, near a trickling spring, he shook his head and said, "The ant can devour a mountain," and then plunged his head deep to drink.

Temeraire continued futilely to search for the high command; there was nothing which might have been called a headquarters visible to the eye. They flew over an artillery company rattling sluggish upon the road; Dyhern caught sight of Prussian soldiers and clambered down from Temeraire's neck, and went to speak with them. He returned to say, "Barclay de Tolly has been replaced: it is General Kutuzov, now, and they say he is in Elnya, to the south."

Kutuzov was not in Elnya; but much of the army had concentrated north of the town, and spilled into its limits. Laurence and Dyhern and Tharkay went into the streets together, to try and find some senior officer. A deep smoldering atmosphere emanated from the soldiers and officers alike, somewhere between misery and wrath; the burning of Smolensk was on every tongue, a collective mourning, and Laurence heard Kutuzov's name repeated every few steps with more desperation than hope. They at last found a ferociously busy colonel engaged in directing the fortification of the northern approach to the town. "General Kutuzov is in Vyazma," he said: another fifty miles, back the way they had come.

"I begin to see," Chu said in dry irritation, "why you use such heavy couriers; they must carry enough men to hunt down the one you are looking for, who may be under a table, or in a basket." The Jade Dragons might have flown the distances trivially, at much less cost to their joint energies, but speaking neither Russian nor French could not themselves communicate, even if Russian officers would have deigned to speak with them; they could serve only as couriers among Chu's own forces.

Temeraire and Chu reached the town as night was falling, weary. Two of Shen Shi's supply-dragons had accompanied them, carrying sacks of wheat and a dazed pig, for which they had ample cause to be grateful: the few Russian dragons they saw, their encampments merely crushed fields, were snarling and hissing at one another with belligerence over a scanty supply of dead cavalry-horses. They made their own camp upon a low hill not yet tenanted by any other company, and the supply-dragons dug a cooking-pit.

"If you will come with me," Laurence said to Dyhern, "we will try again: I suppose when we have looked in every town between Smolensk and Moscow, we will find him eventually."

He scarcely hoped for success, but they made Kutuzov at last, his pavilion planted atop a low rise among three companies of artillery, with two courier-dragons, red, drowsing beside it and a great flag waving brilliant white and red. But the way was still barred. Dyhern attempted to persuade the guards to let them through the perimeter without success; Laurence's French gained them no better result.

"Well," Chu said, when they had returned to report their failure, "this general can talk to me, and we can settle upon our ground, and I can summon the three *jalan* to assemble there in four days. If he does not want to talk to me, I can call together ten *niru,* here, and let them feed themselves off the countryside for three days. And if he does not talk to me *then,* we will turn around and go home, and I will apologize to the Emperor. I will not spend my soldiers for fools, nor expose them to those guns for no purpose."

He said this last very flatly: to have failed his orders so thoroughly would certainly condemn him to disgrace and exile from the Imperial court, even if the fault had been none of his own. But Laurence found he could not argue the decision. He had recalled too clearly, as Chu spoke, the dreadful slaughter of the French dragons at Shoeburyness: the smell of sulfur and fresh loam overturned, the rain of dirt flung high into the air as the British guns brought down the Grand Chevalier. He could scarcely fault Chu for not wishing to hazard his soldiers to such a fate without some assurance of support and the achieving of some desirable end.

"Laurence," Tharkay said abruptly, "do you have those particularly magnificent robes with you somewhere?"

"Oh! Oh, yes! That is a splendid notion," Temeraire said, lifting his head with as much eagerness as might be needed to supply the want of Laurence's own. "Of course they will not turn you away, Laurence, when they see you properly dressed. And I have the robes with me; at least, I ought to: Roland, you have made them quite safe, I suppose?"

"Yes, of course; they are wrapped in oilcloth and in the batting chest," Roland said, before Laurence could begin to protest. "Shall I fetch them out?"

"At once, if you please," Temeraire said, while Laurence drew breath. However desperate the circumstances, all feeling revolted at the notion he should trick himself out in the panoply of the Imperial court and use it to present himself as a prince of China—and not merely in that court, where all involved knew and perfectly understood the polite and fictional nature of his status, but brazenly to the government of a foreign state, to none other than the commander-in-chief of the Russian Army, appointed by the Tsar himself.

"Besides which, you can scarcely expect the Russians to believe me a prince of China on sight," Laurence said, "and they are not likely to listen or accept so fantastic a story as my adoption must seem, on first blush." But Temeraire was inclined to be mulish; Temeraire did not see any reason why anyone should doubt Laurence's claims.

"I beg that you will forgive my presuming to raise a small difficulty, Lung Tien Xiang," Gong Su said, coming quite unexpectedly to the rescue, "but there can be no question of His Imperial Highness presenting himself in such a manner."

Temeraire paused, his ruff flattening, but undeterred Gong Su added gently, "I am sure that if not for the urgency of our situation, and the small amount of time your duties have permitted you to enjoy at the Imperial court, you would recall that the honor of a formal Imperial visit cannot be lightly bestowed, and requires most careful arrangements. The foreign officials should have to be instructed in correct protocol," meaning of course they should have to agree to prostrate themselves before Laurence, an event unlikely in the extreme, "and appropriate gifts should have to be presented on the Emperor's behalf and offered in return. Of course such a remarkable mission cannot be sent forward without the Emperor's will."

"Certainly not," Laurence said, with deep relief. "Temeraire, you would not in the least ask me to do such a thing."

"But when the war depends upon it," Temeraire said, "I am sure the Emperor would understand if one were to make an exception—and all to carry out his orders," he added quickly, with the air of one seizing upon an excellent argument.

"I think we must be guided in such matters by Gong Su," Laurence said hastily, "whose experience of the Imperial court dwarfs our own."

Temeraire turned to Chu in appeal, but he shook his mane vigorously. "Oh, no," he said. "You are not going to get me to quarrel with the crown prince's envoy: I am keeping out of it. You are a Celestial and he is a prince; *you* can disagree. I am just an old general who wants a quiet life, and to retire to a place in the mountains."

Temeraire snorted at this. "But how otherwise are we to get in to see Kutuzov?" he said, turning back to Laurence, who was grimly aware he had no answer, other than perhaps bringing Temeraire down over Kutuzov's pavilion and pulling it up into the air, which should certainly provoke a response of some kind: more likely a cannonball than an invitation, however.

"If I may cut your Gordian knot," Tharkay said, with a glint in his eye. "Bring down the robes, Roland. You are not going to wear them, Will. You are going to lend them to me."

"I do not see why anyone other than Laurence should wear them," Temeraire grumbled, while they unpacked the indeed very thoroughly wrapped garments from their layers and layers of oilcloth and sacking. "They are *his* robes, and *he* is the Emperor's son; it seems to me quite wrong that you should present yourselves in any other manner. Laurence, if you are worried about causing the Emperor any distress, I am sure he should object to your lending out his gift. And is it not in any case quite illegal for Tharkay to wear them?"—half-pleadingly.

"Tharkay can hardly be considered guilty of violating the sumptuary laws of a nation of which he is neither citizen nor servant, and when we are not even within its borders," Laurence said, "and I will present myself to General Kutuzov, as I am, a British serving-officer, here with our nation's allies to assist in the war effort; Gong Su will present himself as the Emperor's envoy. We will not *claim* any position falsely for Tharkay. Whatever conclusions the Russians might choose to draw, from his looks, and his having borrowed certain garments of mine, will create no obligations of state on either side."

He spoke to convince himself as much as Temeraire: but his conscience smote him badly for this undeniable piece of sophistry, and still more when Tharkay had been rigged out in the red robes: he did indeed look a very imposing potentate. "You look as wretched as a cat, Will," Tharkay said. "You need not borrow so much trouble; I dare say we will be run out of camp at bayonet-point before ever we announce ourselves."

When he ran so dreadful a risk, Laurence could hardly begrudge him the right to extract what black humor might be found in the situation: they were far more likely to be shot, than laughed at, in the prevailing mood of the Russian Army, and Tharkay, in assuming a deceptive rôle, most likely to be held culpable. "Are you certain you wish to go forward with this?" Laurence said to him quietly. "If the Russian command are determined to reject help offered with an open hand, it need not be our concern to deliver it to them in the face of all obstacles which they put before us."

"And go back to China, with three hundred dragons at our back?" Tharkay said. "No, Laurence; it would be an unconscionable waste, and I find I have committed too much to the enterprise to see it fail now." He paused, and with less levity added, "You must know, Laurence, that if we cannot stop Napoleon here, likely we can never stop him. If he has time to establish a Kingdom of

Poland, and feed it the rest of Prussia little by little; if he can ship over a hundred Incan dragons—" The sentence required no completion; Laurence nodded. With the wealth and power of the Incan Empire merging with his own, and his conquests in Europe secured, Napoleon's position would grow the more unassailable; his fist would close ever tighter. Russia was the last great counterbalance left in Europe; if it fell, Napoleon would turn all his attention to Spain. And when Spain had been crushed—he would look to Britain once again.

He settled on his own sword, then flanked Tharkay on one hand; Gong Su took the other, with Dyhern, Forthing, and Ferris behind, all of them in the best show they could arrange. They were preceded into the camp by two Jade Dragons: the size of drafthorses and utterly foreign with their lean vulpine heads and dragging wings, bearing suspended between them, on chains slung from their necks, a fence-post on which they had rigged Chu's banner, framed on either side by lanterns in the Chinese style.

Their procession met with bewildered astonishment as they began it, and collected up a number of strays and camp-followers in their train as they went through the encampment: boys running alongside staring and calling in Russian. One of them, rather daring, darted forward to touch with a finger the wing of Lung Yu Fei, the Jade Dragon nearest the side; she whipped her head on her long narrow neck around and hissed at him for this effrontery. With her jaws of serrated teeth scarce inches from his face, the boy paled and fell backwards in alarm, scuttling away on hands and feet like a beetle while his friends jeered him good-naturedly.

They were very nearly as good as a circus coming up the hill for pageantry, and the very growing noise of their approach removed the necessity of passing some challenge: the inhabitants of Kutuzov's pavilion came out themselves to see and to stare as they climbed the hill towards them: the field marshal himself a portly and beribboned gentleman in front, white-haired and with a large, high-browed face, the nose and cheeks and jowls bulbous, one eye milky; epaulettes and medals and sash proclaiming his identity. Beside him was a tall lean man with a smooth-pated head: Barclay de Tolly, Laurence thought. Their party came to a halt some several arm's-lengths away, and the Russian high command regarded them in silent astonishment while not a word was said.

Tharkay carried the event in high aplomb, his face set in the sternest lines as he regarded the assembled Russian company with a searching air, and then said over his shoulder, in Chinese, "I think that will do; you had better be the first to break the silence."

"Gentlemen," Laurence said to them in French, "I am Captain William Laurence, of His Royal Majesty's Aerial Corps. I am here on behalf of our ally, the Emperor of China, in the company of his envoy, and I have the honor to offer you three hundred of the Chinese aerial legions, who can be on the battlefield in four days: if you will use them."

Temeraire could not help but feel a little dissatisfied the next morning, even though Kutuzov had personally come to see them, accompanied by several of his staff officers: the general inspected them all with an air of suspicion, studying Chu and Temeraire especially with narrowed eyes. He looked over the supply-dragons and the Jade Dragons, and then demanded of Laurence, "The numbers of this force are in these proportions? Two middle-weight to eight light-weight and four of these—"

He gave a wave of his arm up and down, baffled by the Jade Dragons, who regarded him and the Russian officers with doubtful expressions of their own; Lung Yu Li said to Temeraire very quietly, "Surely that man has forgotten to put on all his clothing?" Kutuzov was wearing snug trousers and a waistcoat all of brilliant white, excessively tight upon a figure which was not good and showed to even less advantage as he lowered himself into a field chair put down for him, low to the ground, and stretched forth his legs and reclined back so as to make the mound of his belly protruberant under his folded hands.

"No, sir," Laurence said to him. "There are only a few more of the couriers, and they are not counted in our numbers; it is three middle-weight fighters to one light-weight for supply."

"Well, well. You are generous fairies, indeed. All the more so that he has brought almost no heavy-weights, himself," Kutuzov added, meaning Napoleon. "All right, so where is this Chinese general of yours? As long as I am here, let me talk to him. Why is he hiding?"

"I beg your pardon, sir," Laurence said, "*this* is General Chu."

An absurdly long amount of time was required to make Kutuzov believe that Chu was indeed their commander; the Russians looked increasingly disdainful, and several of them began to speak in low voices to Kutuzov, again proposing that the whole force was imaginary, until Temeraire, still smarting at *middle-weight*—he was by no means middle-weight; no-one could possibly have called twenty tons *middle* weight even if he were not as enormous and lumpen as the Russian beasts—broke in.

"If we were inventing it all, for what reason I cannot imagine," he said coldly in French, "you would not be any worse off believing us than you are now, with Napoleon chasing you across your own country, and, it is plain to see, giving your dragons a drubbing. If you *did* have a dragon general yourselves, I dare say he would have put matters into better train."

With morning, Temeraire had been able to see a little more of the arrangements of the Russian beasts in the rough coverts they had arranged for themselves: they were all outrageously quarrelsome with one another, at least the heavy-weights were. There did not seem to be very many of them, and all had wounds of some sort, some of which had not yet been treated properly: he had seen at least three with swollen bulging places where a pistol-ball had not been extracted, although he remembered quite well his own surgeons Keynes and Dorset saying that it was of great importance to remove them swiftly.

Vosyem and her regiment had been summoned up overnight,

and Temeraire had seen the small dragon from her clearing again, laboring under a heavy tun of water which he was bringing her to drink, though she certainly could have more easily carried it herself, or for that matter gone to the pond to drink.

The little dragon had stopped by their own camp: his was the only friendly greeting they had from any of the Russians. "I am glad you have found us after all," he said, in his small chirping voice, "and that it is all cleared up: so you *are* here to fight with us?"

"Yes, of course," Temeraire said, "but pray tell me, whatever are you doing with that water?"

"Oh, I will bring you some, too, I promise—only pray do let me get a little supper, first," the little dragon said, misunderstanding. He spoke with his head tilted, peering sidelong up at Temeraire as though he expected to be cuffed, and then glanced with even more anxiety over to where several other of the small dragons were now picking over the remnants of the carcass of a large moose which had just been abandoned by one of the heavy-weights.

"I do not need any water," Temeraire said; the Shen Lung had jointly chosen a campsite near a small stream, which had taken not the work of half-an-hour to divert into forming a convenient pool, "and if you are hungry, you may have some of our breakfast, if you like; we have plenty. Only I have seen you fly back and forth seven times in the last hour past our camp. I beg your pardon," he added, "if I seem rude for inquiring, but I cannot make any sense out of it."

"Oh, I am doing whatever Vosyem would like me to do," the little dragon said, meanwhile turning to stare at the immense pit full of porridge and meat. "Is that really food? But there is so much of it."

Shen Lung Chi, who could not understand him, nevertheless could read his hungry expression perfectly well, and dished out a large bowl of the porridge; after having devoured this and licked it bare, and refreshed himself at the pool, the small dragon was induced to reveal that his name was Grig, though he seemed half-alarmed even to confess he had one at all. It seemed that the light-weights were meant to answer to the whims of the bigger dragons, and ordinarily fed only on what leavings they could snatch.

"She wanted some water," Grig said, "and then she wanted me to fly back to camp and be sure that her treasure was under proper guard; but Captain Rozhkov would not give me leave to do that, so I had to go back and tell her so," he hunched his shoulders as if in the memory of a blow, as he repeated this, "and then she had me carry him a message, and say that if he did not let me go, she would go herself; so then I had to come back and tell her that if she left, he would call off the guard and let *all* her treasure be stolen—"

"Well, it seems to me a perfectly wretched arrangement," Temeraire said, "and I do not see how any of you are going to fight properly, when we have any fighting: you will be too tired."

"Oh," Grig said, "but I will not be *fighting;* I am too small to fight."

"You aren't smaller than those Cossack dragons, over there," Temeraire said.

"No; but they are irregulars, and I am too big to join them; they cannot feed a dragon my size," Grig said. Temeraire looked over at the Cossack camp: it seemed a far more hospitable place, their dragons tucked around the campfire in amongst the people, and if they did not have enormous heaps of treasure at least had neat harness, and most of them wore handsome woven blankets. But it was certainly true they were considerably smaller: the size of Winchesters, courier-weight beasts by British standards.

Certainly the Russian heavy-weights all looked very imposing—no-one could deny it, and Temeraire had observed that, despite their size, they demonstrated a remarkable speed. Their steel-taloned claws and long necks lashed out very much as though, as Forthing put it, there was gunpowder lit behind them. But as they demonstrated their fighting qualities, for the most part, by quarreling with one another and knocking about the smaller beasts, Temeraire nevertheless felt entirely justified in making his criticisms now, although the Russian officers evidently did not enjoy hearing it, and several of them scowled and spoke again to Kutuzov in their own tongue instead of French, with passion; but the general waved his hand and silenced them.

It seemed that the Russian Army had been retreating all this time, ever since Napoleon had crossed the Niemen—all summer long. Their first plan of battle, which to Temeraire sounded quite sensible, had evidently been to give battle at Vilna and then withdraw a little way into their countryside, luring the French to a final battle at a fortified encampment, where the Russians should have had the advantage. Why they had decided instead to only run away, Temeraire could not in the least understand, when they did have a very substantial army; surely it would have been better to at least try and fight, even if it did seem that Napoleon had a much larger army than anyone had expected.

Evidently many of the Russian officers shared his sentiments, and General Barclay had been superseded as the senior commander for having failed to give battle; but it did not seem to Temeraire that Kutuzov was in a great hurry to fight, either: they were still arguing whether the battle should be given here, or at the nearby town of Tsarevo Zaimische, which evidently offered good ground, or somewhere else entirely.

In any case, though they had been running away as hard as they could, Napoleon's army had nearly caught them a dozen times. He had refined still further the use of dragons in his operations. From what the Russians described, each regiment now traveled with its own beasts, infantry and artillery alike. Men and light-weights foraged, while the heavier dragons leap-frogged companies down the road, and occasionally bore up the guns and heavy loads. Napoleon had eschewed larger magazines; his supply depots were instead numerous and lightly defended, each of them vulnerable perhaps, but as a whole able to withstand even many losses.

"He builds them in the woods, where there are no roads at all," General Barclay said. "A heavy-weight knocks down a few trees for them and goes on; the middle-weights come, deposit some goods and cattle, assist in building a little fortification, and go on; a few light-weights strike out across the countryside for whatever of substance they can steal, leave it, and go on; then a company remains with a couple of light guns and a few couriers, enough to carry supply forward. If our Cossacks strike, they defend themselves. If we come in force, they snatch whatever they can carry and flee, dispersing to the nearest other depots and reinforcing these, and call for a heavier beast to strike in return."

The Russians had only evaded Napoleon through good luck and desperate contortions, and because he and his generals had thrown away several chances by arguing with one another. Napoleon's own brother Jerome had simply run away from his corps on the eve of battle in a temper and gone back to France; or so the Russians said—they had evidently learned of the incident from their spies, and it was repeated with great enjoyment. Then, too, thanks to heavy rains, the Russian roads had become quite impassable with mud at several points, slowing the French advance and forcing Napoleon's dragons to carry the guns nearly all the way by air. Temeraire had carried a twelve-pounder himself once, in the retreat from London, and it had been quite exhausting; one could not lug something so heavy and then fight again straightaway, particularly not without a healthy dinner.

It seemed that Napoleon had tried to repair the sluggishness of his advance, as much as he could, by personally flying about to the different parts of his army, when he could, to take command directly; he had been at the battle of Kliastitzy, and smashed the Russian corps there, opening his Marshals' road to St. Petersburg; and a week later at Smolensk, where by the narrowest of margins the Russian Army had escaped him. And now he was closing in ever more swiftly; he would be on them within a day, perhaps two, and it seemed the Russians had decided at last to fight.

Chu, when Temeraire and Laurence had finished translating the Russian accounts of the campaign so far, hummed deep in his throat, skeptically. "Are they sensible men?" he demanded.

"I know it seems peculiar that they have been running away all this time," Temeraire began, but Chu snorted.

"Nonsense," he said. "What is peculiar is that they have been planning to fight an army larger than theirs in every way, with inferior air support. If they did not know we were coming, they had much better have kept running!"

Temeraire was taken aback; Laurence said, "General Chu, Moscow is in some sense the central city of their nation—it is not formally the capital, but the Tsar is crowned here; they cannot let it fall without some resistance."

"Oh, I see; politics," Chu said. "Well, at least find out for me why they have organized their aerial forces in such an absurd way, for there must be *some* reason. I see they do not have any proper system of supply, but they could at least field forty middle-weights, instead of those fifteen hulks and so many of those little fellows."

The Russians looked irritated to be questioned on this point. "Does this beast of yours not know how long an egg takes to hatch?" General Tutchkov said to Laurence, impatiently. "How does it suppose we should have got fifty middle-weight beasts under harness since they crossed the Niemen?"

"You might have gone to your breeding grounds," Temeraire said. "I dare say if you had offered even a little of all that immense treasure to your retired beasts, or your ferals, they would have been delighted to fight for you." This suggestion met only with stares, and a great comprehensive snort from Kutuzov out of his bulbous nose, which was quite rude; but at any rate, it answered Chu's remaining concern: the Russians had not thought to do so.

"So, they are *not* sensible men," Chu said with finality. "How do they expect to properly oppose a nation whose aerial forces so outweigh their own? They may be victorious in this war, thanks to our assistance, and yet find themselves in the gravest difficulty in the next season once again.

"But," he added, "that is not my business, but theirs! My business is to win now, and if that is the only reason, and these numbers are correct, I am satisfied with our prospects for battle. But I must yet have four days to concentrate upon the battlefield."

Kutuzov was silent a moment, when this information was conveyed: the great massed corps of Napoleon's army were hard upon their rear, and even falling back might not gain them sufficient time along the road to Moscow. "Well," he said finally, "if we cannot win the time from our enemy, we must ask him if he will be so kind as to give it to us." And he called over one of his pages, and took up a pen and paper, to write swiftly a letter to the Tsar.

A large tent had been erected upon neutral ground outside Vyazma, a field cleared half-a-mile in either direction and policed watchfully by dragons of both parties: for the French part, Laurence saw, nearly all middle-weights of no breed which he recognized, most of them with large broad foreheads. Deep chests and heavy shoulders were common as well, but their hides were of peculiarly motley appearance, muddied greens and yellows and browns.

He thought grimly that he detected Lien's hand at work there, though there was no sign of her either at present or reported by the Russian scouts; at least one spy report not three weeks old had positively placed her at the Château de Saint-Cloud, outside Paris, in the company of the new Empress and the infant heir. "I can believe nearly anything of her," Temeraire said, "but she cannot have let Napoleon go to war without her: I am sure she cannot. I dare say she is hiding somewhere, and will find some way to do something dreadful to us before the end. Not," he added, "that I will not be entirely ready to meet her, Laurence, of course."

Gong Su had not disagreed with him openly, but quietly told Laurence afterwards, "It is considered the foremost duty of every Celestial to guard the Emperor's line, a duty which precedes even the ties of companionship: and Napoleon has now but this one child. I think it likely that Lung Tien Lien has indeed remained in

Paris, to protect him and to forward his education," a stroke of great good fortune for which Laurence could not but be grateful.

But Lien had now had charge of Napoleon's aerial forces and his breeding programme for a full five years, and the fruits of her labor were everywhere to be observed not only in the looks but in the wide intelligence and education of the French dragons. These were frequently to be seen sitting up high on their haunches and peering into the distance, getting the best look they could at the disposition of the Russian troops, and then putting their heads together to murmur and exchange thoughts. They were all of them under harness, but many of them bore no evident captain, and several of them emblems which might have been symbols of rank.

Indeed one of the dragons, a grey-and-green beast not quite a middle-weight, sat quietly and unobtrusively in the corner of the field, unremarked; but Laurence saw with disquiet that besides a very cursory harness, only enough to take up perhaps a few riders, it bore a wide red sash pinned with a large silver star: a Marshal? Napoleon had granted Lien the baton years before, establishing the precedent; a dragon of sufficient military gifts to have merited another such grant would surely make a deadly opponent.

There were also three heavy-weights beside: a Petit Chevalier and a Chanson-de-Guerre, each holding one corner of the French line, and anchoring the center was a dragon as different from every other beast upon the field as could be imagined: an Incan dragon, with its long lapping scales like feathers gleaming a brilliant sky-blue and tipped with scarlet, looking more like some immense sort of brooding phoenix, wearing a kind of golden headdress and its belly armored in a mesh washed with gold and bearing many decorations: surely an officer in the Incan armies, and if not yet wholly familiar with Western warfare, likely to be an able commander in the air.

But there were enough signs of weakness visible to hearten a Russian ally, too: hard use had worn many a harness-strap and tarnished many a buckle; the men aboard the dragons looked thin, and they were fewer in number than they ought have been, for so many beasts. However skillfully they had stretched their supply, however swiftly they had moved, still their ranks had dwindled during their long march, and Napoleon could not easily get more men to swell them out again. Laurence had taken a short flight aloft with Temeraire, earlier, and spied out a little of the enemy's artillery: nearly all nine-pounders or lighter, although there were many of them, and the number of cavalry astonishingly small; Bonaparte was relying heavily upon his aerial advantage.

And to this encouragement, Hammond had sent a welcome dash of joyful news: Placet had arrived breathless from Moscow the night before, with Captain Terrance, wide-awake sober for once, spilling off his back; he had seized Laurence by both arms. "Wellington has smashed Marmont, at Salamanca," he said. "On July the twenty-second. Routed him foot and horse and wing: the French lost thirteen thousand men, and they say Marmont is dead, or at least so gravely wounded we will not see him again in the field this year."

If that news had yet reached Napoleon, or his men, to discourage them, there was no evidence of it to be found in their soldierly demeanor across the field; but it had been inexpressibly heartening to men facing the might of France. Laurence would have been drunk still this morning if he had swallowed every toast offered him the night before, in Wellington's health and the King's.

Chu had under cover of darkness taken himself and the rest of his forces to the back of their lines, out of sight of French spies; he now napped comfortably, too old a campaigner to fear the event and satisfied with his arrangements, while Shen Shi and her staff, even further back, had begun the work of organizing cooking-pits and water, and medical stations; the blue dragons were ferrying supplies from the depot near Moscow. The Jade Dragons had gone already to pass the word amongst the *jalan* to gather.

Temeraire stood anxiously amongst the dragons on the Russian side of the field: incongruous in his smooth black and clean-lined conformation when lined up with the bristling, armored Russian heavy-weights, whose own suspicious attentions were nearly all devoted to him and to one another, rather than the enemy. The Russian beasts were laden with men, grim officers in thick leather coats, who held thick riveted straps of leather which had been chained on to the rings driven into the heavy plates of horn that grew upon the dragons' shoulders. Others dangled from grotesque bridles, made of chainmail with spiked steel bits, which Laurence no less than Temeraire could only regard with disgust.

Vosyem was of their number; Temeraire had tried to speak with her, and propose helping her remove it. She had snarled at him around the bit, and fiercely said, "You would like it, that I should be shamed, and refused a chance to do battle and win my share; one less to divide the plunder with, is that it?"

"That is a very quarrelsome beast," Temeraire said in some irritation, withdrawing, "and if anyone could be said to deserve to wear a muzzle, I suppose she does; but no-one *can* be said to deserve it, Laurence. What are they about?"

"I cannot tell you." Laurence watched the line of Russian dragons: the snarling, savage twists of head giving them a look of restive cavalry-horses; the crews gripping hard upon the lines with their faces as set as men facing down artillery, as men looking into the maw of death, though they stood upon no battlefield: they were afraid of their own beasts. "I have always heard the Russian aerial corps mentioned as one to fear," he said, low. "The dragons, it is reputed, will not cease fighting if their captains are taken and cannot be seized by boarding; they have often been seen to fight wholly unmanned."

He had thought, by that reputation, that they might expect to find some greater degree of enlightenment here in the treatment of dragons, perhaps some influence from the East; instead it was plain the dragons would fight on in such circumstances because they had no affection for their officers, or their crews, at all. They cared nothing for the cause of battle, and only for the reward which might be theirs at its conclusion.

"I cannot deny," Temeraire said, "that their treasure is magnificent beyond anything; but it is not enough for any sensible dragon to put up with *this*. No wonder they did not think any of their ferals would fight for them. Laurence, I must say, if only he were not such a tyrant, and always beginning wars, and invading people's countries—"

"Yes." It was hard indeed, for anyone who had affection for a dragon, to look upon this field and not feel the keenest sympathy with the French and their emperor's more enlightened regime, in that regard at least. And yet behind the noble ranks of that army lay a track of near ten thousand miles of wasteland, of death and ruin for man and dragon alike, and if Bonaparte were not stopped, it would march across another ten thousand. There would never be an end to his ambition. "It is time," Laurence said.

From the northern end of the field, the French dragons had made way for a small company to come out: three courier-weight dragons, bearing the flag of France and the standard of the Imperial Guard; a company of the Imperial Guard on foot watchful behind them, polished and brilliant in their red cloaks. And sitting on the center dragon, a man in a grey coat, with his bicorn hat worn athwart.

"Pray do be careful," Temeraire said to Laurence. "Even if Lien is *not* here, I dare say Napoleon will think of something dreadful to do, if only you give him the least chance."

"Recall that for once, this is our trap, not his," Laurence said, "and we can only be grateful that he seems to be walking into it." The grass of the field was yet wet with dew and left streaks upon his Hessian boots as he strode across it towards the gathering Russian party.

Napoleon was altered still further from the last occasion Laurence had seen him, in the Incan capital city of Cusco: older, fatter, and more tired; his voice was thick with a bad cold, and he pressed a handkerchief often to his face, coughing. He showed all the ill-effects of the strain which he had placed upon himself, by flying at such frequency from one part of his army to the next. Standing to greet him, Tsar Alexander was the taller by a head, his face set in stern lines and handsome, though his curling hair drew back a little already from his high brow; young and vital and with an intensity in his looks, romantic in flavor, and a flush on his pale cheeks that stood stark against the high black collar which he wore. The contrast they offered to the eye only increased the impression, looking upon the French Emperor, of fatigue, of a man past the days of his youth, and perhaps his prime.

And yet somehow when Napoleon entered the pavilion he diminished his company, rather than the reverse: a subtle and yet sensible movement traveled around him, a shifting of weight, eyes turning towards him, which made him somehow the center of the stage.

He discarded formality: reached out his arms and embraced the Tsar and kissed him upon both cheeks, though Alexander received the gesture only stiffly, and with a set mouth. "*Mon cher,*" Napoleon said to him, and keeping a hand upon his arm spoke to him directly of his regret, disregarding quite all other men in the room: all sorrowful familiarity, nearly paternal. "You have desired this war, I think," he said, "as little as I have. I know the love you have for your people and your country; no less than mine for France, and so dreadfully have both suffered from our disagreements, and to what end? To whose satisfaction?"

He turned and beckoned forward one of his young aides-de-camp, who carried a long, thin draped package forward. "I have the honor," Napoleon said, "to return this to you: a token, if you will take it as such, that we would gladly be not your enemies, trespassers and thieves in your land, but your guests, cherishing your possessions as dearly as those of any well-loved host."

It was indeed the icon of Smolensk, the frame a little blackened with smoke, carefully laid on a bed of white velvet. "It was saved from the fire by Murat himself," Napoleon said, "who ran into the cathedral to snatch it from the smoke and amidst the falling timbers: a scene of such destruction I yet am anguished to recall, and had no power to prevent; God forbid another such occasion."

The threat, standing as they did not a hundred miles from Moscow, could not have been more pointedly delivered nor received, and Alexander, though handling the icon reverently, gave only short thanks; he had it swiftly removed from the tent, when an aide had been sent out to bring a Russian priest to carry it away. "I think you know Mikhail Illarionovich," the Tsar then said, meaning Marshal Kutuzov, and made punctilious introductions to every other officer of the general staff present, even through the ranks of brigadiers: at once serving to make a greater delay, and to deflect Napoleon's attentions from himself.

Napoleon addressed Kutuzov with a jovial note, congratulating him on his recent appointment to the command, and a little slyly saying, "It is a long while since we met, you and I, on the field outside Austerlitz," an unnecessary reminder of that devastating victory, which had first established him as the master of Europe.

He had for nearly every man there a word of recognition, most without any malicious flavor behind them. He knew their battles and their decorations, and when a brigadier general named Tzvilenev was presented to him, he said thoughtfully, "Ah! I hope you will permit me to congratulate you, young man," and kissing him added, "You have a son. Your wife was in St. Petersburg when it fell to us, for her time came upon her and she could not flee; I am happy to be able to tell you they were both in excellent health, and under the protection of Marshal Oudinot there."

That poor young man, who had labored under a preoccupied and anxious look which Laurence now could well understand, stood dazed by the intelligence and the low congratulations of his fellows, who looked a little wary at venturing to make them in the present circumstances. But Kutuzov made his own loudly, clapping the young man upon the shoulder, and calling at once for a toast, which necessitated glasses and bottles and camp-tables; so through Russian machinations and Napoleon's vanity in turn, the introductions alone were so prolonged as to devour nearly two hours of time.

Napoleon paused during the long proceedings, on seeing Laurence standing behind the ranks of the senior officers, and called him forward to be embraced. "My gratitude," he said solemnly, "does not fail. I have not forgotten what I and perhaps all the world owe to you, Captain Laurence, though I must yet deplore your presence here and the influence of your masters, who sit upon their island fomenting these quarrels amongst nations, and destroying from their fastness the peace and security of Europe. Would that you were now a subject of France! You know well," he added to Alexander, with a hint of reproach, "how the efforts of England have been bent to divide us from one another, and how I have spent myself and France, to try and remove their power to do so."

Laurence could hardly receive Napoleon's sentiments with satisfaction: well might the Emperor regret having failed, in his invasion of Britain; Laurence could only rejoice at it, and the wound which it had inflicted on Napoleon's dominion. And yet with all the cause in the world to hate the man before him, Laurence could not deny the power of his presence. If there had been any smaller advantage to be won by this conference than a force of three hundred dragons, if they had played for lesser stakes, anything not so sure to bring them victory, he thought this encounter might have been as destructive to the morale of the officers as if Napoleon had brought poison to put into their cups.

Alexander himself was not unaffected; evilly so, while the meeting proceeded through drawn-out paces. Impossible not to see that he felt even now a kind of instinctive yearning towards the conqueror as Napoleon concentrated all his attentions, all his intent focus, towards him, not unlike the direction of batteries of artillery; and yet he was resentful of his own feelings, a resentment silenced but diminished not at all by the necessity of deceit.

He played his rôle thoroughly and well, speaking at length and only of intangibles—of the honor of Russia, of his duty to his patrimony, of philosophy and of religion—so that all the while the conversation was kept carefully inconclusive. Napoleon, it was evident to see, saw himself a seducer; and to oblige him Alexander made himself out a maiden to be courted, and as coy as any skillful courtesan played off his suitor's ardent attempts to reach a consummation.

He deferred any explicit offers, which should have to be rejected; he made none himself; and yet he conveyed appealingly all the willingness to make peace which Napoleon, at the head of a tired army thousands of miles from their homes, might hope for. His reward was the success of their aim. When the sun began to sink, nothing had been resolved upon, and they agreed to meet again: Napoleon departed, and they had won the first day.

But Alexander afterwards was in a rage of humiliation, so overcome that he sat silently and unmoving, saying not a word, until the word came that Napoleon was well away with all his escort. Then Alexander flung the camp-table with a savage jerk of his hand upwards and over, startled men scattering away before the toppling dishes and the smoking candles, and rose to pace the opened space like a tiger upon a leash.

His ministers hastily made efforts to clear the pavilion, ushering out the aides and junior officers; Laurence half wished to leave himself, but there was no easy way to do so, standing as he was with the senior officers.

"As though," Alexander said low, "as though Holy Russia were to be bought like a girl, for the price of a few compliments—as though we were to come like the cringing dog to heel, servile beneath him, and allow him to march forward this vile philosophy, this blasphemy, across all Europe—to overthrow all Christianity, and set a—"

The men who remained were all silent before the tirade, their heads nearly bowed; only one of the diplomats, a Greek nobleman named Kapodistrias, at last ventured to step forward and speak to the Tsar quietly, reminding him the goal had been achieved. "Buonaparte's vanity and contempt will soon receive their just reward," he said.

But Napoleon was not to be deferred so easily for a second day.

As though he felt he had paid sufficient lip service to his courting, the next morning he grew swiftly more insistent, and Alexander's patience was by no means equal to fending off his approaches. They had not yet made noon when Napoleon cut short the diplomatic dance, thrusting aside with a sweep of his arm the carefully wrought speech which Kapodistrias and several of Alexander's other diplomats had engineered, outlining without commitment the nearly innumerable small points of conflict and how these might perhaps be resolved—a catalogue which, if permitted to continue, might have consumed another day all on their own.

But Napoleon interrupted with a brusque, "Enough; enough of this," and leaning forward to Alexander said bluntly, "Come, Your Majesty: these matters are for other men. Oudinot governs in St. Petersburg, and we speak here less than one hundred miles from the great city of the Moskova. Must the very throne of your ancestors fall into the hands of my army before you will cease to listen to warmongers? Shall we not again be friends? Give me only your oath that you will uphold again the Continental System, that you will recognize the Kingdom of Poland, and we will proclaim peace to these brave assembled soldiers. Then let the diplomats argue what they will!"

"In the sight of the Holy Mother," Alexander said, springing from his chair, "I will chop the throne into kindling with my own hands before you sit upon it, and for the rest, you may take what you can. But before I give you peace while you stand with an army on my soil, I will grow my beard to my belt and go and eat potatoes with my serfs!"

The conference was shattered. The diplomats on both parts made small abortive attempts to bring their monarchs back to the table, for their several causes; but Alexander could scarcely make apology now without becoming a liar, and Napoleon, at first only surprised, grew swiftly choleric when he understood Alexander's intransigence had not been a mere flourishing of temper but an expression of true feeling, and an outright rejection of the most central terms which should have formed naturally the core of any serious negotiation.

Napoleon's face colored; he looked as though he would have liked to upbraid the Tsar like a junior officer, and nearly took a step towards him; Berthier put a hand upon his arm, prudently. Still hot with anger and breathing quickly, Napoleon said to Alexander's back, "When you have thought better of your choice, I will not let this harden my heart against you," and turning stormed from the pavilion.

The Russian courier-riders outside the pavilion had of course heard all the proceedings; Laurence saw one young enthusiast, as angry as Alexander himself at the indignity offered the Tsar, jerk deliberately upon the chain of his dragon's bridle, and jab it with a spur, so the dragon snarling lashed its head forward to pull the rein loose, placing its jaws directly in Napoleon's path scarce half-a-foot from his head. Napoleon jerked back from the gnashing teeth, many of them jagged and broken and stained; two of his aides caught him, else he would have fallen, and the French couriers opposite their Russian counterparts all rose snarling on their haunches.

For a moment, the battle might have been joined directly, on the field before the pavilion; Laurence put his own hand on his pistol, and saw many another officer do the same. Then Napoleon said, "No," sharply, and waved his own couriers down; he gave one look to the brazen young officer, who defiantly raised his chin and made no apology, though he had better have hung his head at so nearly breaking the state of truce; and then another harder to the dragon, who had pulled its head in towards its chest, and was mouthing the bit with sullen irritation and a cold look for its own handler. "No," he said again, more thoughtfully, and turning went to mount up on his own courier, and departed for his lines.

"More than the heart could bear, Sire," Kutuzov said to Alexander, out of the silence; they were all of them aware that the hammer of the French Army stood ready to fall upon them. "But the point has not been lost. We have been falling back all this day; they will not catch us to-night or tomorrow. Bagration's men have been making fortifications at Borodino. We can hold him there—until the dragons arrive."

He glanced at Laurence as he spoke, a narrow gleam in his one good eye, which Laurence did not wholly know how to interpret. But he and Temeraire carried the report back to Chu, with a borrowed map to show him the location of the little village: scarcely a pinprick on the outskirts of Klin, a little way off the road to Moscow.

"Well, it will have to be good enough," Chu said philosophically, when he was given the news, and dictated new orders to one of the Jade Dragons, instructing half of the first *jalan* to concentrate and approach at a quicker pace. "I would rather have the entire force at the outset, and in the meantime a frightful number of these men will die, I imagine, but ah well! There are a great many of them, and we can manage for a day," he added, a little callously.

"Sir," Laurence said after a moment, "I must tell you I think the Russians as yet doubt the arrival of our oncoming forces. I fear they may not intend to organize their forces so as to provide that ground support which they have promised." He spoke half-reluctantly: his duty to bring the Chinese aerial forces to bear warring with his sense of what was owed them.

"I do not see why they should not support us properly," Temeraire said; he turned to look at Grig, who had become something of a fixture of their encampment, drawn by the regular helpings of porridge. "Grig, surely they do believe us *now,* they must know we are telling the truth."

"Oh," Grig said, doubtfully, looking up from his bowl, "I would not know about that. Are you *sure* that all these dragons are coming? It does seem very strange that there are so many of them, and we still have not seen them on the way."

Temeraire flattened his ruff. "Of course I am sure," he said, "and anyway, Laurence," he added, "even if they *don't* believe us, they may as well prepare: after all, they must give battle somewhere."

Tharkay had been sitting beside the dragons, reading; he looked up and raised an eyebrow. "Why?"

Temeraire paused, doubtfully. "But they cannot simply keep running away," he said.

"Why not?" Tharkay said, and Chu gave a snort of laughter; Temeraire put back his ruff.

"Ha ha," Chu said, to Temeraire, "young fellows like you are the only reason why not, and probably that Tsar of theirs is clamoring for a fight, too. Well, I see that fat old general is not so stupid after all. If we come, why then, he will win a great battle and the war will be over; and if we don't, we have given him an excellent excuse to run some more without losing face."

"But if we did *not* come, and he ran, then Napoleon would win the war!" Temeraire protested.

Chu snorted. "We had to fly over three thousand miles of this country just to get here!" he said. "This Napoleon would have a long way to go to conquer the whole thing, a long and hungry way. No: I begin to think a little better of this Kutuzov fellow, even if these people don't know anything about dragons."

Chapter 18

LAURENCE SLEPT ONLY ILL, the night of the seventh September; his head was pillowed on his folded coat, where he stretched on Temeraire's arm, and he raised it at a dozen sounds, a dozen noises, all his mind alive to the wide road of possibilities opening before them. In the distance there was the occasional sound of musketry, now and again a faintly heard roar: the Cossacks on their dragons and horses were harrying the French lines.

The Russians had previously established a small redoubt at the town of Shevardino, a meager fortification of only a few logs piled atop one another, which now Kutuzov meant to use as a lure to dangle before the French—another day's distraction before the great conflict unfolded, and another day which might allow him to slip away if the dragons did not materialize.

Laurence slept again, woke again, this time to the sound of resonant dragon voices near-by. He roused to see another of the scarlet dragons, wearing the symbols of a *jalan* commander, speaking low with Chu and bowing deeply. "No, Shao Ri, it is not to be supposed we might travel without attracting any attention," Chu said. "You have done all that you could. Establish your camp and bring forward your troops."

"As you command, General," Shao Ri said, and with a final bow went aloft again; Laurence sat up as Temeraire lifted his own head, and Chu looked over at them.

"So you are awake? It's just as well," Chu said, "for we have had some bad luck. A patrol of those French dragons came upon the leading edge of Shao Ri's *jalan,* late last night, and three of them escaped. He says," he added, "they are good fliers: too bad! You had better go and tell Kutuzov. The French will be falling back at once, of course, unless they are very stupid; but if he moves quickly enough there may be a chance to strike him on the road."

Temeraire flew very quickly indeed. "It would be the outside of enough," he said as they went, the air tearing with great violence at Laurence's hair and the skirts of his coat, "for Napoleon to escape, after all the trouble we have gone to, and when he has come all this way."

"We will bring him to battle sooner or late," Laurence answered, but he felt as much urgency as Temeraire did, and sprang down from his back with jarring haste directly they had landed, to push his way into the camp; he waited impatiently while a cold, reluctant aide went to rouse Kutuzov, and counted every dragging minute as a blow.

There were many of these: he stood for nearly three hours in the cold, damp morning air, watching others go in and out, all the while the sky lightened; the coming day's heat was still only a distant promise. At last the tent-flap was raised, and he was admitted; Kutuzov was not yet finished dressing, and sat at the remnants of his breakfast in the company of several Russian officers, nobles all, and most of them to Laurence's eye useless hangers-on. "Good morning, Captain?" Kutuzov said, very placidly, almost sleepily, but there was a hard note to the words.

"Sir," Laurence said, without preamble, "we have been made: the French reconnoitering behind us spied the first *jalan* on the approach. They will have fallen back at once, certainly, unless we move to engage. It may already be too late."

One man, a colonel named Toll, gave a half-snorted laugh, stifled; a few other men of the company smiled with a kind of gentle condescension, as though to say that Laurence's little joke had been amusing enough, but wasn't it stale by now? Kutuzov folded his hands together over his belly, leaning back in his chair, and contemplated Laurence with the careful expression of a scholar at a rare specimen, trying to make it out properly. "Hahm," he said. "I wonder if Napoleon is so easily to be put off the battle he has been seeking for so long."

"By all means," Laurence said grimly, "if his alternative is destruction, and if by doing so he can fall back on better ground, knowing that *we* will now make ourselves the pursuers, and come to meet him on a position of his choosing."

"Be that as it may," Kutuzov began, in mild noncommittal tones, which Laurence might with pleasure have shaken out of him; already the candles in the tent were growing dim and unnecessary. The sun was up outside.

The tent-flap was thrust aside, impatiently; a young captain of hussars pushed inside and said, panting and breathless, "Sir, the Cossacks report the French have left their pickets; they are gone—there is a cloud on the road for ten miles, going west. The French are falling back everywhere."

Kutuzov paused; the tent was silent. Laurence saw every man of the company staring at him in return, as though they began at last to believe: it was nearly anticlimax when scant moments later a young courier captain stumbled in, pale, and blurted, "There are a thousand dragons coming from the east."

The weather was choking-hot and the clouds of dust upon the road, stirred up by many marching feet, rose so high that Temeraire coughed and coughed as he flew; he could make out nothing at all of the French Army, and very little even of their own directly below.

It was splendid nevertheless to be flying once more at the head of the assembled *jalan,* and flying now not to some contrived mission but to a real battle, where he and these dragons should fight properly and win a magnificent victory and defeat Napoleon at last. He would like to see what the Ministry should say to Laurence *then,* Temeraire thought with an intense private sensation of delight.

Nothing could have been more satisfying than the behavior of the Russians, when at last they had seen the ranks of the *jalan*. The heavy-weights had been quite abashed into silence, looking overhead as the legions came on, singing their flying-song and the beat of their wings making a great hollow rushing sound like the wind in the tops during a gale. The Russian soldiers had many of them formed, quite without orders, into their defensive squares with bayonets held aloft bristling, until General Kutuzov had sent men around to tell them all that these dragons were their allies, and some old men in very long beards and robes had gone out amongst the troops and made loud speeches.

"Those are priests," Dyhern said, "and they are telling them that you are sent by God to smite the enemies of Russia."

"Oh," Temeraire said in strong indignation, "we are not; why should they suppose God had anything to do with it? We are sent by the Emperor. I do not see why God should get the credit of it, at all." But in spite of his objections on this score, he could not deny being pleased when slowly the soldiers instead began to cheer lustily, and clash their bayonets together in an unmusical sort of welcome. Kutuzov was even so kind as to order a salute fired, from the great guns; although this startled the dragons nearest those guns a great deal and caused a degree of confusion as they recoiled and tangled with the *niru* nearest them, and it required half-an-hour to quite smooth out the resulting disarray.

"Of course they had no business not to believe us," Temeraire said to Laurence, "but I cannot deny they are proving ready to make handsome amends for it, and I do not know it is not more gratifying to have such a change."

"I should be more ready to enjoy it," Laurence said, "if not bought at such a cost: Napoleon will make us pay dearly for this mistake."

Napoleon had evidently no sooner received the news of his deadly danger than he had at once leapt into action and flung his men back onto the road—an immense gamble on his part: if Kutuzov had only moved more quickly, the French should have been vulnerable to an attack in their rear. But with the crisis upon him, as so often before, Napoleon had disdained the smaller course and seized the one avenue of obtaining some compensatory advantage, which the choice of ground might give him, against the suddenly altered balance of power between himself and his enemies.

And he had been rewarded, for the moment of great danger had passed. The bulk of the French Army, falling back west by forced marches, had been already well away before the Russians had roused, and as soon as the sky had grown even a little light, the French dragons had begun their quick hop-scotch portage of men and guns, and sped them even further away.

Temeraire could not but regret the opportunity lost, but after all, they would win in any case, and in some way it seemed more sporting, that Napoleon should know what force would meet him, and have a chance to do his very best, and then be defeated anyway. "Not, of course," he said hastily, "that I mean we ought not have taken advantage of the opportunity, or that it would have been unfair; this is war, after all, and I do not mean to be romantical—but as it has been lost, anyway, we may console ourselves that the quality of our victory will be the greater, if no-one can say Napoleon did not have a fair chance to win, that he was only taken by surprise."

"When we are in battle with the greatest general of this age, and perhaps of any," Laurence said, "I will be glad enough for victory of any kind; we can ill afford to sacrifice this chance or any other."

Temeraire refused to be so pessimistic: Napoleon was not trying to get away entirely, which would have been maddening; he had only fallen back on a nearby town, Tsarevo Zaimische, and soon the battle would be joined properly—although it seemed, not to-day, but tomorrow. Kutuzov was advancing their army, but they would not be in position properly until late, and then there would not be enough time to engage the enemy.

Chu growled deeply in his throat. "And where are we to get supply, if we do not defeat him the next day?" he demanded, and summoned Shen Shi to join him and Temeraire in proceeding to Kutuzov's tent; although at least General Kutuzov came out at once to speak to them now, and listened with attention to their difficulties.

"We have four days' adequate supply on hand, and of that we require three to reach our nearest resupply point," Chu said, his tone glacially polite.

"Which means, sir," Laurence said, having translated this, to the perplexed pause which received it, "that the legions should have to quit the field by mid-day tomorrow, regardless of the circumstances of the battle."

Kutuzov at once sent for his own quartermasters, and an urgent conference was held. "General, we cannot procure three hundred head of cattle overnight!" one of these worthies protested. "Not unless you mean to starve the entire army for three days to feed them."

"What do we want with three hundred head of cattle?" Chu said, with a disparaging snort.

"Twenty would serve excellently, if they are animals like this one," Shen Shi said, indicating an unhappy bullock in the near distance, intended for the Russian couriers, "and ninety tons of grain. A hundred and ten, if we must transport it ourselves, so long as the supply is within forty miles."

This list of requirements was so at war with the understanding of the Russian supply-officers that some argument was required even to persuade them to believe it correctly conveyed to them; then at last with some doubtful reluctance one said to the others, "The magazine at Mozhaisk is sufficiently supplied. We might get pigs from the farms near Kozhukhovo—"

Some seven of the supply-dragons set off at once, with a few rather alarmed Russian officers flung aboard with the crew to smooth the paths of the requisition, and the immediate crisis was averted; but Chu shook his head disapprovingly as they went back to their own campsite. "If they don't have enough dragons for their infantry, of course this kind of sluggish maneuvering must be the consequence," he said, "but what a mess! I expect those French will have dug in like moles by the time we get started in the morning."

Indeed, when Temeraire went aloft shortly afterwards to have a look, he could see the French working frantically on earthworks and fortifications—the heavier dragons were holding entire trees in place, lengthwise, piled upon one another while men lashed them with rope and the middle-weights heaped up dirt to either side. "That is an inordinate number of trees," Tharkay said to Laurence, as they took their turns peering down through the glass.

"Those trees have been cut, not torn up," Laurence said, after some further study. "How the devil have they managed to cut down a hundred trees—"

"They are cutting down another, over there," Gerry piped up, and looking Temeraire saw not a heavy-weight but three light-weight dragons instead, who were using a kind of saw which was little more than a long toothed chain with one end run around a wheel, which two of them turned rapidly by a crank while the third steadied the tree; the trunk was being torn through at extraordinary speed, and when it had been reduced to only a thin sliver, a heavy-weight was waved down; when she had seized it, several men chopped at the remaining portion with axes until she was able to break it off and carry it away.

"They will have a palisade by morning, at this rate," Laurence said.

As they returned towards their own encampment, towards the Russian rear, Temeraire stopped briefly to speak with Grig, who with his fellows was perched on a hill watching not the preparations for the battle, but the Chinese supply operations, behind their lines: the thirty cooking-pits, spaced at intervals so three *niru* might gather to eat around each one; two pigs and a great deal of wheat had gone into each one, and the bubbling stews were now being attended by five of the Shen Lung, who were stirring at occasional intervals, while another five were busy digging additional watering-holes with the assistance of their crews; the rest were napping while their crews worked on spare harness or cleaned them, or tended to the fighting-dragons who had come back with wounds to be tended.

"How *many* of you there are," Grig said to Temeraire, in amazement, "and how well all of you eat! I haven't seen so many dragons ever, except in the breeding grounds when I was hatched, and no-one gets enough to eat there."

He looked down at his own covert as he spoke. The twenty Russian heavy-weights were presently feasting on what Temeraire could not deny were some very handsome cows, which would have been splendid if properly roasted, or perhaps stewed with some potatoes. But the Russian aviators plainly had no notion of anything of that sort, and the resulting scene was little better than an abattoir, the heavy-weights all tearing the cows apart violently, snapping and hissing at one another in arguing over the best bits of the innards in a very showy way, meanwhile scattering and wasting a great deal of the meat, and most of the blood sinking into the ground. Temeraire sniffed and turned aside.

"There is no reason that a great many dragons cannot partake in battle, and eat well, too, if only things are managed properly, and everyone has a fair share," he said. "Our supply-dragons are paid for their work, too," he added to the assembled dragons, who had cautiously edged a little closer to hear, "which is like being given treasure."

Grig and several of his companions tittered softly together at this, as though Temeraire had made an excellent joke; Temeraire put back his ruff and said severely, "I am not making fun! They are paid wages, which are put into a bank account, and which they can take out as gold and silver, whenever they should like. Look!" He pointed at one of the Shen Lung just then flying in with a load of rocks, which she meant to use for damming up a stream. "Look, you can see for yourselves, Lung Shen Mei, there, has a very handsome gold chain about her neck."

The Russian dragons looked, and were silent; one of them said, low, "It is enough to make one think," and many of the others rustled their wings uneasily, and eyed Temeraire and one another sidelong; they edged in towards one another and away from the speaker, who flung his head back defiantly, though he also threw a nervous look at Temeraire.

"Well, you should think," Temeraire said, "that you needn't live in such a wretched manner as you do. You ought to have liberties, and be paid wages if you *do* choose to obey orders—which you needn't, if you do not want to—"

"But if we do not obey, they will send us back to the breeding grounds," one said, "to go hungry."

"If they do not give you enough food, they cannot complain if you go and take some, elsewhere," Temeraire said. "It is not as though they can make you stay there, if you do not like to."

They all stared at him, as though he had said something very peculiar; but before Temeraire could inquire further, a Russian aviator came out from his tent and saw them speaking together, and began shouting and pointing at them, cracking his short whip. He jerked on the chain of one of the heavy-weight dragons, rousing him up and turning him towards the assembled group, and the small dragons burst away in a frightened cloud, dispersing.

"Come away, Temeraire," Laurence said, "before that fellow comes up here, and demands to know what we are about. I am damned if I will apologize to him for interference, and more so if I will tell him what you were saying to those beasts: the poor wretches have enough to bear, without being cuffed about further."

"Laurence," Temeraire said, leaping aloft, "do you suppose that they *do* keep the dragons in the breeding grounds, somehow, even if they are hungry?"

Laurence was silent, then heavily said, "I imagine they might set the heavy-weights upon them, if they try to leave."

"But how could the heavy-weights agree to hurt a dragon so much smaller than they are, and who was only hungry, and not taking anything of theirs?" Temeraire said. "Surely they would feel perfect scrubs for doing such a thing. Although I do see," he added, "that it would be hard to refuse anyone who had given you *so* much treasure, and helped guard it; one would feel the most extraordinary sense of obligation. Laurence," he said suddenly, with dawning realization, "Laurence, is that why you do not care anything for fortune?"

"I cannot claim to be so unworldly as to care *nothing* for fortune," Laurence said, "but I hope that I am unwilling to be a slave to it."

The notion that fortune might enslave had not previously occurred to Temeraire, and it did not sit very well, but he could not deny that the Russian heavy-weights seemed to be quite willing to put on chains, all for treasure. "But I cannot believe," he decided, "that they are so dreadful as to pen up small dragons for it; not, at least, without giving them a chance to refute it: I will ask Vosyem."

"Pray save your inquiries for after the battle," Laurence said. "We cannot hazard a division among our forces now. *That* might indeed offer Napoleon an advantage he would be quick to seize; and you may be sure that no argument or quarrel could have so powerful an effect, towards your ends, as the demonstration you and the legions—and for that matter, the enemy—are presently setting forward before the eyes of the Russian high command and so many of their young officers, of the immense advantage to be gained by an honorable and just treatment of dragons."

Temeraire did see the necessity of defeating Napoleon, first, before they tried to do anything else; but that only made it all the more aggravating that Napoleon refused to be properly defeated. Anyway he did not see why the Russian dragons had let things get into such a fix, in the first place: even if the heavy-weights *did* behave so badly, surely the little dragons could sneak out, one after another—or they might mass themselves into groups, and all but a few dash past—there were any number of ways Temeraire might imagine, for them to slip out of the breeding grounds, and once out, they might go anywhere they liked.

He devised several dozen such strategems, that afternoon, while there was nothing to do but wait: Laurence had urged him to rest, but Temeraire found he could not sleep properly with the enemy so very close—with victory so very close. He drowsed only a little, and ate his porridge unenthusiastically—he did appreciate, of course, how efficient porridge was, and how necessary to supply a force as large as their own, but he was growing rather tired of it—and then looked around for distraction: but Laurence was closeted with Tharkay and his officers, discussing their positions in the coming battle. That was a somewhat delicate matter, with Tharkay and Dyhern and Ferris not properly officers, although in Temeraire's opinion that ought not count for much when one considered how ragged the proper officers were, and anyway—he sighed—it seemed they would very likely not have much to do. General Chu had hinted very strongly that Temeraire needn't expect to do a lot of fighting, himself. It did not seem fair, somehow, that he and Laurence should have made it at all possible for them all to have such a splendid battle, and now have no real share of it themselves.

He decided to discuss his thoughts with Grig—in an entirely hypothetical manner; he would not at all provoke a quarrel—and looked for him; Grig was for once not directly in their camp, but sitting on the edge of it, and watching a couple of other Russian dragons hanging about with the long and messy supply-train of the army. They were a sort of dragon Temeraire had not seen at all amongst the Russians before, closer to middle-weight and without any bony plates, colored in green and fawn brown, and they wore only light harness.

"Why," Temeraire said, coming over to join Grig, "those fellows look likely: why are *they* not fighting? I dare say they would be more use than those heavy-weights, if we had enough of them: where did they come from?"

Grig gave a start when Temeraire came down. "They aren't Russian dragons, at all," he said, ruffling his wings to his back, and indeed Temeraire had scarcely landed before a man, very portly and red-faced, in high boots and a brown waistcoat and no coat at all, was stomping over with an angry expression, from the waggons, to shout in broad colonial English, "I've already told you fellows to be off: they aren't for sale, and I'll be damned if—" only to halt in some surprise when he saw that neither Grig nor Temeraire had any officers.

"Why, you are Americans," Temeraire said, rather doubtfully. "Whatever are you doing here?"

"You may be sure we aren't here by any choice of mine, that is blasted certain," the sweating man said. "Where else can we be, with Oudinot and Saint-Cyr in St. Petersburg all but confiscating goods, and standing between us and our ship? I would rather get thirty cents on the dollar for my wares than ten; but if you scaly brutes and your rotten pack of whip-happy overseers don't keep off Josiah and Linden, I *will* take my cargo back to Boney's gang and make them welcome to it, and I'll call in my ship and sell them every last bale of wool in the hold, too, see if I don't."

It seemed that the Russians had already made several attempts to buy the merchant's dragons, who eyed Temeraire with some understandable nervousness and edged back from him, refusing to say a word, even though he explained quite clearly he had not the least interest in delivering them to the Russian service. "I don't suppose," he said at last, "that you are acquainted with John Wampanoag?" which produced something of a thaw.

"We are out of New Jersey, ourselves," the fat waistcoated merchant said, mopping his forehead, when he had at last sat down, somewhat more assured of their peaceable intentions, "but I have heard his name, of course; I don't suppose there's many Yankees who haven't. Well, if you are a friend of John Wampanoag, I guess you are all right; and it's true you don't have a look of those other big fellows, always snapping and yelping in that queer gabble of theirs that a man can't fit his tongue around. But what are you doing mixed up in this business, then?"

Explanations made, Temeraire wished to be introduced to Josiah and Lindy, but they only spoke a language called Unami and not English; their employer was a Mr. Calvin Jefferson, and when Temeraire tentatively asked that man, he stridently denied their having any interest in taking part in the battle. "Get themselves shot, all for someone else's quarrel; I should think not," he said, bristling.

"Well, I will not pretend to understand it," Temeraire said, somewhat doubtfully; he wondered if maybe the dragons would have expressed different sentiments, if only they could have spoken for themselves in the matter, "but naturally they should not fight if they do not like; I suppose the Shen Lung will not be fighting, either. Only it seems a shame for them to be here, just when we are sure to win a splendid victory, and not have a share in it."

Jefferson snorted. "It's soon enough to brag of your victory after you've won it," he said. "I don't set myself up as an expert on the matter, but it seems to me that Bonaparte's done pretty well for himself on these occasions in the past."

He gave them a very nice cup of tea, however, and he had some very fine woolen cloth, of which he made Temeraire a present large enough to make Laurence a new coat; as a sample, he said. "I have three thousand bales of it," he said very mournfully, "sitting just out of cannon-shot of St. Petersburg harbor; and if these Russian fellows would only make me a reasonable offer, I guess I could land it north of the city, and they could ship it down to Tver: if the French don't take *that,* pretty soon."

"I do call that handsome," Temeraire said to Grig, as they flew back to his own camp, very pleased with the use of his afternoon, "and I am sure I do not know why your people have not bought his wool."

"Well, he has no-one else to sell it to," Grig said, "except Napoleon, who is offering less," which was a point that Temeraire had not quite considered. "Of course, I do not know much about these things," Grig added.

Laurence received the gift with pleasure, although he professed himself surprised by the presence of the traders. "I suppose I ought not be," he said. "They seem to be everywhere in the world, these days; and in the article of speed their ships are scarcely to be outmatched. Blaise told me he crossed paths with one of their schooners, in his Atlantic crossing to Brazil, and he would have sworn she was doing fourteen knots, in a light wind.

"But this merchant may have gambled badly," Laurence added, "if he was hoping to see his price driven up: God willing, we may end the war tomorrow. Come, my dear, you must try and get some rest."

Chapter 19

TEMERAIRE JOLTED OUT OF sleep the next morning with a start: the thunder-roll and the low terrible whistling of the field guns. It was just dawn. "Twelve-pounders," Laurence said, listening: not as great a noise as the enormous sixty-eights which could be carried by a dragon transport like the *Potentate,* or even the thirty-six-pounders which had made up most of the guns of the *Reliant,* on which Temeraire had hatched, but they were certainly loud enough for all that. When Temeraire put his head out of the pavilion, he saw many of the other dragons sitting up on their haunches, looking a little uneasily to the west where the noise of the guns came steadily.

"How they go on!" Chu said. The guns were firing in nearly a continuous stream; as soon as the reverberation of one shot had died away, here came another. "At least when dragons roar, we have it over with, and then you can hear yourself think again. But I am ready to bear the noise, if that means we can get started. Come, we had better go and have a look."

They had encamped at the Russian rear, as they could reach the fighting more easily than might the infantry or the cavalry, and this way refresh themselves during the battle and tend to injured dragons without being exposed to the artillery. As Chu issued his orders, the *niru* began at once to go aloft; Temeraire flew alongside him swiftly the five minutes to the front, and there halted to hover: the battlefield looked quite different than the previous afternoon. The

French had thrown up three rows of fences nearly all about the highest ground, constructed as they had seen of heavy logs and piled stones and dirt. And as a final insult, they had even seized and improved upon the very fortifications which the Russians had built and abandoned, not a week before.

The ranks of infantry stood arrayed now behind the heavy fences, deployed into broad lines, and great batteries of artillery stood upon raised ground behind them, with several redoubts piled up; their felling of trees had removed the few obstacles which remained to their clear prospect in every direction, while the Russians had been obliged to take up positions crowded up against a heavy stand of timber to the north and with marshy ground not distant from their rear. But the French dragons were massed towards the center, in a peculiar concentration, which it seemed to Temeraire should make it possible to encircle them entirely.

He ventured to point this out to Chu, who said, "Yes, so why has he done it?"

"You have forgotten the guns," Laurence said, pointing: many of the great massed batteries of smaller guns stood behind the infantry ranks, aiming skyward. "Those will surely be firing on us: they are elevated too high to fire on the Russian infantry."

As the Russian dragons made their own first pass, carrying heavy loads of bombs meant for the French infantry positions, the raised artillery began to roar: canister-shot, filling the air with smoke and the flying balls and scraps of metal, and even though these nearly all fell harmlessly into the field between the armies, the hail barred an approach to the French forces from more than half the sky: only the center, where the French dragons were massed, was open air.

"Hah," Chu said, "so he is making a mountain pass, out of gunfire. Yes, I see; we will have a hard time coming at him." The Russian heavy-weights were already being stymied, their approach towards the French falling back before the blistering fire, which would have torn their wings apart if they had continued.

But Chu signaled nevertheless, and Temeraire watched with rising joy as six *niru* flew forward to make the first sortie, and two other wings of four *niru* apiece broke away to either side of the battlefield, to probe at the French defenses. They were fighting, at last they were fighting, and then Chu said, "Well, let's go back and sit down and have a morning drink; is there any tea, Shen Lao?"

"What?" Temeraire said, outraged. "But the battle is joined! Everything has begun!"

"And it will be a long while going, too," Chu said, unperturbed, "as long as we can't come at them more than twenty at a time." He waved towards the engagement: the *niru* had closed with the front ranks of the French dragons, and were skirmishing with them skillfully though as yet cautiously, all the dragons on both sides working out a sense of their unfamiliar enemies. There was indeed no room for any other Chinese dragons to attack. One of the *niru* was already falling back a little from the fighting to give the rest more room for maneuvering.

"But then surely we ought do something to open a wider front, on which we might attack," Temeraire said. "We might—" He paused, and looked upon the field: perhaps they might go around to the west—but there were guns on the heights there covering the French rear, with a forest of sharpened stakes rising up around them. "Well, we ought to do *something*, anyway," he finished a little lamely, even if he could not immediately see what that something might be.

"Certainly," Chu said. "Go find that Russian general, and tell him we had better arrange supply for another two days." And then he turned around and flew back towards the campsite, as though there were no fighting going on at all.

The rest of the morning was equally deflating. Even Laurence only said, "We could scarcely give Bonaparte a better gift than to accept the extraordinary losses which it would require on the part of the Chinese legions to seize and overwhelm those artillery positions as they stand: pray notice, if you will, that the French have secondary guns waiting against just such an attempt, and crews of pikemen in support.

"Time is our ally: they cannot hold against us indefinitely. They have sixty dragons here, you five times that number. Even if we allow the French dragons to be the equal of the Chinese, which we ought not, as the day progresses we can send fresh beasts against tired, and by slow tide wear them down; and all the while, the Russians will be executing their own assault upon the French ground positions."

This was a very sensible and practical explanation and by no means satisfying. Temeraire without much enthusiasm agreed to Laurence's suggestion that they should indeed go and assure additional supply, for the Chinese legions, largely in hopes that the Russians should protest and insist on some more useful course of action. But Kutuzov was sitting in his own low chair with no more hurry in his manner than Chu; he only nodded to Laurence's request and said, "I think Colonel Ogevin has already put it in train. Vasya," he added to one of his aides, "see that it is done."

So Temeraire, with enthusiasm still more diminished, returned to the campsite, where Chu was now eating a large helping of porridge as placidly as—as a *cow,* Temeraire thought, meanly; he scornfully refused the bowl which Shen Lao offered him. He had not in the least regretted Iskierka's absence, all this while, but in the moment he missed her quite acutely. He was certain *she* would not have tolerated merely sitting about, but would have insisted on their going to join in somehow or other.

He ventured quietly to Laurence that perhaps they might try a pass against the French artillery. "For I am quite sure," he said, "that I would be able to break some of those earthworks, with the divine wind, and bowl over a great many of the gunners, so the Russians might be able to come at them."

"Yes," Chu said, having overheard and demanded to know what Temeraire was saying, "and you could also go and dig some ditches, for latrines; and I dare say if you wanted, you could try and cook our dinner, though it might not taste very well; and also you could go and dance for the troops, which at least would entertain them. None of that is your business: it is your business to stay here, and learn how a battle is managed properly, and then *if* a moment should arise where you may, through a decisive action, alter the course of the battle, you will be ready to act, and not worn out and too distracted to observe it."

Temeraire flattened his ruff, but even Laurence did not disagree, saying gently, "My dear, you must see that in the present situation, where the enemy's positions mean we cannot bring to bear even the better part of the forces which we have, it would be folly to risk you to no purpose. Recall that we are here not merely as soldiers, but as envoys; it would be as wrong for us to go foolhardy into battle now, when our destruction could cast into serious disarray all the cooperation between the Russian army and the legions we have asked to follow us here, as it would be in another situation for us to evade battle out of cowardice."

So Temeraire had nothing to do but sigh, and put down his head, and wait, while the Jade Dragons darted back and forth, bringing Chu reports of endless tedium, and the sun crawled by overhead.

"What a hideous noise," Tharkay said. The artillery had not ceased to fire, all this time.

Temeraire went aloft again after noon had passed, only to have a look; although privately he thought perhaps he *might* see an opportunity, of making a particularly significant attack. The battlefield was so thickly obscured by smoke, by now, that it was nearly impossible to see what any of the soldiers were doing on the ground. One could only guess at it, by listening to the roar of the guns, which went on and on and on. His own ears rang with it, the unpleasant brassy noise: he had never heard anything like, save at the battle of Shoeburyness, during the final great bombardment, which had lasted half-an-hour; here so far it had gone on more than half the day.

"Oh, there," Temeraire said, when a breath of wind stirred and blew a great rolling cloud of powder away from before the French earthworks on their left flank, "now we will be able to see something, at any rate." And then he paused, and was silent. The ground was littered thickly with the shattered bodies of horses and of men in both uniforms.

"Dear God, what a slaughter," Laurence said, low. And the soldiers were yet fighting, bitterly, around the fence: the Russians had seized one end now and were striving forward with bayonets and swords and even in some instances bare fists to push back the French further along it.

"Surely we might help them," Temeraire said, unhappily, but even as he half-stooped towards the struggle, involuntarily, another roaring sounded below, and he backwinged, recoiling instinctively: a hail of canister-shot went whistling by not a hundred feet distant.

"We have already helped them," Laurence said to Temeraire, as they drew back. "We have put a stop to Napoleon's aerial attacks: the French would otherwise be enacting a terrible bombardment against the Russian troops. And the guns which he is using to keep the Chinese legions off, he cannot direct against the infantry."

"But he seems to have enough of them to do both," Temeraire said: there were hundreds and hundreds of field guns, it seemed, on both sides. "Laurence, whyever is Napoleon insisting on such a battle? Surely *he* can see, as well as we can, that he is lost: that he is only dragging things out dreadfully, for everyone, and killing so many on all sides."

"He has little alternative," Laurence said, "save if he chose to abandon his army, and flee back to France in a state of ignominy: in a pursuit, our aerial advantage would shortly begin to tell ruthlessly against him; we would have been able to overwhelm his rear-guard, and catch him and his army strung out upon the road. Most likely he yet hopes for some mistake upon our part, which would permit him to use his own advantage in artillery and in ground troops." But the Russians were being quite careful to avoid that: as the fortifications and the heavy woods kept them from coming at the full body of the French Army, General Barclay had positioned his soldiers along the road to Moscow to the south, to guard against any attempt on the part of the French to slip away again during the night, or to sneak some substantial portion out to flank the Russian Army.

Junichiro had unexpectedly begged to be allowed to come aloft with them, on every one of Temeraire's passes: he had become, to Temeraire's gratification, quite a reformed character, and in the course of their journey from China to Russia had acquired a great deal not only of English but of French; to-day he had been avidly studying the order of battle of the armies on both sides. He ventured now, from Temeraire's shoulder, to say, "This seems something between a battle and a siege," and Laurence nodded in agreement.

As a siege might take months or even years to lift, that was by no means encouraging, and it was only meager consolation when Laurence said, "They cannot have the supply to hold out for more than a few days, Temeraire, even if they eat the cavalry-horses: you can see for yourself they have virtually no cattle amongst their baggage."

It did not make Temeraire feel much better, either, to see Vosyem and the rest of the Russian heavy-weights sitting disgruntled in their own encampment, sullenly tearing at the ground and snapping at one another, when he came past them: Chu had sent a word to the Russian generals hinting that perhaps it would be easier for the Chinese legions to operate if they were not being fouled and harassed by their own allies. The Russian heavy-weights had several times bulled through the *niru* formations to engage the enemy directly, with nothing but ill-effect all around.

Temeraire sighed and looked back towards the battlefield: the guns had begun roaring more energetically. The front row of the fences had at last fallen, but the French had got away their guns, and raced back behind the shelter of the second row; the artillery were now pounding away at the Russian troops who had seized the first row, before those men might even have enjoyed a moment's respite from their victory. The batteries of artillery aimed against the sky were yet sheltered behind a third row of fences, and overlooking them were the massed ranks of Napoleon's Imperial Guard, as yet withheld from all the fighting. But aloft, the *niru* were battering steadily and systematically away at the French dragons.

"Ah, there you are," Chu said, when Temeraire came down in the encampment. "This is Colonel Zhao Lien, commander of the third *jalan,*" he said, presenting Temeraire to one officer, a heavyset dragon of pale green, with a bristling spine of tendrils and a mane not unlike Chu's own, in scarlet; she bowed her head politely before continuing her report.

"The quantity of smoke produced by the guns has made it most difficult to obtain a clear understanding of the organization of the enemy's forces," she said, "but their reserves are substantial, and I have determined their supply may be a great deal better than we have supposed to be the case. I sent a small foray against their rear, upon the ground, which was repulsed swiftly by the repositioning of their guns, but one of my dragons was able to seize a packet from their supply-waggons—"

She indicated this, a large square bundle which had been hastily rewrapped; when one of her crewmen opened it up again, Temeraire bending down to sniff found it full of long hard strips of some dark brown stuff that smelt strongly of spice; pieces were handed around, and when Temeraire chewed it, he found that it was meat: quite tough and dry and salty, but perfectly good to eat.

"Hm," Shen Shi said, inspecting it. "That is very clever: they do not need cattle, then."

"No," Zhao Lien said, "and they had fifty pallets of a similar style on hand."

Chu made a low grunt. "Well, then they can hold out at least a week," he said, "but why would they have had so much meat, for this number of dragons—" He fell silent, scratching at the ground ruminatively.

"I will say, General," Zhao Lien said, "that it seems to me the enemy are fighting very conservatively."

"Hm," Chu said. "Colonel, I wish you to take four *niru* and scout—where are those maps? What is to the north of our position?"

Temeraire looked back and forth between them, conscious that he had not quite followed their train of thought, and wondering how he might ask without looking somehow foolish. Chu was bending low over his maps, and then suddenly, very near-by, a blasting of thunder erupted, a cannonball-whistling. Temeraire looked up and around, in surprise, and then recoiled with a cry as something hot and terrible seared along his side. Roars of pain went up on all sides of him—canister-shot was flying down all over the rear of the camp. "Aloft!" Laurence was shouting from his back, through his speaking-trumpet. "All aloft, at once! Get into the air!"

Temeraire flung himself up, blindly, backwinging, and took up the cry himself as he went, roaring it out as loudly as he could; as soon as he was up, and out of the flight path of the balls, he could see the guns firing upon them: a tiny clearing, some four hundred yards to the north, where the French had established a small battery of three-pounders. They were firing at a furious pace: not even pulling their guns back into place after they fired, nor even trying to aim, merely reloading and firing again and again; all they cared for was to hit anything in the Russian rear at all, and even more guns were being dragged out from the trees behind them.

But they had as yet no covering-fire, nor aerial defenders; Temeraire hissed in fury and circled towards them, out of their line of fire. Plunging towards them, he drew in his breath, once and twice and three times, swelling all his chest with air, and roaring fell upon the line of guns, sweeping them and seeing men and horses fall screaming to the ground before the divine wind, while he caught at the hot guns and tipped them over into a clanging, tumbling heap.

Musket-fire spat against his flank, hot stinging bursts of pain, but he was through and pulling up and away, the guns silenced, their crews shattered. Looking back he saw the wreckage they had already made in that brief span of time: the cooking-pits clogged with dirt and smoking metal, many spoilt; a dozen of the Shen Lung moaning upon the ground, bleeding, many of the wounded dragons injured again also; and near the half-collapsed pavilion—

Temeraire flung himself down again next to Chu: the general's great scarlet side was heaving, and with each breath a gush of blood rose up and spilled black from three gaping wounds, clustered near the top of his back; his wings lay limp against his sides. "No, no," Temeraire said, wretchedly. Five of the Chinese dragon-surgeons were already at work, digging their arms within to bring out the shot: one was calling for long tongs to be brought. Another managed to draw out one, which had struck upon a rib; the ball had burst like a star, and another torrent of blood followed it when the surgeon pulled it out.

Chu's eyes were closed; he coughed, rattling, and blood trickled from the sides of his mouth; one of the surgeons was thrown from his back. Temeraire almost nosed at him, but timidly held back; he did not know what to do. Zhao Lien landed beside him and said, "I have ordered five *niru* to the north, accompanied by couriers, to scout for more of the enemy attempting to flank us, as General Chu directed. What are your commands?"

She was speaking to him, Temeraire realized; she was asking him for orders. Abruptly, Temeraire felt rage swelling hot in his breast; he imagined with burning satisfaction throwing himself to the front, commanding all the legions to fall in behind him and overturn the French defenses, smash their artillery and then slaughter all their ranks, no matter what the cost. He would drive them forth with the divine wind, and avenge—

"Temeraire," Laurence said softly, a hand on his neck, and

Temeraire dragged in a breath; he looked at Zhao Lien, and saw her regarding him narrowly, warily, as though she feared what he might do. He swallowed and said to Laurence, in English, "Laurence, what ought I do, now?"

"If you will be counseled by me," Laurence said, "we will determine which of the three *jalan* commanders is senior, and appoint them to the command."

Temeraire took another breath, and nodded; he said to Zhao Lien, "Who is the senior commander, of the three *jalan*?"

She sat back upon her haunches, relaxing a little. "I am," she said.

"Then—then you shall take command, until General Chu is quite recovered," he said, though he could not help but think longingly, one more time, of the glorious vision of his charge. "And I am quite sure," he added savagely, "that there *are* more soldiers coming; it is just the sort of thing Napoleon likes to do, so you had better plan as though there were."

Zhao Lien turned to a limping Shen Shi, who had one badly torn wing, and conferred with her about supply; then she turned and said, "If the soldiers who approach are a substantial force, our situation will be extremely precarious."

"But we still outnumber them so heavily in the air!" Temeraire said, uncertainly. "Of course we must still beat them, surely."

"We cannot be assured of doing so in the present position," Zhao Lien said. "An immediate assault upon the artillery must lose us half our fighting troops. This, having diminished our aerial advantage, may permit the enemy to hold their well-fortified positions against us. If they have sufficient ground forces to strike against the flank of our allies' ground soldiers—"

Interrupting her explanation, Lung Yu Fei came blazing into the camp as swiftly as a rocket, skidding in the dirt as she pulled up: Temeraire regarded her with dismay even before she opened her mouth and said, "There is a whole army coming, from the north-east: they are coming through the trees on foot."

. . .

Once again now the advantage changed hands, as abruptly as before; but Kutuzov's caution had not deserted him even in an apparent moment of triumph: he had placed his rear-guard to cover the road to Moscow, and had kept a great many of his forces uncommitted to the battle. Even before the French reinforcements had completed half their advance, the Russian Army was melting away again eastward, escaping the trap.

Laurence and Temeraire scarcely touched ground the next four hours, trying as best they might to create a unified action with the Russian forces: a coordination almost impossible to achieve when the two of them were nearly the sole interlocutors between the two bodies of troops. The battle had lent itself to a sharp separation between commands; the retreat by no means did so, for the Russians badly needed air cover, and the French had been reinforced by some forty dragons more, under the command of the very dragon Laurence had noted at the false negotiations: Marshal Ombreux.

"We cannot keep flying about in this manner," Laurence said, when they had made the fourth frantic pass back to Kutuzov's headquarters, trying for some clarification in orders which had already seemed inapplicable. "Temeraire, see if you can find Grig, and persuade him and the rest of those Russian light-weights to go-between for us."

What the officers of those dragons should think, of his summarily appropriating their beasts, Laurence cared little; he had already privately resolved that if their conditions were not ameliorated, he should ask Temeraire to offer the poor creatures safe passage back to China, with the *jalan,* on the conclusion of the hostilities. "And if the officers at headquarters do not care to listen to them," he added, "I dare say they will be persuaded, at the next moment when they wish to send us orders."

Grig was easy to find: he had been trailing them, and he and several of his companions were by no means unwilling to help once

Temeraire had assured them of sharing the dinner of the Chinese dragons that night; they soon worked out for themselves an effective rotation whereby each dragon went in turn to the high command. To the credit of Kutuzov's staff, whatever dismay they might have felt at seeing their old order overturned, they did not allow it to deter them: Grig returned from his flight carrying a Russian officer with him, a young man of noble family from Kutuzov's staff, who had with real courage tied himself onto the smaller dragon's harness-rings with nothing but his belt, the better to convey the orders.

As the withdrawal advanced, the *jalan* were pressed into service to carry away the guns and thereby speed the pace of the retreat. The Cossacks carried out a whirling and ferocious defense in their rear; but the heavier French dragons massed for a sortie now and again, and in such occasions, Temeraire would quickly call out and send back a few *niru* to engage and drive them away.

But Laurence was well aware of the dangerous falseness of their position: if the French surged forth from their defenses, and flung all their strength upon the Russian ground troops, success might well be theirs: a quick shattering blow could give them the complete mastery in artillery which should make them impervious even to the continuing disadvantage in the air.

He half-waited for Bonaparte to act, to move; waited at every moment for the French to come pouring forward over their fences; but the moment did not come, and then the ground had opened wide between the armies, and at last the guns fell silent.

The army was yet moving, all that night. Laurence came to ground with Temeraire in Mozhaisk. "Remain here," he said quietly, laying a hand on Temeraire's muzzle. Temeraire had been aloft, flying and maneuvering vigorously, without a halt for seven hours; they had come fifty miles. Temeraire did not answer aloud, but let his eyelids sink shut; Forthing slid down from his back and said, "I'll see about his dinner, sir; will we encamp here?"

"Assume a short halt only, for the moment," Laurence said.

"Roland," he added, beckoning to her; her command of Chinese, having unwillingly suffered Temeraire's tutelage in that language for several years, was by far superior to Forthing's. "Have a word with the supply-officers, and see what they can tell you about our circumstances."

Tharkay fell in with him, as they walked towards the headquarters established in a large farmhouse, some half-a-mile distant; the night was still hot, and the air thick with dust. All around, Laurence heard soldiers coughing, heavily, and long lines stood at all the wells, of men desperately thirsty from dust and gunpowder in their mouths. But the lines were patient, well-ordered; the ranks had not disintegrated, though the circumstances might have been discouraging enough to depress the spirits and morale of any army.

"I can only wonder," Laurence said, "why Bonaparte did not come forth. Even if he were ever to have another chance at smashing their army, he could scarcely hope to find himself at better relative strength. Can he be seriously ill, perhaps?"

"As pleasant a possibility as that might be to contemplate," Tharkay said, "I hope you will forgive me for discouraging it. A man who has seen three hundred enemy dragons appear without warning does not need to be on his death-bed to discover a little caution, even if he is a Napoleon."

The farmhouse was the scene of enormous activity: officers rushing in with reports on the number of troops, the losses; the activity observed among the French by the Cossacks on their light dragons and horses. Bonaparte's army had certainly been reinforced by more than twenty thousand men: now identified as the Sixth Corps, which had last been sighted in Petersburg not a week before. General Saint-Cyr had managed to bring them south so quickly they had outdistanced even the reports of their travel, which uselessly had trickled in that very day. Three separate witnesses had glimpsed him upon the field, that evening, as Napoleon had embraced him and bestowed on him a Marshal's baton, which he had won by the enterprise.

The initial goal of those troops had likely been Moscow itself: a neat pincer-trap for the Russian Army, which would have cut off their supply and likely secured for the French the great magazines of the city, full of food and munitions, which they themselves so desperately required. Napoleon had sacrificed that ambition for the rescue of his army.

In the dining chamber of the house, Kutuzov and his senior generals had gathered about the table; Barclay was speaking impassionedly of the necessity of retreating, and therefore of sacrificing Moscow. "We cannot take the wholly unjustified risk of the destruction of the army—the only way in which this war can now be lost. We know Bonaparte's numbers have already been diminished by half during this campaign; he has lost more cavalry even than that. He can take Moscow, but he cannot hold it; he cannot hold St. Petersburg. He has overreached—"

"Overreached!" Another general, Bennigsen, was already roaring at him, before he had finished. "You would let him walk through the gates of Moscow without giving battle, without challenge—" He broke here into a torrent of Russian, savage, which made Barclay's cheeks flush hot with color, before he returned to French. "Listen to me, General," Bennigsen said, turning towards Kutuzov, "it will not be so simple a matter to get Bonaparte out again, once we have let him in. He may be diminished in numbers, but those who remain to him are the best of his army, seasoned men. If we give him so splendid a resting place as Moscow, his stragglers will gather in to him, he will secure his supply with all the stores laid up for the use of our own army—dear God! If any of us had ever thought there should be danger of them falling into the enemy's hands!"

The argument could not fail but be impassioned, in such circumstances as these: the Chinese legions were still enough advantage to make the Russian Army seem the superior, though on the ground they were as yet perilously outnumbered, and the losses on the previous day had been immense. The French had known they fought a holding action; Bonaparte at every turn had conserved his men, and yielded ground judiciously to preserve them: ground which the Russians had bought dearly in blood while exposing themselves to the withering French artillery.

But no man could easily have borne sacrificing, even in worse circumstances, the very heart of the nation; though the government had been seated in St. Petersburg some years now, Moscow remained to nearly all of them its foremost city. "To have lost Petersburg was bad enough; if we lose Moscow as well, without a shot fired, you may as well send a courier to ask Napoleon which of his brothers we shall see upon the throne, by the New Year!" General Docturov said bitterly: his infantry had borne the brunt of the day's hot work; his own arm was bandaged, and his face spattered with powder-burns.

Another officer, a younger man named Raevsky who had led the assault upon the French fences, said quietly to Kutuzov directly, "We must cover the southern provinces to permit General Chichagov and General Tormassov to unite their forces. Without Saint-Cyr's forces at Petersburg, Wittgenstein has sufficient numbers to drive back the French there—"

"Before we are subjected to more of these counsels of—let us say retreat, instead of surrender," Bennigsen said to him, with acid bite, "perhaps we might first ascertain if the retreat can be accomplished. If Bonaparte were to overwhelm the rear-guard—"

Kutuzov sat impassively while they argued it out, his heavy-lidded bad eye giving him an appearance almost half-slumbering and his face resting upon his fist, elbow propped against the arm of his chair; the fingers of his other hand touched gently the many reports which had gathered up before him, and now and again he lifted one of these to his eyes. But Laurence did not think he read them; and when at last the voices fell silent, he did not answer them, but looked to Laurence. "What is the state of your legions?" he said.

"Sir," Laurence said, "we remain at your service, constrained only by supply. General Chu's injuries are grievous, but I have every confidence in Colonel Zhao Lien, and our losses otherwise were slight: ten fighting-beasts and seven supply wounded past flying."

"Will they carry infantry?" Kutuzov asked; Bennigsen made a small jerk, a half-abortive movement.

"Certainly, for a short distance," Laurence said. "For any longer march, sir, that may materially alter the requirements of supply."

Kutuzov nodded, a little. "We must be in Moscow by tomorrow," he said, "and we will take the road to Riazan," he held up a hand, to forestall argument, "and then cross to the Old Kaluga Road, and make for Tarutino."

Bennigsen checked his first reply without speaking; Raevsky nodded. Laurence looking at the map upon the table picked out the roads, the cities, and understood: Kutuzov would make it seem as though he were retreating eastward, deeper into the Russian steppes, the safest course; and then would turn south again sharply while the French were busy with their occupation of Moscow—and surely its looting as well—and seize a strong position to the south, protecting the supply of food and munitions coming to his army from the rich southern provinces, and ensuring his communications with the large portion of the Russian Army which yet remained in the Empire's south.

There was much to like, in the strategy, and nothing better recommended itself; only sentiment stood in its way—only sentiment. Barclay's own expression was of relief and weariness combined; the other officers remained silent, giving a dull and unhappy consent.

Kutuzov looked around at them and nodded. "To yield Moscow is not to lose Russia," he said. "And if Bonaparte should think otherwise, so much the better."

But if Bonaparte did, he was not alone: so, too, plainly did the soldiers as they marched through the streets of Moscow, sharing the roads at every turn with a terrified and appalled peasantry and merchants all desperately trying to evacuate themselves and their goods before the French arrival. The great square before the red walls of the Kremlin was a solid mass of people, the glorious twisting domes of the splendid cathedral rising like an island out from among lowing cattle, struggling horses, waggon-carts loaded with goods.

Temeraire had insisted on taking a carrying-harness himself with all the rest of the dragons; he bore nearly two hundred Russian soldiers over the city, and Laurence saw many of the young officers openly weeping with rage as they looked down and saw the thronged streets, the masses of men and horses and carts pouring out of the city, the River Moskva crammed with barges and smaller boats. To the west behind them, guns yet spoke sporadically, all the day, and the French advance guard under Murat continued harassing the rear.

They left their load of soldiers on the far side of the city, the *niru* behind them descending each in turn and practicing a maneuver Laurence had never before seen. As they came close to the ground, the dragons' crews went below and detached the lower straps of the carrying-harness; much to the alarm of the soldiers craning their heads to look. Each dragon then made a quick expert hop just before landing, flinging the sides wide—the soldiers shouting wildly as they swung out—then immediately flattening themselves low upon the ground, so the startled men at the ends found themselves already down, and even the soldiers higher up on the dragons' backs might the more easily clamber off.

"How clumsy they are," Laurence overheard one of the dragons murmuring to another, not unjustly: the Russian infantry were not even skillful at mounting their own dragons, plainly as yet uneasy with the entire business, and often tripped over one another in their haste to disembark even without the addition of acrobatics.

The morale of the Chinese forces was as yet untarnished: they did not suffer those same pangs as did the Russians, on seeing the city fall, and they had come off the better in their skirmishing against the French dragons. They plainly were confident in Zhao Lien, although Laurence overheard a little soft grumbling by the first *jalan* that their own commander Shao Ri ought have been the choice: there was a little rivalry, it seemed, between the scarlet dragons who made the bulk of the southern troops, and the green ones who preferred the northern climes.

The attack upon their rear had not disheartened but inspired all the legions with the desire for revenge. General Chu had been gently and tenderly borne to the new camp on a litter by four dragons: he had not yet roused, save to ask for a little water, now and again, and his body was hot with fever; his loud labored breathing was a constant reminder to them all of the treachery which had struck them. But for all that, when they encamped at last for the night, Laurence heard many of the dragons and their crewmen murmuring softly, doubtfully, about the retreat and their allies.

"I cannot like it at all," Temeraire said, unhappily. "It seems to me nearly wicked, Laurence: do you know, Grig has told me his captain was saying the French will take *a hundred million* rubles in treasure out of the city—which I suppose are like pounds—"

"Nothing like," Laurence said, "—not in the least; five in one, my dear."

"Well, I am very glad to hear it," Temeraire said, only a little mollified, "but even so that is more money than I have ever heard of, and they can settle in very comfortably, and eat well there all winter if they like as well: it certainly looked a very splendid city, from above."

The retreat continued, the next day, although a temporary armistice held off the French advance behind them. It was tiring work, and sorrowful; as the day went on the dragons began to be loaded with the wounded, and had to witness their agony at being put aboard. And yet they were the fortunate, not to be dragged over the dreadful roads in horse-carts. Temeraire was drooping before the last flight, as the bloodied and weary men dragged themselves aboard, or were heaved up by their few able-bodied comrades; night was coming on, and the sun had sunk low. He gathered himself and heaved aloft, wings beating, and slowly began to fly. A deep red-orange glow rose against the sky ahead of them; the wind had grown stronger yet again. The riot of color did not diminish as they went, though the sky was sweeping to black above, the stars emerging, and as they drew near the city they heard a great crackling noise, punctuated by sharp explosions like shattering glass.

"*Boze Moje,*" one of the men said, low. "*Onii goryat Moskvye.*"

Laurence put the glass to his eye as they came overhead, a rolling wave of baking heat rising, lifting Temeraire soaring high: a handful of Russian soldiers were dashing through the city streets ahead of the line of leaping, hungry flames, carrying torches; there were heaped piles of hay and tinder at corners, and they were firing them as they went. They were burning their own city. Napoleon would find no shelter in Moscow, after all.

Chapter 20

LAURENCE PAUSED A LONG moment in the empty street, caught by the sight of a swinging, blackened lantern and the shape of steps leading up to a gutted doorway, opening onto the rubble of a house. For a moment he thought it another old memory returning, some flash of the destruction of Portsmouth; then he recognized abruptly the home of Countess Andreyevna, where he had dined his first night in Moscow. Of the palatial house there was nothing left but jagged timbers thrust up into the sky, heaps of tumbled brick and cinders, one corner in the back where a narrow servants' staircase and a corner of the second floor stood alone, a few feet of space.

"Do you see something?" Tharkay asked quietly. His own face was half-covered; only his eyes looked out above the scarf he had wrapped over his nose and mouth: not too incongruous a costume in the city, for there were yet quantities of dust and ash lingering in the air.

"No," Laurence said. "No, it is nothing; let us go on." He put his shoulder back to the yoke of the small cart they were dragging behind them, with its few bags of grain: their safe-passage and the only one required; the French had mastered their own maurauding troops and now were offering urgent and enthusiastic welcome to any of the local peasantry who offered to sell them any food—there being very few such offers; those who made them were meeting with savage reprisals from Russian partisans.

The streets of Moscow bore little resemblance to the thronged narrow lanes which Laurence had seen from aloft, only a month before: now half-deserted, frequented more by rats than men and full of rubble, lined with ruined houses and gardens still choked with ash. Some three-quarters of the city had burned, and if that disaster had denied the French its comforts and supply, Laurence found it hard to accept the price. Little better illustration could be wanted of the cost of Napoleon's pride.

A troop of grenadiers marched past in good order, though their uniforms were an unholy mess: coats in a dozen different colors, most of them threadbare and patched, boots cracked and wrapped about with string; only their muskets still shone brightly. Their eyes drifted to the cart as they passed, with an interest more than academic; when they turned the corner, one man even detached himself from the end of the column and came back, and pointing at the bags said, "*Qu'est-ce que c'est là?*"

Without answering him, Tharkay silently presented him with a paper which had been prepared for them by one young Russian aide-de-camp, in that alphabet, and embellished with all the official art which his creativity had permitted; the name *Louis-Nicholas Davout* was the only legible Latin on the sheet. It was a name to conjure with, for Davout's harshness with indiscipline was legendary, and reports had reached even the Russian camp of the executions he had ordered for pillaging. The soldier thrust the paper back and assumed an officious mien, saying coolly, "*Le Maréchal est avec l'Empereur, en la place Rouge,*" and pointed them along another street before hurrying to rejoin his vanished troop.

Tharkay raised an eyebrow to Laurence as he put away the paper: should they take the chance? Laurence hesitated a moment, but nodded. They had intended only a general reconnoiter, to gain a sense of the French strength and the imminence of action—a sense which could not presently be gained, not reliably, from their Russian allies.

Morale in the Russian Army had rebounded and even swelled

as the French showed no inclination to foray past Moscow, and steady reports of the disintegration of their supply reached the Russian camp every day—often at the same time as their own supply-waggons arrived from the south, loaded with shipments of bread and boots and uniforms. Even the rank and file now had gradually come to share Barclay's view: that Napoleon had indeed overreached, and delivered himself and his Grande Armée into as neat a trap as was ever devised for an enemy. Each day meant the death of another hundred of his cavalry-horses, and three days before he had sent away fifteen of his dragons, traveling together to defend themselves against Cossack harrying: their departure had been observed, and had occasioned great cheer amongst the Russians.

But even as the soldiers grew more satisfied, their commanders grew less so. The intrigue at the Russian headquarters had risen to a fiery pitch; despite having managed the singularly effective retreat through the city, General Barclay had at last resigned his command entirely, in indignation at the disrespect he had met from both Kutuzov and Bennigsen, and those two men were at logger-heads themselves.

Kutuzov's position was an unsettled one: he had been nearly forced on Alexander to begin with, and he had sacrificed Moscow to the enemy. With both Moscow and Petersburg lost, the enemy everywhere west of the Volga and north of Moscow, the Russian nobility had been scattered upon the countryside, many of them cut off from their estates and fearing personal ruin. It was his task not merely to plan the Russian counterattack, when time had done its work, but to keep those nobles and even the Tsar himself placated, and fight off all the loud and urgent cries for an immediate battle.

He was resorting to a kind of outrageous propaganda: mere skirmishes between his men and Murat's advance guard were magnified into great victories—even if his forces came back with but a single prisoner and having lost several men themselves—and he exaggerated even the already-heartening reports of the French decline, filling his dispatches with such numbers as would have shortly ended with Napoleon sitting in Moscow alone but for a single mule and a barrel of beer.

And he was concerned, above all, with ensuring that the Chinese legions remained with the army. If Napoleon were to once again have the advantage in the air, the French position would by no means be so desperate as it was. They had great magazines of their own at Smolensk, and elsewhere through the south. If they did not need to fear being pounced upon by half-a-dozen *niru,* Napoleon's dragons might have been put to supply work, or even to swiftly relocate his army to Smolensk, there to winter and regroup for a fresh campaign in the spring.

Laurence did not wish to abandon Kutuzov in the least, but neither could he feel it at all consistent with the duty he owed the Emperor of China, to strand his borrowed legions in the midst of Russia with inadequate supply during the oncoming winter. October had so far been beautiful, warm and mild; but in the last two days the trees had with startling speed begun to shed their leaves. The Russian countryside was taking on a grey and gloomy character, unrelieved by the enormously tall pine trees looming with their cold dark needles, the increasingly barren birches rattling in the wind.

With the full cooperation of the Russians, Shen Shi had now established depots to the east and west both, which she estimated could carry the legions at their full strength for a month. But there was no reason to expect that Kutuzov would have struck even then: the old general was perfectly willing to permit Napoleon to sit in Moscow as long as he wished. And once they had begun the counterattack, the road back to the Niemen was a long one.

"How much longer will we be required?" Zhao Lien had asked Laurence bluntly, two days before. He could not tell her, and he felt too strongly that he could not trust whatever answer Kutuzov might make him.

"Bonaparte is our best hope, for the campaign to begin," he had said ruefully to Temeraire that evening. "If he has any sense, he must try and fight his way back to Smolensk sooner than late, and westward on from there swiftly. He cannot long suppose that the Russians will make peace with him now."

Such a peace would have allowed Napoleon to withdraw without humiliation, surely all that he could now hope for; but that peace was as surely to be denied him. Alexander, with his government-in-exile in Tula, was intensely, savagely delighted by the growing evidence of French discomfiture: he had already written out many long ambitious schemes to Kutuzov and his other generals for retaking Moscow, for the pursuit and destruction of the remnant of the French Army, and indeed even the capture of Napoleon himself.

Kutuzov received these directives placidly, and stayed just where he was. He had done his best to assist Napoleon in deceiving himself about the prospects of peace: he had received a French envoy affably, and agreed to a temporary armistice, but the false negotiations of Vyazma had done much to close that door. Alexander refused to receive such an envoy himself, or to write so much as a note, feeling that he had already stretched his own honor to bear as much as he could. Napoleon's pride alone could keep him in Moscow—but of that, he had an ample supply. When desperation and the growing certainty of disaster would overcome it, was nearly impossible to tell.

"We could hope for no better opportunity to learn his mind," Laurence said softly to Tharkay now, in the ruined street; together they dragged the cart onto the main street leading towards the Kremlin.

Here the devastation altered in character: the buildings had been more preserved than not, evidently by the labors of the French dragons; great puddles of dirty water yet stood in the gutters. Yet they had still been looted: scraps of silk and shattered porcelain might be seen on the steps, broken furnishings. How the French supposed they should carry away such an immense store of plunder, Laurence could hardly imagine.

The street itself was better tended; looking west towards the bounds of the city, Laurence could see a troop of dragons laboring to clear away the rubble and men behind them repairing the worst of the damage to the cobblestones: perhaps making ready the road for retreat? He and Tharkay went plodding on with their heads down into the vast square around the onion-domed cathedral which, though blackened with smoke, had also been saved: Laurence saw in some disgust that the building was evidently being used for a stable.

The remains of many smaller wooden buildings still lingered at its base, and resting against the high walls of the Kremlin some forty dragons were drowsing together in heaps, while their crews silently prodded at large cauldrons simmering with their poor thin dinner: they were eating dead horses mostly half-starved or sick, stewed with flour. The dragons looked too weary to be called indolent, slumped in the heavy attitudes of exhaustion.

One more-alert beast stood before the cathedral, beside the great city fountain, while some few peasant women, cringing, took their buckets of water before hurrying away: a heavy-weight Papillon Noir in black with iridescent stripes. "That is Liberté," he murmured to Tharkay. He had seen the beast once before, during the invasion of England: he was the personal beast of Marshal Murat, and beside it stood the man himself.

The pair were standing beside one of the Russian light-weights, white-grey. Laurence thought for a moment it might be a prisoner, but as he and Tharkay drew their cart a little closer, he saw the poor beast had no harness and was nearly skeletal in appearance, deep concavities between its ribs. It had a bowl of thin soup, which it was licking up with slow, painstaking care, one foreleg curled around the bowl and a wary watchful hostile eye turned up towards Liberté. Its wings were drawn up tight to its body, as though it might at any moment flee.

Murat was evidently waiting to see the Emperor, and following the line of his gaze Laurence saw him: Napoleon was near the

Kremlin gates, in his dust-grey coat and flanked by the still-glittering ranks of his escort, the Imperial Guard. Davout was a tall thin figure beside him, and his chief of staff Berthier as well.

A French officer then approached the cart, and they were forced to stop: Laurence engaged the man before he could notice Tharkay's foreign looks, pulling back the cover to show him the ten sacks of grain, pantomiming numbers with his hands to indicate many more than these were on offer. "*Cinq cent?*" the Frenchman asked. Laurence nodded, and then held out a hand flat and tapped his palm, asking for an offer; the officer said, "*Attends,*" and went away to confer with another.

Napoleon looked himself as heavy and morose as the dragons of his army; he seemed to only be giving half his attention to an anxious speech which Berthier was making him, full of gestures and intensity; the Emperor glanced away often at the somnolent dragons, at the few companies of soldiers equally dispirited and yawning against the walls. He knew, of course; surely he knew the hopelessness of his position. He was not a fool. He had his hands clasped behind his back, his chin lowered upon his breast; Berthier gestured, down the square, and following his arm, Laurence saw a nearly medieval train of waggon-carts, already loaded and with their covers lashed down.

Bonaparte stood a moment more, and then gave a short nod; Berthier, after a speaking look of relief exchanged with Davout, hurried away back into the Kremlin. Davout seemed as though he wished to say something; Napoleon jerking a hand forestalled him and turned abruptly away, his face hard, and strode out across the square towards Murat, who rose to meet him.

The French quartermasters were still discussing amongst themselves. Laurence looked at Tharkay and, receiving a nod, hazarded the risk. He strode across the square towards the city fountain, as though to have a drink of water, where he could overhear a little.

Napoleon had put his hand on Liberté's side, patting the dragon with easy familiarity as he spoke with Murat; the beast nosed at him with pleasure. "Well, brother," he was saying, with a ghost of a smile, "the last die is thrown, we must stand up from the table! We will have to fight our way back to France, and no rest after that."

"What else is a soldier for?" Murat said, with a wave of his arm: more generosity than Bonaparte deserved, having pressed them all on towards destruction. "We'll sleep a long time in the end. Will you want us to give them a bite on the flank before we draw back?"

Fortune did not smile on Laurence's adventure to so great an extent as to permit him to overhear such invaluable intelligence; Bonaparte only raised his hand a little and wagged it to either side, noncommittal, and jerked his head towards the small Russian dragon, asking Liberté in a deliberate tone of levity, "What is this, your prisoner? A fine battle you must have had!"

"I have not fought her at all," Liberté said, in some indignation, "even though she tried to steal one of our pigs, when we camped near the breeding grounds; and I carried her here myself."

"I couldn't stomach leaving her to starve, poor beast," Murat said to Napoleon, "and it's not as though she could do us any real harm. I've sent for one of the surgeons. Look at what they do to them."

The surgeon, a man in a long black frock coat carrying the grim instruments of his trade, still stained with the blood of some recent patient, came past the fountain even as he spoke; Laurence averted his face, quickly, until the man had gone around him. The dragon hissed at the surgeon and snapped as he approached, only to subside when Liberté put his foreleg on her neck and pinned it to the ground. The man climbed carefully upon her back, between the wings.

Laurence could not see, at first, what the surgeon was doing there; the dragon bellowed in pain and tried to thrash, but Liberté held her fast. A few minutes passed, perhaps three, and then the man flung down over the dragon's side a chain, dripping black blood, with two large barbed hooks on either end still marked with gobbets of flesh: a hobble, simpler but not unlike the one which had held Arkady, when they had found him held prisoner in China. The dragon made a low keening noise, shivering still, but her wings gave a small abortive flutter, as if suddenly freed.

Napoleon made an exclamation of disgust, looking down at the hobble. "And she was not the only one?"

"All of them, in the breeding grounds," Murat said. "And they look as though they do not get enough food to keep alive a cat; I wonder they get any eggs out of them at all."

Temeraire could not but fret anxiously at Laurence's absence, though he had for comfort a splendid dispatch newly arrived from Peking, in which Huang Li had not only reported the egg's continuing perfect condition, but even, to Temeraire's delight, enclosed a small illustration of the pavilion in which the egg was housed, at the Summer Palace, showing it attended by four ladies-in-waiting and four Imperial dragons, and being fanned by servants against the late summer's heat.

"Of course I must keep the original," Temeraire said to Emily, "but perhaps we might make a copy of it, for Iskierka. Surely one of those aides could knock something up?" He was dictating her a letter to pass along the comforting reassurances he had received, and trying as best he could to describe their own success, giving it better terms than he really felt it deserved. "Do you suppose they have reached the Peninsula by now?" he asked wistfully. It was very hard to think that Iskierka might at this very moment already be with the Corps in Spain, which was evidently winning one brilliant battle after another, and he could report nothing for his own part but one battle, from which they had retreated.

"I don't think so," Emily said, with sufficient promptness to suggest that she had thought about the subject before. "They left China in July, just as we did. They might have gone by air from

Persia, if they stopped there, and have just been able to reach Gibraltar. But if they have gone round Africa, they cannot be in Spain before Christmas."

Temeraire did not say, but felt, that this was a small relief: perhaps they would have had another battle before Iskierka did finally have a chance for one of her own. But Emily herself sighed and said, "So it isn't surprising, that we shouldn't have had word from them yet," and looked down at the letter she was writing with a discontented expression, fidgeting with her quill in such a way as to scatter ink across the page.

While she was blotting up the spots, Temeraire said a little anxiously, "I hope you are not changing your mind—I hope you have not thought better of refusing Demane. I am sure that marriage cannot be so wonderful."

"No," she said, downcast. "No, at least, not marriage; but—I suppose I am sorry, a little; I wish I'd had him, while I had the chance."

"Emily," Mrs. Pemberton said, raising her head from where she sat near-by, working on her sewing. "I must beg you not to say such things."

"Oh, I know it isn't my duty; and it should have been a monstrously stupid thing to do," Emily said, "and so I didn't. But I shan't see him for years now, I suppose; if we ever serve together again at all." She sighed. "And one gets curious," she added.

"I ought to be turned off without a character," Mrs. Pemberton said to herself, half under her breath, and then to Emily said, "Even if you must think such things, you needn't *say* them, at least not where anyone might hear you. The last thing a young gentleman requires is any encouragement in that direction."

Temeraire was entirely of like mind with her. He had considered briefly whether perhaps it might be just as well to have Emily marry one of the officers of his own crew, but after some cautious inquiries about the etiquette of the matter, he had determined that this could not really serve to keep her with him when Admiral Roland decided to retire, and it was perfectly likely that she would instead take her own husband away to Excidium with her: so it was not at all to be wished under any circumstances.

He raised his head, alertly, catching some movement through the encampment: Laurence and Tharkay had come back, he saw with much relief, although Laurence's expression was dreadfully grim, and as he came near, already stripping away his peasant cloak, Temeraire asked anxiously, "Napoleon will not retreat?"

Laurence did not answer at once, only shook his head to say he could not immediately answer, and went into the pavilion, and into his tent; Temeraire in surprise went after him and lowered his head anxiously to peer inside: Laurence was putting on his uniform again, his movements short and sharp, angry. He said to Temeraire briefly, savagely, "They are chaining their dragons in the breeding grounds; they are keeping them hobbled."

Temeraire did not understand, at first, until Laurence had explained; and then he scarcely could believe it, until he had found Grig again and demanded a confirmation. "Well—well, yes," Grig said, edging back and looking at him sidelong with some anxiety at Temeraire's anger, though it was not directed at him. "If one won't go into harness, they don't let one fly. Whyever would anyone stay in the breeding grounds, otherwise?"

"It is quite beyond anything," Temeraire said, furious. "Laurence—"

But at that very moment, the courier arrived from headquarters, breathless, with fresh orders: the clamoring demands for action had at last overcome Kutuzov's inertia. They were ordered to attack.

Laurence regarded the orders silently, Temeraire peering down beside him. He knew his duty; it was not to liberate the miserable and wretched Russian dragons, nor to tell the Russians how they were to manage their own beasts: it was to secure the defeat of Napoleon and his army, and see them reduced beyond the ability to threaten either a renewed invasion of Britain, or further warmongering upon the Continent. That defeat was now within their grasp.

"But afterwards," he said to Temeraire, "—afterwards—" He stopped, and then sent for Gong Su and asked him, "Sir, would the Emperor consent to receive these dragons into his Empire?" He gestured to Grig, who looked back with an uncertain expression.

Gong Su looked at Grig with a cool, assessing eye. "He speaks more than one tongue?" he asked. "Will you inquire at what age he acquired them?"

"Well, the dragon-tongue, I learnt that in the breeding grounds before I was hatched," Grig said, doubtfully, "and as for Russian, and French, I cannot rightly say; I suppose I have just picked them up bit by bit the same way that the others have: one does, hearing them every day."

As this was by no means characteristic of most dragon breeds, particularly not in the West, Gong Su nodded in some appreciation. He said to Laurence, "Of course I cannot speak with any official weight. But these beasts appear to be of respectable qualities, and moderate size. There is a great hunger for village porters in the countryside. If they did not consider laborer's work in such small settlements beneath their dignity, then there should be no difficulty in finding employment for them."

"Will you write and inquire if I may extend an offer of such hospitality?" Laurence asked bluntly; Gong Su bowed.

Laurence nodded and said to Temeraire, "Then afterwards, when we have done, we will go to all the breeding grounds which Grig can lead us to—you will explain to them the conditions of their welcome in China, of their employment there—and those who wish to depart, we will free from their hobbles and take with us on our own return to China.

"And if the Russians do not care to lose all their breeding stock," he added, low with anger, "they may amend their treatment."

He knew the condition of the Russian peasantry, very little removed from slavery, was nearly as pitiable as that of the dragons; and yet there was something intolerable in the spectacle of hundreds of beasts so hobbled that they might not even fly as was their nature, but instead were confined to scrabbling in pits; save for those beasts who, cowed by the horror of their circumstances, would consent to be slaves for scraps and at least a little freedom of movement. The sensation was much as though, laboring with all his might upon the rigging of a ship and in her upper decks, keeping company with her crew, Laurence had suddenly seen through an open ladderway the faces of captives chained and looking up at him with accusation, and discovered himself in service upon a slaver.

He and Temeraire flew together to the headquarters, where a ferment of activity was going forward: Bennigsen and his staff were in an ill-suppressed condition of delight, Kutuzov more phlegmatic; he had appointed Bennigsen and Colonel Toll to the command of the operation. Their target would be Murat himself and his corps, encamped not far from Tarutino, who had grown incautious after a month-long informal truce, their patrols slack: a heavy forest near-by offered cover for a surprise attack.

"Ah, Captain," Kutuzov said, and beckoned him out of the tumult, "come and let us discuss your orders."

"Sir," Laurence said, following him into a separate chamber, formerly the private library of the master of the house, "I will carry out your orders, if you continue to desire our assistance; but I must beg permission to speak frankly, as the price of that assistance may no longer be one you willingly accept."

Kutuzov settled himself comfortably in his chair and waved a hand for permission, his face settling into its habitual slack lines; he listened in silence while Laurence laid out both his objections to the abuse of the Russian ferals, and his intentions towards them. "I hope you will understand, sir, if Temeraire and the other dragons should have that fellow-feeling towards their own kind, which absolutely must have prohibited their making themselves allies of a nation which so maltreated them. This project is the only manner in which I can conceive of reconciling that repugnance with our continued service to you.

"But I am by no means willing to provoke a confrontation between nations, wholly undesirable to either; if you should wish us to depart at once, without engaging in what you may call interference in your affairs, we will do so," Laurence added, "and I hope you will believe me nevertheless entirely desiring your victory over Bonaparte, in such a case."

He finished slowly, a little surprised to find Kutuzov still listening to him with an attitude almost of complacency. The old general snorted at his look and said, "Grig is a clever little creature, you know: Captain Rozhkov raised him from the egg."

While Laurence with a sense of strong indignation digested this, Kutuzov continued, "It is not as though we have not heard of you, Captain Laurence. We have all had a great many arguments, whether your aid would not be too expensive, to begin with."

"Sir," Laurence said, now baffled, "I beg your pardon; however should you know me from Adam?"

"If the world had not heard of you, after your adventure at Gdansk," Kutuzov said, meaning Danzig, where they had rescued the garrison from the wreck of the Prussian campaign, "or after the plague, we should certainly have heard of you after Brazil. Where you go, you leave half the world overturned behind you. You are more dangerous than Bonaparte in your own way, you and that beast of yours.

"It is awkward you should have seen that feral just now, in Moscow, but in the end, it seems it will not make so much difference. The Tsar means us to chase the French all the way to Paris, and I cannot do that without four hundred dragons or more. I must get them out of the breeding grounds somehow.

"So! You will show us how to feed dragons on grain, and I will speak to Arakcheyev," the Tsar's chief minister, "and we will cut them loose."

Laurence almost did not at first quite comprehend Kutuzov's

answer; he had long felt—long known—the many practical advantages offered by a more humane and just treatment of dragons; he had recognized the danger to Britain and any other nation in the stark comparison between the increasing consideration offered to French dragons, and the ill-treatment of their own. He had indeed made these practical matters his argument on many occasions, but he had grown so used to failure, to meeting with only a stolid, blind resistance, that to find not only a tolerant ear but agreement left him more nonplussed than rejection; he did not at once know what to say. "Sir," Laurence said, and halted, overwhelmed by a perfect reversion of feeling, as though he had faced a mortal enemy, and been offered from his hand a priceless gift; he could cheerfully have embraced the old general with Slavic passion.

He with difficulty tried to express his sentiments; Kutuzov waved them away. "Don't be too quick to rejoice," he said. "We can't cut them loose until we can be sure we can feed them. It hasn't been so long since the Time of Troubles, you know; half the country would rise up if they saw dragons flying all over unharnessed." He indicated with one thick finger a painting upon the wall, which depicted a band of pikemen heroically massed and their commander pointing aloft at a looming, snarling dragon, which stood with outspread wings over the broken body of a horse and clutched in one taloned hand a screaming maiden, her trailing white gown a banner stained with blood and her arms outflung in supplication as she cast her eyes up to the heavens.

"Sir," Laurence said dryly, "permit me to assure you that the most vicious beast in all Russia would not prefer to make its dinner out of a lady of six or seven stone over a horse of one hundred."

Kutuzov shrugged. "There were not always horses," he said bluntly.

Laurence was nevertheless able to return to Temeraire with a spirit no longer weighed down with guilt, and share with him the satisfaction not only of having carried their point, but having won it in such a manner as founded the victory on the most solid of ground: that the Russians had freely recognized the necessity of reforming their treatment of their native dragons. "Well," Temeraire said, "I am very glad to see that they have some real sense, Laurence; Kutuzov must be quite a good fellow, particularly as he means us to attack. And now we can do so wholeheartedly.

"Although," he added, with a lowering frown, "I cannot like hearing that Grig has been carrying tales of us: whatever did he mean by it, and pretending that he was so wretched, if he is really quite the pet of his captain? I do not know what to make of it at all."

"You must take it as a compliment," Tharkay said, "that you are of sufficient importance to have spies set upon you." He had expressed just such a sentiment on first learning that Gong Su had been all the while an agent of Prince Mianning; Laurence could not partake in those feelings, however, and was not in the least sorry to find the little dragon had prudently taken himself off and vanished into the general mass of the Russian forces.

But it was nevertheless with a gladdened heart that Laurence went to his tent, to clean his guns and sharpen his sword before the engagement, and was surprised to find Junichiro there. "I have neglected you, I find," Laurence said, in apology: it had not escaped his notice that Junichiro had made extraordinary progress in his study of English, and had furthermore devoted himself with great attention to mastering not only aerial tactics, but learning as much as he could of all others as well: he had seen the boy make persistent overtures to the Russian artillery-officers, in particular, and questioning any he found who could speak at least a little French.

He had in short done all that anyone might have wanted, to make him an officer; but Laurence had realized, too late, that he was by no means a valuable mentor: the Aerial Corps would be more likely to scorn Junichiro than embrace him, for having Laurence's good word.

"But," he said, "I will write to Admiral Roland, and see if I can solicit her influence on your behalf—"

"Sir," Junichiro said quietly, "I beg you do not concern yourself further with this matter: I cannot serve in your Corps."

Laurence paused, startled, and was even more so when Junichiro added, "I have come to ask your permission to depart; and if you refuse it, I must nevertheless end my service to you, even if by a final means." Laurence realized with appalled astonishment that Junichiro spoke of ending his own life: that he would die, by his hand, rather than continue with them.

"Good God," he said, "whatever should make you even contemplate so desperate a course of action? I know of no reason why I should refuse you the right to depart; I might counsel you against it, but you are a free man, and you have made no oath of service to the King: indeed, I am rather indebted to you, than the reverse."

"Captain," Junichiro said, "you may feel differently when I have explained, but it would be dishonorable of me to conceal my purpose from you: I intend to go to France."

"You mean to take service with Bonaparte," Laurence said, half-disbelieving: although he did now see why Junichiro had thought he would object. It sounded like treachery, and yet the confession made it not so; a true traitor would have gone, silently, slinking away. But if Junichiro truly meant to go to Napoleon now, with so much intimate knowledge of their force, their positions—

"No." Junichiro shook his head. "I mean to ask him to send an envoy to my country."

Laurence sat down slowly on the camp-chair, disturbed. "Pray explain yourself."

"I am masterless," Junichiro said, "—a criminal and an exile. But it is still my duty to serve the Emperor—*my* Emperor. It is still my duty to serve Japan. And your nation is not the friend of mine."

He gestured a little, towards the tent entrance. "Your position in this war is now superior," he said. "It is likely that you will be victorious, and cement your alliance with China. And long have they coveted dominion over Japan. I have seen the might of their dragons. Soon they will have Western ships, and Western guns.

And we must have them, too—and if not from you, it seems we must have them from France."

"We need not be your enemy, only to be China's friend," Laurence said, but Junichiro raised his eyes and looked at him straight-on.

"You require alliance with them," Junichiro said. "You require their dragons. Whatever you might hope to get from us, you do not need, not in the same way. If they demand that you choose, you will choose them." He made a short cutting gesture with one hand. "My decision is made. I have only waited so long because I did not wish to depart while your situation was yet uncertain, or bleak: I would not leave you in defeat. If you wish to prevent my leaving, you can. I will not attempt to steal away like a thief in the night. But I will no longer serve Britain."

Laurence was silent. He knew what Hammond would have said, to the prospect of sending so priceless an ambassador as Junichiro would make straight into Napoleon's hands: a man not merely versed in the language of Japan but intimately familiar with its customs, and of high birth; a man who despite his exile still had friends among the nobility of that nation, and whose opinions might be privately respected, even if he could not officially be pardoned. It could easily be as much as handing Napoleon a new ally, one who could threaten China's coasts and British shipping.

"You have sacrificed everything," Laurence said finally, "home, position, friends; and if not for my sake, to my benefit. I have no right to keep you, and I cannot dispute your conclusions. But my first duty is to see this war won. If you will give me your word of honor, not to reveal any information about our forces or those of the Russians, I cannot stand in your way."

Junichiro said, "I swear it," very simply.

Laurence nodded a little; he had no doubt of that promise being kept. "Then I will bid you Godspeed," he said quietly, "and I hope with all my heart that your fears will not come to pass."

Junichiro bowed to him deeply, and slipped away; Laurence sat silently in the tent with his sword across his knees, and wondered if they would next meet again as enemies, across a battlefield.

Temeraire was all the more relieved, that Kutuzov's good sense meant that he could properly continue to fight: he was sure now of their ultimate victory. The strike against Murat's forces proved a great success, although a great many of the Russian infantry got themselves lost in the woods and did not reach the battlefield in time: but that scarcely mattered, when Shao Ri came back with not only four captured dragons, and all their crews, but a golden eagle still with tatters of a tricorn attached and sixteen guns; and the rest of the infantry had done well for themselves also, having taken nearly two thousand prisoners and twenty guns, and three eagles. One could not compare, of course, for there were so many more of the French infantry that Napoleon was obliged to give them more eagles to carry, and the eagle which Shao Ri had captured was nearly three times the size—perhaps a little closer to twice—and in any case truly splendid. Temeraire had rarely felt so much delight as when Shao Ri lay the captured standards before Laurence and himself, with a low bow: he felt his breast quite bursting with pride and satisfaction.

The mood in the Russian camp was also nearly exaltation, and everyone was pleased, except the generals, who were quarreling again: General Raevsky, whom Laurence thought a great deal of, and who had dined with them on several occasions, even told Laurence he avoided headquarters as much as ever he could. "It is a nest of vipers," he said, "and they have not yet reorganized the command, even though Barclay is gone."

But however much they quarreled, at least they had won their first real and clear victory, unquestioned, and in the shadow of this defeat, Napoleon had to begin his own retreat from Moscow at last, quite as humiliated as the most ardent Russian patriot might have desired. Of course, they had only defeated his advance guard, but for the moment it seemed as good as if they had routed his entire army, and Temeraire now looked forward with the most eager anticipation to an opportunity to do just that. The question before them now was which way Napoleon would withdraw, along which road; and only a few days later, Temeraire was woken a little way into the evening by a courier coming: there was fighting in Maloyaroslavets, a little town south of their camp along the Kaluga Road, and Napoleon's whole army was there.

"Nothing could be better," he said to Laurence jubilantly. "Now we will properly fall upon him; and perhaps he will be there himself, and we can take him prisoner."

Of course, they had been obliged to disperse the second *jalan* back to the east, because Shen Shi felt too uncertain of supply. But Temeraire privately felt that was all the better, because it should mean more of an excuse for him to take part in the battle, directly; however little he wished to disregard General Chu's last advice to him, he could not help but think he would have quite an awkward time of it explaining, when next he saw Iskierka, if he did not have at least a little fighting himself.

"And we cannot be blamed now, Laurence," he said, "for Kutuzov has got those aides who can speak Chinese, even if their accents are perfectly dreadful; so I do not see that we must sit about behind the lines. Indeed, they are by far the better placed to do it, since they can speak Chinese and Russian, and I have not worked Russian out yet."

He had been very careful to avoid doing so: he did not in the least want to be able to go-between any more than he already did.

"So long as we can be of material use," Laurence said, "I will not scruple to say I share your feelings: and God willing, this battle will see Napoleon's army broken."

Laurence had a note from General Raevsky, while the *jalan* were assembling: *Will you carry us?* was all the message, and he was glad to return an affirmative answer. Raevsky had ten thousand men in his corps, lately denied the opportunity to partake in the attack upon Murat and all of them filled with passion; they flung themselves aboard the Chinese dragons with a will, as enthusiastic seeking battle as they had been miserable in retreat.

The dragons snatched up the guns, and launched aloft: Temeraire nearly trembling with excitement beneath him and only with difficulty keeping to the pace that Zhao Lien watchfully set, to avoid wearing out her forces under their burden; the Russians began to sing as they flew on, deep young joyful voices, and traded off with the Chinese crews, one after another, all the length of their flight.

"He must have meant to march on Kaluga," Raevsky said to Laurence, as they flew: that city being presently the main supply base of Kutuzov's army, and the gateway to the munitions factories of the south. "God favors Russia at last: if Dokhturov had not caught him, he could have done us some more mischief yet."

The distance was only twenty miles: two hours put them in sight of the town, and the plumes of smoke rising; several of the buildings were burning, and the cannon roared ferociously on both sides. Zhao Lien brought them around wide, to the south behind the Russian advance guard which was ferociously holding the small town against Napoleon's advance. More prepared this time for the hop-skip of the Chinese landing, Raevsky's corps were disembarked in not half-an-hour; his sergeants were already bawling for order and forming the men into their regiments as the Chinese dragons lifted off again, to form up aloft.

Temeraire hovered longingly beside Zhao Lien as she sent forth the first *jalan* through the climbing smoke. Dokhturov had only one aerial regiment of six heavy-weights, and with them two dozen light-weights whom, in defiance of tradition, he had flung into battle to give his men a little cover against the French skirmishing attack. The French dragons, some twenty in number and wearing the emblem of the corps of Eugène de Beauharnais, had been handily outfighting them and dropping bombs upon the Russian troops, who were taking a dismal shelter against a handful of buildings now all of them in flames.

The Chinese legions drove in and at once turned the tide in the air: the French infantry fell back and dug themselves grimly into the stone monastery at the center of town behind their guns, and the French dragons turned tail and simply fled, as quickly as they could go. "Look, Laurence, you see they are just running away!" Temeraire said, in rather exultant tones, as they watched the retreat from the southern end of the town.

Five *niru* set off in pursuit; but the crews of the French middle-weights abruptly swung below and cut loose their belly-netting, dropping their munitions. And thus lightened, the French middle-weights could just barely outdistance the Chinese and began to pull away. One *niru* did manage to pounce on a lagging beast, however, and skillfully dragged him down to the ground. The remainder escaped: but meanwhile the soldiers below were now exposed, and the Russian supply corps had labored to some purpose in these intervening weeks to provide the Chinese legions with their own bombs, which now their crews began to hurl down on the entrenched Frenchmen.

The French answer came in the form of round-shot. The French used stones and bricks from the shattered walls and streets of the town to elevate their guns until they were pointing nearly directly over their heads, and in so doing managed to inflict a casualty of their own: a ball tore into the belly of one of the Shao Lung and erupted through its back, and the poor creature fell stone-dead from the sky, smashing through a burning building and leaving its wreck sprawled across the streets of the town. Raevsky's men had now dragged their guns into position, with the aid of horses snatched from Dokhturov's corps: the battlefield was no place for cavalry, with fire on every side and the narrow streets choked with rubble nearly impassable even for men on foot. Their guns began to thunder in company.

The French—whom Laurence realized, when the smoke cleared well enough to see their uniforms, were not Frenchmen but Italians, recruited from another of Napoleon's conquests—would surely have retreated in the face of their disadvantages, if any opportunity offered them; but as they were behind the only stone walls in their vicinity, they could get no better shelter than where they were, and by removing themselves from it would have exposed themselves both to the relentless artillery and to the snatching talons of the dragons above.

From necessity they held their position, answering as best they could, and so valiantly that they could only be winnowed down a little at a time, and the fires of the town crept ever closer towards them.

They held for an hour, pushed back slowly, and then Laurence through his glass saw movement through the immense towering clouds of smoke. "Temeraire," he said, "take us aloft, if you please," but Zhao Lien's scouts were already darting back to report to her: Davout's corps had arrived, with fifty French dragons in support.

For the next four hours, the battle roared back and forward through the town: at first the French fell back, under their newly arrived air cover, and the Russians with a shout charged into its narrow lanes and took possession; then they themselves were forced back by the terrible weight of the French artillery and their advantage in infantry. The town changed hands five more times, that dreadful afternoon: many of the wounded could not be rescued, and a sudden change in the wind drove the spreading flames abruptly further on. As those who could not walk were engulfed by the spreading flames, the shrieks of the dying rose like a noise out of perdition from the smoke.

"Dear God," Laurence said. "Temeraire—Temeraire, can you interrupt them? For God's sake, we must have a cease-fire, and get those men out of the way."

They passed the word to Zhao Lien, and then Temeraire flung

himself aloft and roared terribly, shatteringly: so hugely that all those below halted a moment and covered their heads against it. Emily and Baggy flung out a great white trailing sheet and waved it in the wind, and for a moment the guns fell silent; Zhao Lien sent in four of the supply-dragons, to snatch up the wounded of both sides, and bear them limp and half-scorched out.

The pause stretched on for a moment, for a minute, for three. Laurence half-wondered if perhaps it might go on, no-one wishing to continue: if a little space might break through whatever illusion it was permitted men to desire battle and to give it. It seemed as though all the world held its breath; and then a small company of artillery from de Beauharnais's corps touched off a primed gun, near the center, and the conflict was rejoined even as the wounded—and the many dead which had been taken up from among them—were laid out moaning upon the ground.

"Laurence, when we do not even want this town anyway, particularly," Temeraire said, looking sadly over the miserable wretches. "There is nothing splendid in it; if there ever were, it is surely quite ruined now, and if we *did* win this battle, we should have gained nothing but to say that we had won: that cannot be enough."

"The town may not be of significance in itself," Laurence said, "but it is immensely so as a gateway to our main sources of supply and beyond that to the Russian munitions-factories; if Napoleon managed to seize a great magazine for himself, and so hamper our own supply, he might well cripple the Russian Army."

As the battle continued, Zhao Lien directed her dragons steadily and conservatively: their advantage against the French was no longer so overwhelming, for besides the removal of the second *jalan,* they had been reduced by injuries: the Chinese armor, though excellent against talon and tooth, which it deflected easily, did not withstand rifle-fire as did chainmail. Of the 200 dragons of the remaining *jalan,* 150 were fighting-beasts, of whom nearly 30 were presently in the care of the surgeons; and their scouts and spies had recorded nearly 80 beasts in fighting trim still to Napoleon's tally, though not all of those were to be seen. So she was careful not to commit her entire force: 50 beasts presently were napping on the ground below, conserving their strength, leaving them 70 against 50 in the air.

Laurence had kept all this time scanning the town with his glass: even with all the advantages of elevation, he could scarcely make out anything for the smoke, layers upon layers of it, white and grey and smudged black, except when the blaze of cannon-fire briefly illuminated a company. "The French are presently heavily committed to those streets in the north-east," he said, having made out their positions, "and I do not see any of their guns pointing to their rear. If we should come around for a single pass, and level the buildings behind them with the divine wind, we should likely roll them up: and they are supporting the right flank of their army."

"I will ask Zhao Lien at once," Temeraire said, eagerly, and shot to her side; she looked more than a little anxious—small wonder; Laurence could well believe she would not like in the least to return to China with the news she had lost a Celestial, and even a dubious sort of Imperial prince—but there were nearly twenty guns established in the exposed position, and she could not fail to see the advantage of knocking such a hole in the French artillery.

"Very well," she said, reluctantly, at last, "—only wait a moment: the seventh and the fifteenth *niru* have performed with particular excellence, and deserve the honor of escorting your pass." She waved aloft two companies from the resting dragons below, and recalled those two named companies from the battle; surrounded thus by six beasts flying in protective pattern, Laurence almost felt himself back in England, formation-flying, as they swung out around the town.

Sweeping his gaze over the battlefield as they flew, Laurence saw, aboard one of the French middle-weights, a tall captain in flying-leathers looking at them through his own glass who plainly recognized the danger they posed; his ensign began at once putting out urgent signal-flags. The smoke concealed these from the men below, however; and the French were too hard-pressed to send enough relief to overcome Temeraire's escort. The captain bent forward over his dragon's neck, and the beast fell back from the fighting and turning flung itself gallantly towards the ground, going to warn the artillery-men in person.

"Quickly," Laurence said, "quickly, before they can turn round the guns—"

Their course by necessity was taking them wide around the town, as French artillery range covered nearly every inch of it and beyond its limits; Temeraire increased his speed, while his escort struggled to keep pace with him. Below, the middle-weight had managed to perch for a moment upon a collapsed building, hopping from one foot to the other and trying to keep her bell-men from being scorched while the captain shouted down to the artillery company.

The men were frantically dragging round several of the guns, to aim towards their approach, but their horses were stumbling with drooping heads, already weak, and the guns were surely scorching-hot from their work. Temeraire threw himself forward, roaring, and the buildings, weakened already by fire, began to shatter as the divine wind struck: the center of the walls collapsing inwards and the half-burnt roofs falling after them, until the whole went tumbling forward in a sudden crashing wave of burning tinders, a great blinding rush of orange sparks and ash spraying up, very much as from a fire stuck by a poker and stirred, and buried the guns and the men with them.

The French dragon had snatched one gun from the wreck, crying out with pain at the heat; the bell-men stretched their hands out to seize a few of the soldiers as she flung herself aloft. She was laboring away as Temeraire pulled up again, and Laurence alarmed called, "Temeraire! Temeraire, we must pull back!" for Temeraire was plainly unsatisfied with the immense success of his maneuver and half-instinctively had begun beating in pursuit, though this course should bring them too close to another battery of French artillery.

"Oh—" Temeraire said, stifled, and turned away: but a little sluggishly, and the roar of guns came from beneath as they came briefly into range.

Laurence caught Baggy, when he would have ducked, and kept him standing straight; the boy abashed glanced to see if anyone else had noticed his brief lapse. But his nearest neighbor, Roland, was hanging halfway out over Temeraire's shoulder, her carabiner straps extended to full length, and shouting enemy positions down to Forthing below: he was directing Laurence's handful of bell-men in flinging bombs down.

A whistling of round-shot came nearly past Laurence's ear; behind him another struck one of the dragons on Temeraire's left, scored its side, and as it jerked away, crying, tore a terrible gaping rent through its wing. Temeraire nearly turned back to catch him, but the other dragons of the *niru* were already closing in to support their wounded comrade. "Onward straight!" Laurence shouted through his speaking-trumpet: the other dragons would try to stay with Temeraire, and if he turned backwards they would find themselves snarled and vulnerable. The guns below had been meant for firing on the enemy infantry, at the other end of the town, but in a moment they would be reloaded with canister-shot, and a second volley would be sure of doing terrible damage among them.

Temeraire put on a burst of speed, and carried them back out of range; they swung back to Zhao Lien, who said nothing, but looked at the wounded dragon as he was helped tenderly to the ground; Temeraire hung his head, and as plainly did not require the lecture. He flew down to stand beside the wounded dragon, asking his name unhappily—"Lung Zhao Yang, Honorable One," the dragon said, trying despite his injuries to bow his head.

"I am very sorry I should have led you too close to the guns," Temeraire said, low, and stayed watching anxiously while the surgeons inspected the terrible damage to the wing, shaking their heads with concern.

"Do not wholly reproach yourself," Laurence said quietly. "We have silenced eighteen guns, and made a material change to the course of the battle; their position has been badly weakened. It must be counted worth the cost."

Temeraire nodded a little, unhappily, but did not say anything; he went back aloft watching, until abruptly a small panting Russian dragon came flying wildly towards the village from the north-east, and threading their own ranks dropped himself unceremoniously onto Temeraire's back amidst the crew, sending them all scrambling and himself nearly trembling with his speed and the effort of his flight: it was Grig.

"Oh," Temeraire said, coldly, having craned his head around in astonishment to be so boarded, "—you."

"Yes, but pray," Grig said, between his gulped breaths, "pray don't be angry, not now: they are all coming. I couldn't stop them; they won't listen to me. If only you can persuade them—"

"What has happened?" Laurence said sharply, and looked back the way that Grig had come: a low grey cloud, moving fast, approaching.

"Murat went to the breeding grounds on the Motsha River," Grig said, "and let them all go. He told them—"

The cloud was resolving into a great mass of dragons, most of them grey-white beasts with also a handful of smaller black dragons like the Russian couriers, flying raggedly and slowly but coming onward for all that: not towards the battlefield, nor towards their army, but heading directly for the supply-train in their rear. Temeraire flung himself towards their path, but even as he tried to intercept their course, they were already flying past like hurtling comets, lean and swollen-bellied and hollow-ribbed, some of them with eyes nearly shut and others dripping a kind of trailing slime from the sides of their mouths.

The Shen Lung, though ordinarily not combatants, were nevertheless well prepared to guard the supply against enemy attack: the twenty of them in the rear rose up swiftly to form a knot of protection over the cooking-pits, but preparation was no match for the number and desperation of the loosed ferals, in a battle whose sole question was, whether the supply should be ruined, or not. Some ferals blindly flung themselves heedless of claws and teeth down, and dragged quartered pigs dripping from the pits, then fled with their prizes away; others avoided the defenders and threw themselves instead further on to fall upon the rearing, terrified carthorses of the supply-train stretched down the road to the south.

These, too, were defended promptly by their drivers, who despite the little warning they had been given with courage unshipped their pikes and began to thrust at the snatching ferals; but there were not dozens of dragons, but a hundred and more, and though maddened with hunger they were not dumb beasts. They quickly began to form impromptu bands: one beast or two would draw the defenders, and the other snatch a horse away in that brief opening; then all three together would dart off bearing their trophy.

In the span of ten minutes, all had been reduced to utter chaos in the Russian baggage: carts unhorsed or overturned, and the rest trying both to defend themselves and keep their frantic horses from destroying themselves with their plunging, desperate attempts to break loose from their traces and escape. The Cossack aviators were trying to do what they might, but even massed, their small beasts could not stand against the grey dragons when the latter were so blindly determined to bull their way through.

The ferals were indiscriminate in their hunger: Laurence saw, looking back, that there was some chaos also in the French rear, where a few knots of starving dragons had hurled themselves against their supply-train; but Murat had evidently aimed the beasts well, and the general course of their flight was leading directly to the Russian rear. A dozen afflicted the French; it seemed near a hundred and more had fallen upon the Russians.

The *niru* who had been held in reserve had now come aloft. "Pray do not hurt them, if you can help it!" Temeraire called to them, as they joined him and began to swiftly work to envelop the rampaging cloud of ferals. "Let us try and force them to the ground:

I am sure if only we can, they will listen to us, once we give them a little food."

But the ferals had no intention of staying either to listen or be recaptured, as surely they must have feared. Those who had already snatched some food were darting away in every direction, like fish escaping from a closing net; only an especially ragged few, who had not been able to seize a prize and had reached the limits of their strength, were borne down. Others yet unsuccessful began to abandon their attempts, and then, to Laurence's horror, he saw them turning away from the well-defended supply, and falling upon the rows of the prone and bloody ranks of the wounded soldiers in their hospital.

Temeraire roared in protest, and led the *niru* in a scattering charge: but a dozen dragons fleeing carried off men screaming for aid and rescue in their talons. "God in Heaven," Laurence said, sickened, as he saw one wild-eyed creature raise a thrashing man to its jaws even as it flew, and with a snap of teeth and a savage jerk tear him in half.

Temeraire with a surge caught two of the beasts, and seizing them by the necks with his talons dragged them down to the ground. Laurence saw Ferris raise his rifle to his shoulder and take aim at one of the dragons, who was still trying even pinned to the ground to eat its victim. They were perhaps twenty yards distant. The gun spoke, with a burst of grey smoke; the dragon's head jerked back like a kicking horse, a spurt of blood and ichor coming from its eye, and fell limp. The man it had seized fell to the ground with it, and began to drag himself sobbing away, pulling his leg from between its teeth.

Nine dragons of the *niru* at Temeraire's rear together managed to bring down another five, along with their hapless captives; but by the time they could save the men and go aloft again, there was no hope of catching any more. The ferals were all of them vanishing again, as swiftly as they had come, dispersing to all corners of the countryside.

The battle was dying behind them, in the confusion and horror brought on by the unexpected swarming attack. The day was drawing to a close; the Russians began to fall back to the south, taking up positions across the road to Kaluga, and left the French to possession of the streets, choked with bodies and running with blood.

Their dinner that night was a thin and scanty one. The ferals had not acted with malice: they had not deliberately spoilt the cooking-pits nor the supply they could not themselves carry off, save accidentally, but accident had been more than enough. Their attack had taken or ruined more than half the army's food, for that night. Reports were yet coming in, from all around the countryside, of further depradations against the farmers and nearby villages: terrified peasants were even coming to the army, with their children and their cattle, begging for protection.

"And there are breeding grounds also on the Ugra River," one Russian aviator said: a river which ran on past Kaluga itself. "Heavy-weight breeding grounds."

The Cossacks were laboring valiantly all that evening, despite nightfall, to bring them further intelligence of the movement of both the French Army and the feral beasts. Late in the night, while Kutuzov yet sat looking heavily over his maps, one of their captains came in weary and in his dirt, his mustaches stained with tobacco, and reported to him in Russian. Kutuzov nodded a little.

"The French have put out cooking-pits for them," Kutuzov said briefly to Laurence.

Despite all the barriers of language, evidently the French had managed to make a simple bargain understood: if the ferals brought them grain, which they could not ordinarily digest, the French added some meat to the stew, and shared it out between them and their own dragons.

"And like as not throwing our prisoners and our slain into the pits, the monsters," another Russian said, a grotesque fantasy, but one which Laurence heard more than once repeated in the camp.

Kutuzov said heavily, "We fall back towards Kaluga, at once. Captain," he said to Laurence, "will you go to the Ugra grounds, and secure them?"

Laurence was silent a moment: to make himself a gaoler, for starving and chained beasts, was work he could scarcely bear to contemplate, and yet the faces of the screaming wounded haunted him. "We will, sir," he said.

Temeraire did not disagree; he and all the Chinese dragons, and their crews, had been very silent and shocked since the battle: what was yet a lurking fear in the heart of most Westerners, who had grown up on tales of maurauding dragons and heroic knights standing forth to slay them, and who thought of aviators as the handlers of savage beasts, was to them so unthinkable and vile as to be unacceptable even as a subject for fiction.

They left at once, despite the late hour; so, too, did the army. They saw a few torches moving upon the road below for guidance, the light reflected here and there off pikes and bayonets that bristled in every direction; in the hospital-waggons, those less grievously wounded rode sitting up, holding weapons aloft. There was no sight of French pursuit or forward motion: they remained ensconced around Maloyaroslavets, or what was left of that town after the ruinous combat.

Three roads now stood open to Napoleon: he might retreat himself towards Moscow and from there retire to Smolensk along the road which had brought him, or he might instead try and take a southern route; or if he had not yet lost the heart for a final adventure, even strike out for Kaluga after all, and throw a gauntlet once more in the teeth of the Russian Army.

"I could scarcely imagine it, even of Bonaparte," Laurence said to Tharkay, as they flew through the night; he had sent most of the officers below to sleep, as much as they might, in the belly-netting, "after he was halted in his tracks yesterday, except—"

Tharkay nodded minutely. Dragons could not fly long distances day in and out without steady provender, and their assembled host was so large that if their supply were destroyed, even an instant dispersal to all directions with the liberty of pillaging could not feed them all. And their own supply depots, intended as they were for the feeding of great numbers of dragons, would in any case now be appealing targets for the ferals. Shen Shi already looked grave, and after private consultation that night, Zhao Lien had sent away some twenty dragons to be a guard upon their nearest depots—and with instructions that should they be overwhelmed, they were immediately to begin to retreat eastward instead of trying to rejoin the main body of their *jalan*.

So at a stroke, Napoleon had already managed to whittle down their aerial advantage to a thin margin, now composed not very much of numbers but only of the greater experience and skill at maneuvering which the Chinese forces brought to battle, as compared to his young legions.

The night was very clear, and very cold: Temeraire's breath streamed away behind them in long trailing gusts as he flew on. The first hard frosts had come at last; before they had gone aloft, the ground had been frozen beneath them to a depth of seven inches, and many of the Shao Lung, unused to the cold climate, had been grumbling. It was the twenty-fifth of October. Laurence had to check their course against the stars, several times, until at last they struck the line of the Ugra River and turned to follow it southeast; a gibbous moon hung pale white, shining off the water and more translucently the skin of ice forming over its surface.

"When we arrive," Laurence had said to Temeraire and Zhao Lien, "we must first give them something to eat; we cannot expect beasts who are starving to hear any reason, but having been fed might listen, when Temeraire and Grig can speak with them in their own tongue."

Shen Shi had looked even more grave, but had at last agreed to release an additional quarter-day's ration from her already-strained depots; the grain and drugged cattle were now being carried by the dragons following them along with their own supply. The sixty remaining dragons of the first *jalan*, under Shao Ri, were coming with them; the rest, and Zhao Lien, had remained with Kutuzov's army to cover the withdrawal south. A withdrawal which could all too easily end in disaster, if Kaluga's storehouses were struck.

"Temeraire," Grig said, laboring to catch them up, "Temeraire, there is someone there on the river, I think."

"Where away?" Temeraire asked, and stooping they landed to find a Cossack dragon, barely the size of a Winchester, lying smashed and dying upon the bank half in and half out of the water: his side riddled with bullets, and his two riders both broken beneath his body. The dragon was already nearly gone; one man, who had been half in the frigid water, was dead; but the other opened his eyes and turned his head to look Laurence in the face.

"We will have you out in a moment," Laurence said to him, kneeling to put a hand on his shoulder, the best comfort he could give; ribs were protruding from the man's flesh, and the dragon lay over his legs. The Cossack only seized him by the collar with a desperate final straining effort and tried to pull him close; Laurence leaned in, and the man whispered, "*Murat,*" and released him, falling back; a little gush of blood came from his lips, and he was still.

Laurence rising to catch at the harness and climb back aboard said, "Temeraire, we must go at once. Send half the *niru* along the river, quietly, until they see the other end of the breeding grounds, and then we must close in on all sides: and let us pray the quarry has not yet escaped us. And pass the word: douse all lights."

Lanterns all extinguished, they flew low and quietly over the tree-tops, until coming over a hill they reached a wide shallow valley of the breeding grounds; a massive Russian heavy-weight nearly the size of a Regal Copper was crouched low, its head hanging to the ground, as four men labored frantically upon its back, working on a massive chain of iron stained with rust. They were not surgeons, but blacksmiths: Laurence realized abruptly that the French had forgone removing the barbs for the practical expedient of merely cutting the chains off them, and leaving the difficult hooks where they were.

A small portable forge glowed orange-red where they hammered on the second link, having already broken the first; the dragon was already moving its right wing, experimentally, and looking over with a craning head at its own back to watch the work: it was nearly quivering. The beast did not look quite so starved as had the grey light-weights: if maddened past fear of maiming by starvation, a heavy-weight might have been able to break even the strongest hobble, and then could have done enormous damage. But it certainly looked lean and hungry enough, and eager for its freedom.

The smiths were working with desperate urgency, and around them all the crew and company of twelve dragons in harness were looking anxiously in all directions, around Liberté himself; but on the ground before him, as nonchalant as if he was in the midst of Paris instead of engaged in a wildly reckless and dangerous enterprise behind his enemy's lines, Murat walked back and forth whistling unconcerned. Laurence put a restraining hand silently on Temeraire's neck, and kept his glass stretched out, watching the far side of the breeding ground, for any glint of the other half of their own company; he did not mean to lose this chance through excessive haste.

At last he caught a glitter of moonlight on a bared sword-blade waved at him. The smiths had nearly cut through the second link, below. "Ready arms, and on them," Laurence said, and with a glad and terrible roar, Temeraire surged forward, while below them the French dragons sprang desperately for escape.

The Russian heavy-weight, jerking up its head, saw them approaching and tried its other wing: the smiths were thrown off their feet as the chain went flying from beneath their hands, and with their smoking, sparking forge went sliding down its back to the ground as the massive dragon reared up. It bent down and snatched them all up together in one claw, four men and forge tumbled together, and with the other caught the loose hanging end of the chain; and then it flung itself into the air.

Laurence signaled to let the beast go—he had not the heart to return the creature to its chains, and they had better prey before them. Liberté had snatched Murat off his feet and flung himself into the air, and all the other dragons of the division were doing their best to make of themselves a screen between him and their attackers.

But the net had been drawn too tight: one *niru* after another skillfully surrounded and carved away each French dragon, nearly in minutes, with the skill of a surgeon cutting away limbs: until Liberté was all exposed, flying desperately, but not quickly enough. Ten more dragons surrounded him and began to cut off his flight, no matter which way he turned, tiring him and slowing his movement: a great stag, surrounded by wolves. Then one of the Shao Lung, especially large and with a jagged pale white scar running enormous the length of his left flank, made a full-body leap onto Liberté's back and with a roar knocked his crew off their feet; he sank both foretalons deep into Liberté's back, behind his wings.

Liberté shrilled with agony, and his wings faltered. Another Chinese dragon made a raking pass at his side, knocking air from his body; a third caught his tail and then they all closed in upon him and above him: he sank down at last helpless from the air, and having fallen to the ground resorted to curling his entire massive body tight around Murat, still held within his talons, with a pitiful hunted desperation.

Temeraire landed before him, nearly quivering with excitement, and murmured, "Laurence, I have never taken anyone so important prisoner: what ought we do?"

"Nothing more nor less than with any other man or beast: we must require Liberté's surrender," Laurence said, "and his giving Murat into our hands; and we must have both of their paroles."

Temeraire straightened, sweeping back his wings, and rather grandly said to Liberté, "We will accept your surrender, if you please; and your parole."

"Do you swear you will not hurt Murat?" Liberté demanded

anxiously, looking at them both, though he could scarcely have prevented it. Murat's own opinion on the circumstances as yet could not have been obtained, because only a faintly muffled noise was emerging, from the tight coils of Liberté's body, to confirm that he was still even there.

"I am confident the Russians will treat him with all the consideration due to a prisoner of his rank," Laurence said, "and I will give you my own word, he will be neither abused nor pillaged."

A faint voice was heard saying, in French, "Damn you, you silly python, let me out!" and Liberté unwillingly uncoiled himself; Murat pulled himself up and over one great foreleg, and sprang down to the ground in the open. Laurence slid from Temeraire's back to meet him.

Laurence bowed and said, "Your Majesty—" Napoleon had put him on the throne of Naples, "—I am obliged to require your parole."

Murat reached out and seized him by the shoulders. "What are you saying," he said. "Can *you* truly mean to prevent us?" He turned Laurence almost bodily, and flung out an arm to where Laurence saw a heap of five broken chains scattered on the ground, massive and monstrous links of brutal iron. "Have *you* a heart to see these magnificent beasts chained and starved like rats, for even another minute? I know you, Captain Laurence—I remember when you brought the cure to France, and saved my own Liberté thereby, and so many others. Once you had the courage to seek justice, more than only obey; will you not find that courage again?

"You and these," he gestured to the hovering and watchful dragons, "ought to aid us, not stand in our way. Will you truly make common cause with men as would do such things?"

Laurence said, quietly, controlled, "You are right, sir, that this treatment cannot but appall any sense of justice and decency. But what *you* have done, in merely striking their chains and throwing them upon the army and the innocent peasantry of their own country, is to set them upon a course whose certain event is their destruction at the hands of a furious and determined nation. And you have done this, not for their benefit, but to make them weapons to serve your own unjust ends and thirst for conquest."

"Oh, villain!" Murat cried. "Where else should they turn, but on the holders of their whips? I told the Emperor I would not walk out of this country, without striking the chains off every beast I could find, if it cost me my life and him my service. March me away, then, and have me shot if you like; *I* have no regret. *Vive la France!*"

He flung his saber at Laurence's feet, delivering this speech in parade-ground tones; it roused an answering cheer from his men and their beasts, despite their captivity. Laurence could not but shake his head: he found he did not question Murat's sincerity; so wild an impulse seemed all of a piece with the very recklessness which had led him to expose himself and his men so deeply in enemy territory.

Roland with a quick jump leapt forward, and picked up the sword to give to Laurence, so he would not need to bend down and pick it up. "Sir, if you will give me your parole, I should be glad to return it," Laurence said, mastering his own anger, and when Murat haughtily acquiesced, did so: he could not take insult from a man made prisoner, and Murat's courage could hardly be denied; he had been at the fore of the French dragons, at Tsarevo Zaimische, time and again.

The *niru* had been swiftly going over the breeding grounds, in the meantime; and now one of Shen Shi's lieutenants, a man named Guan Fei, quietly approached Laurence. "I must advise against preparing our cooking-pits here," he said. "This place is unhealthy: there are many dead, who have not been properly buried. We should go along the river to the south, and find some clean ground."

"The remaining dragons here will be unable to fly," Laurence said, "and we ought still to feed them; and then free them ourselves and take them along with us, if they will come. If we can catch any of the rest, perhaps their fellows will be able to induce them to pause and listen, rather than fight."

But Guan Fei said, "There are only four dragons we have found yet remaining within the grounds: we can arrange to transport them a short distance, but they are in any case ill and close to death. I have arranged for them to be tended."

"There ought to be fifty dragons here," Temeraire said in alarm. "Where are all the others?"

Laurence looking at Murat's face, which showed no small degree of satisfaction, said grimly, "Kaluga. He has set them on Kaluga."

It was not until the next day that Laurence had the pleasure of delivering his prisoner to Kutuzov in Kaluga: a thin and insubstantial pleasure, in the face of the disaster which had unfolded about them.

The town had been utterly unprepared for the sudden and thunderclap descent of forty heavy-weight beasts: the great magazines had been smashed open and ruined, immense quantities of munitions and grain taken, cattle and horses slaughtered and devoured; and much of the town itself smashed in the frenzy of destruction.

Temeraire and his fellows had driven on the last few miles from the breeding grounds to Kaluga, despite their fatigue and hunger. But even so they had come too late, and found a scene of wreckage only: the heavy-weights had come, the townspeople told Laurence, and plundered swiftly, and as swiftly fled back towards the north—perhaps carrying their stolen goods towards Napoleon's army.

Temeraire had tried to go aloft again, in pursuit; he and his fellows had gone half-a-mile, heads drooping progressively lower, and then Shao Ri had roused up and shaken his head and turning towards Laurence and Temeraire had said, "We must halt."

Laurence himself started from a half-doze and realized the folly of their attempt: after a day of hard fighting, little food and less rest, followed by a cold flight in the dark and a battle to end it, the dragons were at the limits of their strength. "Put out the signals, Gerry, if you please," he said, and to Temeraire's half-drowsing protest said quietly, "We cannot throw ourselves at nearly our own number of fresh heavy-weights, in this state; we would be destroyed. You must all have some rest, and something to eat, before we can continue on."

The exhausted dragons slept eight hours, in four watches, with the French dragons always under a wary eye; Laurence had put their captains and crews aboard the swiftest of the dragons of the *niru,* and kept Murat himself aboard Temeraire, but he was mindful that not all the French dragons might have been harnessed from the shell, and might not feel the intensity of attachment to their captains which ordinarily served to render a captured beast meek. He was well served by his caution: a little while after dawn, he roused to find two of the French dragons being wrestled to the ground again, having made an attempt to creep away.

In the morning, they returned to Kaluga, where the army was slowly marching in, and Laurence delivered their noble prisoner to the headquarters. Murat had been considered by the Russians an honored foe; they saluted him in the air and on the field, when they saw him: a great horseman, a great swordsman, a great soldier, fearless in battle and gallant in his personal manner, he was in most respects the romantic ideal to which young Russian officers aspired.

But now as Laurence escorted him past many of those who had cheered him, not long before, and into the building of the headquarters, silence followed them: a hard, angry silence. In his office, Kutuzov said, very briefly, coldly, "Your Majesty," and then paused; he then said, "The Tsar has commanded that you be sent to Tobolsk," a city which Laurence recalled: they had passed it, in the earlier stages of their journey from China, deep in Siberia's wastes, "there to await the conclusion of the war; you depart in the morning."

Murat's courage, to do him credit, flagged not a moment; he only said, cheerfully, "I am sorry to miss the rest of it! May I write a letter to my wife?"

He did not wait for permission, but brazenly reached for pen and paper on Kutuzov's desk, and scribbled out a careless note:

My darling Caroline! My luck has gone sour; I have been taken prisoner and am being shipped away to some distant corner of beyond, whose name I have already forgotten—

"Tobolsk, was it?" he asked, and scribbled it in.

I am perfectly well; Liberté has not a scratch; tell your brother to win the war as quick as blazes and bring me home before I die of boredom. Ever yours, Joachim.

He folded it once and handed it over. "You are welcome to read it over, but I promise there are no secrets," he said. "I've no head for ciphers. I don't suppose there are any pretty women in this country?"

Laurence could not but feel some sympathy, seeing him sent away: he knew the bitter pang of being sent away from the field to linger in remote exile in an alien land, and felt an echo of the misery of his own transportation, the heavy bowing weight upon his shoulders, the knowledge that he and Temeraire would be denied the chance to be of any use. And Murat had not even the comfort of his own dragon's company; Liberté would be kept imprisoned far from him, and very likely in one of the same dreadful breeding grounds they had emptied.

But Laurence felt nothing but coldness for Murat's acts: the impulse to free the dragons might have been a noble one, but it would not have been carried out, if it had not so neatly aligned with his interests and those of Bonaparte, and if truly motivated by disinterested affection would never have been done in so crude a way, which showed so much disdain for the evil consequences that would fall on those dragons themselves.

"Sir," Laurence said to Kutuzov, when Murat had been escorted away to await his transport, "will you tell me where we stand?"

Kutuzov shook his head. "Thirty ferals were seen at Maloyaroslavets this afternoon, with cartloads of grain from Kaluga." Answer enough: that meant the Russian dragons were accepting the lures which the French had thrown out to them. Laurence was silent. He could no more reproach the beasts for pursuing a course of liberation, than the Russians for wishing to defend themselves against Napoleon's invasion.

He returned to his own encampment and found an unhappy Grig lingering there, having managed to beg Temeraire's pardon, and wanting company: twenty Russian light-weights had vanished from the muster. "They are leaving," he said, low. "I think—I think they are going over to Napoleon."

"How many of them speak French?" Laurence asked, grimly.

"So many of our officers speak it," Grig said, "I dare say nearly all of us know a little, at least."

Meaning that by serving as go-betweens, they might permit Napoleon to turn the ferals into more than simply a wild foraging party, scarcely under his control; they might allow him to weld them into a true fighting force, and use them effectively in battle.

The day was drawing on; Laurence spoke long with Shen Shi, and several officers of the Russian general staff, upon the one essential note: supply, supply, supply. The roads from the south were slow and choked with mud, and more attacks had already been reported, against their supply depots. At last he fell asleep for a few hours of rest, on Temeraire's arm; at eleven in the night, Roland woke him.

"I'm sorry, sir," she said, quietly, "but there's a dispatch," and handed him the note; he broke it open and read: Napoleon's army had begun to move south, along the Kaluga Road. He was coming. He had chosen the great gamble. A cold and stinging wind was blowing into Laurence's face; he rubbed away sleep, and found his hand wet; he looked up. Snow was falling.

Winter had come.

ABOUT THE AUTHOR

Naomi Novik was born in New York in 1973, a first-generation American, and raised on Polish fairy tales, Baba Yaga, and Tolkien. Her first novel, *His Majesty's Dragon,* the opening volume of the Temeraire series, was published in 2006 and has been translated into twenty-three languages and optioned by Peter Jackson, the Academy Award–winning director of the Lord of the Rings trilogy.

She has won the John W. Campbell Award for Best New Writer, the Compton Crook Award for Best First Novel, and the Locus Award for Best First Novel. She is one of the founding board members of the Organization for Transformative Works, a nonprofit dedicated to protecting the fair-use rights of fan creators, and is herself a fanfic writer and fan vidder, as well as one of the architects of the open-source Archive of Our Own.

Novik lives in New York City with her husband, Edgar Award–winning mystery novelist Charles Ardai, their shiny new daughter, Evidence, and a recently and ruthlessly winnowed set of ~~four~~ five computers.

You can find out more at her website (http://naominovik.com) and follow her as naominovik on Livejournal, Twitter, and Facebook.